Ruined Lives

Best Wishes, Marey
Enjoy!
Thorpe Higgins
Aug. 29, 2003

Ruined Lives

Grayce Higgins

Copyright © 2002 by Grayce Higgins.

Library of Congress Number: 2002092653
ISBN :   Softcover   1-4010-6326-8

All rights reserved. No part of this book may be reproduced or transmitted in any form or by any means, electronic or mechanical, including photocopying, recording, or by any information storage and retrieval system, without permission in writing from the copyright owner.

This is a work of fiction. Names, characters, places and incidents either are the product of the author's imagination or are used fictitiously, and any resemblance to any actual persons, living or dead, events, or locales is entirely coincidental.

This book was printed in the United States of America.

To order additional copies of this book, contact:
Xlibris Corporation
1-888-795-4274
www.Xlibris.com
Orders@Xlibris.com

TO MY CHILDREN.
THANKS FOR EVERYTHING.

Author's Note

The Central Intelligence Agency (CIA), the Federal Bureau of Investigation (FBI) and their agents do exist. However, any references to those agencies or the training of their agents mentioned in this novel are purely fantasy from the depths of the author's sometimes malevolent imagination. The futuristic repairs of the leg and ankle mentioned in this book may be possibilities one day according to an article by Doctor Peter Ivanovich, president of the International Society for Artificial Organs.

ONE

In 1982 I was free, white, twenty-one and obnoxiously cocky. A college graduate with a degree in criminal justice, I was positive a foreign country was going to test one too many nuclear bombs and blow the world to bits. The only thing that could save America, hot dogs, and mom's apple pie, was if I, Cassandra Shores, joined the CIA. My parents weren't happy about it, my boy friend wasn't happy about it, but what could I do? The world needed me to save it from itself, right? Honestly, I was so full of myself, it's a wonder I had any friends.

After becoming a member of that esteem organization, I went through several months of rigorous training to become a counter-intelligence agent, better known to the general public as a spy. We had been training for about three months when they selected a few of us to take part in an experimental class on self-hypnotism. It was an attempt to find some way to keep our servicemen from giving away secret information to the enemy while being tortured.

First, they wanted to see if we could learn to put ourselves under hypnosis. Secondly, we needed to learn to go under so deeply that we wouldn't feel any pain, no matter what happened. It didn't sound plausible to me, but I was willing to try it. It was during that training that they discovered I had a rather strange gift. I could put myself in the trance, but my eyes would remain open, staring, devoid of all expression. The instructor told me I made his blood run cold the first time I was successful. He said I moved my head, watching every move he made, never blinking. When he pinched my arm or lightly slapped my face, I didn't seem to feel any discomfort. The odd thing that really upset him was that when I came out of the trance I was able to recall everything he did to me.

The instructor worried that if, God forbid, I should fall into enemy hands this ability of mine would cause them to beat me to death while trying to get the information they wanted. He told my superiors, "They will undoubtedly think she is just refusing to talk. Her open eyes are totally void of any expression. Her head moved to watch every move I made. It reminded me of those old zombie movies."

The other thing my superiors didn't like was that no one could bring me out of the trance with a special word the way they did with the rest of the trainees. Nothing worked on me. I came out when I was good and ready. Sometimes it was much sooner than anyone else because in some strange way I was able to sense when the session was over. It took a lot of discussion and what seemed like a thousand more tests before I finally convinced them I should continue my training.

Near the end of our instruction when their attempts to bring us out of our trances increased in painful intensity, I still didn't feel a thing. As much as I wanted to go out and save the world, I'm not an overly brave person. Thinking about watching someone mutilate my body while I remained unfeeling was not my idea of the perfect party. I could only pray I'd never have to test the trance to its limits.

It was a proud day for me when we "graduated", so to speak. No actual ceremony, of course. After all, the CIA claims we spies don't exist, that there is no James Bond prototype in *their* organization. Be that as it may, I, Cassandra Shores, was now a counter-intelligence agent assigned the duty of protecting the United States of America from all foreign threats against democracy. Mom and Pop were still unhappy that I had chosen to be a spy. Just the word "spy" conjured up all kinds of dire pictures and nothing I said could change their minds. I could hardly believe it when they consented to come to Washington, DC to see me before I left on my first assignment. I knew they loved me in their own way, but they were so in love with each other that they seldom remembered I was around. I received an occasional arm around the shoulders, but nothing like the love I saw other parents lavishing on their children. It surprised and deeply touched me when they both hugged and kissed me goodbye with tears in their eyes as they were leaving. It was as if they never expected to see me again.

Over the next fifteen years I became one of the agency's best agents. Several times I received a commendation for my work. I must admit that the first few times were thrilling and I almost burst my buttons with pride, but after that it became embarrassing. The barbed teasing I received made me want to blunder slightly on my next assignment, but I valued my life too much to take that chance.

Today, sixteen years later, it's a totally different story. I'm thirty-seven, no longer cocky nor a first class agent. I've always been a slim five foot six inches, but now after a year in the hospital recovering from injuries and an unknown poison, I am a walking bag of bones. My mousy brown hair hangs limp, my brown eyes have lost their sparkle, and my Jane Doe face, which normally reminds everyone I meet of someone else, is haggard. I have gone through a lot in the past year and I admit I look terrible. Even my best friends in DC, Sue and Jake Cummings, say I looked like hell. I can take that from them, but not when CIA Director Wendell Bradford Smyth told me that in my condition I wasn't worth the powder to blow me to hell. Somehow, coming from him, it destroyed what little bit of self-worth I had left. True, on my last mission I received horrendous injuries, but what a terrible thing to say to one of his best agents. I should say former agent because when I refused the desk job he offered, choosing to retire instead, I immediately became useless in his eyes. Okay, granted, maybe he was trying to be funny with his remark, but I never liked the man, so his remark hurt. He had always been civil to me prior to that time, but nothing about him appealed to me. His short, compact frame, his tiny mustache, his erect military bearing, his upper-crust British way of speaking were characteristics some women love, but not me. There is something about the man . . . something that makes my skin crawl.

Since the day I received my commission I have been in several situations from which I doubted I would return. True, none of them required me to use the trance, but they were scary enough to make me fear for my life. When things got bad I would find myself thinking about the lake, and home and Art, my first love. He had asked me to marry him the night we graduated from college, but I turned him down. I was going out and save the world, I told him. Sorry, but marriage was not part of my immediate future. We didn't part on the best of terms, something I've regretted. I've fantasized often about what our reunion would be like. Those were the dreams that kept me going during the rough times.

Did I ever think of quitting the agency? Sure. There were times when I would promise God that I'd never accept another assignment if He would get me out of the jam I was in alive and, hopefully, in one piece. But, I'm like the guy who, flying a plane in trouble, says, "Please God, let me land safely and I promise I'll never fly again!" Well, he would fly again, and I always accepted another assignment. Too bad I didn't have the foresight to quit instead of accepting just one more assignment, which did turn out to be my last.

My mission in North Korea had been going well. In a few more weeks I would have been on my way home, pleased with myself for having completed another fine job.

I had been enjoying the apartment pool when a group of army soldiers burst through the gate leading from the street. They leveled bayonets at my mid-section, and told me in to get out of the pool, get dressed and come with them.

"Why?" I asked in Korean. The only answer I got was a crack of a gun butt on the back of my head.

One of them jerked me to my feet and insisted on being in

the bedroom while I got dressed. I'd endured a lot of things during my years with the agency, but that man's slimy eyes on me while I dressed was one of the worst. Rape was in his eyes. I think the only thing that saved me was that his superior was waiting to talk to me.

I could hear the rest of the soldiers tearing through the apartment, probably looking for electronic equipment to incriminate me. I knew they could look for a month without finding a thing. I sent my information out in letters addressed to the home of my "brother", who was actually another agent. When my letters arrived, Jake delivered them unopened to the agency.

How I would slave over those letters. They were in code, making it difficult to get the needed information down in sentences that made sense. I knew the Korean officials would censor them before they sent the letter on. If I valued my life, they had to be perfect. There was no margin for error.

When I finished dressing, the soldiers escorted me to a black stretch limousine waiting at the curb. When I saw who was waiting for me, my heart stopped. I knew I was in for a rough time. I could only hope I'd survive. Waiting for me was a general I had nicknamed "The Executioner." I had seen some of his handiwork up close and realized his recipients would have welcomed death, hence the nickname.

"Good afternoon, Miss Carmichael . . . or should I say Miss Shores?"

When I heard those words I knew I had just heard my death sentence. "Why are you calling me Miss Shores? Who's she?"

"Don't waste my time with your lies. I know you are Cassandra Shores, agent for the Central Intelligence Agency of the United States. How I found this out is of no importance to you. What I want to know is what you are doing here? My men have been unable to find any evidence in your apartment that you have been spying on us."

"Spying?" I laughed. "I wouldn't know how to spy if I had a book with pictures."

The slap that followed my attempt at levity seemed to come from nowhere. I tasted blood. His smile was vicious.

"Don't be facetious, Miss Shores. I have it from a reliable source that you are here to spy on my government for a reason unknown to me, but not for long. Please understand, we can get the information I want in a civilized manner or we can do it the hard way. It is entirely up to you, *my dear*." The way he said "my dear" made my skin crawl.

"I don't know what you are talking about . . . "

His struck the back of my hand forcibly with the steel cane he always carried. For a minute I thought he had broken my fingers.

"Enough of your lies," he hissed. He rapped on the window between himself and the driver. Apparently, the driver knew where we were going because the car pulled noiselessly away from the curb. I could only pray I would live through the torture I knew was coming.

TWO

The limo stopped at an old warehouse down by the waterfront. I had to give the General credit; he had picked a perfect spot. In the late afternoon's fading sunlight, hundreds of fishing boats were docking, their catches weighed, and the boats cleaned. Hundreds, no, make that thousands of excited questions and answers about the day's catch floated loudly up and down the wharf.

My captors were intent on making me stumble and appear drunk. I received my share of snide comments from the fishermen. The soldiers forced me down, down, down to the subterranean bowels of one of the many buildings lining the wharf. The air was stale and cold. After the heat of the day, my skin felt clammy. After tying me tightly to my chair, they focused bright lights on my face. Everyone around me seemed to disappear. The Executioner's disjointed voice came from out of the blackness.

"Are you comfortable, my dear?" he asked sarcastically, then continued without waiting for my answer. "Good. Now are you ready to tell us, Miss Shores, what are you doing in this country?"

"I tried to tell you earlier . . . " The sound of his fist smacking into his palm sounded like a gunshot.

"And I told you, I don't want your lies. Give me the truth or you will suffer such pain you will beg to die."

His voice seemed to fill with pleasure contemplating what he was planning. However, he could have threatened to shoot me and I wouldn't have changed my story. Under no circumstances does an agent admit to being anything other than what she is pretending to be. The agency decides on my story before I begin a mission and that's what I repeat, again and again, no matter what happens. I knew from day one of my training that there was the possibility I might die in the line of duty, but my first loyalty was to be to my country.

My story for this mission? I had fled the States because federal warrants were out for my arrest for bank robbery and the murder of a bank guard. I faced twenty-five to thirty years in prison or a possible death sentence if I ever returned to the U.S. It was a good cover and had worked before. If anyone did check on me, there were persons in high places to vouch for me. This time I don't think the locals had made any attempt to verify my story. Had someone snitched on me? That was an uncomfortable thought. Whichever way it played out, I was certain "The Executioner" wasn't buying anything I had to say.

For what seemed like an hour he barked questions. I was getting tired of being asked the same questions over and over; he was getting tired of getting the same answers. He shouted a command.

Suddenly, a soldier ripped my blouse and bra from my body. I hadn't expected anything like that and for a moment I forgot a prime rule: never show anger. It's too easy to let something slip if they can find a way to get to you. Okay, fine, but how was I supposed to keep from getting mad enough to kill when some devil was shooting questions at me while his henchmen were running their hands over my breasts. Another command came from the General and two of his men started licking my breasts, even sucking on the nipples. If their purpose was to make me tell them what they wanted to know, they were way off base. Oh, I got excited all right . . . fighting mad excited and more determined to keep repeating my cover story.

Again and again questions the General shouted questions, undoubtedly trying to catch me in a lie. I was becoming dead tired, but if I seemed to be dozing off, hard punches came from nowhere. Most of the earlier punches he aimed at my head and face, but now I suffered repeated blows on my breasts. My God, how it hurt. I had been in enough situations to know when to twist my head, making most of those blows slide past, but there was no way to ward off the hits on my breasts. I began praying that my signal had gotten through.

One of the James Bond toys I did have was my table lamp. If no one turned it on by nine p.m., a silent signal went out to activate an alarm across the bay. Agents there would immediately contact the Navy, who would send their Seals in on a rescue operation. I knew that several hours might elapse before the Seals could reach me. The trick was to stay alive until they arrived. I didn't worry about them finding me while I had my watch on. I had pushed the button that turned on that signal when I was on the way to the warehouse. That signal would pinpoint my location for the rescue team.

Time passed in a blur of pain. Blood dripped from my broken nose, one eye was swelling shut, and it hurt to take a deep breath. "The Executioner" finally got tired of playing with me and decided to get down to business. At his command someone turned off the bright lights that had been giving off a slight amount of welcome heat. As my vision cleared I saw someone hand him what appeared to be a small sledge hammer.

"Perhaps, Shores (he had stopped being polite long before), I can convince you to tell the truth with my little persuader. Either you start talking or I will be forced to tap your foot with my little friend." Quickly he turned, bringing the hammer down on a small table, smashing it to bits. "Imagine that was your foot," he snarled. I knew he wasn't kidding.

I knew the time had come for me to use the trance. I could only hope I would be able to clear my mind in preparation under these circumstances. I barely made it.

I don't know how long I was in that warehouse before the Seals arrived to get me out of there. "The Executioner" had done a bang-up job on me. Blood was oozing from my ear and my nose. With his little hammer, he had broken my legs, my left arm and my ribs. My left knee and left ankle looked like pulp, and he had broken nearly every bone in the left foot. The right leg had two broken bones but, at least, they were clean breaks; none of the smashing the left leg had endured. It wasn't until several minutes after I received a pain shot that I brought myself out of the trance. Too soon! Immediately, I was in excruciating pain. Thank God, the medic brought several pain shots with him. He had confronted the General's handiwork before, he told me, so he had come prepared. The second shot brought blessed relief from the pain, but nothing helped the nausea I was feeling. I was sweating one moment and shaking with chills the next. It wasn't two minutes later that the nausea became more than I could handle. When the first wave of sickness past I tried to tell them what had happen in those last few minutes I was with the General.

"Shot," I murmured, while they were cleaning me up.

"Sorry, I can't give you another this soon."

"No. In my butt."

Quickly, he turned me on my side to check for a puncture wound. "Yes, I see. Do you know what it was?"

"No. Shot . . . when they heard you."

Immediately, the Seal contacted the doctor on the ship across the bay. "We have Miss Shore on board. She has been given a shot of something which has her vomiting every few minutes. Chills, high fever. I'd say it's some kind of poison. Yes, sir, I do have that with me. Yes, Sir. Well, Miss Shore, you do get another shot, after all. This is a universal antidote which has recently been developed. If it was poison that was given to you, this may help."

He neglected to tell me that the minute I was on board the ship they planned to pump my stomach. Not that it mattered. It probably saved my life. Even today it makes me shiver when I think how close The Executioner came to winning.

On board, after they got me stabilized, I agreed with what the doctor planned: casts on my broken right leg and left arm, and taping the broken nose. The broken ribs would heal on their own, he informed me. He was going to recommend an implant to replace the injured inner ear, and amputation of the left leg.

"Whoa, whoa." They had me doped up, but no way would I

allow anyone to amputate a part of my body. "Do what is necessary . . . cast, brace . . . but no amputation."

The doctor did his best to convince me that with an artificial leg I would be able to walk normally, to do anything I wanted.

"Will I be able to . . . dance?"

"Of course."

"How about that. I never could before," I mumbled. I don't think he appreciated my trying to joke when I was so physically ill.

The doctor gave up and made me as comfortable as he could. He put my left leg in a temporary cast, and left it to the doctors at Walter Reed Hospital in DC to try to talk sense to me about having it amputated.

"Do you know what happened to my captors," I whispered as he was casting my leg. It was too painful to take a breath to speak loudly.

"I know several of them are dead, but whether our boys got them all, I can't be certain."

I didn't say it aloud, but I would have bet my last dollar that "The Executioner" had an escape route planned.

The doctors at Reed couldn't believe the antiquated tortures that the General had used on me. I told them they should meet the General, then they might understand. They, too, did their best to convince me to have the leg amputated. Again and again I refused. Finally, they gave in, and told me about a new procedure that a Doctor Harrison O'Conner in Seattle, Washington, was trying to perfect. His process would allow the broken bones to adhere to a metal rod coated with encapsulating cells from the patient's own body. The cells would then form a new and stronger leg around the metal rod. However, they were quick to point out that the procedure was still experimental. I asked if they had an idea when this man's process would be ready to test on a human. They had no way of knowing, they told me.

"Do what is necessary to enable me to get around. I'll wait for that doctor to need a human guinea pig." I put up a good front of being brave and willing to wait until the procedure was available.

My roommate, Ann, told me, "Brave—phooey-stupid is more like it." Yeah, maybe she was right, but I couldn't agree to the amputation.

They gave me a new knee, enabling me to bend my leg, but the bone from the knee down was beyond repair. Without the brace they gave me, my foot flopped around like a fish out of water. I couldn't walk without the brace and the use of a crutch. Without them I could only crawl. Once down, I couldn't get up unless I had something solid to pull against.

True, if I had agreed, they would have cut off the leg and I would have received a prosthesis and would now be walking normally. But no, I had to do it my way. Crazy as it seems, I'm sure I would make the same choice today. I may be stupid, but there is something about the thought of cutting off my leg . . . I can't imagine ever giving them my permission. I guess it's because I haven't given up hope of being married someday and I can't see taking my leg off before getting into the wedding bed. If ever there would be a turn-off to sex that would win the prize in my book.

After several weeks in the hospital, and endless hours of therapy, the doctors conceded they had done everything they could for me. The day I left the hospital they told me that when that new procedure became available, the government would foot the bill. That struck my funny bone, " . . . the government would *foot* the bill." It was so appropriate, I laughed until I cried.

In the hospital I went over and over my last mission trying to figure out where I went wrong. How did the General identify me? My final consensus was that I hadn't goofed in any way. After talking to several of my cohorts who dropped by to visit, I found out I wasn't the only one the enemy detected. In the past two years, the enemy had killed four operatives outright, and maimed seven others so badly it forced them to retire. There was no way that many operatives would unknowingly tip their hand. There had to be a leak within the agency. When I came to that decision, I knew what I had to do.

I enlisted the aid of my best friends in the Agency, Sue

Cummings and her husband Jake, the agent I had sent my letters to while in North Korea. We got in touch with the injured who had retired. Two had died from their wounds within six months after retirement. Our question to the remaining five was: "Would they sign a letter addressed to Director Smyth, detailing what had happened to each of us, with a suggestion he investigate his organization for a possible informant?" We received five confirmations immediately. We slaved over that letter to Smyth the way I did my letters home to "brother". After several revisions, the final draft was acceptable to all seven of us. Someone suggested that the informant might be Smyth, which brought the rest of us up short. If that were true, not one agent was safe. To cover that contingency, everyone agreed that without Smyth's knowledge, a copy of the letter should go to President Wilton with a note detailing our fears. If there was anyone that would understand our position, he would, having been an agent himself. I think that's what makes him such a maverick. Many times he has disappeared and a few days later we would hear he'd gone off on a golf or fishing trip by himself. I'm sure that was enough to drive the Secret Service men, whose job it was to protect him, out of their minds.

The last thing I did before leaving for home was mail those letters. We felt we had done everything we could. We prayed we were wrong about Smyth, but like I said earlier, I'd always thought he was a sneaky devil. Still, I hoped I wouldn't be able to say I told you so.

THREE

After some cautionary meetings concerning what I could and couldn't say to my friends when I got home, they released me. I stopped by to see Sue and Jake before leaving DC. Jake and I had been making plans to open a private investigator's office in Mountain View, Oregon, when we both retired. Sue thought the plan a good one. She felt DC was no place to bring up their two children. Now, those plans would have to wait. Jake still had two years to go before retirement, so I would have to open the office by myself. After many hugs and promises to come and visit me, I left for home. Home. Home meant Art. Memories kept crowding in on my thoughts as I drove onto the freeway and started the long trek West.

I had been on the road for a week and had done a lot of thinking as I drove across the country. I decided I would open an office as I planned, but in Myrtle Woods, instead of Mountain View. There are only eighteen miles between the two, but I had investigated and found that Mountain View had ballooned to a population of a hundred thousand. I made the decision while driving through Wyoming, that I didn't want to tackle that large of a place by myself. Besides, I doubted I'd know my way around anymore. Money-wise I wasn't hurting. Actually, I didn't need to work, but I knew I'd go crazy if I didn't have something to do. The way I figured it, an office in Myrtle Woods, population of four thousand one hundred and two, wasn't going to overwork me. I'd probably be lucky to have three or four cases a year, if that many.

It was mid-day of day seven. A short way out of Sisters, Oregon my trusty Toyota began climbing through the Cascade Mountains. The scenery, a multitude of green shades with a few golden aspens sprinkled here and there, blue sky, and deeper blue lakes had a picture post card look. I breathed deeply of the cool, clean mountain air blowing in my window. I had forgotten how good the smell of pine and fir could be. I pulled off on a side road that led to Blue Lake. I parked close to the lake and hobbled to a big log by the water. Looking around, I had to admit that God was a master painter. This was one of the sights I was positive I would never live to see when I was in that warehouse with that butcher standing over me with his hammer.

I spread my lunch out beside me on the log, contentedly watching the fish jump, listening to the blue jays screaming at each other, the quail calling in the brush. I must have been very quiet because suddenly a doe stepped out of the bushes and looked at me before bending down to drink. Once again she raised her eyes to mine, then she turned her head back to the trees. She must have made a sound, although I didn't hear one, because her twin fawns stepped cautiously out to join their mother at the water's edge. I was afraid to breathe for fear I would frighten them away. The moment was so sacred it brought tears to my eyes.

After the doe and her babies left, I took off my right shoe and soaked my foot in the cool water. I have automatic drive, but my foot was beginning to cry for a few days off. I played in the water for a few minutes before getting back on the road. Only a few hours, I thought, and I'd be home. God, that sounded good. I hadn't realized how much I had missed it. Living in DC must have dulled my senses.

When I pulled into Mountain View, I got a room for the night. I wanted to drive into Myrtle Woods early the next morning. That way I would have time to look around and bury old memories before any of my friends knew I was in town.

I reached Myrtle Woods about nine the next day. My first stop was the cemetery. Both of my parents had died while I was on assignments. After placing flowers on their graves, I stood there thinking about the last time I had seen them and of their teary good-byes. They were right in thinking they would never see me again, but they thought it would be me that would die. Only a few months after I saw them in DC, my father was killed by a drunk driver. My mother died six months later, I'm sure, of a broken heart. She had no desire to live without her love beside her.

I drove aimlessly around for an hour before heading for the house they left me. When I learned I had inherited the house, I told the folks' lawyer to hire a caretaker couple. I had written him two weeks ago to inform the caretakers that I had retired and was coming home to stay.

I pulled slowly into the driveway, momentarily surprised by the memories that came rushing out to greet me. The house hadn't changed. Still the same big, dark brown rambling structure softened by a riot of flowers blooming around the lush green yard. A wide porch stretched across the front increasing the old-fashioned look. The porch swing was in the same place, I noticed. How I loved that swing. How many times had Art and I sat there, swinging gently, solving the worries of the world? That's where Art had asked me to marry him. For a moment I wondered, looking down at my leg, what my life would have been like if I had accepted his proposal. I'm sure I would have ended up making both of us miserable. My family and friends kept me informed on what was going on in his life, but he and I never wrote.

A few minutes lapsed before I could force myself to get out and limp up to the front door. I worked my way up the front steps, knowing they would have to go. I kept feeling like I was going to tumble backwards—not good for someone using a crutch. Before I could knock, a short, grandmotherly-plump, white-haired lady of about sixty opened the door. She had the smoothest face I had ever seen on a woman her age. Honestly, she didn't have one wrinkle. Unlike the elderly people in Korea and other Asian countries, who seemed to age twenty years overnight, somewhere this woman had discovered the fountain of youth. I'd have to get her secret.

"Miss. Shores?" she inquired in a sweet, soft voice.

"Yes. Mrs. Applebee?"

That much settled, she ushered me into the coolness of the house. I noticed that nothing had changed since the day I left. The front room was still large and gloomy, overflowing with massive pieces of furniture. I decided to do something in here also. A lot of the old furniture I would send to the Salvation Army, then I'd paint the rooms in light, bright colors.

Mr. Applebee brought in my suitcases. "Where do you want these, little lady?" He was the exact opposite of his wife: tall, skinny, completely bald, his tanned wrinkled skin weathered by many seasons, his blue eyes undimmed by time.

After making sure they weren't using the room I wanted, I told him to put the suitcases in the big bedroom at the rear of the house that had the best view of the lake. After so many years away, I wanted to see that beautiful body of water the first thing in the morning and the last thing at night for the rest of my life.

Before I was born, the founding fathers decided to dam the river that flowed through town, making a lake for summer recreation. They felt it would be a tourist attraction and bring extra money into the town coffers. It had worked like a charm. The folks had written me about the hefty new fines imposed on those who left trash lying around and on boat owners who didn't take care of their boats, thus fouling the water. Across the lake were the storage sheds for those wealthy enough to have a fancy pleasure boat. We had nothing but a small skiff that we kept moored at our dock, but I wouldn't have traded straight across. Too many happy memories connected with our little boat.

Mrs. Applebee took me into the kitchen where the muffins she was taking out of the oven flooded my sense of smell with delight. Over cups of coffee and several muffins, we graduated to first names: Sandy, Frances, and Al. They asked if I wanted them to find another place or did I plan on them staying? I hadn't planned to continue the relationship, however, that was BTM (before the muffins). I suggested that we give each other a one-month trial, then we would talk again.

"No matter what the final decision is, you'll have plenty of time to find other employment before you need to leave. I better unpack a few things. Al, there will be some large boxes and a trunk coming in a few days. Have the movers leave them in the front room until I get them unpacked, please."

He grunted an okay of sorts. I found that Al was a man of few words, unlike Frances, who elaborated in great detail. Could be that's why he's the way he is.

After I put away the few things I brought with me, I stood at the open window taking in great gulps of the sweet, clean air, much like a pelican gulping fish. I couldn't wait to go down and walk along the edge of the lake. I hadn't realized how much I had missed it until I saw that incredibly blue water beckoning me from the window. I gave in to temptation and in no time found myself leaning back against a large boulder marveling at the clean, clear water. From nowhere came the memory of the young girl who used to race up and down this shore. A lithe, homely, little elf of a girl, with long brown hair blowing in the wind. How strong those young legs were, I mourned.

Stop it! Wake up to the real world, I rebuked myself. What's done is done. Remember, lady, you wanted to save the world. You have only yourself to blame for what happened. Yeah, yeah, yeah, I knew that, and I had always prided myself on being able to take anything those foreign bastards threw at me. Standing there in my special place by the lake, tears filled my eyes, and I gave in to my inner pain. I wept convulsively—great shuddering sobs—for that little girl and her dreams. When I felt I had no more tears in me, I blew my nose and scrubbed my cheeks with my handkerchief. I longed to wash my face with that beautiful water, but my brace wouldn't allow me that pleasure. Not for the first time I found myself wondering what was the use of a new knee was that would allow me kneel down, but was no help when I wanted to get up.

Stop it! Quit being such a crybaby, I told myself. Forget the past, the present is what's important. How true, I thought. Squaring my shoulders, I worked my way slowly back up to the house.

I didn't think I could possibly be hungry after the muffins, but being down by the lake must have stimulated my appetite. Lunch, consisting of fresh shrimp salad, deviled eggs, home-grown sliced tomatoes, and hot French bread disappeared quickly. I even found room for a lemon tart. By the time I finished lunch, I knew I wanted to keep Frances and Al forever, if they wanted to stay.

"I'm not going to need a month to decide if I want you both to stay on here. I can't boil water and I'm worthless at gardening. You two would be doing me a favor if you would stay. We could see about renovating the apartment above the garage and I could have an enclosed walk built between it and the house. That way you would have your privacy and I'd have mine. Will you think about it.?"

"Don't need to think about it. Already decided to stay, if you liked us," Al stated in his blunt way.

Frances was beaming. "I'm glad it's working out. Anytime you want to have guests for dinner, give me an hour notice and they will be welcome. Al and I will take a look at the apartment this afternoon and we can talk this evening."

I told them of my plans to remodel the house with more and larger windows, new paint, inside and out, plus different steps on the porch. I gave them a thumbnail sketch of what I had in mind; they both had helpful input that made the whole idea better than I had imagined. We decided each of us would think about it during the rest of the day and discuss our ideas at dinner.

FOUR

With those decisions made, I started my walk-about of the big city of Myrtle Woods. Al told me to call and he would come and get me if I got too tired. Walking along, I noticed that the shade trees were much taller and broader than I had expected. A few of the sidewalks needed replacing. Several of the houses I could remember from my childhood, but there were many more where there used to be empty lots.

By the time I got close to the sheriff's office, I was walking slower and slower. I didn't know if it was because I was getting tired or because I would see Art again. My heart was beating wildly. I felt like I was sixteen.

My hand was sweaty as I opened the door of city hall. I asked the lady at the counter to direct me to the police department at the back of the building. I stepped into the office of the Chief of Police, immediately recognizing the broad shoulders of the man sitting at the desk. He was going through his files and hadn't heard me come in.

"Hello, Art."

He turned in his chair and we stared at each other. "Sandy!" For a tall man, he moved fast. He caught me up in a bear hug, with me hugging back. He drew back to look at my face. For a moment I thought he was going to kiss me, and I realized how much I wanted him to, but he didn't.

"Art, how are you? It's good to see you." I hardly recognized my trembling voice.

He was still the best looking man I had ever met. Granted he had a few gray hairs at the temples, but he still stood straight and slim, his steel-blue eyes clear, that dazzling smile I remembered so well, the little movie-actor cleft in his chin that I had loved to touch. I realized that, subconsciously, I had been comparing every man I met to him, and none of them had come close to measuring up. I had thought my line of work was what kept me from getting involved; looking at Art, I knew how wrong I was. I loved him as much, if not more, than I did fifteen years ago.

"Come, have a chair. We have a lot to catch up on. Are you back on vacation or back to stay?" he asked.

"Back to stay. The bureau doesn't have an active place for someone who uses a crutch. Somehow, we don't blend in too well with the natives. They offered me a desk job, but I was sure that would drive me crazy. No, I figured with my degree and past experience, I shouldn't have trouble getting my Private Investigator's license."

"I don't know if there will be enough work to keep you busy." He was serious.

"Sh-h-h, don't let this get around, but I don't need to work. Having an office will keep people from thinking I have turned into a bum. I have my disability pay plus my retirement. I'll be okay."

"Did you ever marry, Babe?" Babe. The old nickname. It sounded right.

"No. You?"

"Nope. I've been waiting for you to get tired of cleaning up the world and come home. Looks like it's finally happened." His eyes were twinkling; I felt myself blushing.

We spent the next couple of hours reminiscing, catching up on important events, and remembering old friends. Art asked about my leg. Concisely, I gave him the details.

"How could you stand the pain? How did you keep from going out of your mind?"

I told him about the trance, about how my eyes stay open which undoubtedly drove "The Executioner" to hurt me more than he would have otherwise. "Had I been conscious during that ordeal, I'm sure I would have gone insane."

"That's probably true, Babe," he said, with tears in his eyes. "Well . . . , it's to bad I wasn't there to protect you." He cleared his throat and tried to smile. "Say, I've a couple of new detectives I want you to meet. They may be of help to you when you open your office." He called in the two detectives he had recently hired, and once again, I was greeting friends from long ago.

Ed Bagley and Billy Ray Williams were two from our college class. Both had gone to the big city to work after college, but with their kids growing up they wanted to get away from too many people, too many cars, too many temptations. They had written Art to see if he had an opening. Fate must have played a part. A few days before they called, the Myrtle Woods City Council had given him the funds to hire two more detectives.

The three men wanted to know about some of the assignments I had been on. I told them about a few of the lesser ones. I'm sure they knew I was leaving out a lot of the dirty details. When Ed asked how I had hurt my leg, I begged off. That hurt was still too fresh for anyone except Art.

"I'll tell you some day, but not yet. Okay?"

They understood, and changed the subject.

It was four-thirty when Art told his deputies he was taking the rest of the day off. Something he must not have done too often, judging from the surprised look on their faces. After hugs from Ed and Billy Ray, we slowly walked the two blocks to the drugstore, stepping from the sun into the dark coolness. I didn't see her until I heard this hoot and saw a body hurtling at me.

"Sandy! Sandy! Oh, God, I can't believe it. How are you? What happened to your leg? Come here and sit down. Roger, Roger, hurry up. Come see who's here."

Beautiful, crazy, wonderful, non-stop Marie. My best girlfriend since I was seven years old. I felt tears spring unbidden to my eyes.

"How are you, Marie?" I asked, unwinding myself from her arms. She brushed her hair back from her face, and reached for a napkin from the counter to wipe her eyes. By that time Roger was there and I repeated everything again. I hadn't realized how emotional my homecoming was going to be for all of us. Art stood there with a silly grin on his face. Darn him, he knew this would happen.

They wanted to take me to dinner, but I told them I'd have to call my housekeeper. That statement called for an explanation about Frances and Al. When I called Frances, she suggested they all come home with me. The menu—stew, homemade biscuits, tomatoes vinaigrette, iced tea and strawberry shortcake—convinced them to show up at seven.

Art drove me home, filling me in with the details about Marie and Roger's son, Adam. "Marie wrote me that he had died, but she never explained what happened."

"It's a sad story. Adam was a terrific kid. He had Marie's red hair and Roger's calm personality. On his ninth birthday they were having a party at City Park, when Adam and a bunch of his buddies decided to swim out to the platform. They were goofing off and at first he wasn't missed. It wasn't until they were climbing up on the platform that they became alarmed. The cry went out and several adults, including myself, Marie and Roger, jumped in to find him. Twenty minutes passed before Roger brought him up. The rescue truck was there by that time, but they weren't able to revive him. The sad part is, because of the trouble Marie had carrying Adam, she was warned not to have more children."

"She didn't tell me she couldn't have more kids. How were she and Roger able to survive?"

"If anything, their love for each other grew stronger than ever. I thought they would try to adopt, but I guess not, and now they may be getting too old to be considered. It's a shame. They would be ideal parents."

Art dropped me off at the house. He wanted to go home and get out of his uniform before returning for dinner. The story about Marie and Roger broke my heart. Frances and Al remembered the drowning, and the sadness the whole town felt for the young couple. I told them about Marie being my special friend since childhood.

I had always gone to the lake when something was bothering

me, so of course, that's where I took this new pain. Until Art appeared beside me I didn't realize how much time had passed. He took one look at my tear-streaked face and took me in his arms. He held me close, while I sobbed out the grief I felt for my friends.

"Come on, Babe. They will be here shortly. You don't want them to see you like this, do you?"

I shook my head. Using his handkerchief, I mopped my face and tried a wan smile. He took my hand and we hurried to the house as fast as my crutch would allow.

By the time Marie and Roger arrived, I was presentable ... barely. We had a wonderful time during dinner while they brought me up to date on some of my other friends who had remained in Myrtle Woods.

"You've got to be kidding," I laughed, when they told me Oscar Wheatland owned the Feed and Seed store, and Margaret Pick had a small florist shop on the north edge of town.

"What do you mean?" they asked.

"Someone by the name of Wheat-land owns the seed store? And how about Margaret? A Pick sells flowers! And Keith Drumm owns the music store! Good God, I can't stand it." I was laughing so hard my sides hurt. "Thank God your last name is Owens, Roger, instead of Pill. That would take the cake!"

They had never thought of the names that way, but since I had brought them to their attention, they couldn't help laughing along with me.

"I'll never be able to look any of them in the face without remembering this conversation," Marie giggled. That giggle. I realized how much I had missed it.

I told Marie and Roger about my plans to open a P.I. office. "I'll have to find an office. Some place where people will feel comfortable coming to see me and, most importantly, dirt cheap."

"Marie, how about the old Graham place?" Roger asked. Turning to me, he explained, "It's in a good part of town, but in dreadful condition. You would have to do a major overhaul before you could move in."

"Sandy, I'm sure it would be perfect." Marie still had her positive attitude. "Want me to go with you tomorrow and see what we think?"

We made arrangements for me to pick her up about nine in the morning at the drug store. The rest of the evening was so pleasant that I hated for it to end. I stood on the porch for several minutes after they pulled away, thinking how precious those old friends were to me.

Before I headed for bed, the Applebees and I discussed the apartment.

"Do you think there will be enough room?"

It would be perfect, they informed me. "That little bedroom will be perfect for the grandkids when they come to visit," Frances said.

Their living quarters decided, we discussed what I wanted to do with the house.

I thought larger windows in the dining room that overlook the lake, bright paint, and new furniture should do it. Al, never using more words than necessary, stated, "Front room needs a bigger window." I realized immediately that he was right. Also, I wanted to see about having a deck added to the back of the house.

Frances asked if they could have first pick of the furniture for their apartment. I told her to take what she wanted. Everything was in good shape, but big—and hard—and old.

"I'll keep a few of the smaller pieces for their sentimental value. After that, you can have anything that is left."

Al recommended Dan Corbett, a well-known builder, to do the remodeling. I made a note to call him the first thing in the morning. I wanted his input on a remedy for those steep, narrow front steps.

FIVE

I took one look at the Graham house the next morning, and told Marie what we should do is tear down and rebuilt. She convinced me to look it over before making a final decision. As we made our way to the door, I think we both expected the ghosts from the past to open it and usher us inside.

It had to be the tiniest house ever built. The front room was about twelve by fourteen. Big enough for two desks, I decided. Behind that was a smaller room, which would make a good store room for those files I hoped to accumulate. The kitchen and bath were minute.

There were three things going for it: the foundation appeared solid, the roof looked in good shape, and the location was ideal. I decided if the rent was cheap enough and the owner would give me free rent for a couple of months in exchange for repairs, I'd be able to make the place presentable.

"Before I put money into this place, I'd want to have a contractor check to make sure it's solid," I told Marie.

We hurried to the real estate office handling the renting details. I told the agent, Kent Olsen, I was interested, but that I wanted a contractor to do a thorough inspection before I committed myself. If the contractor gave his okay, I would want the first month rent free, in exchange for the repairs I would make.

"I plan to paint the place inside and out, lay new linoleum and plant flowers."

A call to the owner gave me the first three months free in

exchange for all the work I had mentioned. Would I be interested in an option to buy, he wondered. That was an idea I would consider later, I told him. It would depend on how much business I had.

I contacted Dan Corbett and asked him to check out the building. His findings were what I had hoped to hear: solid foundation, roof in good condition, and no pests or dry rot. He decided that he could fix the building up into a fine office.

All I talked about at dinner was that tiny house. I think Art thought I'd bitten off more than I could chew. After dinner, we piled in his car and went to see my recent acquisition.

"Doesn't look like much, does it?" I asked them. "Oh, well, I always was one to steam ahead and damn the torpedoes."

"Amen," Art said.

The following Monday I signed a lease for a year with an option to buy.

I think I drove everyone who worked on the office, crazy. I couldn't stay away from watching the metamorphosis of that old, rundown building. What emerged was a quaint cottage; a neat white house with an inviting porch, a tiny lawn, and geraniums bobbing their heads in the window box.

I was standing there admiring the finished project when three car loads of people came screeching up to the curb. With a lot of laughter and shouting, they piled out and trooped up the walk. In Art's hands was a sign to hang from the porch. The sign was plain, but the beautiful lettering more than made up for it. The words read simply:

> Kassandra Shores
> Private Investigator

"We thought this porch was the best place to hang this sign. We hope you like it, Sandy," Art told me.

Like it? I loved it. With tears in my eyes, I did my best to tell them how much.

It has been a year since we hung the sign and I've had more clients than I ever dreamed possible. I've helped track down delinquent dads, aided people in tracing back their roots and, once in a while, helped the police on a case. Nothing earth-shaking, but encouraging enough for me to take out a loan to purchase the building.

About six months ago Art asked my help in solving a local murder, which we managed to do fairly quickly. Now, if they don't solve a case within the first few days, Art calls and we start working together before the clues get too cold.

Today is a hot July day that was giving every indication we could be frying eggs on the sidewalk before dark, something we don't do often in Oregon. Even the dogs don't have the energy to chase the cats. The old-timers are predicting rain; I'm praying for it.

Business was slow, so I had stopped by the police station and brought two of the unsolved cases from the archives with me this morning. I'd been trying to read one of them, but I couldn't seem to concentrate. I kept reading the same two pages again and again. I guess my brain doesn't work well in the heat. Instead of taxing my brain further, I was intently watching a spider, who looked pregnant, build a web in the corner of the porch when my phone rang. I jumped a foot.

"Hi, Sandy. You busy?" Art asked.

"Never too busy to talk to you."

"Flattery will get you everywhere," he teased. "Could you drop by when you have a minute?"

"Sure. I'll be right there." Within three minutes I was on my way.

Art got right to the point. "I'd like you to take a look at this new case, Babe. I imagine you have read about Doreen Fuller who disappeared about three weeks ago?"

"The lady everybody thinks left town?"

"Yeah. She lived in South Point before her marriage, so I doubt you would remember her. Supposedly she left this cryptic note saying she was going to go find herself. Both the parents and the husband say it's not her writing." He pushed the note across to me.

She had torn the paper from some kind of a notebook, the ink was lilac. "Dear Dale, I'm sorry, but I feel I must have time alone to see if I can't come to terms with the blows life has dealt me. In my own way, I love both you and Tracy. I need to get away and try to straighten out my life, so we can be happy. Please don't be angry and try not to worry. Tell them at work I had to go away for awhile. I'll be in touch. (signed) Doreen."

"Her parents and her husband, Dale, are driving us crazy. Her father calls two or three times a week, while the husband's in here practically every day wanting to know what we are doing to find her. We have checked the house from stem to stern, talked to her parents and the neighbors, checked every type of transportation out of town, checked the freezers of Fuller's meat markets. He owns four, one here and three in Mountain View. The only thing we know for sure is that she didn't leave town in her car. It's parked in the Fuller's garage. We've hit a dead end. Would you take a look and see if you can think of anything we haven't done?" Art was practically begging.

"You bet. Sounds interesting," I answered. He gave me copies of the reports done by members of the police force. "What does she mean by the blows life had handed her?"

Art shook his head. "You've got me. Her parents and husband say they don't know, but I think they're lying."

"I'll let you know if I find anything," I promised. With a wave I headed back to my office.

I got an ice-cold pop from the 'frige before settling back in my desk chair. Pulling my yellow pad close to make notes on, I began to read the report on Doreen Fuller.

Name: Doreen Emily Fuller. *Age*: thirty-five. *Hair*: blond. *Eyes*: green. *Weight*: one thirty. *Height*: five eight.

Occupation: Employed by Paul J. Logger Company for fifteen years. One year in secretary pool, four years private secretary to owner, Paul J. Logger, ten years administrative secretary to Vice-President Ronald Miller. (Why the change from president to vice president?)

One child: Tracy, a son, ten years old.

Married to Dale Donald Fuller. Age: fifty. Hair: bald. Eyes: brown. Weight: two fifty-five. Height: six foot five. (I don't remember this guy.) Occupation: butcher. One shop in Myrtle Woods, three in Mountain View. Well liked by employees.

Fingerprints: Fuller house checked. Prints found belong to members of the household. No sign of forced entry or signs of a struggle. Mr. Fuller visibly upset when shown warrant to check his meat market freezers. Search negative.

Date of disappearance: Sunday, seven July. Church in a.m. At one p.m. Mr. Fuller and son went to Mountain View to visit Fuller's sister. Maybelle Snook. Address: 145 Bethel St., Mountain View. When Fuller and son returned at four-thirty they were unable to find wife. Husband says very few clothes are missing. Mrs. Fuller's car is in garage. Nothing unusual in the car. Dusted car and the note for fingerprints. Found only Mrs. Fuller's. Fuller says she was only one who ever drove vehicle. Mr. Fuller's alibi checked out.

End of report.

I was curious, but where to start? I should go do a little house to house neighborhood canvassing, but this crutch and my underarm don't do too well in the heat. In minutes, I'm rubbed raw. Granted the police have talked to everybody, but sometimes people remember little things later, after the excitement has died down. The best I can do in this heat is get in my air-conditioned car and cruise the Fuller neighborhood.

Cruising down Pleasant Street past the Fuller house, I noticed most of the houses were in good repair, but several needed painting. Homeowners could only water once a week, so lawns were turning brown, flowers were dying. Even the trees along the curb were drooping; their leaves dusty. The only bright spots were flower boxes here and there. It surprised me that a man who owned four meat markets lived on Pleasant Street. I would have thought he would live on Skyline Boulevard where the successful business people lived.

As I drove past his house two things caused me to go slower. The flowers in his window boxes were dying from lack of water, and, although the house looked recently painted, the grass looked like it hadn't been cut in weeks. Every window blind I could see in the two-story house was down. That didn't surprise me in this heat, but every single one? That seemed like over-kill to me. Why, I asked myself, does the house look deserted? If good ol' Dale was expecting his wife back, wouldn't he have kept her flowers watered and the lawn mowed? And where was the boy? Surely, Fuller didn't keep him shut up in that house alone.

Maybe I have the wrong address, I thought. To eliminate that possibility, I stopped at a phone booth in the parking lot of a small neighborhood grocery store a few blocks down the street. Nope, right address. Something was haywire, I was positive. I gunned out of the parking lot and drove quickly back to the Fuller house.

I decided to see if anyone would answer the door. I had no idea what I'd say if someone did open the door, but something would come to me, I was sure. I rang the bell. There was a scurrying movement inside, but nobody answered. I tried the bell again. Still nobody came. I drove away slowly. Before turning the corner I glanced in the rear view mirror and the hair rose on the back of my neck. A small, white face was peering out from under the shade in one of the upstairs windows.

So-o-o, I whispered to myself. Somebody *is* hiding in that house. Possibly the boy, but why hide? I was beginning to have a sneaky hunch why Art gave me this case. And sneaky was the operative word here.

SIX

I had barely returned to the office from checking out the Fuller residence when I heard a noise at the door. I looked up to see a woman waltz into the room and I *mean* waltz. She was a puppet with an unseen person manipulating the strings. She appeared to be in her late sixties, slender, a well-proportioned body, pure white hair, black eyebrows and beautiful deep brown eyes. Her eyes fascinated me. They reminded me of the eyes of a frightened deer caught in someone's headlights. She was nice looking, but rumpled. I think under different circumstances she would have been stunning.

"Are you the detective?" she asked me.

I felt like asking her if she saw anybody else in the room, but I was polite.

"Yes, ma'am, I am. Won't you sit down?"

Well, she didn't sit. She collapsed onto the chair, the way a puppet does when the puppeteer releases the strings. She sat there a minute looking at me with those big, brown doe-eyes.

"Miss. Shores—or is it Mrs?"

I assured her I was Miss and asked if I could get her anything. Perhaps a glass of water? I thought maybe I had a fainter here. No, no, she assured me she was fine—well, not in those words—but I got the drift.

"Miss. Shores, a week ago they found my husband's body floating in the lake at City Park. They are trying to tell me he committed suicide, but I know that's not possible."

"And why do you say that, Mrs . . . ?"

"Oh, I'm sorry. I have been under such a strain lately, I sometimes forget who I am. My name is Harriet Logger. My husband was Paul Logger of the Paul J. Logger Company. Do you remember reading about him in the paper?"

The Paul J. Logger Company was the largest grass seed processor in the Willamette Valley. Yes, it did ring a bell, since it was the same company where Doreen Fuller worked. Was there a connection here?

According to the paper, a jogger found Paul J's body last Wednesday morning floating in the lake with nothing on but his necktie. The police found the rest of his clothes neatly folded on the bank. I had read the police report last Thursday, and there was a detail she had not mentioned. Someone had cut off his penis with a very sharp knife.

Things like that didn't happen to the caliber of people the Logger's represented. Lots of money, owned most of the town, and what they didn't own, they contributed to heavily each year. The Boys and Girls Club, the library, the hospital, the Boy and Girl Scouts—all of these organizations were delighted that the Loggers lived in Myrtle Woods.

"Yes, Mrs. Logger, I remember reading about your husband. But why come to me? Is there a piece of information you haven't told the police yet? Something that would make you feel he didn't commit suicide?"

"I know he didn't," she insisted. "My husband never took off the gold chain I gave him for a wedding present. That chain had been in our family for years and Paul treasured it. When they found his body it was gone. They tell me there were no marks on the body, but I'm positive my husband was murdered."

Now that she had mentioned the "M" word, her strength seemed to drain away. She seemed to age twenty years before my eyes; not a pretty sight. I didn't ask this time. I got a glass of water and made sure she took a sip or two.

"Thank you. Miss. Shores, I must know what happened to him. He was a good man and a good husband. Please, will you help me? The local police and the other two detectives I spoke to in Mountain View don't seem to think there is anything unusual about the missing chain. However, I'm positive it's a clue that would tell us what happened to him. If only I could get someone to listen to me."

Abruptly, she became a different woman. She straightened up, squared her shoulders and, in the blink of an eye, went from sad widow to the new president of the Paul J. Logger Company. "Something must be done to clear Paul's name." She spoke in an entirely different voice. "I can't have the world thinking he killed himself. The stock value of the company would plummet. It's already dropped several points. I've been buying the shares that the investors have sold to keep the value from going down still further. Well, I can't keep that up indefinitely, can I?" She became the weeping widow again. "Won't you please help me?"

The first thing I decided was that I would never turn my back on her. This woman has more sides to her personality than a chameleon, I told myself. In reality, she might be a black widow spider. I made a note to ask Art if she was a suspect in the death of her husband.

The second thing that amused me was how she breezed over contacting two other detectives. I decided not to let that bother me. She could have talked to six other P. I's, and held a seance for all I cared. This case intrigued me. Big-time civic leader, lots of money . . . I was itching to get to work.

"Of course, Mrs. Logger. I'll do everything I can to help you, but you must know if I find out anything that may be damaging to you or your husband's reputation, I must report it to the police."

Yes, she understood that. I told her my going rate was two hundred a day plus expenses, which didn't seem to phase her. After we got the details out of the way, I started asking the preliminary questions.

"Was your husband involved in any new business deals? Had he suddenly become involved with a different crowd of people? Was he seeing another woman?" That last one got her riled.

"No, never. Paul and I loved each other very much. He always came home by four-thirty in the afternoon. We would go to the club and play a round of golf in the summer or a game of tennis in the winter. Two or three times a week we would have dinner there. Sometimes we would go elsewhere to eat, if we were feeling especially romantic. So many wonderful memories." She paused for a moment, her smile sad. "When he didn't come home Tuesday afternoon by five, I knew something was wrong. When he wasn't home by seven I called the police to report him missing. They refused to take the information until twenty-four hours had passed. By that time they had found his body. I knew before they came to tell me that he was dead." Tears welled in her eyes. "We were making such great plans to go to Hawaii for our thirtieth anniversary next m-mo-month." With that, the dam broke, and she sobbed. I could only sit there, after handing her a box of tissues, and wait. I had the feeling this was the first time she had let herself give in to her grief. There is nothing better than a good cry, I always say. Kind of lets you come together and focus on your problem.

"I'm sorry," she hiccuped.

"No problem. Can you think of anything that your husband did differently within the last month or two? Anything that might get me started on the right track? Even if you think it too insignificant to matter. Sometimes the smallest key opens the door to the truth."

We spent an hour going through their last few days together, but nothing seemed out of the ordinary. She was getting ready to leave when she remembered something.

"Paul liked to keep in touch with the groups we donated to. Once a week he'd visit each place to see for himself how things were going. When he came home a few weeks ago, he told me about a young boy about ten years old who had started coming to the Boys and Girls Club. Paul thought he had great potential to make something of himself. He told me the boy was smart and quick; good with numbers. He had decided to keep an eye on him and see how he made out. Then last Monday, when we were playing golf I asked Paul about the youngster. He didn't answer.

When I spoke his name again, he shook his head and told me he didn't want to talk about that boy again. He was quite emphatic, so of course I agreed. We continued our game, but I could tell his mind was elsewhere. For the rest of the day and during dinner he was like that. That was our last evening together," she sobbed.

I finally got her calmed down and sent her home with the instructions to call me if she thought of anything else. I shook her hand and her grip amazed me. If playing golf and tennis gave a person muscles like that, I decided I had better take up those two games. Well, okay, maybe not tennis, I admitted to myself.

I reread my notes. A smart kid, huh? Not much to work on. But wait, what did she mean "no marks on the body"? Didn't she know about the little knife job done on her husband? I made a note to check with Art. And why this big hubbub about that chain? I placed a call to Henry Oliver, the medical examiner.

"Hi, Henry. Sandy here. Did you find scratches or other marks on Paul Logger's neck?"

"Let me check my file." He was back in a minute. "Yes, I did. A slight scratch along the hair line."

I told him about Mrs. Logger's claim that someone had murdered her husband because his gold chain was missing.

"Well, the scratch could have been caused when it was jerked off or by a fingernail, if it was unclasped in a hurry, I guess. Not much to go on, though."

"It's something I will share with Art. Who knows, it may mean something later on," I said.

Earlier, I was complaining because I didn't have anything to do. Within the last hour I have taken on two cases. That's the way things happen in my business. Before I get started though, I must go out and replenish my tissue supply. Harriet Logger had cried me dry.

SEVEN

It was five-fifteen in the afternoon and the temperature was still eighty-five degrees in the shade. When Art came through the door I got two cold ones from my little 'frige, opened them and handed him one. After he swallowed better than half of it, he settled back in the chair.

"Thanks, Babe. I needed that," he sighed. "It's been one helluva day. This heat is making everyone edgy. We had more domestic violence calls today than we had all last month. Stupid men, anyway. If they want a punching bag, why don't they go to the gym. Although, there was one . . . I swear the guy came out on the short end of the deal. By the time she'd finished with him, his face resembled fresh hamburger. Well, enough of that. What happened around here today?"

I told him about my caller and her chameleon ways. "I don't know if she is a heart-broken widow or a hard-hearted business woman or plain nuts. Whichever she may be, the case intrigues me. Do you know anything about the Boys and Girls Club?"

"Not much. I believe the fellow that runs it was a year or two ahead of us in college."

I'll find out tomorrow, I told him. Did he know anything about Paul J.? No, nothing except what was in the reports. This was the first drowning since Adam died, he told me. I didn't mention the meeting I had had with Marie in which she had cried like a baby in my arms. I don't believe she will ever get over losing Adam.

"I need to know what Mrs. Logger was told about the condition of her husband's body. While we were talking, she made the remark that she knew it was murder because the chain he always wore was gone. Doesn't she know about the amputation?"

"No. That information is being withheld. If we get a crank call, we will know it immediately because they won't be able to tell us about the mutilation. You know how that works, Sandy," he answered tersely.

He was right, I did know how it works. "All right, I'll keep mum about it."

I proceeded to tell him about Mrs. Logger's claim about the chain and about the scratch that Henry found.

"Yeah, Mrs. Logger came to us about that chain theory, but I didn't think it was anything. Paul J. did drown. There were no other marks on the body, no bruises, which meant no one held him under. Why his body part was cut off—you've got me. Maybe he was trying to punish himself or some crazy thing like that."

"What do you think about Doreen Fuller being employed by the Paul J. Logger Company? Think there might be a connection there?"

Art was slow in answering, "Not likely. There aren't many places for secretaries to work around here. I think it's a coincidence. However, it won't hurt to keep it in mind."

We talked about the case a few more minutes, and decided to check the microfilm of old newspaper stories to see what we could find written about the Loggers. I called Frances and told her I would be late for supper and to go ahead without me. No problem, she assured me, she would save me something.

Art and I spent over two hours in the station archives department viewing film until I thought I would go blind. We went back ten years and discovered several things about the Loggers. One: Yes, Mr. & Mrs. Logger truly seemed to be the ideal couple. Two: Mrs. Logger was a fantastic cook, putting on dinners for up to sixty people for one benefit or another. Three: She played in golf and tennis tournaments, and bowled a one-eighty-two average. No wonder she had the grip of a boa constrictor, I mused. We were unable to find one derogatory item about them during that time. I found it odd that although there were numerous pictures of Mr. Logger, nowhere was there one of Mrs. Logger. When I mentioned this to Art he shrugged it off.

"Maybe she doesn't think she's photogenic."

"Maybe. Well, I've had it for today. I'm tired and hungry. I think we've gone back far enough. If they haven't done anything involving the police in ten years, they must have been what Mrs. Logger claims—the happiest couple in town."

We didn't know it, but we were that close to finding the needle in the haystack everyone is always talking about. If we had only gone back one more year. Funny little word, "If."

My dinner consisted of chicken pie, green salad, iced tea and brownies, everything as delicious as always. I told Frances and Al about accepting the Fuller case and about the drive past the house on Pleasant Street.

"I'm certain I saw someone looking out of the upstairs window when I was driving away. I'm sure it's the boy. I think I'll drive by there when I finish here."

When I turned on to Pleasant Street, it was getting to be that time of the day when there is still a little light outside, but you can't see to read in the house without turning on a light. If there was anyone in the house, I should be able to tell it this time.

I was one house away when suddenly, slowly, inexplicably every shade in the Fuller house started going up. It surprised me so much, I almost rammed into one of the cars parked along the curb. What the heck, I thought, is the place haunted? What else would explain the phenomenon I had just witnessed? No wonder Mrs. Fuller left, I shivered, feeling cold in the hot evening air.

I decided to try knocking one more time, although my feet wanted to go the other direction as I headed for the front door. Nothing. No movement, no sound. I walked back to the car, knowing I was going to come back in the morning on my way to the office. I tried to come up with answers as I drove home. Every time I thought of all those shades winding up ever so slowly, I got goose bumps and my mind refused to try to think of a logical explanation. The whole thing was utterly crazy.

Art called the office in the morning to hear my report on the shades.

"I don't understand it," I told him. "This morning they were all down again. As the king said in "The King and I," this is a puzzlement."

After we hung up, I pulled out the reports that he had given me about Doreen Fuller. When I finished reading them, I had to admit the guys had been thorough. Each one mentioned that the note, written in lilac ink, was checked for prints, and that Doreen Fuller's were the only ones found on it. They had checked all modes of transportation out of town, checked for old boyfriends, checked to see if there was a new boyfriend hidden somewhere, talked to her parents and the people in the neighborhood. No one claimed to have seen anything out of the ordinary. They talked to her friends and business acquaintances to no avail. The woman had suddenly disappeared without a trace. Period.

I leaned back in my chair, put my hands behind my head and thought, but no great ideas came bounding out. I decided it was time to get Art's input.

"Good morning, sir!" I snapped in my best military style when he answered the phone. In my mind's eye I could see him sitting in his chair in front of that huge, cluttered desk of his. Yet if I asked for anything he could put his finger on it in an instant. It was a fascinating thing to watch.

"Yes, Babe. What can I do for you?"

I knew he was swinging around to gaze out the window at what he called his view. Actually it is the library parking lot. He has told me many times how envious he is of my little front yard.

"I have a couple of questions about the Fuller case. Was the pen used to write the note checked for prints? Did anyone mention anything odd about the window shades on the Fuller house? And, if she didn't leave town, and you haven't found a body, have you considered that she might still be in town?"

"Whoa, Whoa, Whoa! One question at a time," Art said.

"About the pen, I don't remember anyone mentioning seeing one. Good point, Babe, I'll follow up on that and get back to you. No one has mentioned the window shades to me. I doubt, however, if anyone was there during the times of day that you have noticed them. Yes, we have considered that she might be hiding out in the area, but where?"

Who knows, I told Art. Promising I would keep him posted, I hung up. I spent the next hour coming up with, and discarding, numerous answers to the mystery of the shades.

The next day, I stopped by my office to check the answering machine. Nothing doing there, so I was off to the Boys and Girls Club. When I walked into the building I realized that the fellow in charge was Jack Wild, a good friend in my college days.

"Jack, what a pleasant surprise. I didn't know you lived in Myrtle Woods."

"Sandy, it's good to see you. Are you home on vacation? Are you still doing that secret government stuff?"

I told him I was home to stay. After reminiscing for a bit, I got down to the nitty-gritty of why I was there. What I learned in the next hour was almost unbelievable. I could hardly wait to get back to the station to discuss it with Art. When I left the club I told Jack that he had been a big help. Promising to stop by again, I hobbled quickly to my car.

When I got to the station, I could have screamed. Art was appearing in court, his secretary informed me. She didn't expect him back until late afternoon. I left a message for him to call me the minute he got back, that it was of the utmost importance.

Why is it, when you want time to pass quickly, it crawls slower than a snail? I thought the day would never end. Shortly after five, Art walked through the door.

"Finally! Sit down, because what I learned today puts a whole new slant on everything." I was so excited about my news that Art had to get his own drink from the 'frige. "You were right. The club director is an old classmate, Jack Wild. Remember him? Anyway, we had a very informative conversation. The young man that Logger was interested in? Would you believe he is the son of Doreen Fuller? Not of Doreen and Dale, only Doreen."

The bottle he was holding slipped in his hand. "How did he know?"

"Doreen was there the day she disappeared, when Paul Logger walked in. Jack said he thought for a minute or two that she was going to faint. Then she kind of shook herself and walked to where he was standing. She was civil when she first spoke to Paul J, but her voice went up an octave as Jack overheard her tell Paul J. that the boy he was watching was his son. The one he refused to claim when she became pregnant. Then she said something about him being deaf and how it was Logger's fault. Jack thought she was going to attack him, but you could tell that Logger hadn't realized that the boy belonged to Doreen nor did he realize that the youngster was deaf. When that got through to him he looked ill and left immediately. Jack said that Doreen followed him outside, looking like she wanted to kill him on the spot.

"I asked what she was doing there. He told me she had stopped by to make sure the boy was there. I guess she was worried because he had come down by himself.

"Anyway, she had turned to walk to her car, when this other car drove up. A tall guy stepped out and called to her. Jack said she froze for a minute. Then she let out this big whoop, ran and jumped on this guy, practically knocking him down. They talked for a minute, then she got in his car and Jack hasn't seen her since.

"I asked if he knew when she came back for her car, but he'd gotten busy with the kids and didn't notice. It had to be before her husband came home from work or he would have noticed her car gone when he pulled into the garage.

"I asked Jack to describe the guy she drove off with, but he said he was an ordinary looking guy. He didn't notice anything outstanding about him. He was more interested in the guy's car because he was driving a new Corvette. Seems he was drooling over one like it in a dealer's showroom on his day off last week.

He said he wouldn't be surprised if it was the same car. It should be easy to spot if it ever shows up here again because it was a bright cherry red. I asked him if he remembered the name of the dealer and he did better than that. In his desk he had one of their cards. It was Honest John's on River Road in Mountain View.

"Anyway, we got to talking about the boy again. Jack told me he hadn't seen him since that Saturday. He went on to tell me that the kid has been in a special school for years and only came home a few days ago. The kid's name is Tracy Fuller." Art's eyebrows went up. "Yeah, it seems that good ol' Dale knew she was pregnant when he married her. I guess Dale was always in love with her, and when she found herself in trouble, he stepped in."

Art couldn't believe my news. "Good, something new to go on. I think the first thing we need to do is visit the car dealer. If it's the same car, we can find out from the dealer who bought it. The second thing we need is information on the boy. How long did he live at home before he was sent away? What happened at the Fuller house when he came home? For that matter, why did he come home after being gone for what sounds like several years?"

"Jack wasn't sure, but he thought it had something to do with the kid becoming ten years old. I guess he's a real whiz with anything electrical. You should have heard Jack when I was leaving. He asked me if he had helped me. When I told him more than he'd ever know, he was so funny. He lowered his voice about three octaves and told me he loved this cloak and dagger stuff.

"There is one thing I don't understand though. How did Doreen and Paul J. avoid meeting in the past ten or eleven years, when they worked for the same company? Especially in a town the size of Myrtle Woods?"

"I don't know, Babe. But, think about it. How often do you see people outside your circle of friends."

"True, but, not seeing him during the day must have taken a

conscious effort by Paul J. or both of them, for that matter. It's unbelievable, isn't it?"

Art didn't argue.

This case was growing like a fungus. Now we are looking for Doreen Fuller, a cherry red car, an elusive young boy, and a murderer. Art wanted to send someone out to talk to Dale Fuller immediately and . . . right there I stopped him.

"Listen, why don't I go talk to him? Since I was the one that talked to Jack, it would seem to me I would be the logical one to do the follow up. Besides it will give me a chance to find out about the kid." I would have begged if I'd thought it would have helped. I was curious about the boy. This would be the perfect way for me to get my questions answered.

Art said there was no reason why I couldn't handle it, if he filed a report on what I found. We decided we would check out Honest John the first thing in the morning. Then, when we got back from Mountain View, I would go interview Dale Fuller.

EIGHT

There was no red car in the showroom when we got there, which gave us hope. A young salesman came hurrying to meet us. "Good morning. May I help you?" he asked.

"Have you sold that red Corvette?" I tried to look crestfallen.

"Yes, Ma'am. I sold that about three weeks ago." he boasted.

"Oh, darn. See, honey, I told you we should have come sooner."

"Sorry about that, sweetheart. I know you had your heart set on it. By the way, between us guys, how much did it go for?" Art asked of the salesman, in a low tone of voice.

"It sold for $52,000. That baby was equipped," the salesman informed us.

Art whistled. "Man, that fellow must be looking at powerful big payments."

"Nope. He paid the full amount in cash."

"In cash?" Art acted like he didn't believe the kid.

"Well, you know . . . by check."

Art started looking over the car that was on display. "I'd be afraid to take a check that big. What if it wasn't covered? You sure could lose a bunch on that deal." Art acted like he didn't care one way or the other.

"What do you think we are—a bunch of hicks? We called the Arizona State Bank in Phoenix, made sure it was covered, and had them put a hold on the funds. We weren't born yesterday, you know." He was indignant.

I spoke up, excitedly, "Honey, I'll bet Horace bought that

53

car. You remember when we were talking to him a few weeks ago. He told me he was going to stop by here on his way out of town and see about trading."

"No, it wasn't your friend. This guy's name was Jasper Grant. About forty-five, I'd guess," the young barrel of information told us.

I felt like throwing my fist in the air and shouting: YES! We had hit the jackpot. I wanted to tell that young man he shouldn't give out that kind of information, but I didn't. Who knows, I might want something else from him sometime.

After giving the salesman mutterings about not wanting anything but the Corvette, we left. Nasty persons that we are, we listed the phone number of the police station as our home number.

"Can you believe it?" I said, as we were pulling away from the car lot. "How lucky can we get?"

"That kid sure has a loose mouth. Makes me think he won't last long in the car business or, for that matter, in any business," Art told me with a smile.

We went right to the police station when we got back in Myrtle Woods. Art contacted the Arizona police chief, and asked to have Jasper Grant picked up for questioning in the disappearance of Doreen Fuller.

While Art was busy with the police in Phoenix, I drove out to the Pleasant Street house and was rewarded with a car in the driveway. I stepped up on the porch and had my finger ready to ring the bell, but before I could push the button, the door opened. A handsome young boy about ten years of age stood before me. The elusive Tracy Fuller, I was willing to bet.

"Hello there. May I speak to your father?" I asked him.

Without a word, he opened the door wider, indicating I should come in.

"Hello, Mr. Fuller?" I asked the tall man coming in from another room.

"Yes, I'm Dale Fuller."

"I'm Sandy Shores, a private investigator. I have been asked by the police to see if I could help them locate your wife. I'm sorry, but I do have a few questions."

"Questions, questions. Is that all you people know how to do? Have they helped the police find my wife?" He sounded more defeated than angry.

"No, sir. I'm afraid not. May I ask who this is?" I asked, motioning to the boy.

"Oh, I'm sorry. This is my son, Tracy. He can't hear or speak. *He's been in school learning how to sign and to read lips. He's very good at both, aren't you, son? And he's a whiz at anything electrical. Going to grow up to be an electrical engineer, aren't you, Tracy?*" He spoke the last few sentences for my benefit and signed to his son.

I surprised Tracy when I signed how glad I was to meet him.

"You know how to sign?" Dale acted like he couldn't believe his eyes. "I was beginning to think I would never find anyone else in this town who could talk to him. I think he gets a little tired of talking to me all the time. His mother wouldn't try to learn. It was a bone of contention between us.

"I know she left because Tracy had to come home to live. Since the day she was told he couldn't hear, she refused to care for him. She kept saying he was her punishment for getting pregnant before she was married. I took her to counseling, psychiatrists—the works. The last doctor we saw told us she was psychosomatic or something like that. He seemed to think it was caused by her emotional state. Well, there wasn't anything I could do about that." He sounded so defeated I felt sorry for him.

"I hired nurses to care for him during the day while he was a baby, and I took care of him at night," he continued. "His grandma, Doreen's mom, tried to help out, but it was too hard on her to see the way Doreen acted. I finally told her not to come anymore. When he was old enough, I sent him to a convent near here where I knew the nuns had a school for deaf children. I was sure they would take good care of him, and he would also get a good education. It about tore me apart to have to do that, but it was best for the boy. I went up every Wednesday and Sunday to see him. Doreen thought I was in Mountain View visiting my sister on Wednesday. Then on Sunday, she thought I was having meetings with my managers, but both times I was at the convent seeing Tracy. I had alibis set up if she should ever check up on me, but I don't believe it ever occurred to her to wonder where I was. I often thought she was seeing someone else. She is such a beautiful young woman. I wouldn't blame her if she has left town with another man. Anyway, about a month ago there was a fire and they had to send the kids home while the convent is being rebuilt.

"Well, Doreen went off the deep end. She screamed she wouldn't stay here if Tracy came home. Well, I slapped her. It made me angry, her acting like that. Most of the time she is gentle and sensitive, a real nice person. But she froze around Tracy." He stood up and walked aimlessly around the room, straightening an article here, a picture there. I could tell he was trying to make up his mind about something.

He must have decided I needed to know everything because he suddenly turned to Tracy and sent him to get a glass of water. While he was out of the room Dale Fuller verified what Jack had told me yesterday. "I'm not his real father, you know. I don't know who is nor do I want to know. I love this boy like he was my own flesh and blood. I was sorry for Doreen, knowing how she felt, but there was nothing else I could do. Tracy had to come home. I guess she wasn't kidding though, was she? She did leave, one week to the day after Tracy came home. I am worried sick because that note she left doesn't sound like her, and the handwriting looks different somehow. I can't quite put my finger on it. I think if she was okay, she would call." He took time to drink the water Tracy brought him.

"I don't know what to think anymore. On top of that, I've got to find somebody to stay with Tracy during the day. He refuses to go to the Girls and Boys Club anymore. Won't even go outside. He sits in here during the day with the blinds drawn. It's not healthy for him to act that way. I don't want to lose him, too." Tears rolled slowly down his cheeks. "Sorry," he said, wiping them away.

I sat still, giving him time to compose himself. I had come to the conclusion that the boy could lip-read because Fuller made sure he talked above the boy's head most of the time. When he sent Tracy after another glass of water to eliminate the chance that he would catch what he was about to say, it confirmed my suspicions.

"I've been staying nights at my sister's in Mountain View, but she works too, so I don't want to leave Tracy there where he doesn't know anybody. If I have him stay here, he can go to the Boys and Girls Club, but something must have happened to him there. He won't talk about it, but he hasn't wanted to go back since the day Doreen disappeared. I don't understand it. He seemed to enjoy it in the beginning."

This talk about the club reminded me of the Corvette.

"Have you noticed a cherry red Corvette around anywhere since your wife disappeared?"

"Yes, I did see one about a week ago, but where was it?" He thought for several seconds. "I'm sorry, I can't remember. Is it important?"

"Possibly. Try to relax. It will come to you and when it does, get in touch with me immediately. Day or night," I instructed him, handing him my card.

"One more thing, Mr. Fuller. I've noticed that all the blinds in the house go up and down at certain times of the day. Could you explain?"

Mr. Fuller started laughing. "It's Tracy. I told you he was smart. He has rigged up a device that pulls them down before sunrise to keep the heat out, and rolls them up again when it gets dark. Works off of a sensor. Way beyond me, but he wanted to try it. He's quite a boy, Yes, sir, quite a boy."

Fuller signed to Tracy that he loved him. The most engaging grin spread across the boy's face.

So, Dale Fuller was not the bad guy we were making him out to be. He seemed genuinely worried about his wife, and he was gentle and loving with the boy. It gave credence to the old saying: Blood does not a father make.

"Mr. Fuller, I would like to spend the days with Tracy. I would have to take him with me to my office in the mornings, but I'll never take him anywhere that he might be in danger."

"You'd do that?"

"Yes, I'd enjoy it. Besides I have a wonderful couple that work for me in my home by the lake, and I'm sure they would love to have him visit. Does he swim?"

Fuller kept looking for a catch in my offer. The final decision was that I would come at seven-thirty in the morning to pick up Tracy. I could take him anywhere I wished, except to Doreen's parents in South Point, Dale had informed me.

"I will tell you what you need to know later." He nodded at Tracy.

That mysterious remark about Doreen's parents sounds interesting, I thought, heading for the police station.

After Art and I discussed my meeting with Fuller, we almost decided to let Doreen Fuller stay lost. However, when I told Art that Fuller had possibly seen the Corvette last week he got excited. He convinced me we needed to concentrate even harder on trying to find her.

"I'm going to be taking care of Tracy during the day since I know how to sign," I told him. His mouth dropped open. "You better shut your mouth before a fly gets in."

"You continue to amaze me, Babe. Will I ever know everything about you?"

I told him I hoped not.

NINE

Seven-thirty sharp the next morning I pulled into the Fuller driveway. Both Dale and Tracy were waiting for me on the porch. He was a little shy, but I could understand that. I decided to keep him home for the first few hours, figuring it would be easier for us to get acquainted if he was in familiar surroundings. I had my notes with me, so there was no need to rush to the office.

Tracy was sitting on the front room floor trying to come up with a design of something that would make my life easier, he told me. Bless his heart, if he only knew that getting rid of this blasted crutch without losing my leg would solve ninety percent of my problems. I sat reviewing my notes on both the Fuller and the Logger cases, while Tracy worked. I felt sure the two cases were linked, but the only thing I knew for certain was that Doreen didn't run off with Paul J. Thinking of Paul J. reminded me that I hadn't been earning my money from Mrs. Logger, so I decided to pay her a visit. My thoughts stopped me. Did she know about Tracy? Paul J. had ten years to tell his wife that he had gotten his secretary pregnant. However, his anger when Mrs. Logger asked about the boy while they were playing golf, made it apparent that she didn't know about Tracy. It still seemed incredulous to me that in a town the size of Myrtle Woods, especially with Doreen employed by his company, that Paul J. had never run into her before that fateful Saturday. Was it possible that Paul J. had something to do with her disappearance? That was a whole new angle I would have to consider.

It was getting close to ten o'clock when I decided to take a chance and take Tracy with me to see Mrs. Logger. He seemed happy to get out of the house, despite what his father had told me. Today was going to be another scorcher, so I decided we'd be smart and get our visiting over early.

The difference in the neighborhood between Pleasant Street and Valley View Drive was like night and day. The spacious homes, surrounded by well-manicured lawns and riotous flower beds, were a far cry from the drabness of Pleasant Street. What was their secret? Maybe if you had money, the city didn't ask you to conserve the water. I surely hoped that wasn't the answer.

The Logger house was the biggest and the best on the block—two-story colonial with columns, circular drive—it looked a southern plantation. It sat further back from the street than the others. Two beautiful old shade trees stood majestically in the front, while the backyard butted up to the forest. It was a picture out of a magazine.

I'd like to have one like that someday, I signed to Tracy.

Me, too, his fingers answered.

We pulled in the driveway to find several other cars lining the way. Mrs. Logger was having a party or a wake. When I rang the bell I could hear laughter in the house. It didn't sound like the widow was too unhappy.

The person who opened the door had to be the biggest man I have ever met. He was seven foot tall, if he was an inch, and positively ugly. In addition to his height, the giant must have weighed better than three hundred pounds. Tracy shrunk back behind me and I didn't blame him. This guy was enough to scare the daylights out of a ghost. Was he the butler, the bodyguard or the bouncer?

He glared down at us. I smiled sweetly and handed him my business card. "Would you please tell Mrs. Logger that Sandy Shores is here?" I asked in my most upper crust voice. My knees were knocking together so loudly I was afraid he would hear the racket.

Within three minutes he returned, followed by Mrs. Logger. "Miss. Shores, how nice to see you. Do you have news for me?"

This was an entirely different lady from the two I had talked to in my office. This Mrs. Logger, looking ten years younger with every hair in place in an elaborate hairdo, had on a dress that had to be an original. She was most gracious to both of us. I knew she was curious about Tracy, but was too well bred to ask.

"No, ma'am, I'm afraid not. What I need is a picture of your husband's chain. I have determined that it was either jerked off or your husband's neck was scratched by a fingernail when it was removed."

"Of, course, won't you and your friend come in."

"May I introduce Tracy Fuller?" I held my breath.

I've heard of a multitude of expressions racing across someone's face, but had never encountered it before. It was like watching a movie. First surprise, followed quickly by curiosity, shame, shock, anger and, finally, rage.

"How dare you bring that child here?" She was holding tightly to the door frame, looking like she might fall to the carpet if she didn't have it for support.

"I'm sorry. I don't understand." All the time I was thinking: Oh, Lord, I've really messed up this time. She does know about Tracy.

"That child . . . don't tell me you didn't know that boy is my husband's only child. One that I didn't know about until last week. Oh, my God, I can't stand it. Please leave. I must have time alone." I heard her tell the butler to inform her guests that she would be unable to continue with their bridge game.

Well, I thought, I got more from that visit than I expected. I hope I didn't cause her to have a heart attack, I thought regretfully. On the way back to Pleasant Street several thoughts were running through my head. Was the shock of finding out about Tracy enough to cause her to kill her husband? It would explain the amputation. But, wait, she said she found out about Tracy last week. How did she? Did Doreen come to the house to confront Paul J.? Not likely, after all this time. Besides, Doreen was missing before he died. The question was: who told her?

Deep in my own thoughts, I'd forgotten about Tracy. He was

a statue sitting beside me. His eyes were staring straight ahead. Then it hit me. Damn, I had forgotten Tracy could read lips. Oh, dear, I thought, I hope I haven't harmed him. I hadn't expected the reception we got. I had been fairly certain that Mrs. Logger didn't know about him.

Hey, guy, I punched him lightly on the arm, *how about an ice cream cone?*

That got him started. His fingers were going a mile a minute: *Who was that lady? What did she mean—I was her husband's child? I'm not their child. I belong to Daddy. Why did she look like she was afraid of me?*

I pulled over to the curb to answer his questions, and I fibbed to him like a Dutch uncle. I told him she was most likely confused. That she had him mixed up with someone else. I kept signing until he finally began to calm down. When I asked him again if he wanted ice cream, he indicated he thought that would be nice. Poor kid, I thought, sometimes he acts and talks like an adult.

After we got our ice cream, I asked if he wanted to go to my house and play in the lake. I got the same answer. *That would be nice.*

I watched a multitude of expressions flitting across his face on the drive to the lake. *Has your dad brought you downtown since you came home*, I signed to him, stopping for a traffic light.

Yes, on the way to the Boys and Girls Club, he told me.

Why don't you want to go back to the club anymore, Tracy?

He didn't do anything for a minute, then he turned to face me. I was able to see most of his words while I drove. He started: *People fight and say bad things to each other when I'm around. It makes me sad. My mother and father are always fighting when I'm home. It makes me think I'm what causes people to get mad. I should never go where there are lots of people because I always cause trouble*, his fingers told me.

Poor little boy, I thought. That's a heavy load for one that young to carry. I wanted to stop in the middle of the street and give him a hug. Since that wasn't possible, I took his hand and gave it a little squeeze. When we reached the house and walked toward the lake, it surprised me how many people were there. Children, I expected, but not that many adults. It was Friday, why aren't these people at work, I wondered.

I watched them swimming, and thought: how can they swim in water that held a dead body a few days previously? Okay, maybe they and the rest of the town could, but not me. No way. I would feel like a hand was going to come up, grab my ankle and pull me under.

I decided I would never get Tracy down to the lake with that mob there. I turned back to the house, signing I had someone I wanted him to meet.

Tracy touched my sleeve. *I want to go home. I don't want to meet anyone else.*

Darn it, I thought. I was suddenly angry at those who were enjoying the lake, and I didn't even know them. I wanted to jump up on the hood of the car, and yell at them to go home. I signed that to Tracy, and got a small grin in return.

We were getting back into the car when Frances came around the corner of the house. Her face lit in a big smile when she saw us. I turned my back to Tracy, and quickly explained to her about him, warning her he could read lips. Frances took over like I hoped she would.

"How do you do, Tracy. My name is Frances. I do hope you will come to visit sometime. I would love to have you come and help me make gingerbread men someday. I'm sorry you have to leave, but you'll hurry back, won't you? Bye, bye." With that she gave me a pat on the arm, and walked back to the house.

On the way back to his house, he kept me busy answering questions about gingerbread men and who Frances was. After I explained, he decided it might be nice to go back there someday. Bless Frances, I thought.

On the way to Pleasant Street I got to thinking of Fuller's unkempt lawn, and those equally wilted flowers. If I could get Tracy to help me, we might be able to make something of that yard, and do something for his self-confidence.

When we arrived back home I broached the idea to Tracy. He wasn't too wild about it. I suggested we make a big pitcher of lemonade. Every twenty minutes, or sooner, if he got too hot, we would take a break, I told him. What I didn't have the heart to tell him was that he would have to do all the mowing. I was no help to him with my crutch. We were in the garage looking for the lawnmower when he informed me I would be in charge of the lemonade. He would be in charge of the lawn. What a sweetheart, I thought.

It took him two hours to finish mowing the lawn. Poor little fella, I was afraid he was going to have a heat stroke. About halfway through I tried to get him to quit, but he informed me: *If I quit, I will never get started again.* Bless his heart, he did finish. While he was taking a shower, I went to start the sprinkler on that part of the lawn that was in the shade. I must admit starting the water on the lawn is quite a stunt when you need a crutch to get around. But, by darn, if that little kid can mow the whole thing, the least I could do was start the water, I told myself.

Well, I was wrong . . . again. I got that darn hose wound around my good foot, and down I went. I was struggling to get up when strong hands on my arms helped me stand. It was the mailman. Bless his heart, he helped me to my feet, put the sprinkler in place and started the water. On a hunch, I asked him if he had noticed a red Corvette in the neighborhood.

"Well, yes, ma'am. Let's see. I get paid the last Saturday of the month, which was the twenty-ninth of June. The next day was Sunday, and since June has thirty days, that Sunday would have been the thirtieth. It was the following Sunday when my wife and I went by here on our way to the lake. So, let's see, if I've calculated correctly, it must have been the seventh of July. Yep, I remember it like it was yesterday. It was sitting right here in this driveway. I thought maybe Mr. Fuller bought a new car, but I only saw it that one day. It sure was a beaut. I've always wanted one, that's why I remember it. Well, I got to be on my way. You take care of yourself, little missy."

I nearly fell again when he nonchalantly announced that he

remembered seeing the Corvette in Fuller's driveway. Talk about God working in mysterious ways. If I hadn't decided to try to do something about the lawn, if I hadn't sent Tracy in to shower, if I hadn't tried to set the sprinkler myself, if I hadn't fallen . . . it was enough to blow my mind. Wait until Art hears this, I thought.

Tracy and I were sitting on the front porch when Dale Fuller pulled into the driveway. The expression on his face when he saw the lawn and saw Tracy sitting outside, made me want to cry. I felt like I had won the Nobel Peace Prize.

"How did you talk him in to coming outside," he asked me, giving Tracy a monstrous hug.

I shrugged. "I have no idea. I guess it never entered my head that he wouldn't come with me. After what happened this morning, I don't think he wanted to get too far away from me."

While Tracy ran to get his Dad a glass of lemonade, I told Fuller quickly about going to Mrs. Logger's house. "I hesitate to tell you what happened . . . "

"Tell me," he demanded.

"Please, Mr. Fuller. There are things I'm not sure you want to hear."

"TELL ME!"

"Okay, okay, take it easy. Please, for Tracy's sake, try to control your temper. He already feels that he is the cause of people getting upset whenever he's around."

"Oh, my God. I had no idea I was doing that to him. Okay, okay. No matter what she said, I'll try to control myself."

I told him then what had happened. When he heard that Tracy was Logger's son, he seemed to age before my eyes. He took a long drink of the lemonade that Tracy had brought and wiped his hand over his eyes. When he looked at me, I knew the news was a violent shock to him. I needn't have warned him to control his temper. He was past feeling anything.

I noticed Tracy staring at the man he knew to be his father. He realized something was going on, but he had no idea what. I signed for him to go to his daddy; that his daddy needed a hug.

Tracy put his arms around him; Fuller drew him fiercely into his arms. "I don't care what she claims. This boy is my son. Mine, you understand? No one will ever take him from me. Maybe I can't give him fine houses in fancy neighborhoods, but I can give him more love than all of them put together."

I nodded. "Yes, I can see that. I think it's wonderful. From the way Mrs. Logger acted today, she won't be trying to claim Tracy. He loves you a great deal, you know. I think one of the greatest gifts you can give him is to learn to control your anger."

"Yes, I can try to do that. I can see where I have been doing Tracy a grave injustice. I've always had trouble controlling my temper, most of the time it controls me." He grinned ruefully. "Well, I'll have to change that." He pushed Tracy back a step so the boy could see him signing, and told him rapidly: *I love you, son. Don't ever think otherwise, even if you think I'm angry. You have never been the cause of my anger, never. Will you remember that?*

Mr. Fuller had tears in his eyes; I had tears in mine. Tracy was the only one smiling.

"Have you found any clues while you were prowling through my house today?" his voice was menacing.

"Please, believe me," I assured him, "I didn't come to stay with Tracy so I could check out your house. The police have done that. I'm trying to find avenues that they overlooked. I'm hoping I can get acquainted with the neighbors, and maybe find out something that will help find your wife."

Dale stood up and went to look out the window for what seemed to me to be forever.

"Miss. Shore . . . "

"Sandy, please."

He nodded his head. "Sandy, I think there is merit in what you want to do. I know Doreen was especially friendly with Jane Farmer, who lives in the yellow house next door."

I smiled. "Have you remembered where you saw the Corvette?"

"No-o-o." Then I saw the light dawn in his eyes. "Yes, it was at the Logger house. I was delivering a large order to Mrs. Sheridan on Valley View Drive when I saw it parked in the Logger driveway."

The Logger driveway! "When was this?" I asked.

"Let's see. It was last Wednesday. Does that help?"

"It might," I told him slowly. "I'll need to talk to Mrs. Logger again before I know for sure. Oh, one other thing. Can you tell me if there was a pen close to the note your wife left?"

"No, I don't remember seeing one. That's strange, isn't it? It should have been right beside the note." He turned to Tracy and asked him if he saw a pen near the note, but he hadn't. "What does that mean?" he asked me.

"There is always the possibility that whoever wrote the note used their own pen and then stuck it back in their pocket or purse. Is there anything you can tell me about Doreen's childhood? The favorite places she liked to go. That sort of thing."

Fuller returned to his chair and took Tracy up on his lap. "I'll tell you what I know."

TEN

"Doreen was born to Emily and Peter Grant ten years after their son, Jasper."

"Whoa, wait a minute. Jasper Grant is Doreen's brother?"

"Yes. It seems he disappeared when Doreen was about ten. No one has heard from him since. It seems Doreen was what people call a mistake or a surprise, depending on how you look at it. Peter told me that he and Emily were quite set in their ways and, although they tried, it was difficult for them to fit a baby into their life style. They are quite rich. Old family money on Mrs. Grant's side, plus they owned and operated the South Point Inn for years. To make up for ignoring the child, they gave her everything she wanted. Consequently, Doreen told me, she grew up a spoiled little brat. She acted like other people were to do her bidding, no matter what it was she wanted. Her brother, Jasper, worshipped her from the day she was born. Her mother told me that Jasper jumped to do Doreen's biding, even though he was often the brunt of her unkind jokes.

"Doreen was actually brought up by a succession of nurses and governess', none of whom stayed long. They couldn't stand her or the tantrums she threw. Her parents contributed to the way she was because, believe it or not, they informed the nurses and governess' that they wouldn't tolerate spanking or, for that matter, any form of punishment. Under those circumstances, it's a wonder any of them stayed longer than a few weeks.

"Doreen told me that it wasn't until she entered the first grade, that she learned the world did not revolve around Doreen Emily

Grant. The first few years of school were torture for her, her parents, and the teachers. No matter how much Emily and Peter tried to throw their weight around, it didn't work, which was an eye-opener for them also. Finally, when it was time for Doreen to enter the fourth grade things came to a head. She refused to go to school, and if the truth be known, the school didn't want her. After a lot of soul searching, Emily and Peter admitted that they had failed in her upbringing. They had created a little horror that they didn't want around either. A private school seemed to be the only answer.

"Peter told me that if Doreen had been a boy, they would have sent her to a military school. Can you believe that, although they realized they were the ones who were responsible for her attitude, it made them angry that the school wasn't able to straighten her out?

"In the long run, it was decided to send Doreen to a school called Rotten Apple Ranch in the Arizona desert. There were two reasons why they chose that site. First, it was a working school, and, two, it was way out in the middle of nowhere. She couldn't run home even if she tried. It was then that Jasper disappeared. He only stayed home to be with Doreen. He worshipped the ground she walked on. To this day they have no idea where he is."

"Rotten Apple Ranch? What a strange name," I interrupted him.

"Doreen told me it was called Rotten Apple because it was for kids that everybody had given up on. The motto of the school was "Give us your incorrigible, uncontrollable child and we will return a well-behaved adult." They called it a working school because that's what was expected of the kids. I guess they worked their butts off. I couldn't believe half of what Doreen told me. The kids got up at five a.m. to milk cows or do other assigned chores starting at five-thirty, breakfast at seven, studies seven forty-five to noon, lunch twelve to one, studies one to three-thirty, a half-hour free time until four o'clock, then they milked cows again at four-fifteen. Those not involved in milking did other chores: fed the cows or the chickens, collected eggs, or worked out in the fields until five-thirty. Dinner at six, chapel, which everyone was expected to attend, from seven to eight, lights out at nine."

"Holy cow. It's a wonder they didn't all run away," I exclaimed. "If someone did run, what happened?"

"The people at the ranch let them go," Dale continued. "Yeah, I know. That sounds kind of scary, huh? But it wasn't that bad. Someone was sent to follow, but they were not to pick up the kid. The runaway was left out in the desert all night. Normally the night sounds and the cold were enough to drive them back to their beds. If they did tough it out, they were picked up the next morning and brought back. Whether they came back of their own free will or were brought back, they were moved into a special bunkhouse that had bars on the windows. Each day for the next week they were assigned double chores, and were locked in at night."

"I'm surprised her parents left her there, feeling the way they did about punishment," I interjected.

"I guess Peter and Emily thought this was the last chance to straighten her out. They sure didn't want her back home. But, for some reason, Doreen fell in love with the ranch, the duties, and the regulations. During her first few days she did try to run away. However, one night alone in the desert, listening to the coyotes howling, the bushes nearby rustling by God only knows what, and the freezing cold, she was willing to return to the school and take her punishment. She still had a smart mouth that often got her into trouble during her first few months there, but gradually her whole attitude changed.

"She became a model student, and a hard worker during chores. She often took new pupils aside, and told them the story of her first few days there. She elaborated on the night she spent in the desert, making it three times worse than it had been. She told me several students, who were thinking of running away, changed their mind after she talked to them. She got a kick out of scaring the wits out of them.

"There were two things I thought strange. The kids were not

allowed to write, phone or contact any member of their family for the duration of their stay. They weren't allowed to bring any clothing, except underclothes, shoes, socks, and coat. Everyone there wore a uniform coverall."

"What a strange place," I mused.

"Doreen went to Rotten Apple Ranch a ten year old, and returned to South Point when she was eighteen," Dale continued. "I guess the difference between the snotty-nosed little brat that was sent away, and the composed, well-mannered young woman that returned was like night and day. Those that knew her when she was young couldn't get over the change. Her parents didn't know how to react to this new Doreen, anymore than they had the nasty child.

"While she was there she had taken the courses she would need to enter college in the fall. She had decided that she wanted to be an administrative secretary. All the local girls wanted to get a job working in the office of the Paul J. Logger Company because it was about the only decent paying job in the area. Oh, there were other jobs around, like working in the Logger grass seed plant, or becoming a housekeeper for one of the rich retirees moving into the area, but Doreen didn't want anything to do with those.

"She enrolled at the community college in Mountain View and, from what I understand, she was a good student. She knew how to study despite outside noises—knowledge she put to good use at both home and in class, I was told.

"One day when she stopped by the market to pick-up meat her mother had ordered, I was teasing her about falling for one of those young men in her classes. She informed me in no uncertain terms that she had no interest in those guys. She was going to marry a guy with money. The kind she wanted, she said, wouldn't be caught dead at a community college. She did have a few dates with one of the fellows, but it didn't last.

"After we married, her parents told me they had nothing but praise for her while she was in school. She studied hard, got good grades, and spent little money on herself, except for a few compact discs. Doreen loves music. One of the gifts I got her was a compact disc player with the most beautiful sound you will ever hear. You would have thought I had given her a million dollars." He paused, then murmured more to himself than to me, "It worry's me that she didn't take it with her." One of his big hands wiped tears from his eyes, "Sorry, I was thinking of something else for a moment," he said, apparently not realizing he had spoken aloud.

He cleared his throat and continued. "Graduation day seemed to be one of the happiest days of her life. "She and her parents stopped by the store on their way to the college for the ceremony, to order a special cut of meat. Doreen came in with the order, and she was so beautiful it took my breath away. I told her how pretty she looked, and to come and see me if she should ever need a job or anything. She told me she might take me up on that.

"About a month later she told me she had been hired by the Logger Company. It wasn't the dream job she wanted, but she had a job, which was the important thing. Now she had to make herself indispensable, she told me.

"It didn't take her long. I have a friend who works there, and he told me she was the perfect secretary. Her work was immaculate; she was willing to work anytime of the day or night; and she could be trusted to keep sensitive information concerning the company to herself. Two years later she was promoted to private secretary to the owner himself, Paul Logger. I guess I can't blame her for falling under his spell," Dale sighed.

"If it's not too painful, after what you learned this evening, can you tell me what he was like?" I asked softly.

"I can give my impression." He shifted Tracy to a more comfortable position. "Paul J. was a man who caught your attention no matter what the occasion. He wasn't a tall man, maybe about your height, but his presence made him seem much taller. When Doreen went to work for him, he had just turned forty-five. His dark hair was barely sprinkled with gray at the temples then. He had steel-blue eyes that seemed to bore right through you, but he had a nice smile. He was, I think, a friendly person. He used to come into the market to pick up orders for his wife and was always pleasant. I did hear though that he was known to be a hard man to deal with when it came to business. Doreen did say that he seemed to love his wife, Harriet, a great deal.

"I don't know what happened between Doreen and Paul J. Doreen seemed to love her job in the beginning, but one day after she had been there about three years she changed. She lost that bubbly personality, and smiled less and less. I kept asking her what was wrong when she stopped by the store, but she refused to tell me. That's when I told her that if she ever needed help to come to me. I told her I would do about anything for her, no questions asked. She had no idea I was in love with her. Emily told me one day that she wasn't eating enough to keep a bird alive. She and Peter were worried sick about her, but Doreen told them she was fine and refused to go to the doctor.

"It wasn't more than a month later when she stopped by the market and asked if she could speak to me privately. Of course, I told her yes, but I wasn't prepared for what she told me. She was six weeks pregnant, and the father wouldn't claim the child. Poor Doreen, she was crying so hard that I could barely understand her. She said she had never had sex before. How could the father deny it? He knew she was a virgin, and they only did it one time. She told me that she couldn't have an abortion, that it would be like committing a murder. That's when she asked me what to do."

ELEVEN

We didn't realize how late it was getting until Tracy sat up and informed us: *I'm hungry, Daddy.* "Would you have supper with us?" Dale asked. "It will give me a chance to finish telling you about Doreen."

"Sure, Mr. Fuller, I'll be glad too. Let me make a phone call to Frances to let her know I won't be home for dinner," I told him.

"Francis?"

"That's Frances with an 'e'. She's my housekeeper. That's a story I'll have to tell you sometime," I smiled.

A short time later we were seated in a booth at Mom's Country Inn. It wasn't fancy, just good old American food and lots of it. We ordered before Fuller continued his story.

"Before I continue with Doreen's story, I'd like it if you would call me Dale. Mr. Fuller sounds stuffy."

"Of course, Dale. Thank you." If the truth be known I was getting tired of using Mr. Fuller, but my mother brought me up to be polite.

Dale continued with his story. "When Doreen asked me what to do, I told her in a kidding way that she could marry me. She looked at me with those beautiful eyes of hers . . . I mean, really looked at me for the first time. She asked me through her tears if I knew what I was saying and I told her I sure did. I told her I had loved her for years; that I knew she didn't love me, but maybe she could learn to after awhile. Well, anyway, she finally consented and we got married one week later. One time she tried to tell me who the father was, but I wouldn't listen. I told her it didn't matter.

When Tracy was born, I felt such a feeling of love wash over me. I can't explain it. It was awesome. I knew that no matter what, this child was mine.

"For the first six months after the baby was born Doreen was great. You could tell by the way she nursed him and held him that she loved him. Then we started noticing little things, like he didn't turn his head when we spoke his name, but he would smile when he saw us. Then we saw that sudden noises didn't seem to bother him. He didn't jump or anything. We finally took him to the doctor, and found out he was deaf. I thought Doreen would go crazy. She started crying and screaming it was her punishment for having sex before she got married. From that moment on she wouldn't have anything to do with him. That's why I had to hire nurses and later, when he was old enough, to send him to the convent to get his schooling. It broke my heart to send him away. As I told you earlier, I saw him on Wednesdays and Sundays, but it was never enough for me. I was even happy when the school caught fire. I thought if Doreen could see what a fine young man Tracy had become, she might forgive herself and love him again. I couldn't have been more wrong. He was only home a week before she disappeared, and before that she stayed in her room most of the time, except when she was working, so she wouldn't have to see him." Dale was quiet for a minute. "It's a good thing Logger is dead. The way I feel right now, I could kill him myself for ruining Doreen's life."

I could hardly swallow because of the lump in my throat. Poor man. Poor little boy.

"Dale, I would like to take Tracy to see the Grants tomorrow, if that's okay. Maybe they will tell me things they haven't told the police, especially if I have Tracy with me."

I could tell he was not overjoyed with the idea, but he finally consented. He told me he would call when he got home, and let them know Tracy and I would be coming tomorrow.

"Don't . . . ," Dale started to say. "No, I'm not going to tell you anything ahead of time. I don't want to prejudice you before you meet them. Promise me you will be careful."

After those instructions I wasn't sure I wanted to go, but I must admit my curiosity was peaked. I knew I could take care of myself, but what was I getting Tracy into? I'd have to keep my eyes open, that was for sure.

While we had been talking Tracy had been looking around with wide eyes. Dale told me when we had entered the restaurant that this was the first time the boy had ever eaten out. Oh, they had gone to drive-ins before, but never inside. Watching him, that much was obvious. Tracy was having a ball. He found everything new and exciting, from the silverware to the menu to the plate his food came on.

I had driven my car to the restaurant, so after dinner we went our separate ways. Before we parted, Dale told me he would check with the Grants. If tomorrow about eleven wasn't a good time, he would call me.

Driving home, I tried to assemble all the information Dale had given me. Too big a job, I decided I would have to wait until I got home and started making notes in my journal to sort it out. Rotten Apple Ranch. I couldn't get over a place like that. Not to let the kids correspond with their families seemed excessive to me. I prayed I would never feel like I had to send my child there. Not that I had to worry, I thought. My biological clock was nearing the witching hour, and Art didn't seem the least bit interested.

When I pulled into the driveway, I noticed Art was visiting. Actually, what he was doing was eating the dinner Frances had prepared for me. I joined them in having dessert. I've never been one to pass up lemon pie. In between bites, I told them about my talk with Dale Fuller.

Art was surprised to learn that Jasper was Doreen's brother. Apparently the Grants hadn't told the officers who went to talk to them anything about having a son. Probably because they thought he was dead. When I told him about the mailman seeing the Corvette in Dale's driveway, he decided he would send his men out tomorrow to follow up on that lead.

"It sounds to me like Mr. Fuller would be better off if she didn't come back," Frances exclaimed.

"That's how I felt after I talked to him the other day. However, Art changed my mind. He informed me he wants her found, dead or alive, so the case can be closed. You hate unsolved cases, don't you, honey? Tomorrow Tracy and I are going to visit his grandparents in South Point, unless Dale calls to tell me otherwise. I'm going to stop by the station on our way out of town and take a good look at the note Doreen left. Then tomorrow afternoon when we get back, I'm going to search the Fuller house for that pen. Dale didn't remember seeing a pen, but it won't hurt to look," I informed them.

"Won't that be like looking for the needle in the haystack?" Art asked.

"Maybe yes, maybe no," I shrugged.

Art slipped his arm around my shoulders. "I wouldn't mind being in on that visit to the Grants, but I'm on duty tomorrow."

I took advantage of his arm and kind of snuggled close. "Not to worry. I'll fill you in on everything. That Tracy is such a sweet kid. I wouldn't mind having one like him."

"I don't think you should think of having kids until you're married," Art said. "So, how about it?"

"How about what?"

"Getting married." Art took my hand. "Would you marry me, Sandy? I have always loved you. There was never anyone else for me."

I was stunned. Frances and Al were stunned. Then we all started talking at once.

"Yes. Oh, yes, Art. Of course, I'll marry you. I love you, too. I think I've loved you since the first time I saw you when we were kids," came from me.

"Marry?" from Frances.

"About time," from Al.

For the next hour, we talked wedding plans. Frances suggested we have the wedding and reception in the garden. I suggested the wedding be by the lake and the reception in the garden. Art didn't care one way or the other; when was his question. He wanted it soon, like yesterday. I kept pinching myself to make sure I wasn't dreaming.

Later, Art took me for a walk by the lake. "Whenever I was in a tight spot, and wasn't sure I was going to get back, the thing that kept me going were thoughts of this lake and you. Kinda crazy, huh? That's why I would like to be married down there. We could have the wedding at ten in the morning. The haze will have burnt off. It will be as peaceful and quiet as a church. Then we could have a brunch for the reception. What do you think?" I asked.

"I'm for anything, anyway you want it. Be it here, in the garden or in a church, I truly don't care, but make it soon. We've wasted too much time already," he told me, giving me a long kiss. He reached into his pocket and brought forth a small white box. Inside was the most beautiful ring I had ever seen, but I suppose most newly engaged brides-to-be say the same thing.

We decided the first thing to do was to contact Art's parent's and see when they would be able to come to a wedding. I didn't have a special day in mind. Yesterday would have been fine with me, too. Art told me he had informed his parents when I came home to stay that he was going to marry me someday. They had been driving him crazy wanting to know if he had asked me yet. That made me feel better. I was afraid they wouldn't remember me.

"I'm curious. Why didn't you ask me sooner."

"Well, I was afraid that you would get bored here, and want to go back to the big city. I wanted to ask you the first day you came into the station. Aw, Babe, I do love you so very much," he told me.

I tried to tell him I loved him, too, but the words kept being covered with kisses.

We returned to the house, and put in a call to Art's parents. To say they were delighted doesn't even come close. Frances brought us a calendar, and after a lot of discussion it was decided to have our wedding in about three weeks, Saturday, August 31. After we had everything settled, I called Marie.

"Hi, lamb, it's Sandy."

"Silly, I know that," she answered. "What's up?"

"How about a wedding?"

For a full minute there was silence. Then came this scream that I swear they could have heard in Mountain View. I thought my eardrum was broken. "A wedding? You and Art? When? Do I get to be the matron of honor? Where will it be? We must get together to plan this. It must be done right. You two have wasted too much time already," she wouldn't let me get a word in edgewise.

"Yes, of course, Art and I. On August 31. If you can't be the matron of honor I'm not getting married," that brought a frown from Art. I blew him a kiss. "We are going to have the ceremony at ten in the morning down by the lake, and a brunch for the reception here in the garden."

"Oh, Sandy, it sounds beautiful," she was getting weepy. "Can we have lunch tomorrow? We need to find dresses and decide on flowers and . . . and everything. Gosh, so much to do in such a short time."

I told her I was taking Tracy to South Point tomorrow, but why didn't they come to dinner. I glanced at Frances, who nodded an okay. I hung up with congratulations ringing in my ears.

Frances and Al excused themselves to get the dishes done. Art and I wandered out to the front porch, and sat in the swing. For the next two hours we recalled things that went on when we were apart. We spoke of the other people we had thought we could fall in love with, but somehow it never seemed to develop into anything. I described in detail a few of the assignments I had been on, where the only thing that brought me through sane were thoughts of him and the lake. And, of course, we caught up on the kissing we had been missing.

In bed that night I lay there thinking about how much we had accomplished that day. We knew that Doreen's brother was probably the last person to see her before she disappeared. There was a chance that he also had something to do with the drowning of Paul J. I had found out that someone told Mrs. Logger about Tracy. I knew Doreen's life history. However, I reminded myself, I still wanted to talk to her parents. But the best part, of course, was that I was going to marry Art. I went to sleep dreaming about wedding dresses and gardens and frilly things. My dreams lately had been of dead people floating in the water, and of women being cut up in pieces and thrown in the seed elevator. One thing I know for sure: frilly dreams are much better.

TWELVE

The next morning I awoke to the ringing of the phone. It was Art calling to make sure he hadn't dreamed last night. Such a sweetheart. Before hanging up he made me promise to get in touch with him the minute I got back from visiting with Doreen's parents.

I picked up Tracy and stopped by to see the note. Tracy was excited when we pulled up in front of the police station. When I told him I was working with the police to try and locate his Mama, he quit signing and seemed to withdraw from his surroundings. Once more, I didn't give a fig if we ever found his mother, and from his actions, neither did he. I hated her for the mental damage she had done to him. While I talked to Art, I asked a couple of the guys to take Tracy on a tour of the station. They knew he was deaf and needed to watch them speak when they explained things. He came back in a much happier frame of mind.

"Sandy, I was thinking about what you told us last night and I don't know what to say," Art said. "Bill and Gary never heard anything about Jasper Grant being Doreen's brother. I guess they didn't ask the right questions. By the way, I got an answer back from Phoenix. Jasper has not been around his apartment for several weeks. The Chief of Police there assured me they would keep checking and let me know if he shows up. He'd been working as a bodyguard for one of the movie stars who live there. When his boss died, Jasper told his friends he was going to take a couple of months off. He mentioned something about stopping in Myrtle Woods, on his way to go hunting in Alaska, to see if he could find his sister. The Phoenix Chief told me Jasper is approximately six foot three and weighs around two-twenty."

"That's interesting, isn't it? Do we have another missing person?"

"Oh, Lord, I hope not."

I promised I would let him know if the Grants had anything interesting to say. I practically had to pry Tracy away from looking at mug shots so we could head to South Point. On the way he kept me busy answering questions about police work.

Following Dale's directions, we drove directly to the Grant house. The woman who answered the door was beautiful. Her short white hair shimmered like quicksilver, intelligence shone from her brown eyes, her slender body implied a personal trainer. I was about to congratulate Tracy on having such a lovely grandmother, but before I could, she spoke.

"Yes?" That one word sent shivers running up and down my spine. It was a thousand fingernails scraping down a blackboard.

"Mrs. Grant? I'm Sandy Shores."

"Please. Come in." Her voice was, by far, the worst sound I have ever heard coming from a human being. I watched Tracy. He was totally unaware. How I wished I could be for the time we would be there.

"Have you found out anything about our little girl?" She dabbed her eyes, but if she was actually crying, I'm a monkey's aunt. It wasn't even a good acting job.

"No, ma'am, I'm sorry. However, I would like you to become reacquainted with your grandson, Tracy."

"Tracy? This big boy is Tracy? I can't believe it. Peter, Peter, come quickly. Tracy is here," she screeched.

I had told Tracy he would be seeing his grandparents, so he was prepared for the onslaught he received. When they got through with the hugs and kisses, we proceeded into the front room. The sight that greeted our eyes was one of surprise for Tracy; for me, shock. The Grants must have decided to make up for all the Christmases they had missed with him. There was a fully decorated Christmas tree with every toy and game known to humankind—a full sized basketball hoop, football equipment, robots, electric-powered cars—you name it and it was there. Tracy eyes glazed over with amazement. I acknowledged to him that everything was for him, but he acted like he still couldn't believe it. Emily held out her hand to him. He shyly took it and they went to look at his gifts. The further they advanced into the room, the more she changed. She became like a child herself. A child who had found a playmate after many years alone. I stole a glance at Mr. Grant, and was shocked at the look of hatred that flitted across his face. Had I only imagined it?

Peter Grant was a nice looking man, but much older than I had expected. When Dale had told me they had Doreen when their son was ten years old, I guess I was thinking they were in their thirties when she was born. Now, judging from their appearance, I realized they must have been closer to forty, since both of them were in their mid-seventies, at least. Despite his age, Peter Grant was six foot of muscle. He wore his gray hair cut short in a crew-cut. His piercing hazel-green eyes blazed from his chiseled-from-granite face. His manner and posture indicated military training sometime during his life.

"Miss. Shores, thank you for bringing Tracy to see us." He shook my hand. Lord, he had a grip. When he spoke his voice was deep and sophisticated; a true theatrical voice. "We attempted to see him when he was at the convent, but Dale thought it best that we didn't. We concurred with his wishes, although it was difficult to do. Maybe now that he is back home we will see him more often. It might help Emily to get better. She . . . ," he stopped.

"He will be going back to the convent when it's repaired," I told him gently, wondering what he had started to say.

"Oh, no. That will kill Emily. Since Doreen disappeared, she hasn't been the same. We didn't do a good job bringing up Doreen when she was a child. I think Emily was hoping for another chance with Tracy. I wish to explain to you about Emily's voice. It wasn't always like that. Ten years ago they found a cancerous growth on her larynx. The operation saved her life, but left her with that sound when she speaks. She no longer goes out in public because of it."

"I'm sorry to hear that. It must have taken a lot of adjustment for both of you when her voice changed."

"Yes, especially for Emily. We used to act together in local little theater plays. The operation brought that to an end for her, and I won't act without her. I couldn't. It would kill her to watch me perform in a play, with only her memories of how good she used to be." I had the impression he had said those same words many times before. I remembered how I thought the little crying scene when she opened the door was a poor acting job. Had she actually been crying? Perhaps I had misjudged her.

"Mr. Grant, when was the last time you saw your son?" I hoped to catch him off guard if Jasper was staying here.

"Please don't mention Jasper to Emily. It would kill her. She has convinced herself he is dead, and it's better that way. She hasn't seen him since he moved out after Doreen was sent to Rotten Apple Ranch. You know about that?"

I told him yes, I did. Evidently, if Jasper did meet Doreen at the club, he didn't come to see his folks. Interesting. Where in the world was he? If he was still around here, why hadn't someone noticed that fancy car?

"Have you noticed a red Corvette around recently?" I asked.

"Something like that should stick out like a sore thumb. Is it important?" He turned away to pick up his pipe from the table next to his chair. He must be trying to stop smoking, I thought, since he didn't fill it or light it.

I almost told him that Jasper was driving the Corvette, and then quickly decided that would be cruel if it turned out his son was dead. "No, not important. It has to do with another case I'm working on. I thought maybe the man I was looking for might be here in your neck of the woods."

I asked him to tell me anything and everything he could about Doreen and Jasper. Nothing he told me was new. It was discouraging. When Peter and I went back into the living room it was to peals of laughter from Emily and Tracy. It always amazed me to hear sounds like that coming from Tracy. Somehow, I had gotten it into my head that deaf people couldn't laugh, but I can't say why. Tracy was having such a good time, I hated to take him away.

Mr. Grant touched my arm. "Would you like to see their rooms? You will have to climb several stairs." His glance lingered on my crutch.

"No problem. I'd love to see them, Mr. Grant," I reassured him.

"Peter, please."

"Thank you, and please call me Sandy."

He nodded curtly in agreement.

On the way up, I realized what had been bothering me while I was talking to Peter. It was the times he claimed this or that would "kill Emily". Remembering the look of hate I had surprised on his face, I knew it wouldn't surprise me if the Grants became a police case sometime in the near future. I'm a good judge of character, and from his actions I wondered if insanity ran in Peter Grant's family. I didn't believe it would take much to push him over the edge.

When we reached the top of the stairs I was huffing and puffing, but Peter Grant wasn't even breathing hard. Hum-m-m, I thought, he must be in excellent shape. There were four bedrooms, and I could have found the ones belonging to Doreen and Jasper even if he hadn't pointed them out to me.

Childhood dolls and stuffed animals filled the shelves in Doreen's room. Stepping up to a bulletin board I noticed several postcards from Rotten Apple Ranch. It was interesting that she was still keeping in touch long after she left there. I made a mental note to ask Dale if she was still in contact with anyone from there. The bed looked freshly made, everything was sparkling clean; it was ready for an occupant. It gave me the creeps.

Jasper's room was the same way—waiting for him to walk through the door. Walking into the room, I immediately realized guns were young Jasper's whole world. Pictures, newspaper clippings and magazine articles on every kind of gun, gun clubs, and gun meets covered every bit of space—walls and ceiling. There were trophies designating first or second place. Only one gun seemed out of place. Someone had carelessly thrown it on the bed, as if Jasper had gone out before he had a chance to put it away.

"Jasper was always interested in guns," Peter said.

That's an understatement, I thought.

"He was forever winning one award or the other. I don't know why he didn't take those with him when he left. He was so proud of them." Peter sounded more puzzled than sad. It had been a long time since Jasper had left. Does the sadness a person feels when that wears off after awhile? Thinking of Marie, I doubted it.

"There are many, many memories in these rooms . . . but come, let me show you the playroom we had built above the garage."

When he opened the door at the far end of the hall I saw it was about six inches thick. He pulled it shut. "Do you notice anything?"

I stood still for a moment. I couldn't hear anything, not a sound. "Is it soundproof?" I asked.

"Right," Peter smirked. "It gave the kids a place to play, to make all the noise they wanted without bothering us. We often had business dinners that we didn't want the children to attend. You know the saying: children should be seen and not heard? Well, I always preferred that the children were not seen nor heard. That's when this room came in handy. Sometimes we had to lock them in, but not often."

I must get out of this crazy house, I thought. "Thanks for the tour. Gee, look at the time. I better get Tracy back to town."

"Oh, no. Surely you are going to stay for lunch. Emily has gone to a lot of trouble preparing special things," he pleaded.

"Oh? Well, I guess we have time for lunch," I consented reluctantly. "But right after that we do have to head back. I have company coming for dinner."

Peter left me in the front room while he got lunch on the table. Watching Emily, I got the impression that she didn't care if we ate or not. She was having too much fun with Tracy.

When Peter took us in to lunch I couldn't believe what I was seeing. We sat down to a complete Christmas dinner. Roast turkey, dressing, sweet potatoes, gravy, jello salad, green beans with tiny onions and chopped bacon, mince and pumpkin pies, plus a huge coconut cake. Peter was in charge of carving the turkey, and there was none of the fumbling around that my dad used to do. Peter definitely seemed to know what he was doing.

"That's wonderful the way you can carve that turkey. You must have had a lot of practice," I said.

"Yes, I guess you could say I have."

I waited for him to continue, but he concentrated on carving. I was beginning to think he was an evasive person. He had yet to fully answer one of my questions.

Everything was delicious, but while we were eating I kept wondering if they had put something into the food to drug us. Were they planning to lock us in the playroom? I watched them until they tasted everything before I felt I could relax and enjoy the dinner.

I was so glad when the meal was over. They wanted us to stay longer, but I told them I had friends coming for dinner (which was true). I said I had to get home, and get dinner started (which was a lie). I'd have claimed the Shah of Iran was coming to dinner, if that's what it took to get us out of there. Peter loaded the gifts in the car with no more effort than a twenty year old. After several hugs and kisses for Tracy, they let us get on our way.

Talk about your strange people. If I were Dale, I wouldn't want Tracy around them either. Thinking back over the afternoon, I was surprised he let him go this time. Maybe he felt the boy would be safe with me. Ha! Wait until I tell him my fantasies, I laughed to myself.

Tracy was quieter than I expected on the drive back to Myrtle Woods. Finally he started asking questions. *Mrs. Grant—my grandmother—kept calling me Jasper. Why did she do that?*

What kind of an answer could I give to that? That his grandmother was slightly off? I didn't think that's what he wanted to know. Finally, I told him that she had a son by that name that she hadn't seen for a long time, and maybe she got confused.

Maybe you look a lot like him, I signed to him. Then it hit me. There was not one picture of Jasper, Doreen or Mrs. Grant in that whole house or in the Fuller house. The only one I had seen was the one that Dale had given to the paper and that was only a snapshot. Why, I wondered. There had to be a reason, but nothing I could think of came close to being a satisfactory answer.

We stopped by the station on the way back to fill Art in on what I had learned. Of course, Tracy didn't mind one little bit. He wanted to see more mug shots. *Maybe I'll see someone I know.*

Stranger things have happened, I agreed. I watched him follow Billy Ray out of the room, a big smile on his face.

"You know, Art, I realized on the way back that there was not one picture of Doreen or Jasper at the Grant's or at Dale's. Is that crazy or what? I didn't ask them for one because I thought you might want to do so, if it becomes necessary."

"We have this picture of Jasper that was faxed from Phoenix. It's fairly recent, taken when he signed up for bodyguard duty," Art said, sliding the paper across his desk to me. "I don't think we will have to bother the Grants. Not until we apprehend him, anyway."

"That's probably best. You won't believe the strange things that Peter said. I didn't tell them we were looking for Jasper. However, when I asked him if he had seen Jasper lately, he said, she, meaning Emily, hadn't seen him for years. Nothing about whether or not he had seen him. Then when I asked him if he had seen a red Corvette lately, he said that it should stick out like a sore thumb; not whether he had seen it. My little voice is telling me something is going on and it's not all kosher. The entire episode freaked me out."

I went on to explain how they locked the children in the soundproof playroom so they wouldn't bother anyone. When I told him how the bedrooms looked like Doreen and Jasper might walk in momentarily, he shook his head in disbelief.

"They had what seemed like a hundred presents for Tracy, a Christmas tree, and for lunch they served us a Christmas dinner complete with the trimmings. I did worry if the food was drugged and if Tracy and I would end up locked in the playroom. It still gives me goose bumps. Mrs. Grant had to have an operation four years ago, which ruined her voice. She doesn't speak, she screeches. She and Peter used to act in plays, he told me. Now, she never leaves the house. All the time she and Tracy were opening presents, she kept calling him "Jasper". That confused Tracy. He kept asking me about it most of the way home."

"It sounds like you had quite a day, honey. Maybe it's a good thing tomorrow is Sunday. I think you could use a little R&R away from this case." With that Art sent us on our way with a hug for me and a wink for Tracy.

It took Tracy and me several trips before we got the car unloaded. I couldn't wait to hear what Dale had to say when he saw it all. Leaving Tracy to the toys, I started my search for the pen used to write the note. I searched for the next three hours and found nothing. Tracy came to see what I was doing. I put him to work looking under each bed, each chair, each piece of furniture that the pen might have rolled under, still nothing. Finally, I gave up. I informed Tracy that his mother must have taken the pen with her. He agreed, collapsing in a chair. Both of us could have used a nap. It had been a long, long day.

When Dale came home, I told him what had happened to get his input. He was a little upset about the amount of gifts that the Grants had heaped on Tracy, but like he said: "What's done is done." Tracy informed him he was going to take most of them back to the convent when he returned there. He wanted the other kids to have fun with them, too.

He, Tracy, constantly amazed me. He had never known a mother's love, yet he was sweet and generous, thinking more of others than himself. It was a miracle or maybe it was because of the love Dale lavished him, to make up for what Doreen didn't give him.

He continued: *I want to share them with my best friend, Matthew Smith. He has to live at the convent all the time.*

Doesn't he have a home? I wanted to know.

No. He told me he was born there. He doesn't have a daddy to take of him, like I do.

I don't know if Dale noticed it, but I sure did. Tracy didn't indicate anything about a mother. Could be that's why they were best friends, I thought. Born there? Did they take in unwed mothers? I'd have to remember to ask Dale later.

How old is he, Tracy? I asked.

Same age I am. I miss him a great deal.

Dale turned to Tracy. *Son, would you like to drive up there and see if we can find him. Maybe he could come and visit, if Sandy doesn't mind having two of you under foot.*

They both turned to me for an answer. *Why not? The more the merrier,* I signed.

Tracy let out a big . . . well, it wasn't a shout, more like a loud growl. He ran around the front room with his fingers saying: *The more the merrier. The more the merrier.*

While Tracy was acting like a normal kid for a change, Dale told me he had been having concerns about the Grants since the day Tracy was born. He kept feeling that Emily, especially, would kidnap him in a minute if given the chance. How would I feel, he asked, if they kidnapped your son and took him to that house?

"I won't give them the chance to do that," he continued. "That's why I told them I didn't want them to visit the convent. They went up there several times against my wishes, but the nuns wouldn't let them see Tracy. I think the Grants finally got the message. I decided it would be okay for you to take him there because I doubted they would try anything in front of a stranger." He had a good laugh when I told him about my fear of the food.

"I have a question. I didn't see pictures of Doreen or Jasper in the house nor have I seen one here. Why?"

"I don't know about the Grants, but Doreen refused to have her picture taken. I've always thought it had to do with something that happened in her mother's childhood, but Doreen would never tell me. The only picture I have is this snapshot I took one day when I saw her coming to the shop. I took it without her knowing. That was before we were married, and after I found out how reluctant she was to having a picture taken, I never told her I had it. Now I'm glad I kept it."

Tracy was pulling on Dale's shirt: *Will we go see Matthew tomorrow?*

Yes, son. Nice and early.

I think Tracy was wishing they could go that evening.

After giving Tracy a hug, I told him I was looking forward to meeting his friend on Monday. It brought tears to my eyes to see him so happy.

Driving home, I had an inspiration. I would take the boys to visit Marie. I had taken Tracy into the drugstore one day to have a soda, and had caught a look of naked longing on her face. Yep, that's one fine idea, I decided.

THIRTEEN

The next day, Sunday, I decided I better call on Mrs. Logger to find out who told her about Tracy. A phone call, and a confirmation that I didn't have Tracy, got Art and me an appointment for two o'clock.

After church and one of Frances' fantastic Sunday dinners of roast chicken, sweet potato casserole, a green salad, and blackberry cobbler, we arrived for our appointment right on time. A woman we assumed was the housekeeper led us down an entry hall that would have held my whole office, bath included. She ushered us into the library of this magnificent house. Silently comparing this house to the Grant's, I had to admit the Logger home was far more ostentatious. My heels sank into thick carpet for what seemed like two inches. A ladder was on a track that ran along three walls enabling anyone to reach to the top shelf. My first thought was: who reads all these?

The most complete gun collection known to man covered the third wall. Every size, shape, make—you name it—was on display. However, in the far left corner of the room, far to the back, one was missing. We'll have to remember to ask about it, I thought, silently pointing it out to Art.

There was a huge desk in the middle of the room that made mine look like a child's toy. On the desk were the usual blotter, a tray of pens, pencils, paper clips, and a letter opener. A white phone was to the left of the blotter. Two easy chairs were in front of the desk. I was examining the lethal-looking letter opener when Mrs. Logger entered the room. She wore a soft green suit with a ruffled white blouse that framed her lovely face. Her green high heels exactly matched the color of her suit. She looked calm and cool. I found myself thinking: what a beautiful outfit. I'll bet it would pay my rent for months.

She was a gracious hostess when she greeted us, but before our eyes she suddenly became a young girl of perhaps twelve or thirteen. She became nervous and seemed shy when she saw Art. What's going on, I thought. I had made a point of telling her Art was coming with me. When she indicated we were to sit in the two chairs, she seemed afraid to sit behind the desk.

"Mrs. Logger, I want to thank you for seeing us today," I began. "This is my fiancé, Art Landow, the chief of police." Art had told me he had not yet met her. Ed and Bill were the only ones who had talked to her after her husband's drowning.

He got up to shake her hand, and she actually seemed to blush when he said how pleased he was to meet her.

"This is a beautiful home you have," I told her for openers. She ducked her head and in a small voice thanked me. "I'll try to be brief because I know this won't be easy for you." This statement caused her to take a handkerchief from her pocket and dabbed at her eyes. Now who was she? Young girl, widow, chairman of the board or . . . ?

"Would you please tell us how you found out that Tracy Fuller was your husband's child?" I could see a transformation was happening, so I rushed on. "There is a possibility that the death of your husband, and the disappearance of Mrs. Fuller are connected. If you could tell us what happened it might help in solving both cases." I watched as she changed to the angry wife. It was fascinating. For a minute, I thought she wasn't going to answer me. With a sigh, she reached into one of the desk drawers and took out an envelope.

"I received this note about a week after Paul's death telling me about the boy being a result of my husband's infidelity. I thought it was a cruel joke. Then I called a friend of mine who knows everything that goes on in this community. She told me that she had known about it for years." Then her voice became hard and she seemed to draw herself upright. "My friend told me that my husband had begged her not to tell me. He told her it was over, that it hadn't been an affair in the true sense of the word. He had only had sex with his secretary once. It happened about eleven years ago when I was in a bad automobile accident, and unable to take care of his needs. That bastard! Unable to take care of his needs—what a crock of bull. I swear if he wasn't dead already, I could cheerfully kill him." With that she collapsed, becoming the grieving widow. She began crying the way she had in my office. I stood there, stunned. From the look on Art's face, I knew he didn't have a clue what was happening.

Within minutes she had collected herself and wiped the tears from her face. "I'm sorry," she told us. "I loved him deeply. I would never have believed that story if someone had told me before I received the note. His secretary then was the young lady who is missing, the Fuller woman. I understand she was the model of efficiency. She never did anything out of line. She still works for the company or did until she disappeared. She was secretary to the vice-president. I guess from what my friend told me she revered my husband, and would do anything he asked. It must have happened in a moment of weakness on his part." There was a short silence then the angry wife appeared before us again. "The one thing that makes me angry is that he never acknowledged the boy. Did he think I was so shallow that I would divorce him or do something else stupid? How could he think something like that? Well, I hope he rots in hell! You said earlier, Miss. Shore, that there is a possibility my husband's case and that of Mrs. Fuller may be connected. How could that be? That little incident was over years ago. Anyway, here's the letter I got. You are welcome to take it with you. I have no need for it. The words are burned into my memory." She walked to the window and stood staring outside with unseeing eyes.

I glanced down. My God! The ink was the same shade as on the note Doreen had supposedly left. I'm sure my mouth dropped open. Here was proof the two cases were connected! Since there was no postmark on the envelope I felt I had to ask, "How did you get this note, Mrs. Logger?"

The silence seemed to stretch intolerably. "How did I get it? What do you mean?" The president of the Logger Company turned back from the window.

"There is no postmark, which makes me wonder how it got here."

"I'm sure I can't tell you. It appeared with the rest of my mail one day. I can ask William when he comes back on duty tomorrow and let you know. Would that be satisfactory?" she asked haughtily.

I told her, of course, that would be fine. I gave her a few minutes, then asked if she had a description of her husband's gold chain. She went to get me the information they had given to their insurance company. Holding the note by a corner, I showed it to Art and pointed to the ink. Before I could speak, Mrs. Logger was back. She brought the description and a close up picture of Paul J, which showed it in remarkable detail. I studied the beautiful double braided type of design and my mouth fell open. Emily Grant had been wearing one exactly it! I thought Mrs. Logger told me it was one of a kind, a family heirloom. I heard the word What?—What?—What? running through my mind.

"You did say this was one of a kind?" I asked.

"Yes. It belonged to my grandfather on my mother's side. My mother gave it to Paul when we married. He treasured it, and I know he wouldn't have taken it off willingly."

I told myself that I was most likely wrong about Mrs. Grant having one like it. We were getting ready to leave, when Art walked to the gun wall. "This is a magnificent collection, Mrs. Logger. Where did you find them all?"

"I have no idea. It was my husband's collection." She still seemed to be in the president of the company mood.

"I notice there is one gun missing. Do you have any idea what happened to it?" I asked.

Bing—she was the young girl again. "I don't know. I didn't take it. I promise I didn't. Please don't be mad because I can't remember. Maybe William will know. I'll ask William tomorrow. Would that be okay?" Her voice changed—becoming younger and higher.

We told her that would be fine. I was becoming quite concerned about her. She seemed even more tightly strung than she had when I made the mistake of bringing Tracy to her house. I felt that any minute she would snap.

"Mrs. Logger, do you have a relative or a friend who could stay with you a few days?" I asked.

I wish I could explain what happened in the next few minutes. Harriet Logger went as white as a ghost, her mouth opened and closed as if she found it hard to breathe. Suddenly, she threw up her hands as though to protect her face. Her mouth opened in a silent scream as she collapsed to the floor in a dead faint.

I don't need to tell you that it scared us half to death.

Art called the housekeeper, who came running. "Oh, no," she whispered.

I told her of asking Mrs. Logger if she had a relative or friend and what happened afterwards. "Has this happened before?"

"Yes, Ma'am. We are to call Doctor Morton immediately, and not try to help her gain consciousness," she answered.

Art knew the doctor and got him on the phone. In a few concise words he explained what had happened.

"I'll be there in two minutes. Whatever you do, don't try to help her regain consciousness."

I put a small pillow under her head, while the housekeeper got a blanket to cover her. I sat down on the floor beside her to wait.

Before the doctor could get there, her eyes fluttered open. I'm not sure what I expected to see, but it wasn't the composed lady of the manor.

"What happened? Did I faint?" she asked in her normal voice.

"Yes, I think the last few weeks have been too much for you. The doctor is on his way." I wasn't about to mention the word relative or friend, since I didn't know which had caused her to faint.

"There was no need to call Doctor Morton," she said, as Art helped her to her feet.

"I think you have been trying to put on a good front instead of letting yourself grieve for your husband. Why don't you spend the rest of the day in bed? Perhaps you'll feel better tomorrow." I suggested.

"Yes. Yes, I think I'd better do that. Would you excuse me?" One would think her performance had never happened.

We thanked her, and promised to let her know if we found out anything helpful. She assured us she would talk to William and to let me know if he could remember anything about the note. As we walked out the door, Doctor Morton walked in.

Pulling out of the driveway, Art said, "I'll contact Doctor Morton tomorrow. He may be willing to tell me what's going on. I see what you mean about that lady. She has more personality swings than a schizophrenic. I wouldn't want her mad at me, that's for sure."

Handling the paper by the corners, I had been reading the letter Mrs. Logger received. The writer had used the same cheap notebook paper. Even the hand writing looked the same to me.

It read: "Mrs. Logger, Did you know that your husband is the father of a sweet ten year old boy named Tracy Fuller, who was born deaf? Did you know that Doreen Grant, his secretary, became pregnant from the one time they were together, and that she was a virgin. Yet your husband refused to accept responsibility for the child because he was afraid you would divorce him? How does it feel to be responsible for ruining three lives. The mother. The boy. The man the little boy believes is his father? Since you destroyed their lives, why don't you do the same for yourself? Your husband has paid his dues. Go ahead, Mrs. Logger, go ahead. Take your life. No one will miss you. (signed) A Friend."

"It's horrible, Art. The person who wrote this note must be crazy. However, I must admit there have been many times when I've thought perhaps Harriet Logger was the one who killed her husband. She has so many sides to her personality, it's hard to know what to believe. She is strong enough to hold him under water until he drowned, but there were no bruises on the body."

"I know. I think our best bet is to wait until we talk to William and find out how that note arrived. Let's stop by the station. I'll get that note in an evidence bag. Tomorrow, I'll have it checked for fingerprints. What say we forget about this whole mess for the rest of the day? Let's go sit down by the lake and talk about the wedding, each other, and our lives together. What do you say?" he asked me.

I told him that sounded perfect to me. When we got back to the house, we let Frances know we would be back by six for supper, and took off for the lake. What a blessed time we had. It was great to act like a couple of kids again.

Sometime during the afternoon I admitted to Art that I hated the thought of walking down to the lake in my wedding dress with my crutch.

"It ruins the whole picture I have been carrying around in my mind for years," I told him tearfully.

"Aw, Babe, don't cry. It won't make a difference to those of us who love you. I thank God everyday for bringing you back to me. Truthfully, when I look at you, I don't even see that little ol' crutch."

He couldn't understand why that made me cry harder. I explained it away by saying it was a woman thing.

FOURTEEN

The next morning I called Art from the Fuller house to see if he had set up an appointment with Doctor Morton. Yes, he had one for four o'clock that afternoon.

"What are your plans for today, Babe?" he asked.

"I'm bringing Tracy and Matthew to the office with me. I want to stick close to the phone in case Mrs. Logger calls about William. I keep thinking that Paul J. might have met his fate on the far side of the lake near the boat houses. The boys and I are going to take a picnic lunch and go over there. While they play in the water, I can have a look around. We'll be back by four. Call me when you get back from the doctor's office, would you?"

He asked me what I thought of Matthew.

"Art, he's wonderful. I want Marie to meet him. He is an exact miniature of Roger, except for his blonde hair. The same inquisitive brown eyes, the same glasses, the same serious expression—everything. Wait until you see him. And, guess what?" Rushing on, I didn't give him time to answer. "Matthew can speak, but he uses sign language because he is used to it. We have agreed that we will always sign, so Tracy won't feel left out. That was Matthew's idea. I'm constantly amazed by the amount of compassion both boys have for each other. The nuns must be wonderful teachers."

"After that description I'm anxious to meet this paragon of virtue. If Mrs. Logger doesn't call, why don't you and the boys come by the station on your way home. Say around eleven-thirty."

I told him that would be great; we would see him then.

99

Tracy was full of importance while he showed Matthew around my office. *Where did I get my training to be a private investigator?* Matthew wanted to know. I had been waiting for that question, thinking Tracy would ask it, but I still gave it a great deal of thought. I finally told them a few of the simple cases I handled while with the CIA. I think my prestige went up when they found out what I had done in the past. They were full of questions. Some I answered, and others I sidestepped.

We were getting too deeply into one of their questions for my comfort, when the phone rang. It was Mrs. Logger. Could Mr. Landow and I come and talk to William? I couldn't let this opportunity go by. I told her we'd be right there. I hung up, my mind was racing. What to do with Tracy and Matthew? Quickly, I called the station and explained the situation to Art. He suggested they might like to spend a little time at the station, while he and I called on a witness. When I put it to the boys, they beat me to the car. Matthew assured me that they had been having a good time with me, but, well, you know, a trip to the police station, how could they say no. I told him I understood.

"It's a man thing, right?"

"Right," he said, relieved.

When we arrived I let Tracy lead the way to Art's office with Matthew in tow. I wanted to lag behind and get Art's reaction when he met Matthew. It was comical, believe me. Matthew stepped up when Tracy signed what Art's name and title was, and spoke up like he was ten going on forty.

"How do you do, sir? It's a pleasure to make your acquaintance."

Art had a hard time controlling a smile. "How do you do, Matthew? I'm glad to meet you also. I understand you have come to visit Tracy for a few days."

"Yes, sir. I will be staying for a period of one week. I'm looking forward to meeting Tracy's friends."

Good grief, I thought. He must be a forty year old midget! The thing that brought a lump to my throat was that while he was talking to Art he was repeating the whole conversation to Tracy in sign language.

"I hope to see you again while you are here, Matthew."

"Thank you, sir. I will look forward to it, sir." I expected Matthew to salute, make an about face, and march out of the room.

I asked Art what he thought.

"I agree," he chuckled. "The resemblance to Roger is uncanny. And the way he talks. Isn't that something? If I didn't know better, I'd swear Roger had been cloned. Why don't you stop by the drugstore on your way home. It's time those two meet."

There are times when Art's an ornery cuss.

Art and I drove to Valley View Drive to meet William. I tried to prepare him for the meeting, but I don't think it soaked in. It was comical when William opened the door, and Art's eyes went up and up and up to William's face.

"Art Landow and Sandy Shores to see Mrs. Logger," Art told him.

"Right this way, please," the giant requested in a high pitched voice. We followed him down the hallway, trying hard to control our surprise. I don't know what Art thought, but that voice reminded me of one of the guys in our training group who accidentally got slammed in the crotch with a sledge hammer. Poor guy went out like a light, and was in the hospital for several days. Afterward, his voice remained about three octaves higher. He was going to quit the force, but they transferred him to a desk job. The last I heard he'd married, and he and his wife had adopted a couple of kids.

Mrs. Logger was looking like perfection again today. So much for staying in bed and taking it easy, I thought. It had to take a couple of hours to get dressed up like that. The thing that irritated me is that she made me feel absolutely frumpy.

Again we went to the library. We sat in the same chairs we had occupied on our first visit, and declined her offer of something to drink.

"I have asked you here today, so you might hear William's story directly from him. All right, William, tell them what you told me earlier." Her voice was firm, but not unkind.

"Yes, madam. On the fourth of August a gentleman came to the front door, and demanded to see the madam . . . "

"That was the day I came to see you, Miss Shores. Continue, William," she interjected.

"Yes, madam. When I told him she wasn't home, he told me he would wait. I told him I didn't know when she would be back, but he pushed past me. He was a large man, muscular, in his forties, I would judge. I was afraid he was going to attack me, so I led him here to the library to wait. I stood inside the door, and he became belligerent. He told me to get out, and quit watching him like he was a thief. Well, I had never had a situation like this before. Something told me I shouldn't leave, but I was truly frightened of what I might do if he should attack me."

"Did he ever tell you his name?" Art asked.

"No, sir."

"What else can you tell me about him. Color of hair? Scars, tattoos, or other distinguishing marks?"

"His hair was dark, cut kinda long, with a little gray sprinkled on the temples. I didn't see any marks, but his hands were huge and callused, like he worked outside. His eyes were a strange bluish-gray color. He was driving a bright, cherry red Corvette. I remember admiring the car."

"Go on," Art said.

"Well, I stepped out of the library, but I stayed right outside the door, in case he tried to steal something. I'm terribly sorry, madam, I thought I was doing right."

"I know, William, I know." Mrs. Logger sounded resigned to this type of behavior from William.

"I didn't hear a sound from inside, but suddenly he flung the door open, and informed me he couldn't wait any longer. He told me to put a letter he had for the Madam in with her mail. I was to make sure she received it, but I wasn't to say where it came from. He said . . . he said if I told anyone, he would make me sorry. I did what he instructed me to since the mail had just arrived. I didn't notice that he was carrying anything when he went out to his car. I went into the library immediately after he left, but I didn't notice anything missing until the next day when I realized one of the master's favorite pistols was gone. I didn't know what to do. I wanted to tell you, madam, but I was afraid." William was almost in tears. It was sad to see a big man like that so frightened.

"Thank you, William," Art said. "I'm sure you can relax. I have it on good authority that the man you described is headed for Alaska. We found out recently that he was extremely fond of guns. I guess he couldn't pass up the chance to grab that pistol."

You could see the relief flow through William's body. Poor, guy, I thought, I hope he keeps his job.

"Do you know who the man was, Mrs. Logger?" Art asked.

"No. I don't remember ever seeing anyone that matched that description around here."

"Does the name Jasper Grant mean anything to either of you?"

"No," they both answered. "Is that his name?" Mrs. Logger asked.

"Yes. We are sure he is the same man we are looking for in connection with another crime," Art told them.

"That's all, William. I'll talk to you later," she informed the butler.

"Yes, Ma'am."

When he was out of earshot she turned to us, and asked if we would like to know William's history. "Definitely," we both said, in unison.

"William's full name is Thomas James William," she started.

"The kid that played for the New York Knickerbockers, and then disappeared!" Art interrupted. "I've often wondered what happened to him. He was a real good looking kid, if I remember right."

"You remember right, Mr. Landow. William had always wanted to be a big league basketball player. His mother said she would have to drag him away from practice to eat and sleep. He was his college's most valuable player in his senior year, and, of course, the scouts were watching him. When the year ended he was offered a contract with the New York Knickerbockers. He was thrilled and so determined to do well that the coach started letting him play in his first year. It was always the final minutes of the game when he was put in because he excelled at hitting the three point shot.

"It was nearing the final game of the season, and New York was one game away from winning the championship. A group of heavy betters out of Las Vegas got to William and told him if he would miss his final shot so the Knicks would lose, they would make him a millionaire. They told him he would be sorry if he didn't do what they said, but he couldn't do it. He had always played fair and it went against his nature to cheat. He was put in the game in the last five minutes and it was his final shot that won the game.

"It probably would have been better if he had confided in his coach, but he had himself convinced that he was being tested to see if he actually would take a bribe. On his way to his apartment later that night he was badly beaten. The doctors were afraid for awhile he would lose his sight. It took two hundred stitches to close the wounds on his face, and what you see today is the best they could do. He had three broken ribs, a broken left wrist, one knee cap had been shattered with a baseball bat, and there were several slashes on his chest, arms and legs. The gangster's men had also used the bat on William's head, in an attempt to kill him. It might have been better if they had finished the job because William now has the mentality of a twelve year old. However, he was not standing idly by while those goons were messing him up. By the time they were through with him, two of them were dead. William had killed them with his bare hands, while trying to protect himself.

"The police exonerated him completely from any blame in the two deaths, but he has this irrational fear that he might kill again if he were to get into another fight. I believe that's why he acted the way he did when that man was here."

Everyone was quiet for a few minutes when she finished speaking, each of us dwelling on our own thoughts. Art was the first to speak.

"T. J. had a great deal of natural ability. It was a thing of beauty when he would shoot for the basket. I even enjoyed watching him during the warm-up time." Art sat lost in thought for a moment. "What are you planning to do about the loss of the gun, Mrs. Logger? If you would give me a description there's a possibility we may be able to return it to you when we locate Jasper Grant."

"I honestly couldn't care less about the gun," she smiled. "That collection was my husband's, not mine. I actually abhor guns. Don't worry about William. I will reprimand him the same way I would a naughty child. I'll think of something. I don't intend to let him go. Most people are intimidated when they see him. I believe he is what I need now that I'm alone, don't you agree?"

We both agreed wholeheartedly.

"Mrs. Logger, I have one question. Where does William live? I've never seen anyone like him around Myrtle Woods."

"He has an apartment over the garage. On his days off his sister from Mountain View picks him up, and he spends time with her and her family. I've never known him to go downtown here."

While I was talking to Mrs. Logger, Art was having a few personal minutes with William, who looked a lot happier when we left.

"I wish I was chief of detectives," I told Art as we drove back to the station, "then I could go with you when you talk to Doctor Morton tomorrow. You, in your position, have the right to ask questions in the course of your investigation, whereas I don't. I'll have to sit and wait for your report."

"Aw, poor little girl. Is your curiosity about to get the best of you?"

"That's for sure," I told him, giving him a poke in the arm, "and you know it too, you stinker."

I dropped him at the station, collected Tracy and Matthew

and we went to the drugstore. Supposedly, we were stopping by there to show Matthew the old fashioned soda counter; the only one left in the state. When we entered the door I spotted Roger with his back to us, talking to a customer. Marie was behind the soda counter. The three of us slid up on the stools, and I thought Marie's eyes were going to fall out.

I introduced Matthew, and then sat back and let him do the talking. It was the same way it had been with Art. I could see a smile tugging up the corners of her mouth, but she managed to control it. When Roger finished with his customer, Marie took Matthew's hand. Stepping up to Roger, she kept the boy behind her.

"Roger, honey, I have someone I want you to meet."

Marie drew Matthew in front of her. For a few seconds man and boy stood staring at each other. Marie opened her mouth to make the introductions, but Matthew beat her to it.

"You look like me," he said to Roger, wonder in his voice.

"No, son, I think you look like me."

"My name's Matthew Smith, sir. May I ask your name?"

"My name is Roger Owens." He glanced up with a dazed look on his face, saw us standing there and realized this was the boy who had come to visit Tracy. "You must be Tracy's friend."

"Yes, sir. He is my best friend. It's good for a fellow to have a best friend, don't you agree?"

"Oh, yes." We could tell Roger was still slightly befuddled.

I had been repeating this two-sided conversation to Tracy. You could tell by his grin that he was enjoying what was happening between Roger and Matthew. I spoke up and said we had to be on our way if we were going to be back by four.

We decided that the boys would come by the next day, and Roger would explain how he mixed the ingredients for prescriptions. Matthew thought that would be extremely interesting, but he took time to make sure it would be okay with Tracy. After all, he explained to us in his serious young voice, he was here to visit Tracy. Matthew shook hands with Roger and Marie telling them he hoped to see them tomorrow.

When we reached the house, we visited with Frances for a few minutes and picked up our picnic lunch. Tracy and Frances were getting to be such good friends, I told him to introduce Matthew. He did an admirable job, and ended by telling Matthew that Frances was the best cook he had ever met. When Matthew repeated the compliment Frances actually blushed!

Since Tracy no longer had aversion to crowds, we went everywhere. Both of us were looking forward to showing Matthew a good time.

FIFTEEN

It was a beautiful day. Driving around the lake, I was humming a happy little song, thinking how sad it was that Tracy would never know what it was to hum. It wasn't until I started taking care of him that I realized how much a person who can't hear misses. Little things, like his friend's voice, waterfalls, snow crunching underfoot, train whistles; there is no end to the list. Several times I have seen Tracy get frustrated because he couldn't think of the right word to sign that would enable him to get his thought across.

In this continued hot weather we are having, he seldom wears much of anything unless I take him with me to call on a client. Today, both boys wore swimsuits in hopes of playing in the lake after lunch. I had thrown a shirt in for both of them, in case they started to burn, or the weather made a quick change.

We arrived at the first of the storage buildings in time to watch one of the larger boats being winced down into the water. By the time we reached the end of the road and the last of the buildings, it was time for lunch. I spread out the blanket Frances had sent with us, and laid out the fried chicken, cherry tomatoes, little containers of potato salad, rolls, chocolate chip cookies and pop. Tracy and Matthew had gone down to check out the lake, but Matthew hurried them back when I called. We ate like we hadn't had anything to eat for a couple of days, but with Frances' food you can't help it. Oh, to be able to cook like that. I say that, and in the next minute realize with Frances in the kitchen I didn't want or need to learn.

While we were eating I let them know that I didn't want them to go in the water unless I was there. Tracy knew the story of Adam, which he repeated to Matthew. Matthew asked if those were the people he had met at the drugstore, and when Tracy informed him that it was, Matthew whispered and signed, "How sad."

Every once in a while a terrible odor would waft around us on a sudden breeze. I was sure there was something dead close by.

After we finished our lunch we put our dirty paper plates, forks, and empty pop cans back in the picnic hamper. There were a few cookies left, which we put on top, planning to eat them later. We set the hamper on the blanket, and started out to search the nearest building.

I was following up on an idea that had come to me in the night. I woke up thinking: I must go check out the storage buildings. I wasn't sure what I expected to find, but I've learned that when my brain gets these wild ideas, it's a good idea to see what I can find.

The first building we reached was open. Boy, I thought, if I owned one of those beautiful boats I'd sure have it locked up. However, this building was empty. We walked in to check it out. The boys headed for the winch used to bring the boat into dry dock, while I wandered around to see what I could find.

Nothing.

Motioning to the boys, I went back outside. That pungent odor hit me again. I indicated to them that I wanted to go into the forest for a short way, and asked them to wait for me on the blanket. When I get back, I told them, we'll go swimming. That brought smiles. The trees and brush were thick so it was slow going. I found myself following a faint trail and wondered what made it. I had not gone far before the sunshine grew dim. I let my nose guide me and it didn't fail me. I had not gone twenty feet before I found a shallow grave. Wild animals hadn't left leave much of what was once a human being. They had badly ripped the clothing in their attempt to get to the flesh. I looked around quickly, but I couldn't see either arm or one of the legs. One tennis shoe was still on the body, while the other shoe was a short distance away. My first thought was: my God, I think I've found Doreen. My second thought was: poor Tracy, poor little man, never to know his mama. Hurriedly, I examined the shoe more closely. Actually, it looked more like something a man would wear in the summer, so perhaps it wasn't Doreen. I shoved it into my waistband, covering it with my shirt. I didn't want either of the boys to see it.

What was that smell, Tracy wanted to know. I informed him I wasn't sure, but I thought someone had died in there. *What we need to do,* I told them, *is get in touch with Art immediately.* We had gathered up the remnants of lunch, and were starting to put things in the trunk of my car when I heard the sound of another car coming. Somehow I knew it was bad news. I could feel it. Quickly, I told Tracy to take Matthew and hide. *Don't come out, no matter what happens, until I come for you.* He was bewildered at my request because, after all, he hadn't heard the car motor. Thank God, he didn't argue. Both of them quickly blended into the forest. I set the hamper on the floor of the trunk, not taking time to open the lid and put the leftover cookies inside. Throwing the shoe and the blanket in, I slammed the trunk and hurried as quickly as I could to the edge of the lake.

I was trying to skip rocks, looking, I hoped, like I didn't have a care in the world when I heard a car door slam. I was doing my best not to breathe too quickly from hurrying back to the water's edge.

"Well, imagine meeting you here," he said.

I would have known that voice anywhere. Smiling, I turned. "I might say the same to you. How are you, Mr. Grant?"

"Hey, I thought we were Peter and Sandy."

"Of course, forgive me."

"What are you doing here, Sandy?"

"I needed a little time alone. We haven't been able to find Doreen and I thought if I came here alone, I would be able to think of things we haven't done in the investigation. What are you doing here? Do you have a boat stored here?" I looked around innocently.

"No-o-o," he said. "I've been keeping an eye on the turnoff to this road for several weeks, watching who came and went into the storage buildings. Have you found anything of interest?"

"Why, no. I've been standing here enjoying the quiet." While we were speaking I had been watching his face and what I saw there was frightening. Unless my training was failing, Peter Grant was on the brink of insanity. Realizing that, there was no way I was going to bring Matthew's name into the conversation, since apparently he hadn't heard of the boy visiting Tracy.

"You haven't been walking in the woods?"

"Oh, no, it's too difficult for me with my crutch," I lied.

"You're lying," he shouted. His sudden change in attitude surprised me. "When I saw your car turn up this road, I knew you would start snooping around and you'd find the body. You did find it, didn't you?"

I knew better than to lie to him this time. "Yes, I found it," I said softly, trying to calm him down.

"I knew it. I knew you wouldn't be able to leave well enough alone. I don't know why you couldn't have waited for another week. By that time the animals would have picked the bones clean, and I could have bundled everything up, and destroyed it. Then no one would ever have known what happened to Jasper."

Jasper! What a surprise! I'm sure my mouth fell open.

Peter fell to his knee's, tears racing each other down his face. "God knows I didn't mean to kill him. If only he hadn't taken that note to Mrs. Logger. If only he hadn't stolen that gun. I was going to force him to take it back, you know, but he said no way. We got into a terrible argument. When I tried to take it away from him it went off, and he ... died."

He clasped his hands in prayer. "God forgive me, I didn't know the gun was loaded. What was I suppose to do? I didn't mean to kill him. It was an accident. I buried him here in the forest. I was hoping no one would find him until the animals were done. I mustn't be arrested. I can't stand being locked up."

In a flash, he was on his feet. He grabbed my left arm, and twisted it behind my back, causing my crutch to fall to the ground. "In another week I can gather Jasper's bones and get rid of them. No one must know what you found." He began muttering to himself. "Yes, that's what I'll do. I'll take this one deep into the forest where no one will ever find her. The animals will get rid of her for me. No one will ever know what happened to her. I'll put her car in with Jasper's. That way no one will be able to prove I had anything to do with their deaths."

"Don't do something that will get you in more trouble, Peter. If it happened the way you said, it was an accident." I was trying to catch him off guard; perhaps get my arm loose. I knew I wouldn't get far, though, without my crutch. It was a Catch 22 situation for me.

He showed no emotion. "That advice is a little late, Sandy."

"What does that mean?" I asked, though I knew.

Without answering me, he started pulling me toward the trees. Oh, God, he was going to go right by where Tracy and Matthew are hiding. Hide, baby, hide, I thought, hoping Tracy would read my mind.

"I thought you had Tracy with you everyday." Peter stopped and glanced around, his eyes clear. "Where is that dumb brat?"

"In the first place, he isn't dumb," I snapped. "He's with my housekeeper making cookies. I wanted to come here by myself. I don't have much time to myself since I agreed to take care of him during the day."

"That's why we put Doreen and Jasper in that soundproof playroom. Worked like a charm every time."

My God, what a monster. If he feels like that, why does he want Tracy? The thought of Tracy living in that house was nauseating.

Peter was dragging me down an old logging road that I remembered from my childhood. My mind was racing trying to figure out what to do when suddenly, right in front of me was a strange looking pile of brush. Peter had been muttering words I couldn't understand, but when he saw the brush pile he said something about Jasper's car. Making a military left turn, he began dragging me deeper and deeper into the forest. What was he going to do with me? If only I didn't have this darn brace on my leg, I could fight him off, but to get away I'd have to knock him out. How I would get back to the car without my crutch was another problem. I knew I better start thinking of something, or I was positive I was going to die. He had killed once, why not again? Anger washed over me. Why was this happening just when Art and I had decided to get married? The only thing I could do was drag my foot and snap the limbs of the small bushes as Peter pulled me ever deeper into the forest.

"Where are we going?" I inquired.

He ignored me, and started rambling. "Yes, I killed that little bastard Logger. He deserved it—getting my little girl pregnant, and then claiming he wasn't the father. When you asked about Jasper and the red Corvette that day you brought Tracy to visit, I knew sooner or later I would have to kill you, too. But, guess what? I'm not going to kill you. Oh no, I'm going to tie you to a large tree and let the wild animals take care of the job for me. I realize it will be a slow death, but you shouldn't have been snooping around where you weren't wanted." His eyes had a fanatical gleam in them, and I realized I was dealing with an utterly insane human being.

"Humor me, and tell me one thing. How did you drown Paul Logger?" I hoped he wasn't so far over the edge that he couldn't remember.

He had been pulling me for what seemed like forever when suddenly he stopped. Before I could formulate a plan that might work, I found myself being securely tied to the tree he had chosen. He worked quickly, taping my fingers together, knowing that way I wouldn't be able to get loose. That was a trick the CIA had taught me, and it made me wonder what branch of the service he had been in.

He worked swiftly, continuing his story in a crazed tone of voice. "I made arrangements to meet Logger at his storage building when I heard he had his boat for sale. I made sure we were alone, then forced him into my car and brought him to where I met you today. I pointed my gun at him, and told him to take off his clothes. That's when I spied that gold chain he was wearing. I figured no sense in an expensive thing like that going down with the body. When he wouldn't take it off, I jerked it off. I was going to wear it, but it was too small for me. I gave it to that bitch that lives in my house. When Logger was bare-butt naked, I forced him to walk into the lake. He kept crying that he couldn't swim, but a few well-aimed shots from my silencer convinced him I wasn't bluffing. Guess what? He wasn't kidding; he couldn't swim. God, he was stupid. If he had refused to go in the water, I would have shot him. It would have been much quicker." He laughed maniacally. "After he went down for the third time, I swam out and towed him back into the shallow water. I thought it only fair that I get rid of that part of him that had caused Doreen all her problems. I sliced his penis off, just the way I did that turkey leg at dinner." I felt my stomach lurch. Did he have to mention penis, turkey and dinner in the same breath?

Peter started laughing so hard that it was an effort for him to finish telling his story. "Since that sonofabitch never went anywhere without his necktie, I tied his back on. Don't you think that was kind of me?"

Before I could answer his question he slapped a piece of tape on my mouth. That done, he stepped back to admire his handiwork.

"There. I suppose you are wondering what happened to Logger's car, aren't you? I'll tell you since I don't think you will live to tell anyone," he giggled maniacally. "I waited until everyone had left the park for the day then I towed it to the other side of the lake. Using his keys that I had gotten from his pocket, I drove it into the parking lot. I folded his clothes in a neat pile down by the edge of the lake. I knew the police would think he took his own life. Oh, God, I'm clever.

"Now that I'm through with you, I'm going to go get Tracy and take him back home with me. Fuller better not try to tell me he's the brat's father. I know better and I'll tell him so. Then we will go get Doreen, so we can all be together again. Let's see. We need a little something to draw the animals to you, so they will finish you off." Whipping out his knife, he slashed my right leg deep enough to draw blood.

No, I silently screamed, not my good leg. It was another thing I would make him pay for when I got out of this mess . . . if I got out.

"There, that should be enough to draw wild animals in the vicinity. Bye, bye, Sandy. Sweet dreams." He gave me a salute, did an about face in his best military manner and walked away without a backward glance. His laughter floated to me through the trees. An eerie, crazy kind of laugh that remind me of things that go bump in the night.

A short time later I thought I could hear the faint sound of a car motor, and was sure he was hiding my car somewhere. I prayed the boys would stay hidden until he left. Poor Tracy, I could imagine what he was thinking.

It didn't help, as I knew, to try to get loose from my bounds. The way Peter had tied me, any movement seemed to tighten the knots. I don't think my future ever looked this bad. In Korea, I knew the Seals were eventually coming. Today, no one knew where I was, and the cut on my leg was dripping blood into my shoe. The red ants and the mosquitoes were beginning to feast on the skin my shorts and top didn't cover. The urge to scratch was starting to drive me crazy. I knew the smell of my blood would bring any large animals in the vicinity for a fresh lunch.

Immediately, my survival training kicked in. I was well on my way to going into the trance when something Peter told me came through my subconscious: We will go get Doreen, he had said. She was alive! I could only pray I would stay alive until I could tell Art.

SIXTEEN

Tracy couldn't figure out what was going on. He almost came out of hiding when he saw his grandfather drive up, but he remembered Sandy telling him to stay hidden, no matter what. He signed to Matthew who the man was, but indicated they were to stay hidden.

They watched Tracy's grandfather talking to Sandy, but Peter kept turning his head, so there were times when they couldn't read his lips. They weren't close enough for Matthew to hear what Grant was saying. What little he did hear made no sense. Something about a gun, and someone driving somewhere.

Again, Tracy came close to coming out of hiding when he saw his grandfather twist Sandy's arm behind her back, knock her crutch to the ground, and start pulling her into the forest. Wait, what's going on, he wanted to ask, but he suddenly heard a little voice inside him saying: hide, baby, hide. Tracy grabbed Matthew's arm, and drew him silently deeper into the brush. They watched his grandfather dragging Sandy by, not three feet away.

Sandy, Sandy, come back. Don't leave us. I'm afraid, he cried out silently; the trees and brush hid her from view. He felt tears gathering in his eyes. I won't cry. I'm too big to cry, he thought.

Should we go after them? Matthew signed.

No, we will stay right here like Sandy told us and wait, was Tracy's answer.

According to their watches they had crouched in the bushes for an hour before they saw the man come out of the brush. But wait, where was Sandy? Once again, Tracy started to rush out, to grab the old man's arm and ask him what was going on. When he made a forward motion, Matthew grabbed him and held him back.

Wait. We better see what he does, Matthew warned him.

The boys watched while the man started Sandy's car and drove it into the forest. Tracy tried to see where the car went, but after a short distance the forest seemed to gobble it up.

It looks like we've never been here, Matthew signed. The boys saw Peter Grant backing out on the tracks the car had made, using the limb of a small tree to brush the tracks away. He gathered several fallen branches, using them to close up the opening to the forest. One of the branches was so close to where they were hiding that they both thought Peter Grant would see them.

Grant got into his car, drove it down to the lake until he went slightly into the water, then he backed up and drove away. Tracy was certain something bad had happened. He realized the man wanted people to think that Sandy's car had gone into the water.

What should we do, Matthew? What if that man comes back? Both of them knew they must remain hidden. They decided to settled down in the midst of the overgrowth to think of a plan.

Earlier, back at the house, Frances thought it would be nice to have gingerbread cookies ready when they got back. Busy in the kitchen, she didn't hear a car nor did she hear anyone come in. She had taken a tray of cookies out of the oven, and was reaching for another, when suddenly a man grabbed her arm and swung her around to face him.

"All right, old woman, where is the boy? Sandy told me you and he were making cookies. What have you done with him? I've come to take him home and I won't tolerate interference from you. Well, speak up, old woman, before I break your stupid neck," Peter yelled, shaking Frances back and forth.

"Let go of me. I can't answer you when you are shaking me," Frances yelled back. Peter let go of her so suddenly she fell to the floor. "Where did you see Sandy?" she asked, trying to stall for time.

"Never mind that," he snarled. "Get Tracy in here right now or I'll make you sorry."

"You listen to me, mister. I don't know you from Adam, and I'm not about to give Tracy to any yahoo that walks through the door," she said angrily, her brain working a mile a minute. This man says he saw Sandy, but not Tracy or Matthew. Something is wrong. Sandy must want to keep Tracy away from this nut, Frances concluded.

"I," Peter drew himself up to his full height, "am Peter Grant, Tracy's grandfather. I have come to take him out of this den of iniquity, and take him back to where God-fearing people live. We will see that the boy is washed clean of this wickedness, and make sure he learns to fear God." Frances watched him change before her eyes. He was no longer the God-fearing man of a moment ago. Glaring down at her was a snarling, nasty-mouth bully whose voice had dropped to a whisper. "I'm giving you one last chance, you bitch, to tell me where Tracy is. If you don't, I'll beat it out of you."

Frances believed him more when he whispered than she did when he yelled. I better come up with something, she thought. "Well, if you had told me who you were instead of barging in and yelling like a crazy man, I would have been delighted to tell you. Mr. Fuller left with him not twenty minutes ago."

"What? Where were they going?"

"Why, I'm not sure. I believe they were headed to Mountain View to visit his sister. They should be home this evening."

Peter Grant stood quietly. Suddenly without warning, he swept the cookie paraphernalia on to the floor. "Don't lie to me! I know he's here." He started yelling for Tracy, slamming from one room to another.

Frances began cleaning up the mess he made while she waited for him to look through the house. Unexpectedly, he stop yelling. A minute later she heard the front door pulled shut with such force she expected to find it hanging by its hinges. She hurried to the window in time to see him tear out of the driveway, and head for town.

Quickly she dialed the butcher shop.

"Fuller's Meat Market. Dale Fuller speaking."

"Mr. Fuller, this is Frances Applebee, Sandy Shore's housekeeper. Please do what I ask you without asking any questions. It may concern the life of your son, Tracy, and his friend, Matthew."

"What's the matter . . . ?"

"Please, don't interrupt. Get out of the market immediately. Peter Grant may be on his way there and he has gone crazy. Please, please, get out of there. Come here to Sandy's house. The address is 765 Lakeshore. Make sure no one follows you. Please hurry," Frances begged.

"I don't understand, Mrs. Applebee, but I'll be there right away," Dale told her.

Oh, please, let Art be there, Frances prayed, dialing the police station. She identified herself and asked for Chief Landow.

"I'm sorry, ma'am. The chief is in a meeting and can't be disturbed. May I take a message?" an impersonal female voice answered.

"Please, it may be a case of life or death for Miss. Shores. Please take him that message," Frances implored her.

"Okay. Please hold."

Within two minutes Art was on the phone. "Frances, what is it? Has something happened to Sandy?"

"Art, could you come here right away? I'm afraid it's bad news."

"I'll be right there."

Frances, completely unmindful of the mess on the kitchen floor, walked back and forth through the house until she heard the siren coming down the street. Art pulled into the driveway right behind Dale Fuller. Frances hurried out on the porch.

"Mr. Fuller, I think you better pull your car in the garage where it can't be seen from the street," she called to Dale. Taking one look at her face, he immediately did what she asked.

Art took the porch steps two at a time. "Frances, what's wrong?"

"Oh, Art, I'm afraid something has happened to Sandy and the boys," she told him tearfully.

"Okay, Frances, take it easy," Art put his arm around her shoulders, and led her back into the house. Dale, coming in the back door, joined them in the kitchen. When they saw the mess on the floor, they turned to her for an explanation. She told them about Peter Grant, and everything that had happened. By the time she had finished she was weeping quietly.

Art was the first with questions. "He said Sandy told him Tracy was with you?"

"Yes."

"And you told Grant that Dale had picked up Tracy, and they were going to Mountain View?"

"Yes."

"Quick thinking, I'd say," Dale said.

"Frances, where is Al?" Art asked.

"He's at the dentist, thank God. I hate to think what might have happened if he had been here."

"I think you are probably right. Tell me what time Sandy left, and if she said where she was going." Art was trying to be calm.

"I made them a nice picnic lunch, and they left here about a quarter to eleven. She said she was going to the end of the boat storage buildings. She expected to be back here no later than four." Three pairs of eyes went to their watches. It was three-thirty.

Art called the station. In a short time, two of his detectives and another patrolman arrived. "Frances, this is Mike Maloney. I'm going to leave him here in case Grant comes back." He took Mike aside to give him instructions and a description of Peter Grant. "Frances, would you make us coffee to take with us?" Seeing how distraught she was, he thought it best to keep her busy.

"Bill and Ed, if Sandy isn't back here by four-fifteen, I want you to be ready to go pick up Peter Grant for questioning. She is normally so prompt, we won't wait later than that. Grant may have gone by the Fuller house. Swing by there on your way to South Point. When you pick up Grant bring him to the last boat storage building across the lake. If we haven't found Sandy and the boys by then, maybe we can convince him to tell us what he has done with them. Fuller, you come with me. If Tracy is the only one we find, I'll need someone who can talk to him."

The next twenty minutes went by agonizingly slow for those who were waiting. Every time a car came up the road everyone hoped it would be Sandy, that this was a false alarm. Finally, at four-ten Art couldn't contain himself any longer. He nodded at the two detectives. Giving Frances a hug, he signaled Dale to follow him.

Frances was trying hard to control her weeping, but she wasn't having much success. Every time she remembered the look on Peter Grant's face, she knew in her heart of heart, the seriousness of the situation.

Still hiding in the brush, Tracy awoke with a start. For a moment, he couldn't figure out where he was. He checked the time. It was four o'clock. *What is the matter with me? Here we were supposedly coming up with a plan, and we went to sleep instead. What a stupid thing to do,* he chided himself. He shook Matthew awake.

Without realizing it, Tracy had come up with a plan. *I think we better see if we can find Sandy's car, Matthew. We have to have a better hiding place in case that man comes back.* Slowly, they left their hiding place, Tracy walking backwards keeping an eye on the road, while Matthew crept forward. Tracy wasn't taking any chances, in case the old man came back. Slowly they went in the direction Peter Grant had driven Sandy's car. When they felt the trees and brush hid them from view, they turned and walked up the tracks the car had made, both shaking with fright. Tracy knew there were cougars and coyotes in the vicinity. The latter he didn't worry about, but he didn't want to meet up with a cougar. Unable to hear it, the scream that suddenly echoed through the forest didn't faze him, however, Matthew jumped and turned frightened eyes on Tracy.

Someone or something screamed, he told Tracy, his fingers flying. *It sounded like that cougar they killed up by the school last year. We must hurry and find a place to hide.* Even under these conditions he still thought like an adult.

They were busy signing instead of watching where they were going when they stumbled into the back of Sandy's car. Getting in, Tracy noticed the keys were still in the ignition. Yeah! he thought, I can open the trunk, get our shirts, and those cookies left from lunch. These darn mosquitoes are eating me alive. I better bring the blanket, too. First they rolled up the windows, to keep more bugs from getting in.

Wait, Tracy. I don't believe you should step out of the car. What if that was a cougar, and it is near by? Matthew signed.

You keep watch, and I'll get the stuff out of the trunk. If you see anything wave out the back window.

Matthew didn't like it, but he finally agreed.

Tracy was able to get the trunk open, and lifting the basket out, he put the cookies inside. He couldn't reach the blanket. When Sandy had hurriedly thrown it in the trunk, it had ended up way in the back. Tracy had to climb in before he could get it. He was reaching for the blanket when he noticed the shoe Sandy had found, but it had no meaning to him. He grabbed the blanket and both shirts, scrambled out of the trunk and slammed the lid down. Picking up the basket, he realized Matthew was waving frantically from the back window. Not taking time to look around, Tracy rushed to get in the car, his heart pounding. Throwing the basket and blanket in to Matthew, he jumped in and slammed the door behind him.

Is it out there? Did you see it? he asked.

There! Matthew pointed.

Tracy turned to see the wild, yellow eyes of an injured, hungry cat standing in the brush. For a moment, he thought he would faint.

Wow! They signed to each other. It wasn't a funny situation, but they couldn't stop laughing hysterically.

Neither of them realized that beyond the pile of brush in front of Sandy's car was a cherry red Corvette that was no longer beautiful. On the contrary, it had become a safe haven for many of the small animals of the forest.

SEVENTEEN

It was exactly four-thirty when Art and Dale reached the place where Sandy and the boys had enjoyed their picnic. They hurried to the storage building to search it first. When they found it empty they slowly began searching the whole area, looking for a clue that would tell them what had happened there earlier. Dale was the one who discovered Sandy's crutch. When Grant had driven down to the lake and then backed out, he had run over it both times, embedded it in the car track.

"Art, I think I've found Sandy's crutch," he called, digging frantically at the dirt.

"Oh, my God, yes, that's it." Art fell to his knees to help dig it out. He saw the tire tracks in the soft dirt leading to the water and beyond. He drew his breath in sharply. "What did Grant do? Push them into the lake?" Both men jumped to their feet and raced to the edge of the lake. Unmindful of their clothes, they both waded out into the water to get a better look.

"I don't see anything do you?" Dale asked.

"No, I don't. With water this clear you'd think we would see something. I think he made those tire tracks to throw us off."

Dale had to agree. "They aren't in the building or in the water, What has he done with them? My God, they could be anywhere. I wish Grant was here. I bet I could force him to tell us where they are."

"Take it easy. We need our wits about us if we are going to outwit that crazy devil. My guess is . . . " Art stopped speaking when they heard a car coming. It was Al.

"Frances told me what happened. Found anything?"

"We know they aren't in the building, and we are fairly certain they aren't in the lake. They must be in the forest. The question is, did they go willingly or were they forced?"

A light breeze came up, and the putrid odor that Sandy had noticed wafted out of the forest.

"What is that smell?" Al asked, wrinkling his nose.

Art told the two men to stay where they were while he checked it out. A few minutes later he came out of the forest, holding his handkerchief to his nose and mouth.

"Something has been killed in there. Probably an animal. We will check it out after we find Sandy and the boys." *If we find them,* he thought silently. *I only took a quick look, but I'd be willing to bet that's Doreen's body I found. Well, I'm not going to add that to Fuller's troubles right now. This new clue can wait until later.*

Art was doing his best to stay calm. "I think we better say a prayer that we find them before dark. The first thing to do is get more people out here to help search." He hurried to his car to use the mobile phone to call the station. "Kendall, call the Search and Rescue unit in Mountain View. Tell 'em we have three people lost in the woods over by the last of the boat storage buildings. Ask them to get here ASAP. Oh, and tell them we need Wicks and his bloodhounds. Get an ambulance out here too. Okay, Kendall, thanks."

Turning to Dale and Al, Art said, "If I remember right, this road used to be an old logging road, didn't it?" The two men agreed. "Okay. There is a possibility Grant drove Sandy's car into the forest using that old road. Let's look and see what we can find."

Walking along the edge of the forest they were surprised at how dense the brush had become over the years.

"That old road has to be here somewhere," Art muttered.

Dale suddenly started tearing at the brush, trying to find an opening. Working his way up from the lake it wasn't long before he came to the place where Grant had piled brush to hide the old road. When he jerked on it, he unceremoniously sat down hard on the ground with the brush in his lap. "I've found it," he yelled.

The other men came running. "Wait, fellas, go slow. That crazy might have booby traps set in there," Art warned them.

Slowly, they advanced through the dimly lit forest. "Good thing the sun is still up or it would be pitch black in here," Al whispered. "Hope we don't surprise that cougar the farmers were having trouble with last week."

"Me, too," Dale prayed.

"Hey, guys, he won't hurt you if you don't back him into a corner," Art laughed.

"This one will. Last I heard somebody shot and wounded him. You know what a wounded cougar is like." He had no more than gotten the words out of his mouth when they heard the cougar scream. "That cat ain't too far off," Al said, quickly scanning the area around them.

Oh, great, Art thought, another worry. Where are you, Sandy? Hang on, Babe, we're trying to find you.

They had been walking for about two minutes when Dale grabbed Art's arm.

"What is that?"

They could see a light flashing a short distance ahead of them. Art loosened his gun holster; they crept forward. It was a car turn signal light blinking on and off.

"Is it a trap?" Al whispered.

"It looks like an SOS," Art said. "Wait, Dale, it could be a trap." Slowly the three men crept closer. Looking in the back window they could see two figures in the front seat, with a blanket pulled around them.

A hand came out of the blanket and reached for the signal lever. Dale let out a whoop. "That's Tracy's hand," he said, running for the door.

When Tracy saw the men, he unlocked the door and fell into Dale's arms.

Dale grabbed the boy up to hug him tight. *Are you hurt,* he asked.

No, but, Daddy, Sandy is in trouble. His fingers flew as he tried to tell Dale what had happened that afternoon. He soon had Dale hopelessly confused.

Art had trouble getting Matthew to come out of the car because of the cougar. When Art assured him the cougar was no longer around he quickly climbed out to answer Art's questions about Sandy's whereabouts.

"Well, sir, first, Sandy found something in the woods and she said we must locate you immediately."

"That must have been what you saw, don't you think, Art?" Dale interrupted.

Art agreed. I'll bet she knew who it was, too, Art thought to himself. That's why Grant has done something to her. He must be the one who killed Doreen, and now he is trying to get rid of Sandy. If anything happens to Sandy, I'll kill him, I swear I will.

Matthew continued telling the men what took place. Every once in awhile Art would stop him to ask a question.

"Sandy told us to hide and not to come out until she came for us, no matter what we saw. Tracy signed that the man was his grandfather, but Sandy had told us to stay hidden no matter what happened. I couldn't hear the old man too well because his back was to us and they were down by the lake. There was something about a gun, and somebody driving somewhere. Tracy told me he no longer considered that man his grandfather when he twisted Sandy's arm behind her back, making her drop her crutch, and dragged her off into the forest. He didn't come back for an hour according to my watch."

Art had his arm around the boy's shoulders. "That's fine, Matthew. You both were right to do what Sandy told you. Can you think of anything else?"

"No, I'm extremely sorry, sir, that's my report," said this young boy with the grown-up vocabulary.

"Was she still wearing the slacks and shirt she had on earlier?"

"No, sir. She had on shorts and a short sleeved shirt. They were blue in color, I believe."

Pulling Tracy close again, Dale's tortured eyes said what they were both thinking. "She could be anywhere, Art. How are we going to find her? We can't leave her out here all night. These mosquitoes alone are enough to drive a person crazy, especially if Grant tied her up. On top of that we have the added worry of that injured cougar."

"Let's get this car out of the forest. If I know Sandy she has tried to leave us a trail. I have to find out where it starts." Talk to me, honey—he kept sending the message, trying to reach her by mental telepathy. Why does that always work in books, but not real life, he fretted.

No one paid any attention to the pile of brush in front of Sandy's car.

When they emerged from the trees in the little car, the ambulance was just pulling up. It was too soon to hope for the searchers. They probably wouldn't be here for another half-hour or better. Well, Art thought, I can't wait that long.

"Dale, if you want to take Tracy and Matthew home, it will be okay."

"I would if I could, but they won't leave until we find Sandy. Tracy has his heels dug in, so I guess we are here for the duration. If it's okay with the ambulance crew, they could stay with them. That would free me up to help you look," Dale told him.

"I can use all the help I can get. Get the boys to show you where Grant pulled Sandy into the forest. We need a starting point. Al, would you please wait out here for the searchers? Show them where we went in, tell them we are trying to find a clue. Broken branches and stuff like that. She must be in the radius of the distance that can be covered in a half hour, since Matthew said Grant was gone for an hour. When Wicks gets here with his dogs, get something out of Sandy's car for them to smell. If Bill and Ed get here with Grant, tell them to try and force him to say where she is. Okay?" He knew he shouldn't, but he couldn't wait for the searchers. I'll go crazy if I'm not out there looking, he thought. Now I know how parents feel who have a child lost in the woods, he admitted to himself.

Art ran to his patrol car and got extra bullets and two torches.

They would throw a good wide path of light, and would be helpful when trying to find a clue like a broken branch or a drag mark.

The boys had indicated that Grant had taken Sandy into the forest where they had backed out the car. Art was positive there was no sense looking on the lake side of the old road. He told Dale he would go down the track for thirty feet. Dale was to wait a few minutes, then he was to walk along the lake side of the left hand track looking along the far edge for drag marks or freshly broken branches. Art would be making his way back looking for the same thing. It took the two men twenty minutes to meet. Neither found a clue.

"He must have brushed out Sandy's tracks at the same time he did the car," Art said. "Let's step into the brush about a foot, and try it again. Try not to tramp down the brush too much." I know better than to do this, Art thought. I should wait for the dogs, but I can't, I just can't. A sudden thought came from nowhere: go further up the road to search.

Calling to Dale, Art went back to the cars. He was explaining to Al that they were going to go in further along the old road, when several car loads of searchers pulled in. The time was six p.m. There were only two hours of daylight left.

EIGHTEEN

There were about twenty adults who showed up to help with the search, each carrying a gun because of the injured cougar. Immediately the Search and Rescue coordinator, Jim Collier, set up a base in the boat storage building. Art explained the situation to Jim, who decided to form a line of searchers three feet apart.

"I'll space them along the old road." Jim pointed to a map of the area as he spoke. "Everyone will enter the forest when I give the signal. Working quickly in the fading light, they will search the area for clues for forty-five minutes. If they haven't found Sandy or some good solid clues by the end of that time, they will return to the base. At that time, I'm sorry, Art, but I'll have to call off the search because of darkness."

"Yes, of course. I understand," Art agreed. Right, you and your searchers go home, he thought to himself, but I'm staying here until I find her.

Art, Dale, and Al placed themselves at the head of the search line, which put them closer to where they found Sandy's car.

"Dale, I've got a hunch that we still need to go further up this old road. I'm going to go to where we found the boys and enter the forest there. With that injured cat out there somewhere we have to find her today."

"I know, man, I know," Dale consoled him. "I'd feel the same way if Tracy was out there."

Art couldn't speak over the lump in his throat. He gripped the other man's shoulder, nodded in agreement, and turned to walk up the track. He could no longer control his emotions. Crying in great heart-wrenching sobs, he begged: Oh, Babe, hold on, sweetheart. Hold on. Don't leave me. I love you. I love you.

When he reached approximately where he thought they had found the car, he wiped the tears from his eyes, squared his shoulders and entered the forest, swinging his torch from side to side. If I could just find one clue, something to know I was on the right track, he thought. Anything would help this hopeless feeling I have. It was then that Art saw the broken branch, and what appeared to be drag marks in the dirt. Thank God, he thought. Thank God.

His elation was short lived. Within a few feet the ground turned to smooth rock, and the drag marks disappeared. Retracing his steps, he tried going a slightly different way, to no avail. Which way to go? He felt like a mouse in a maze. He knew he was wasting valuable time, but he didn't know what else to do. Again he started out, going to his right this time. There! Another broken branch. Good girl, he thought. He decided the terrain was too unpredictable to try to look for drag marks; he would concentrate on the broken branches. I pray she is the one who is breaking these; that I'm not wasting valuable time following an animal.

He advanced slowly into the forest. Several times he had to retrace his steps and try again. It's probably taking me three times longer than it evidently took Grant, he thought, but I can't afford to miss anything. He often had the feeling that he was going around in circles, which kept him from notifying the Search Coordinator of what he was doing. There was the possibility he was tracking the injured cougar, too. That thought made his forehead break out in sweat.

He was so intent on looking for broken branches that the cougar scream surprised him. Dropping to the ground, he switched off his light. My God, that scream was close, he thought. Slowly, he crawled forward.

He couldn't believe his eyes. The cougar was standing in front of Sandy, reaching out with his paw to push her right thigh. The scent of blood coming from the cut on her thigh that Peter had inflicted was tantalizing to the big cat. Don't move, Sandy, please don't move, he prayed. The cougar went into a crouch, and he realized it was about to attack. He whipped out his gun and fired into the air, hoping to frighten the cat away. The cougar flinched, but still kept its eyes on Sandy. It was hungry and knew that its next meal was right there, tied to a tree. I'm going to have to try and shoot, he thought, not that this pistol is my gun of choice. The big cat screamed again. Art fell to the ground, sighted carefully, and fired. The crazed cougar leapt forward at the same instant the bullet hit. His claws extended, he raked deeply into Sandy's thigh as he fell to the ground. Blood spurted everywhere. Sandy didn't twitch. Art couldn't believe his eyes. My God, am I too late, is she dead?

Art should have known better than to rush past a dying animal, but this time he didn't use his best judgment. He knew he had to get a tourniquet on Sandy's leg before she bled to death. He was so intent on getting to Sandy, he didn't notice that the cat's eyes were watching his every move.

Rushing to the tree, he couldn't believe what he saw. Sandy's eyes were wide open, looking first at him, then the cat as if she was trying to send him a message. What unnerved him was her eyes showed no emotion, never blinked. It was like looking into the eyes of the dead. The rest of her face and body were badly swollen from the insect bites. He felt sick as he watched ants crawl across her eyes, over the lids, and into her hair. He dropped his gun on the ground and took her face in his hands to see if he could get a reaction. What the hell is going on, he wondered. Then it hit him—the trance she had told him about. He could understand why she didn't want to bring herself out of it right now. She must realize how much pain she will be in, he thought. I better get her untied and get that tourniquet on her leg before she bleeds to death. Working swiftly, he had her loose in seconds. Laying her carefully down on the ground, he took off his belt to tighten around her leg, while he hunted for a stick.

Suddenly he felt a terrible searing pain as the badly wounded cat clamped its jaws around his ankle and started dragging him across the clearing. Oh, God, help me, he thought. I can't reach my gun. There is no way to help myself.

Looking back at the tree, he couldn't believe what he saw. Sandy was reaching for the gun, wiping insects off her face. She sighted the gun carefully and fired directly into the cat's brain, killing it instantly, before she slumped to the ground, whimpering from her own pain. Prying the jaws apart, he was thankful he always wore boots when on duty, but that protection evidently was not enough. He could feel the blood running down his ankle and into his boot, but it didn't matter to him. He gently pulled the tape from her mouth. "Honey? Honey, are you okay?" She was like a rag doll and gave him no response. The only sound was her whimpering, which sounded more like an animal than a human. That was more frightening to him than the cougar. Making a tourniquet from pieces of his shirt and a stick, he tried to bind together the two sides of Sandy's leg where the cougar's claw had laid her leg open. Working quickly he managed to slow the worst of the bleeding.

Getting on his radio he notified Jim that he had found Sandy, and they both needed help immediately. The cougar had mangled Sandy's leg, and had bitten his ankle. Oh, yeah, he added, the cougar is dead. Jim told him they were on their way, and to fire his pistol every fifteen minutes. Thank God, I brought extra bullets, he thought.

While he waited for the rescuers, he brushed off the ants that were vying with the mosquitoes for the new blood oozing from her leg. Grant must have been a member of the mercenaries, he thought. He sure knew what he was doing when he tied Sandy up and left her for dead. I swear to God, I'll make him pay for this.

"Poor, poor baby, between the ants and the mosquitoes I don't know how you kept your sanity. You are going to be okay, my love, help is on the way."

The first thing that registered in my mind was that Art was in trouble. The Agency had never found anything that could bring me out of my trance. That was something I always had to do for myself. Now I knew there was one thing: love. My mind had registered that the man I loved above all others was in danger and the only one that could help him was me. Love helped me brush the ants from my eyes. Love helped me pick up the gun in my taped hands, and somehow get a finger on the trigger. Love helped me to keep the hand of my trembling body still while I fired. What love did not do was take away the pain and agony of thousands—no, make that millions of insect bites. I couldn't answer Art. I couldn't gather the energy needed to go back into the trance. All I could do was whimper.

He picked me up in his arms, and holding me tenderly, rocked me back and forth. "Help is on the way, dear one. Please hang on." I don't see how she can stand it, Art thought. It must be bad because she hasn't asked about her leg.

Then in the distance he heard the baying of the bloodhounds. He had never heard a more welcoming sound. Within a short time they arrived. Several searchers, the ambulance crew, Dale, Al, and Wicks with his dogs.

The medics worked swiftly binding the deepest of my wounds. It wasn't until they tried to move me that I realized how much pain was coming from my leg. Art was explaining about the itching. After asking me if I was allergic to anything they decided to give me a pain killer which would put me to sleep. Sweeter words I had never heard, but I made them wait while I told Art that Peter Grant had talked like Doreen was still alive. I knew that was exciting news to him, too. I'd leave it up to him to talk to Peter Grant. All I wanted was to be sedated.

Art refused to take his boot off until they got back to the base, so Dale and Al helped him out of the forest.

The searchers brought back the dead cougar to have it checked for rabies. Someone said Sandy might want to make a rug from the skin, but that was the last thing on Art's mind. He told me later that he was too worried about me to give any thought to a cougar pelt.

When they reached the cars, they found Marie waiting with the boys. The three of them rushed to the stretcher.

"Marie, what are you doing here?" Art asked.

"We heard on the radio that three people were lost in the forest. I somehow knew it was Sandy and the boys. I knew it meant trouble, too, because there's no way Sandy could get lost in these woods. Is she going to be all right? She looks dead." Marie and Tracy were crying. Matthew stood stoic, not saying a word.

"No, listen, believe me, she will be fine."

One of the medics was taking off Art's boot while this conversation was going on. The cat's teeth had gone through the leg to the bone, right above the ankle. Art's wound and the dead cat fascinated the boys, after they knew Sandy would be all right.

"I'm sure you are going to need a few stitches. You better ride to the hospital with us," the young medic said.

Art agreed quickly. He had planned on doing that anyway.

The emergency room doctor told the little group that Sandy was in grave condition. If she were awake she would tell him there had been many times when she had been in worse condition than she was right now, Art thought. The doctor told them her body had sustained more bites than he had ever observed on one person, and apparently she was allergic to the ant bites or the mosquitoes.

"It's not the mosquitoes, doctor," Art told him. "She has less reaction to them than I do."

"Thanks for that information. We can start treatment right away. We may not be able to save her leg. It will depend on whether or not we can control the infection that might develop from the dirt that got into those wounds. That cat did a lot of damage. The other thing that concerns me is her mind. I can't imagine not being able to brush off one of those insects, let alone both of them. She is going to have to be a strong woman to come out of this without side effects."

How ironic, Art thought. Sandy has probably come in contact with more strange bugs than most ordinary women, and the lowly red ant brought her down.

Art told the doctor a little about Sandy's past, and of the atrocities she had endured. "I don't think she will have a problem.

I strongly suggest you don't do anything drastic about her leg until you can talk to her."

"I won't, I promise," he said. "I hope you are right about her mental fortitude. We are going to keep her sedated for a day or two until most of the swelling is gone. We will have to wait and see about the leg. I'll keep you informed. You may go in and sit with her if you wish."

He was sitting beside the bed with his leg propped up on another chair when Frances and Al came rushing in.

Frances was beside herself. "What happened? She is so swollen," she whispered.

Art explained about the allergic reaction to the red ant bites and what the cougar had done to both of them. He didn't mention what the doctor had said about Sandy's leg and her mind. No sense worrying about something before it happened.

"I'm sure she will be fine once they get the reaction under control," he told them quietly. "I'm glad you two are here. The doctor has gone to rustle me up a pair of crutches because I have to get down to the station. We haven't heard from the men I sent after Peter Grant. I've got to see if I can track them down. Please call me immediately if there is a change in Sandy's condition. I'll instruct them to put your call through, no matter where I am."

"You be careful, dear. We can't have anything more happen to you. That cougar bite is enough for you to contend with, I would think," Frances said, fussing over him like he was her son.

"I'll be careful, Ma," he teased, taking the crutches the nurse brought him. "See you soon."

NINETEEN

When Art arrived at the station, Billy Ray and Ed had not yet returned with Peter Grant. Fearing that something had happened to them, he called the chief of police of South Point, Steve St. John, who was one of his Vietnam buddies. After he explained the situation, Steve said he would have one of his officers drive by the Grant residence to see if a Myrtle Woods police car was in the vicinity. It wasn't twenty minutes later when Art got the call that, yes, one of his cars was in front of the Grant residence.

"I'll be right over, Steve. Something is definitely wrong."

"Stop by the precinct. I'll ride out with you. A couple of my men can follow us."

When Art reached South Point he decided to call the Grant house to see if he could learn anything about what was happening. Peter Grant answered on the first ring.

"Sergeant Grant."

For a moment Art's mind spun. Grant thinks he's fighting the war again, he realized.

"Where the hell are you, Sergeant?" Art barked into the phone. "Why haven't you been reporting?"

"Sorry, SIR! Those yellow bellies ambushed us on Hill Thirteen, SIR! Everyone's dead but me. I haven't had time to send a report, SIR!" Grant told him insolently.

"Watch it, solider. I'm still in command here. Give me your exact position so we can pepper it with mortar fire, and get you out of there."

"No can do, General. Those sons-a-bitches killed my men,

and now it's payback time. I have two of those slant-eyed, yellow-livered bastards rigged up as booby-traps. When their buddies come busting in here, we're all going to meet our maker."

"Sergeant, this is an order. Give me your position, NOW!" Art bellowed.

"Sorry, Sir. Something is wrong with my radio. So long, General, it's been nice known' ya'." With that, Grant slammed down the phone.

Art said a silent prayer as he hung up the phone. Concern for his men made his voice ragged. "Peter Grant has gone completely over the edge," he told Steve. "He thinks he is fighting the Japanese again. From what he said, he has Ed and Billy Ray wired as booby traps, so we can't rush him. Well, Steve, any suggestions?"

The time was now eight-thirty, and it was getting dark.

"I think the first thing we better do is evacuate the neighbors in the immediate vicinity, and barricade off the whole block until this situation is under control. I'll get my men assigned, then I suggest you and I drive out to the Grant house in an unmarked car. That way we can see if there is anything we can do that will help us get your men out of there alive."

By the time they got to the Grant house it was completely dark. Walking slowly because of Art's crutches, they stood by the trees and looked into the front room. The scene chilled them to the bone. Peter Grant was rocking slowly back and forth with what appeared to be a 357 magnum on his lap. He was pointing the gun at Billy Ray, who was sitting on a hard kitchen chair with his feet tied to the legs of the chair. A wire around Billy Ray's neck appeared connected to the trigger of a rifle aimed at his head. The two men could see that the wire ran to the front door where Grant had stretched it tightly around the door knob. If anyone tried to attack the house Billy Ray would die instantly when they rushed through the door.

"That's some set up he's got Billy Ray in," Art whispered. "One false move and Bill is a dead man. If he gets tired and tries to doze off, he's had it. Let's see if we can find out what has happened to Ed."

Moving cautiously, they worked their way around the house. They came to the window that gave them a view of the dining room where they saw Ed bound spread-eagle on the dining room table. The only thing he had on was his shorts. Hanging from the light fixture approximately eight feet above him was a large hunting knife aimed at his heart. The lightweight rope tied to the knife went through the fancy light fixture then over to the kitchen door. Art realized that anyone rushing in that way would cause the knife to plunge straight into Ed chest.

"Would that knife actually hurt him if it fell?" Steve whispered.

"Yes, I have one of those knives and it's quite heavy. The weight plus the distance it would travel would surely plunge the knife into his body, especially since he is naked. I don't think it would go through to his heart, but it would certainly cause some damage," Art replied softly.

We watched Peter Grant come in through the door leading to the front room. He placed a drop of what must have been acid on the thin rope. Even from where they were they could see that the rope was already beginning to fray.

"We don't have much time, Steve," Art whispered. "We need to decide quickly how we are going to handle this. I wonder where Mrs. Grant is?" Moving quietly, they looked through windows in the kitchen, in the ground floor bedroom, and in the library before they located her. Badly beaten and securely tied hand and foot, she lay in a pool of blood on the library floor.

"That bastard," Steve swore, "he has gone completely mad. Did you notice how he was dressed? He reminds me of those guerrillas we fought in Vietnam. The way your men are trussed up makes me think Grant must have been in Special Forces during WW2. They were taught a lot of that kind of stuff, my dad told me. Listen, I've got a glass cutter at the precinct. I can have it out here in a few minutes. I think our only hope is to go through one of these windows and pray they aren't booby trapped. What do you think?"

"Agreed. While you go back to the car to call for the cutter, I'll try a few other windows to see if I can find one open. Hurry, time is short."

Silently, Steve melted away into the darkness. Quietly, Art started going from window to window. He let out a sigh of relief when he found the large window into the downstairs bedroom unlocked. Slowly he raised it and pulled the curtain aside to peer inside, looking for booby traps. There weren't any wires that he could see, but directly in front of the window Grant had placed a low coffee table covered with a variety of pots and pans, intermingled with several small pieces of bric-a-brac.

How am I going to move that table to one side by myself without waking the dead? Art wondered. With this bum ankle I can't step over it. I can't hang on to everything and move it, either. Well, shoot, he thought, I'm useless.

Suddenly behind him a branch snapped; he froze. Out of the darkness a figure materialized. Steve! When Steve took a look at the mess inside the window, he swore softly to himself. Reaching in, he slowly began handing things out to Art.

It seemed to take an eternity to remove enough stuff so that he felt comfortable climbing in. Once inside he moved the table quietly to one side before helping Art into the room. Only then did Art realize what a strain it had been to dismantle the table. Steve was wiping away the sweat that ran down his face.

Quietly, slowly, the two men moved to the bedroom door. They could hear Peter talking to Billy Ray in a low monotonous tone of voice.

" . . . you should have known better, you yellow-skinned, slant-eyed son-of-a-bitch. Now, you are going to get yours when your buddies come bursting through that door and you want to know what I'm going to do? I'm going to kill them all with my trusty little machine gun here." He stroked his magnum, treating it like a true machine gun. "The same way you sneaky cowards butchered my buddies. You saw what I can do when I took care of that little Jap wife in there," he nodded toward the library. "Now don't run off," he laughed loudly, "it's time for a little more acid for your friend in there" he said, moving silently through the door into the dining room.

Quietly, Steve stepped into the front room, while Art stayed back in the shadow of the bedroom door. Without a sound, Grant appeared in another doorway behind Steve. Art hollered; Steve fell to the floor, and rolled for cover as Grant got off a shot. Before Grant could shoot again Art stepped out of the bedroom. Using the door jamb to hold himself erect, he aimed his gun.

"Drop it, Grant," he yelled. "Police!" In what seemed like slow motion Grant swung around to face him; raising his gun to fire. "Drop it or I'll shoot," Art warned him. He could see that Grant was starting to pull the trigger and knew one of them was a dead man. It seemed that both guns fired simultaneously. Grant's bullet shattered the edge of the door frame, spraying wood particles into Art's face. The force of the bullet grazed his forehead causing him to lose his balance. His bullet tore into Grant's brain.

Wealthy Peter Grant, former owner of the South Point Inn, member of numerous civic committees, leading man in the Little Theater Group, was dead before he hit the floor.

"Steve, you okay?" Art called. He bound a bandanna around his head and laboriously pulled himself erect.

"I got one in the leg, but I've got it handled."

"Good. I've got to see to Ed."

Calling to Billy Ray that he had to take care of Ed first, he limped through the door into the dining room.

The rope holding the knife had only a few threads holding it together. Loosening the rope, Art let the knife down slowly until it lay on Ed's chest. Pulling the tape off of Ed's mouth brought back the memory of doing the same thing earlier for Sandy. Grant certainly had a fetish for adhesive tape, he thought.

"Hi, Chief. I can't tell you how glad I am to see you. What happened in there?"

"Grant is dead. Chief St. John took one in the leg. Billy Ray is okay, but we still have to get him loose," he said, untying Ed's hands.

"Then go. I can finish getting these bounds off of my feet. You can give me all the details later."

Steve had gone in to see if he could do anything for Mrs. Grant. "I don't know what is keeping her alive. It looks to me like she has lost gallons of blood. I've called for an ambulance, but I've told them to stay out until I give the signal."

It was a little trickier getting Billy Ray free. First, they found a pair of wire cutters in the dead man's pocket. In looking over the setup the men found that the slightest movement of the gun would cause it to discharge. If Billy Ray leaned forward that also would set it off.

"Grant certainly knew what he was doing," Art said. "Thank God, he used thin wire."

Looking things over again, they decided the only way they could dismantle the gun was by cutting the wire going from Billy Ray's throat to the trigger. The instant they cut, Billy Ray would fall to the floor as someone pushed the rifle upward. When they cut the wire they didn't think the rifle would discharge, but there was no way to be positive. So, the big decision was, who would do what?

Ed came in, tucking his shirt into his pants. "Have you come to any conclusion yet?"

Art explained what they needed to do. "Whoever cuts the wire must remain rock steady."

After what had happened in the past few minutes, none of them felt too steady. Art could not stop the blood dripping from his head wound. Steve with his gunshot wound didn't seem like a good candidate. Ed was still shaking from his close call with the hunting knife. Lying there and watching the rope fray hadn't done a lot for his nerves either, however, he decided he was the best choice for the job. When he picked up the wire cutters, he felt the perspiration break out on his forehead.

"Well, old buddy, here we go. On the count of three fall sideways, okay?"

Billy Ray whispered okay. Steve stood at the butt of the rifle ready to push it up into the air when Ed cut the thin wire.

"All right, here we go. One . . . two . . . three!"

Ed cut the wire, Billy Ray fell to the carpet, Steve pushed down hard on the rifle butt, and the rifle shot a hole in the ceiling.

The 911 crew Steve had called found all four of them sitting on the floor, grinning like a bunch of fools.

It was past midnight by the time the ambulances had taken Mrs. Grant, who was barely alive, Steve, and Art to the hospital. The emergency room doctor pulled numerous wood slivers from Art's face, and took three stitches in his forehead where Grant's bullet had grazed him. They managed to get the bullet out of Steve's leg, and determined it was a clean wound, so there would be no permanent damage. Art sent Ed and Billy Ray to the police station to get his cruiser.

"I can't tell you how much I appreciate your assistance tonight, Steve. I couldn't have done it without you." Art gripped Steve's shoulder in a warm grasp.

"Glad I could help out, my friend," Steve said. "It sure brought back memories, didn't it?"

"I'll say. Ones I'd rather forget."

"Amen to that."

"Let me know when I can talk to Mrs. Grant, will you? I've got a lot of questions. Of course, Sandy may be able to answer some of them, but I still want to see her."

"Sure thing, Art. See ya', buddy."

On the way back to Myrtle Point, Art told Billy Ray, who insisted on driving, what had happened to me and the two boys, how Grant tied me up and left me to die, and about the cougar.

When they arrived at the station, Art called the hospital to find out how I was doing. Upon hearing that I was still under sedation and resting quietly, he decided to go home, to get some much needed rest himself. After leaving his home number with the night nurse, he consented to let Ed drive him home. First though, he left a message with the officer on duty that neither he, Ed, nor Billy Ray would be in until noon the next day. Although he hated to admit it, Art realized the cougar bite, plus the gunshot wound, plus all the stress he had been under for the last twelve hours, had wiped him out.

TWENTY

It was noon the next day before Art came to see me. He hadn't set his alarm and didn't wake up until eleven o'clock. He was still one of the walking wounded, with his crutch and his bandage. Kiddingly, I told him we should get married right now while both of us were on crutches. Of course, he said that was fine with him. I was afraid we would get run out of town by Marie and Francis, I told him, if we did that, after all their planning.

"Where are Tracy and Matthew staying during the day? With Frances?"

"No. Marie is taking care of them. They are even teaching her how to sign. Can you believe it?"

"That's . . . great," I replied, feeling more than a little jealous. "So, tell me what happened to Peter Grant. Is he in custody?"

For the next fifteen minutes Art brought me up to date on what had happened to him, Billy Ray, Ed and Steve St. John the night before.

I could hardly believe what he told me. "What about Mrs. Grant? Is she going to be all right?"

"It's still nip and tuck. She's lost a lot of blood plus the mental anguish—they still aren't sure yet."

"Poor woman. Peter Grant surely loved to play with a person's mind, didn't he? I do hope she makes a full recovery."

"I do, too. How about you? Do you feel up to answering a few questions?" he asked.

"Yes, and there is so much I have to tell you. Did you find the body by the lake?"

"Yes, I did. I assumed it's Doreen."

"No, Art. It's Jasper."

"Jasper!"

"Yes. Peter told me he got angry with Jasper because he took that note to Mrs. Logger and stole the gun while he was waiting for her. He tried to force Jasper to take the gun back. When he refused, they got into a fight over the gun, it went off, killing Jasper. It seemed to affect Peter deeply, he appeared to love his son, although you would never know it by the way he treated Jasper as a child. Grant buried Jasper in a shallow grave, hoping the wild animals would pick the bones clean. His plan was to come back in a few more weeks to gather the bones and dump them miles from here."

"Too bad you didn't wait a few more weeks to go over to the storage sheds. Maybe you would have avoided all the pain and misery you are going through right now, my love."

"Yes, but we would have never found Jasper's body, and we would still be hunting for Doreen."

"Correction," Art said. "We are still hunting for Doreen."

"I think I know where she is. Rotten Apple Ranch."

Art looked dubious.

"No, listen. Think about it. Where was she the happiest when she was a child? Rotten Apple Ranch. Who helped her solve her problems? Rotten Apple Ranch. Where would she feel most secure, knowing no one could contact her unless she wanted to be found? Rotten Apple Ranch," I finished smugly.

"You know, you might have something," Art said, thoughtfully. "I think I'll contact the sheriff in Phoenix, and see if he can give me an address and phone number for that place. Oh, by the way, I had Jim Hammer, the undertaker, go over and retrieve the bones. He will hold them until they're identified."

"How is anyone going to do that? Both arms and hands were gone, weren't they, so you have no fingerprints?"

"Yes. When I call the sheriff in Arizona about Rotten Apple Ranch, I'll ask him to find out what dentist Jasper used. I wouldn't put it past Grant to kill someone else and tell you it was Jasper."

"I wouldn't either. By the way, Dale has a postcard Doreen received from that place. Maybe . . . "

"No, I don't want to contact him and get his hopes up, in case we are wrong."

That's my man, I thought, always thinking of the other fellow. We spent the next half-hour telling each other how happy we were that the other was still alive. The nurse came in to do those nuisance things that they do to keep patients awake, so Art left to call the sheriff in Phoenix. He promised to either come back and tell me or call if they found out anything. I don't believe the nurse was even out of the room, before I was asleep again.

A sudden noise that sounded like a gun shot woke me with a start. I could hear people laughing, so common sense told me it hadn't been a shot. Doctor Johnson stepped into the room. "Did we wake you?"

"Yes, you did," I accused him. "I thought it was a gun shot."

"Nope," he said. "A tray of instruments got knocked over. Nothing dramatic as a gun shot. How are you feeling?"

"Pretty good, all things considered."

Doctor Johnson pulled up a chair. Now what? I thought. To me it's a bad sign when the doctor sits down.

"Sandy," he said, "I contacted the CIA in Washington, and they sent me a complete dossier concerning other injuries you have suffered while a member of the agency. Let me say that I am amazed that you remained sane, after what you went through."

I knew right away they had not mentioned the self-hypnosis. That was my cue not to mention it either. I gave him my martyr's smile, letting him go on thinking what a brave girl I am.

He continued, "I understand your reluctance to have your leg cut off. What I want you to think about now is not only keeping the leg, but perhaps making it better than ever. Science has made great strides in the area of bionics. By replacing your crushed bone with bone harvested from a donor, they are now able to hook those new bones directly to your existing bones in the thigh with steel pins. We would use the donor's leg from the knee down. It would be hooked electronically to your muscles and nerves, so the leg will act the way it did before you were injured. What you end up with is a leg that looks like your leg, acts like your leg, but which will be better and stronger than it ever was before. And you can say goodbye to the brace and crutch."

For a minute I didn't get past two words: "harvest" and "donor." Was he talking about putting a dead person's leg on me? Good God!

"I don't understand. I've heard of bionics, of course, but only in relation to existing bones and muscles. Weren't my muscles and nerves destroyed when my leg was damaged?"

"No, I think only the bone was crushed. A friend of mine, Doctor Harrison O'Conner in Seattle, is a well known physician specializing in this field. He is working on a new concept that uses your own cells wrapped around a steel shaft to grow a new and stronger leg. It's extremely complicated. He should be the one to explain it to you. Why don't I see if I can make you an appointment to talk to him?"

"Of course. I've heard about Doctor O'Conner from the doctors in Washington. In fact, I told them I was going to volunteer to be his human guinea pig. If you two can show me how I can keep my leg and make it as good as new, I'm all for that. It still sounds to me like a pipe dream."

The more I thought about that possibility, the more it intrigued me. How wonderful it would be to walk normally once again, but on another person's leg? That would take a little getting used to, I decided. The other procedure—the wrapping of a steel shaft with cells from my own body sounded better, but maybe using a donor bone would be the best they could do. Oh, well, I thought, it wouldn't hurt to talk to the doctor in Seattle.

I about drove everyone—including the Doctor Johnson—insane wanting to get out of the hospital. I was running up and down the hallways in my wheelchair visiting the other patients. They never knew where to find me unless it was time to eat. Finally, for their own sanity, they consented to let me go home.

When Art arrived to pick me up, the nurses got their revenge.

I wanted to walk out of the hospital, but they forced me to ride in a wheelchair like an invalid.

I wanted to go to the lake when we pulled into the driveway, but Art vetoed that idea. I thought, okay, fine; I'll wait until you go home. I was fuming silently as we walked slowly up the steps and entered the house.

"Surprise!" a chorus of voices yelled. Everybody was there, including Dale and the boys.

Marie was the first to reach me with hugs and kisses. "Oh, sweetie, I'm so glad to see you home. You gave us quite a scare, you know. Promise me you will never, never do that again."

"I promise. Scouts honor." I meant it, I really did, but I should have remembered that in my line of work one never knows what the future may bring.

There wasn't anyone there who had not been in to see me in the hospital, so I didn't have to spend time rehashing my story. They settled me in one of the big lounge chairs; I felt like a queen. After signing how glad he was to see me and how much fun he and Matthew had been having with Marie and Roger, Tracy seemed content to sit by my side and watch the others. Everyone came by to say a few words, when they weren't partaking of all the goodies that Frances had made. She had gone all out. There were small sandwiches of turkey or beef, homemade clam chowder, a huge fruit salad, cookies, pies, and a huge sheet cake that said 'Welcome Home, Sandy.'

The doorbell rang and Art went to answer it. He returned ushering in Doctor Johnson and most of the nurses who had cared for me.

"You guys! I can't believe you knew about this and didn't tell me," I exclaimed.

Doctor Johnson spoke up. "They didn't know until after you left today. I was afraid they couldn't keep the secret."

That statement didn't go over well with my nurse friends. They were all over him until he yelled uncle.

The homecoming lasted until Art made the announcement that he thought I should get some rest. Now, wait a minute, maybe I didn't want them to go home yet, I told him. Yes, you do, believe me, he told me quietly. It took better than a half hour for everyone to thank Frances and Al for everything and to tell me goodbye. Tracy asked if he and Matthew would be coming to the house on Monday. When I assured him that both of them would be, he was willing to say good night.

I caught a look between Matthew and Marie. *Tracy, maybe Matthew would rather spend the day working with Roger,* I signed.

That may be a distinct possibility, was his answer. I had to smile. He was beginning to sound more and more like Matthew.

Why don't we have a day to ourselves? You can catch me up on what went on while I was in the hospital. Okay?

Sounds good to me. What do you think, Matthew?

That sounds like a delightful plan, my friend, Matthew signed to him.

Then I got the biggest surprise of the evening. Marie *signed, It sounds delightful to me, too!*

"Marie, that's wonderful," I said.

"I've been taking lessons from both of these fine instructors," she said, putting an arm around each boy. They were all proud of their part in surprising me. "I would like to continue to learn if they are willing to teach me."

Matthew took her hand, and looking up into her eyes he signed, *It would give me great pleasure to continue your lessons in this medium.*

Thank you, Matthew. I would appreciate that very much.

Maybe something will come of this yet, I fantasized, watching the two of them together.

Dale, Tracy and Matthew had one more surprise for me. Dale had contacted the Mother Superior at convent with a request that Matthew stay with Tracy until the convent was repaired and she had given her permission.

"Now, all we need is to find out if it's okay with you, Sandy," Dale said.

"Of course," I smiled. "I think we'd all be lost without Matthew." God works in mysterious ways, I thought, as Matthew turned to Marie to tell her he would be staying.

It wasn't until everyone had gone that I realized how tired I was. Art was right, I thought, not unkindly. But he still had one trick up his sleeve.

I had gone to the dining room windows to look out toward the lake marveling at the beautiful, warm, summer evening when Art came up behind me. "Now do you want to go down to the lake?"

"Yes, please." He took the arm I usually use for my crutch. The look I gave him was an unspoken question.

"Let's try this, shall we?" he said, laying my crutch aside.

"Okay," I said hesitantly. I was leery, but actually it went quite well.

Art walked me out to the end of the dock where I found a railing built in the center of the dock. It stood at an angle to the left side of the dock. What the heck? That was one crazy place for a railing I thought. Art led me to it and turned me so the railing was across my stomach, the lake was at my back, and I was facing the house.

"I know how much you hated the thought of walking down the aisle, so to speak, using your crutch, so I thought we could try this. You and I can walk down from the house in all our finery, then you can use the railing to lean against if you get tired, then we can walk back when it's over. What do you think?"

I burst into tears.

"What? Don't you like it? We don't have to use it, honey."

"No," I sobbed, "it's wonderful. The whole idea is wonderful. You're wonderful. Oh, Art, I love you so much."

He understood how I felt, bless his heart. Gathering me into his arms he gave me a long kiss. "Want to take off your sandals and play in the water a bit?"

That sounded like a fine idea to me. We sat there on the edge of the dock while I told him about the suggestion Doctor Johnson had about the bionics. It sounded like a good idea to him, he said, but right then he had more important things to think about. like catching up on all the huggin' and kissin' we'd been missing. Now that sounded like an even better idea to me.

TWENTY-ONE

Two days later Art's cruiser came screeching into the driveway before I was even up. When I heard his voice I yelled I was awake and for him to come in. His face had the look of a boy who had caught his first fish—wonder, excitement, and that pleased as punch look even grown men get now and then.

"Guess what?" he demanded.

"What?" Both Frances and I said together. She knew something was up by the look on his face, and had followed him into my room.

"You were right! Doreen is at Rotten Apple Ranch!" In his excitement, he was practically shouting. "Clark Redman, the sheriff in Phoenix, couldn't get a straight answer from anyone over the phone, so he drove out there. From what he told me, people use that ruse all the time—I'm the sheriff of some place and I want information—so they don't believe that story any more. When the directors of Rotten Apple realized it was the sheriff this time, they cooperated. Doreen told Clark that she didn't think her husband wanted her to come home. When her brother, Jasper, brought her down there, she had sent a letter back with him to her husband, but he had never tried to get in touch with her. She said that she wouldn't blame him if he didn't want her back; that she had done some extremely stupid things. In her letter she had told him that she loved both him and their son, Tracy, and that she was taking a sign language course so she could talk to the boy. How about that? Isn't that great news?" Art had a grin on his face that, had it been any wider, it would have split his face wide open.

I couldn't believe it. This was so much better than I had hoped. Although part of me was elated, the other part, the part that would have to give up Tracy, was crying. "That's wonderful," I managed to say. "Have you told Dale yet?"

"No, I came right here. I thought we could tell them together when he drops Tracy off."

"They should be here any minute. Scoot out of here so I can get dressed. Frances, will you help me?"

"Sure, if Al will start the coffee," she said, looking at Al who had come in and caught the last of the conversation.

Al grunted a reply of sorts that Frances seemed to understand.

Why is it when someone tries to help you get dressed, it seems to take twice as long? Both of us seemed to be moving in slow motion, but when Dale's car pulled into the driveway, we walked into the kitchen.

Art had gone to let Dale in. Those of us in the kitchen could hear them talking as they came to join us.

"When I saw your car here I was afraid something else had happened," Dale was saying.

"Nope, nothing bad this time. Have you got time for a cup of coffee and a roll?" Art asked.

"Oh, sure. We never pass up one of Frances' rolls, do we, son?" He answered Art, signing the question and his answer to Tracy. Tracy headed for the table and nearest chair to show he was in agreement all the way. I wasn't sure how Dale would take the news, so I took Tracy with me to the counter to put some rolls on a plate. I kept up a chatter with my fingers, keeping him entertained so he wouldn't look at Dale.

"Dale, I have some news for you, but I think you better sit down to hear it," Art took Dale's arm and led him to the table.

The blood seemed to drain from Dale's face. "What . . . what is it? Is it about Doreen? Is she dead?" The questions rushed from his lips.

"Now take it easy," Art told him. "It isn't bad news; it's all good. She is alive and living at Rotten Apple Ranch. She . . . "

"Alive! Rotten Apple Ranch? How did she get there? Didn't you say your men had checked the buses and trains . . . "

"Shut up, man," Art told him. "I want you to be quiet while I tell you the whole story, then I'll answer your questions. Okay?"

Dale nodded his head.

"Doreen's brother, Jasper, came through town the day she disappeared. He is the one who took her to Rotten Apple. He stayed with her for a week, while she talked to the people there that she had trusted to tell her the truth. To make a long story short, she now understands it is not her fault that Tracy is deaf. They believe he might be able to learn to speak—not plainly, but certainly he would be understandable." Art took a sip of coffee. "Doreen has started a crash course in sign language, so she can talk to Tracy, if you want her to come back home."

Dale opened his mouth to say something, but Art held up his hand.

"There isn't much more to tell you. She wrote you a letter explaining everything and asked her brother, Jasper, to deliver it to you on his way to Alaska. We believe he was killed by his father, Peter Grant, before he could bring it to you. That's how Grant knew where Doreen was. It was Sandy who figured it out, and got me to call the sheriff in Phoenix to check it out."

"But I called Rotten Apple. I told them I was the sheriff of Mountain View, but they wouldn't give me any information."

Both Art and I laughed. "They get calls like that all the time. Unless the sheriff comes out there in person, they don't give out any information," Art explained.

"Oh . . . well," Dale said, embarrassed. "What did she say in the letter? Does she really want to come home? Wow, taking sign language lessons. I can't believe it. What a change."

"Yes, she does want to come home. She told you in the letter that she has realized she loves you and Tracy. She is sorry for the misery she caused. She hopes you can forgive her."

"Forgive her?" The look on Dale's face was enough to bring tears to everyone's eyes. "How could she think otherwise?" He turned to Tracy and quickly told him a condensed version of the news.

Tracy was not overly enthusiastic about his mother coming home. She had never shown any love toward him that he could remember, so how could he expect her to be different now, was his question. Dale asked Tracy to at least give her a chance. Did he think he could do that? Tracy nodded, then he ran over and buried his face in my lap.

Poor little boy. I had to blink fast to keep my tears in check.

It turned out to be a wild morning. Art called Sheriff Redman, who called Rotten Apple Ranch to inform them that that Doreen's husband would be calling within the next half hour. After getting the okay from Clark, Art had to practically tie Dale down to keep him from calling immediately.

"Doreen is out doing her chores. We have to wait twenty minutes."

"Twenty minutes? That will seem like a lifetime. What if she has changed her mind? What if she doesn't want to have anything to do with Tracy again. What if . . . "

"Dale, stop it. You're driving us all wild."

"Oh, sorry. I can't believe this. I keep thinking I'm dreaming."

The second the twenty minutes were up, Dale was dialing the Ranch. "Hello, this is Dale Fuller. May I speak to Doreen, please?"

All of us found ourselves holding our breath.

"Hello, Doreen, honey. Is it really you? I can't believe it. What? Yes, of course, I want you to come home." Naked longing sounded in his voice.

We decided all of us better leave the room, and give him a little privacy. I wanted to tell Tracy something—anything about his mother that would bring the smile back to his face, but what could I say? It was true the only love she had shown him was when he was so little he couldn't remember. I decided I better butt out, and let Dale handle this problem himself.

Dale was grinning from ear to ear when he came into the front room. "I have made arrangements for one of my men to take over for me at the market. Tracy and I will get packed and be on our way to Phoenix to pick up Doreen. Sandy, Art, I can never thank you enough for all you've done. Come on, son. Let's go get your mother," Dale said, holding his hand out to Tracy.

Slowly Tracy took his hand. Going out the door, he looked back at me and signed: *I love you, Sandy. I love you.* Tears filled his eyes. It broke my heart. I followed them out to the porch signing: *I love you, too. I love you, little man.* After their car backed out of the driveway, I sat down in the porch swing and cried like a baby. Art sat beside me with his arm around my shoulders and let me cry it out.

"I will miss him so much," I hiccuped.

"I know, Babe. I know. But it's not like you will never see him again. I'll bet Doreen will welcome some more training in sign language, and you can offer to take him places. You could be like an aunt or a godmother."

Of course, he was right. Thinking of doing those things made me feel better. We rocked slowly, my head on his shoulder, as my world came back into perspective. It was right then that Frances poked her head out to call us to breakfast.

After my third cup of coffee I felt up to calling Marie to tell her about Doreen. When she heard Tracy would be gone for a few days, her first concern was for Matthew.

"I would be glad to come and get him."

"Oh, no, Sandy, that's okay. We would love to have him stay for a few days. He truly enjoys watching Roger prepare prescriptions, and Roger gets a kick out of having him there. While Matthew is there, why don't we go look at wedding dresses? You do realize there isn't much time left, don't you? You are still planning on getting married on the thirty-first, aren't you?"

I caught the sound of dismay in her voice. I hastened to assure her that yes, the wedding was still on. To prove my point I told her that the invitations had been mailed to out-of-town guests two weeks ago, that the rest went out yesterday, that Frances had brought some pictures of wedding cakes to the hospital where we picked out one, that Art had built a railing on the wharf so I wouldn't have to use my crutch, that all the flowers were coming from the garden, that . . .

"Okay, okay," she said, laughing. "I get the idea, but we still have to find a dress. I doubt if you feel much like wandering around Mountain View, though."

"You've got that right," I agreed. "Why don't you come over here when you get free this morning. We can discuss it then."

I had a big surprise for her that I couldn't talk about in front of Art. In sorting through the boxes in the attic that Frances and I were trying to clear out, I came across my mother's wedding dress. It was a simple creation: a length of form fitting, glossy white satin from the neck to the toe. It looked so demure from the front with its high collar, and its long sleeves that covered the shoulders. Yet just the reverse was true from the back where it was bare from the collar to slightly below the waist. It changed my entire opinion about my mother. On the bodice and along the bottom of the skirt, tiny seed pearls formed a lovely flower design. It was perfect and fit me like I had special ordered it. The only thing wrong with it was that it smelled to high heaven of mothballs.

TWENTY-TWO

I was released from the hospital long before Emily Grant. The things Peter did to me were mere scratches when compared to her injuries. Besides a severe concussion, she had a broken leg, two broken ribs, one rib had pierced her lung, and, to top it all off, he had shoved a kitchen knife up her vagina, twisting as it went in. How she kept her sanity, I'll never know.

In fact, I don't know how she kept her sanity living with that man. Yes, granted she acted rather strange the day I took Tracy to visit, but I remembered that during dinner she acted as sane as I am. For that matter, there are those who doubt at times that I'm sane, so I rest my case.

Art had no more than gotten to work Monday morning when he got a call from Steve telling him Emily Grant could have visitors. He called to see if I wanted to go with him.

"Of course. Can we go this afternoon after Marie leaves?"

"I'll call them back and set it up for one-thirty. Will that be late enough?"

I assured him that would be fine.

Marie arrived at ten-thirty sharp. Of course, Frances had recently taken a goodie out of the oven that both of us had to try. After passing a verdict of delicious on a cinnamon concoction, I took Marie into my bedroom.

"Okay. You sit on the bed, shut your eyes and don't peek," I instructed her.

Quietly, I slid the closet door open and took Mom's wedding

dress out and hung it on the hook in the bathroom. I was so quiet when I came back to get her that when I touched her hand, she jumped a foot.

"Gees, you scared me," she complained.

"Sorry, sweetie. Now keep your eyes shut and I'll lead you."

"All I got to say is this better be worth it. Did you go out and buy a dress without me?"

"No way. You know I wouldn't do that," I said in an injured tone. "Open your eyes. Ta-da!"

For a moment she stared. "Sandy! Where did you get it? It's beautiful!"

I told her about finding the dress in the attic. Of course, we had to try it on. It seemed to take ages to fasten all the tiny buttons down the sleeves and on the back of the collar.

"I can't get over how well it fits or the fact that is in such good shape. Why don't I take it with me to the cleaners when I leave, and make sure they can get the smell of mothballs out of it?"

"That would be a big help. Art and I are suppose to be at the hospital in South Point to talk to Mrs. Grant at one-thirty. If they can get the odor out, would you be able to store it at your house to make sure Art won't see it?"

She assured me that would be no problem. "I saw a dress in Mountain View the other day that I think might be great for me as matron of honor. It is quite plain, but the material is covered with every kind of flower imaginable. Shall I get it on trial so you can see it?"

That sounded fine to me. From that moment on until after a quick lunch all we did was talk wedding. I even took her down to show her the railing Art had built. When she asked me who was going to be the best man I had to admit I didn't have the slightest idea. I promised I'd ask Art.

It was exactly one-thirty when Art and I walked up the hospital steps for our appointment with Emily Grant. I wasn't looking forward to hearing that terrible voice again, but I wanted to hear what she had to say about her husband.

When we walked into Room 241, her appearance shocked me. Without her makeup, with her hair hanging in strings around her face, Emily Grant seemed to have aged ten years. Granted she had been through a horrible experience, but her face was so old! I couldn't believe that makeup would make that much difference in a woman's appearance.

She looked up as we came in. A sweet smile lit up her face.

"Sandy. How nice to see you again," she said.

I couldn't believe it. She didn't screech, but spoke in a beautiful modulated tone. Once again: what? what? what? was all I could think.

The expression on my face must have told her my thoughts because she laughed softly. "I can see you can't believe what happened, any more than I could in the beginning. It seems this is the only good thing that came out of the beating Peter gave me. In choking me, he realigned the apparatus the doctors put in when I had my . . . accident. It's wonderful, isn't it."

I told her I had to agree with the outcome, but I was sorry that she had to go through so much pain to achieve it.

When I introduced Art to her, she graciously offered her hand. Art took her hand, leaned over and kissed it. I thought what a beautiful, sweet thing to do, and we could tell it tickled Mrs. Grant.

"Mrs. Grant . . . ," Art started.

"Emily, please," she told him. "I've been doing a lot of thinking, and I do believe I will take back my maiden name. I, myself, can't even say Peter's name without being sick to my stomach. Do me a favor and call me Emily."

"Of course. It will be my pleasure, Emily. Will it be too upsetting if we discuss your husband's life?"

"No, I want to help you in anyway I can. I understand Sandy and some of your men went through utter hell because of that man. Anything I can tell you to alleviate their nightmares will be worth it."

Art pulled chairs close to the bed for us. Sitting down, he said, "I would appreciate it if you could tell me when Mr. Grant started to change. Was there any one incident that set him off?"

Emily settled back on the pillows. "Let me go back to the beginning. I first saw Peter at the Debutantes Ball in 1938 where I and many of my friends were presented to society. It was the first great ball since the stock market crash of '29. The wealthy, who weren't wiped out during the crash, were becoming increasingly rich again. They loved to show off their wealth by spending great sums of money on foolish things. I will always remember that ball. I believe it was one of the happiest days of my life; the lavishly decorated ballroom, the young women, each trying to be the one with the most expensive, the most beautiful, the most daring gown. Truly, it was something one never forgets.

"The evening was nearly over when I saw Peter dance by with Tippy McBride. The minute I saw him I knew this was the man I wanted to marry. He was dashing in a swashbuckling kind of way. Six foot tall, beautiful, dark wavy hair, slim, twenty-one years old—he made an enticing picture to an inexperienced young girl of seventeen. Everyone considered him the best catch of the season, and ever so many young women were running after him. When I saw what was happening, I gave up my little pipe dream and started to date others. I wasn't the most beautiful of the debutantes, in fact, I was quite mousy. I had ordinary features and rather drab brown hair. I was timid, afraid of my own shadow because of something that had happened when I was younger. I'm sure the only reason anyone asked me out was because of my father's money.

"I thought the fact that I didn't chase after Peter, or hang on his every word the way those other silly girls did, made me appealing to him. I found out a few months later that I was wrong. After the ball, Peter had done his homework and found that my father was by far the richest man in the area, so he set out to sweep me off my feet. His father had been one of the wealthiest men in Mountain View, but he lost everything during the crash, and chose to kill himself. Peter's mother died of a broken heart a few months later. Peter was forced to leave school, come home, and sell everything. At the time of the ball he was nearly penniless. However, he was ingenious, and crafty, and what he wanted, he got. What he wanted was a rich wife. I didn't try to kid myself that it was my "stunning beauty" that brought him to my side. In fact, I didn't give a hoot if it was the money he was after. If marriage to me was part of the deal, so be it.

"Our wedding night was a horrible revelation to me. Peter was a terrible lover. There was never a thought given to me, what I wanted or needed. I was expected to be ready for sex, any kind of sex, anytime of the day or night that he might want it. It didn't matter to him if what I was forced to do made me physically ill or not. It was pure animal lust on Peter's part. Would you believe, I thought I was the one in the wrong. The day after the wedding Peter's true colors had come to light. He made me sign all my accounts over to him, telling me that in a marriage it was the husband who handled the money.

"I thought about getting a divorce, but my father had told me, not unkindly, that when I got married I was not welcome back in his house to stay. I could return for visits with my husband, but I was never to come alone or plan on staying any length of time. Peter, with his insufferable attitude, managed to cut me off from all my friends, until I had no one I could confide in. If I left Peter, where could I go? I had no money, no close friends, nothing. So I stayed, and continued to accept both his mental and physical abuse. Oh, yes, didn't I tell you? I was also, according to Peter, the most ignorant person in all of Mountain View—no, make that the whole world.

"In 1941 when the Japanese bombed Pearl Harbor, Peter joined the Marines. Before he left, my father made him sign everything back over to me, in case he got killed. What blessed relief the next five years were. I took classes to learn how to handle my money efficiently. I started making friends again, learned how to make myself more attractive, worked for the Red Cross, volunteered at the hospital, and, most importantly, I found out that all men were not like Peter.

"I came within a cat's whisker of having an affair. My friend thought me beautiful and smart. He was gentle where Peter was brutal. I don't know why we didn't consummate our love. Maybe it was because of what happened in my childhood. Maybe because I was taught that when you marry it was to be forever. I don't know. I'll probably never know. He still remains my friend to this day. Maybe now . . . (for a few moments she was lost in a daydream before continuing).

"When Peter was promoted to sergeant, I do believe he was in his element. I couldn't imagine that he was ever well-liked by his men, but I convinced myself I was wrong. After all, he was awarded several medals, among them was the Purple Heart for saving a platoon of soldiers in the battle of Iwo Jima. Later I found out he was only a cook, not the battle weary soldier he led every one to believe. How he won those medals is beyond me. For all I know, they may have actually belonged to someone else.

"After Germany surrendered, I thought the war might be over soon and Peter would be coming home. I began preparing myself to stand up to him when he arrived, to sue for divorce if necessary. Then in the battle of Okinawa he was badly injured. He came close to losing his right arm and leg. After months in the hospital they transferred him to the hospital in Mountain View to finish his physical therapy. I will give him credit for his determination to walk and to use his hand normally.

"His first few months at home were guarded, to say the least. It was if we were both walking on eggs. He had noticed the change in me when I visited him in the hospital, and I think he wasn't sure how to handle the person I had become. After he had been home for approximately two weeks, we went out to dinner. We had a drink before dinner, wine with dinner, and brandy after dinner. We laughed a lot, danced a lot, and when we got home we made love for the first time since he had come home. I was more than a little surprised when he was gentle, sweet, and loving. I'm sure that is the night I became pregnant with my son, Jasper.

"Jasper was a darling baby boy. When he was five, Peter wanted to move his bedroom to the attic. We nearly came to blows over that stupid idea. Peter couldn't believe I would stand up to him the way I did. He backed down in a hurry. I think he was afraid I would leave him, and cut him off without a penny. Although he was a much nicer man than before he left for the service, I still refused to give him a power of attorney to handle my affairs. The lawyers did all that, I told him, and that is the way it would remain. Oh, he had an ample allowance, and to my way of thinking, he didn't need more.

"When Jasper was six, we bought the South Point Inn. Once more Peter was in his element, only this time it was as the best looking man in town that every woman was trying to get into her bed. Sex with me was not enough. He had to have a variety. He was like the flower that attracted the bees. Many times he would disappear for a few hours, and no one knew where he was. It wasn't until he succumbed to the lure of Helen Rawlings that things came to a head. Helen's husband came home unexpectedly, and found them in his bed. Jim Rawlings was so angry he went to his den, got a gun, and came back and killed Helen. Peter had somehow managed to get away before Jim returned with the gun. It came out at the trial that Peter and Helen had been having an affair for months. The negative publicity was embarrassing to Peter. For several months he didn't give into temptation. I think he was afraid to go outside, but as time went by, he became more and more frustrated. He was, once again, stuck with his mousy wife and it was driving him wild.

"It was about this time that he discovered the Drama Club. I'm sure he thought that the Club would be a perfect way for him to make it with other women and still be legal. If he took the love scenes more seriously than the script called for, who would know? He never appeared in a play that I was not in also. I was his cover, you see. Surely, everyone thought, he wouldn't try anything right in front of his wife, would he? What they didn't know was that I couldn't have cared less. The more he left me alone, the better I liked it. I had the business to run, and a darling son to raise.

"Shortly after Jasper's ninth birthday, Peter came home drunk and in a foul mood. He sent Jasper to his room, telling him not to come down if he knew what was good for him. When Jasper was out of sight, Peter walked over to me, and with both hands he tore my clothes from my body. He took me right there on the front room floor, in his old way. I didn't dare cry out, though he hurt me terribly, because I was afraid Jasper would hear. His reason: his latest conquest had ended their affair and he was in a rage. Looking back, I think Irene Dunley was the first woman he truly loved. She was an exceptional talent, a true actress. She had told us at the cast party that she was going to move to Hollywood and try to break into the movies. She did become one of the truly great actresses. Do you remember her?"

We both assured her that we did, indeed, know of Miss Dunley and thought she was a wonderful actress.

I could tell Emily was beginning to tire. "This must be tiring for you, Emily. Would you like us to come back tomorrow?" I asked her.

"No, I want to tell you all of it. Only then can I try to forget it and clear it from my mind. Would you please fluff up my pillow? And may I have a sip of water?"

I fluffed the pillow. Art got the water.

Emily continued, "When Irene left South Point, Peter disappeared. I had the feeling it was for some other reason, but I finally convinced myself that he had followed Irene to Hollywood. Six weeks later I verified with my doctor that I was pregnant with Doreen. It was a peaceful pregnancy. I kept busy at the inn. Jasper was a great help around the house. Neither of us said it out loud, but we were both glad Peter was gone. Too bad it didn't last. When I was in my eighth month, Peter walked back into our lives. With no explanation as to where he had been, he took up where he had left off. Once again he became the fair-haired boy of the Drama Club. It no longer mattered to him whether I was in the play or not."

I know my thoughts must have shown on my face.

"He must have told you about being in plays together until my accident. He lied. Anyway, upon his return, he said nothing about me being pregnant, nor did he pretend to be interested in Doreen after she was born. The only time he even spoke to her was when other people were around. I was so busy that Doreen became quite spoiled and uncontrollable. She had Jasper wrapped around her little finger. He would do, or give her, anything she wanted. Peter was no help. The only time I saw him was in the evening when he showed up to welcome the diners as they arrived for dinner. So suave, so debonair; he made me sick. I knew we were headed for a showdown, but I kept my head buried in the sand.

"When Doreen was to start the fourth grade, everything came to a head. The school would no longer put up with her tantrums. Peter accused them of not doing their duties. After all, he ranted, wasn't it up to the school to straighten her out? How stupid he was. I certainly didn't think that way. There was no doubt in my mind whose fault it was that Doreen was such a little brat. I talked to our physician, Doctor Davidson, who gave me the names of some places that were accepting incorrigible kids. Armed with that information I went home, and told them all I was sending Doreen to Rotten Apple Ranch. Doreen threw a tantrum; Jasper begged me not to send her away. Peter surprisingly agreed with him. However, I was determined. I put my manager in charge of the Inn and we all took off for Arizona. It turned out to be a much harsher environment than I had expected. I almost relented and took her home, but common sense won out and she stayed. The morning after we returned home, Jasper ran away. I nearly went crazy. I had lost both of my children within a twenty-four hour period. Even though I knew where Doreen was, I couldn't call or write to her. It was as if she didn't exist. After all these years, I can still feel the pain. When the police couldn't find Jasper, I hired a private detective. I'm ashamed to admit I even went to psychics. I never saw him again."

Silently, I handed her a tissue to wipe her eyes. Knowing what I knew, I felt like crying, too.

"Years later a grown-up Doreen returned to us. She was a beautiful, sweet young lady. You already know what happened after she returned home. Now it has happened again. My beautiful, mixed-up Doreen gone, and no one can find her."

TWENTY-THREE

Art and I glanced at each other. Apparently, Steve St. John hadn't told her that Peter had killed Jasper, nor did she seem to know that Doreen had been found, although Art had been keeping his friend apprised of the situation. I would leave the telling of that information up to those two. I didn't envy them the task.

Emily continued, "When I got over the shock of Jasper disappearing, I told Peter I wanted a divorce. He had not tried to understand my misery over the children nor had he offered me any comfort whatsoever. I could not forgive him for being so unfeeling. He refused. He knew if he left, his allowance would stop, and he would have nothing. Heaven forbid, he would have been forced to go to work. I told him that was not my worry. I had had it with his chasing other women and making me the laughing stock of the community. I was fed up with his acting like he was actually working at the Inn, when he didn't lift a hand to do any of the actual work. I would no longer tolerate being treated as if I were invisible on the few evenings he was home. I wanted him to pack his belongings and leave immediately. He begged me to reconsider. When I refused, he hit me so hard he knocked me completely off my feet. I struck the edge of the dining room table with my throat. It was no cancerous growth that injured my throat, it was that dirty bastard. I'm sorry. Please excuse my language, but that's exactly how I feel."

We both assured her that was exactly how we felt also. Art told her he could even come up with a few more adjectives that would describe him even better. That brought a smile to her face.

"I won't go into detail about what was done to repair my throat. I was not asked if I agreed with my father and my husband when they made the decision to operate. The device the doctors put in was an experimental apparatus, Sandy can attest to the fact that it didn't work well. Since it was attached to the larynx, it could not be removed, so all these years I have been sounding like a cross between a screech owl and a laughing hyena. I never went out. I refused to see anyone. After I was home for about a month Peter asked me for a divorce. He told me he couldn't stand to listen to me any longer. This time I refused. I told him I would ruin his life. I would make sure that everyone knew that he had left me in my time of need. Furthermore, I would make sure he never got a job anywhere. When he laughed, I told him not to test me. I had the money to ruin him, no matter where he went. Also, he was to quit the Drama Club, help me sell the Inn, and stay home to take care of me. I felt I had finally found the ultimate torture to make up for all those indignities he had caused me in the past. He had to agree, I left him no choice. We both realized at that moment how much we hated each other."

"Weren't you afraid he might kill you," I couldn't help asking.

"I would have welcomed death, I think, after being cooped up in that house day after day, year after year. But, no, he couldn't do that without ending up in prison. I had contacted my lawyer who documented everything that had happened to me in the past. I left a sealed letter he was to give to the police accusing Peter of my murder, if I should be found dead."

Now I could understand the look of hatred I had seen on Peter's face the day that Tracy and I went to visit.

Emily lay back against the pillow, exhausted. We knew we had heard everything Emily was capable of for this first visit, even if Doctor Davidson hadn't come in to tell us it was time to leave. Telling her goodbye, we promised to return the next day. Truthfully, wild horses couldn't have kept us away.

The next day dawned bright and beautiful. The early morning sun was reflecting off of the lake, giving it a shimmering, silver cast. I was rushing to be ready for breakfast when Art arrived. Frances felt everyone should have a good breakfast under their belt before tackling the problems of the day.

Art walked in the front door at the same moment I opened my bedroom door. For a few moments we were the only two people in the world as we moved toward each other. The loving kiss we exchanged was terminated when Al cleared his throat and proclaimed loudly how hungry he was. Grinning sheepishly, we took our places around the table.

We were in the middle of fresh fruit, pancakes, bacon, and coffee when the phone rang. It was Doctor Davidson informing us that Mrs. Grant was too exhausted to have visitors. He recommended that we wait a day before talking to her again. Of course, we acquiesced. What else could we do? Maybe wild horses couldn't keep us away, but her doctor certainly could.

The next phone call was the one Art had been hoping to receive for several days. It was Doctor Andrew Morton, Mrs. Logger's psychiatrist. He was calling to set up an appointment for that morning, if Art was free. Art had an appointment with him the day I disappeared, but hadn't kept it, of course. Then the doctor went on vacation, so this was the first time they were going to be able to meet.

Art explained my interest in the case, and inquired if I might sit in on the meeting. Doctor Morton graciously consented. "I feel that all the people I will be discussing are involved in the cases she has been working on."

Doctor Morton's office was on the outskirts of town and it was charming. The doctor had taken one of the first homes built by the pioneers who settled Myrtle Woods and remodeled it into a first-class office, without losing any of its ornamental gingerbread design on the outside. The room we entered was a restful place. The walls were light gray in color; the carpet was light mauve. The three chairs and a lounge sofa were all large, comfortable pieces, upholstered in a deeper mauve. A round coffee table made a comfortable seating arrangement. The doctor's roll-top desk was against the wall between two ceiling-to-floor bookcases, a setup I thought rather odd. Don't most doctors use their desk to separate themselves from the patient when they are discussing a case? Not Doctor Morton. He asked us to be seated, and when we had chosen our chairs, he took the remaining one.

Doctor Andrew Morton appeared to be in his late seventies or early eighties—much older than I had expected. He had been a tall man, but was now stooped with age. He had snow-white hair and a Santa Claus face with twinkling blue eyes. He even wore his glasses down on his nose, so that he looked over the rims whenever he was speaking to us. The only things he didn't have were the beard and the round belly. I swear he couldn't have weighed over one hundred and forty pounds. His voice reminded me of the actor, James Earl Jones, deep and resonant. I detected a slight Irish accent.

"May I get you a cup of coffee or tea?" he asked. Both of us declined since we had just finished breakfast. "I'm sure you both realize there are some things I can not discuss because of patient confidentiality." We both nodded. "However, I am going to be lenient in Mrs. Logger's case because I feel we may be able to help each other.

"I first saw Harriet when she was nine years of age. She was my first patient after I graduated and opened my practice here. Her mother, Anna Brocall, brought her to me because, she said, Harriet was suffering from severe nightmares. During those times she would call repeatedly for a sister, Emily."

I sat straighter and leaned forward to catch every word. Mrs. Grant's first name was Emily! Could it be that Mrs. Grant and Mrs. Logger were sisters? Now that I thought about it, she did remind me somewhat of Mrs. Logger, especially, through the eyes. Art noticed my movement. His glance was a question. I shook my head slightly.

Doctor Morton continued his story. "Mrs. Brocall told me Harriet had no sister. She claimed she didn't know where Harriet had gotten such an idea. I spoke to Harriet alone and Harriet swore me to secrecy, then explained that she did have a sister and that her mother's husband had taken her away five years previously. Harriet said she and her mother were not allowed to speak of her sister or they would be extremely sorry. She told me she was sure her mother's husband was connected with the mob. I asked her what that meant. She informed me, as if speaking to an idiot, that it meant he associated with bad men. I asked her why she didn't call her mother's husband, "father." She told me he would not allow it; that each time she did, he struck her."

I know I must have drawn in a quick breath or something, because he glanced over at me. "Yes, it sounds hard to believe, doesn't it?

"For the second time I questioned Anna. She did agree that her husband would not allow Harriet to call him "father." Haltingly, she informed me that Harriet was a child of a rape she had suffered years ago. She refused to elaborate further, but once again she swore to me there was no sister. It was a strange case—both of them willing to swear they were telling the truth."

Doctor Morton got up and brought a glass of water to the table. His hand was shaking as he brought the glass to his mouth. I wondered how much was caused by age and how much from stress.

"My hands were tied. I couldn't discuss the case with anyone to find out if there had been a sister. Any patient that came to me had enough problems without me trying to bring the Brocalls into it. Then when Anna passed away I got a phone call from her attorney, Ken Holberg. He said he wanted to meet with me and give me some information that might help me treat Harriet more successfully. He told me he felt free to speak now that both Anna and Luther, her husband, were deceased. On his way to my office Ken was killed in a hit and run accident. A few weeks later, his wife stopped by my office to tell me that her husband had known Harriet Logger's sister's whereabouts, but she was unable to help me because he had never told her. She brought me a paper she found in his desk that stated if Ken uttered a single word to his wife or anyone about the sisters, even after Luther Pritchard's death, Ken and his family would die horrible deaths. Ken's wife was terrified that she or the children would be harmed. She had put her house up for sale and they were leaving town that night. Up until that time I had thought Luther's last name was Brocall. Neither Anna nor Harriet had ever told me otherwise. I had heard that Luther Pritchard was truly a ruthless man, used to having his own way."

"I can't believe there are still men like that in the United States, who are able to have their wishes carried out, even after death," I said. I had run into men like that in many foreign countries, but in the U.S.? I couldn't believe it was true.

"Yes, Sandy," Art said quietly. "I'm afraid so. However, we seldom see any of their kind in a town the size of Myrtle Woods. I remember my predecessor talking about the Ken Holberg case. I don't believe it was ever solved."

Doctor Morton brought the tray he had prepared earlier to the table. Cups, sugar and cream, and a carafe of hot coffee were offered. Coffee sounded good to me. This story was becoming more and more unbelievable.

Doctor Morton continued the story. "When Mrs. Holberg told me there were two sisters and that Pritchard was the father, I went to the newspaper office and searched the back issues until I found information about Anna. The old guy in charge of the archives remembered the Pritchards. He was able to tell me the whole sordid story.

"In 1931 Anna Pritchard, as she was known then, was a well known socialite involved in many worthwhile charities. She and her husband, Luther, gave glittering parties that were well attended by the wealthy from all over the world."

"Yes, I remember my grandfather and my dad talking about the many well-known people who came to town for those parties," Art exclaimed. "I didn't make the connection when you called her Brocall. Wasn't it at one of those gatherings that she was kidnapped and raped?"

"Yes," Doctor Morton replied. "According to my source, some people in town think that Luther Pritchard arranged the kidnapping, trying to scare Anna into obeying him when he commanded her to sleep with his friends. She was a beautiful woman, with a gorgeous figure. I was told that many men lusted after her, but she was true to her marriage vows. I learned that Luther used the offer of his wife's body as an incentive to get certain well-known men to attend his political gatherings. The men who did the kidnapping weren't supposed to rape her, but they did. Two days later they were listed as missing by the police. Their bodies were never found.

"Nine months after the rape Anna gave birth to Harriet. Pritchard never forgave her for getting pregnant. When she refused to abort that fetus, he refused to have anything to do with the child. When Harriet was four, Emily, their first daughter who was ten was nearly abducted. It was the final straw for Pritchard. He packed all of his and Emily's clothes and stormed out of the house. Before leaving he forced Anna to sign a paper saying she would take back her maiden name, that she would never allow another picture to be taken of herself or Harriet, that she would never mention Emily's name again, and that she would convince Harriet to forget she had a sister. If Anna did not do as he said, he would make sure they'd both suffer horribly. There was no mention of money since both of them had their own fortunes."

"My God, he must have been some kind of monster," I said in wonder. "How could anyone be that maniacal."

"My father said he was greedy, ruthless, and temperamental," Art said. "A great guy if everything went his way, but watch out if it didn't. I guess someone who had the political power to make or break presidents thought he could get away with anything. My father was sure he had mob connections."

"That poor woman. Being deprived of one of her daughters, while bringing up the other whose father was a rapist. How did she stand it? How did she treat Harriet?" I asked.

"She loved her dearly," the doctor answered. "I guess she tried and tried to make Harriet forget Emily, but the bond between the two girls was too strong. I'm sure she must have explained to Harriet why they couldn't speak of Emily, so Harriet managed to bury all thoughts of Emily deep in her subconscious. I saw Harriet off and on over the years when she felt she needed help. Then about twelve years ago she became a regular patient. She told me she was losing an hour or two every day when she couldn't remember where she had been or what she had done. During one of her weekly visits two other personalities made themselves known. It didn't surprise me. After all she had gone through, I had been expecting something like that to happen. The way things are now, I have no idea who's going to come in for her weekly appointment. There are certain words or actions that take Harriet back to her childhood, but I never know what they might be. It seems like every week they are different. I'm becoming greatly concerned, however. When Harriet reverts back, it seems to be taking me longer and longer to bring her back to reality. That is primarily the reason I decided to share with you what I know. I'm even trying some treatments that are brand new, hoping one will work Now, I'm hoping you will be able to give me some new information that will help me. I must find some way to help her before Harriet returns to the time she was with Emily and stays there."

Art and I had decided if the doctor asked for any information, he would be the one to answer, with me joining in if he forgot anything. "Let me tell you what we know to date, then you can tell me if you think it will be of any help. I'm sure you read of the disappearance of Doreen Fuller." Doctor Morton nodded. "When I and my men began to investigate that case we got nowhere. That was when I called Sandy and asked for her help," Art continued, smiling at me. "It was she who discovered that Mr. Fuller had a young son, Tracy, who cannot hear or speak. Sandy agreed to take care of the boy during the day because she knows sign language. Unknown to Sandy, someone had delivered a note to Mrs. Logger stating that Mr. Logger was Tracy's father, not Mr. Fuller. Sandy is working on both the drowning of Mr. Logger, and Doreen Fuller's disappearance, so she decided to drive over to talk to Mrs. Logger. She needed a description of a missing gold chain that Mrs. Logger was sure had some bearing on the case. Of course, Tracy was with her. When Sandy introduced Tracy, Sandy thought Mrs. Logger was going to faint."

"Now I know what she was talking about when I went out to see her after William called me," Doctor Morton stated.

"Art, may I interrupt?" I asked. With a nod, he gave his permission. "When you mentioned, Doctor Morton, that Mrs. Logger had a sister named Emily, it made me start comparing Mrs. Grant to Mrs. Logger. I may be wrong, but there may be a possibility that they are sisters. They both have beautiful brown eyes. I know that isn't much, but . . ."

"Is it possible that Harriet's sister has been living that close all these years? What about their voices. Do they sound alike?" Doctor Morton exclaimed excitedly.

"There is no way of knowing. Mrs. Grant was in an accident several years ago, which left her with a terrible voice."

"I would like to speak to her. Ask her about her childhood," Doctor Morton said.

"That's not possible right now," Art told him. "Mrs. Grant is in the hospital recovering from an attack by her husband, who is now deceased. We will have to wait a day or two before she is rested enough to tell us the story that she referred to several times as something that happened in her childhood. What would happen if you were to tell Mrs. Logger that her sister was alive and well?"

"I'm not sure," Doctor Morton said thoughtfully. "If it's true, I will have to give it some thought on how to present the information to Harriet. I would have to be sure I was approaching the idea correctly or I'm afraid I could do more harm than good. When will you be talking to Mrs. Grant again?"

"We hope within the next few days. Her doctor, Howard Davidson, is going to call us when it is possible."

"I know Doctor Davidson. He is a good man, a dedicated doctor. The patient's welfare is always his primary concern. I will be thinking of possible solutions to this problem until I hear from you again. I pray they are sisters. It may be the answer to keeping Harriet sane," Doctor Morton said, showing us out.

"Has Mrs. Logger ever mentioned Luther Pritchard?" I asked.

"No, but that's not surprising. The way the man treated her, it's no wonder she had no problem forgetting he ever existed."

On the way home, I kept ranting about the viciousness of Luther Pritchard. To separate the children was bad enough, but to blame his wife because she became pregnant by a rapist he hired, blew my mind.

"What would you do if that happened to me?" I asked Art.

He gave my question serious thought. "I would probably talk to you about an abortion." When I opened my mouth to speak, he went on, "However, if that was something you felt you couldn't do, then I would try to love the baby. I have to admit it would be difficult. Every time I looked at him I would see the rapist's face. I would hope I would have the grace of God to overcome that feeling, and love the child because it was half you, hopefully endowed with your goodness."

By the time he finished, I couldn't speak over the lump in my throat.

TWENTY-FOUR

We thought the rest of the day would be ordinary. Not much happens on a Tuesday. The weekend drunks are sleeping it off, and the abusers are back at work. Usually it is the kind of day where the police and private investigators take a breather, and check the case load. This Tuesday was far from ordinary.

When Art dropped me back at the house, so I could pick up my own car, Frances had a message for me. I was to call Doctor Johnson as soon as possible. Not giving myself time to conjure up all kinds of reasons he might want to talk to me, I hurried to the phone. When I gave my name, the receptionist put me right through.

"Sandy!" I had never heard Bert Johnson sound so excited. "Can you come to the office right away?"

"Well, sure, but . . . "

"Remember me telling you about Doctor Harrison O'Conner, the orthopedic surgeon from Seattle? He is sitting across from me right now. He is on his way to a conference in San Francisco, and he stopped by to discuss your case. He thinks he may be able to do something for you, and he wants to examine you immediately. How soon can you get here?"

I told him ten minutes, but my heart dropped to the pit of my stomach. The day of reckoning had arrived. I was about to find out if I would ever have a leg better than new. I called Art, but he hadn't reached the office yet, so I left a message saying I would come by after I saw the doctor.

I argued with myself on the way to Bert's office. Sure, I wanted

175

to be able to walk normally again, to dance, to run, but at what sacrifice? Months in the hospital right after my wedding?

My little inner voice asked what good was my leg to me now, and I had to admit it wasn't much good for anything. Don't you want to walk the floor with your baby when he is cranky, the voice asked. That question brought me up short. Baby? Where did that idea come from? Out of my subconscious, I guess. I would love to have Art's baby, and yes, I would want to take care of it without being hindered by a crutch. I was smiling as I pulled into the parking lot. It amused me that after all the reasons I had given to keep the leg, all it took was a tiny baby to make me willing to give it up.

In Bert's office a nurse rushed me into an examination room where Ruth, Bert's nurse, had me take off my slacks, shoes and socks, and climb up on the examination table, where she gave me one of those ridiculously short cover-ups. The two doctors came into the room together. I liked Doctor O'Conner immediately. He was quite short, but good looking in a dark-Irish way. He had an easy-going attitude that I liked. It was as if he was saying: Hey, this is no big deal. Don't worry.

"When the doctors in DC worked on this leg what did they tell you?" Doctor O'Conner asked, after we were introduced.

"They suggested I have it removed above the knee, then they would fit me with a prosthesis. When I refused to consider that option, they told me about a new procedure that was in the experimental stage by a doctor in Washington State." I smiled.

"Well, how about that? My fame is spreading," he smiled back. "Mine is a new treatment that, so far, has been quite successful. I believe my idea is better than any other process being used at this time. I open the leg from slightly below the knee down to the ankle, and remove all the bone. Then a steel shaft encapsulated in cells from your own body is inserted down to the ankle, where I attach a new steel ankle and foot apparatus. Do you follow me?"

"Yes, I think so. Are you saying you would have to cut my foot off?"

"That is a possibility. I will take your x-rays with me, and study them while I'm at a conference I'm attending in San Francisco. It may be, if there is enough of the main bone of the foot left, I can attach the ankle to it."

"What are the risks?"

"You will have to learn to walk all over again, no matter which way we go. It will take awhile to get used to the extra weight of the new leg. The infection risk is minimal. However, if infection should occur we will have to remove the foot or the whole leg depending on where the infection is located and fit you with a prosthesis. Then, of course, there are those risks listed for any operation . . . "

"Yes," I stopped him. "I know all those. What are those cells that you wrap the steel shaft in?"

"They are cells from your own body, grown in a test tube in the lab. This will help fill out your leg to its normal size."

"I think I'm following you. When would you do this, what is the recovery time, and how much does it cost?" I reeled off in rapid order.

"Before I can do the surgery I will have to fashion a new ankle and foot to your exact measurements. This takes approximately four to six weeks. It takes approximately three months for the cells to adhere to the metal shaft. The recovery time will depend on you. As I said, you will have to learn to walk all over again. That could take two weeks to two months. It would be your call."

"How many of these procedures have you done?"

"Only three. It's a new method of replacing the leg and foot bones when both have been damaged beyond repair. I'm the only surgeon in the country, or in the world, for that matter, who is willing to do this type of operation. It is costly, and time-consuming to fashion ankle bones. If your ankle is so damaged I cannot use the existing bones to cover with the encapsulating cells, then I will revert to my first suggestion—the metal ankle and foot. However, I much prefer to use my method throughout the damaged area if it is possible."

"What is the price of the operation?" I asked. Not that I needed to know. I knew the government would pay for it.

"For now, five thousand dollars. That the price of fashioning the ankle bone. I'm doing my best to make this procedure available to all who need it. Right now most insurance companies are not paying for it. Well, what do you think? Does it sound like something you would like done?"

Having decided to do anything to get rid of my crutch, I gave him a quick answer. "Yes."

"That's great, Miss Shores."

"Please, call me Sandy. All my friends do, and if you are going to be replacing some of my bones, I certainly hope you will be my friend."

Solemnly, Harrison O'Conner stuck out his hand. "Hello, friend."

"Hi. When do we start?"

"When I get back from the conference, I'll need to meet with you to get some measurements. I'll call the first part of next week and set up a meeting. Is that okay with you? By the way, wish me luck at the conference. I'm going to be presenting a paper on my new procedure."

"Best of luck, friend. I'll wait for your call."

After handshakes all around, I left the two doctors talking excitedly about my leg, while I hurried off to tell Art the news.

Art knew something had happened when he saw my face.

"I got your message. What's up?"

I pulled the chair even closer to his desk. "What would you say if I told you there was a possibility my leg could be made as good as new?" I laughed when his eyes opened wide in surprise.

"What?"

"It's true," I said. I settled back in the chair, and told him about Doctor O'Conner and his new procedure.

"Boy, I don't know. It sounds pretty futuristic to me. What happens if it doesn't work." Art was dubious, which surprised me.

"Then they would remove the leg and fit me with a prosthesis."

"But, Babe, I didn't think you wanted to do that."

"I didn't until I got to thinking about . . . about some of the things I would miss if I kept the crutch."

"Such as?" he asked.

"I . . . um . . . I want to be able to walk the floor with our baby," I told him quietly.

Art put his head back and roared with laughter. Personally, I didn't think it was funny.

Jumping to his feet, he pulled me up and held me close. "Oh, Babe, how I love you." Wickedly, he asked softly, "When would you like to get started making this little bundle of joy?"

Blushing, I answered him, "Our wedding night. How's that suit you?"

"I can hardly wait," he whispered.

Still holding me close he said, "Seriously, sweetheart, are you comfortable with this operation? You have been so adamant against having your leg removed. I know this must appeal to you because you don't lose your leg, but you must be sure you understand the risk factor. If the doctor should make even one small error you would most likely end up using a prosthesis."

"Tell me one thing truthfully, Art. Would you still love me if I took a piece of me off when I went to bed? I think that's why I didn't want it cut off." I tried to ask it lightly, but I found myself holding my breath. So much depended on his answer.

He held me away, and looked at me as if he was memorizing my features. "The only way I can answer that so you will believe me, is to have you talk to my mother. I told her once that I knew you might be gravely injured, but no matter what happened I would still love you and want to marry you. I prayed every night for your safety, and that God would bring you back to me." We exchanged a kiss. Everybody in the office started clapping. Truthfully, I had forgotten all about them.

"Remember that old song about how the couple married, and on their wedding night she took off her leg, laid her glass eye on the dresser, and hung her boobs on the bedpost?" he asked, smiling. "Even if you were that bad, I'd still want you for my wife."

I punched his shoulder. "You nut! If I was that bad, I wouldn't have ever come home."

"What? And condemn me to life as a bachelor? Surely you wouldn't be that cruel."

"Oh, be quiet. I'm going to the office. Call me if you hear anything from Emily's doctor, okay?" With a wave, I was out the door.

When I got to the office I had a message on the answering machine. I was so deep in thought that at first the voice didn't register, then I realized it was Harriet Logger. I pushed rewind and played it again.

"Miss Shores, this is Harriet Logger. Would it be possible for you to come over and talk to me. I read about your case in the paper and I do have some questions. It is now Tuesday morning, at ten-thirty. Please let me know if you can come."

Oh, Lord, what do I do now? Should I go alone? Take Doctor Morton with me or Art or both? I called Mrs. Logger first and told her I would be over shortly after lunch. Then I called Doctor Morton and asked his advice. I suggested he come out to the house for one of Frances' great lunches, and we could talk. He agreed, after being assured that anything spoken in my house was completely confidential. He thought it might be a good idea to ask Art to come also. I didn't tell him that was to be my next phone call. I called Frances last, and begged her forgiveness for only giving her a half-hour notice before bringing company. I had never asked Frances and Al to leave me alone with my guests before, and I was hesitant to do it now. However, when I explained who was coming and why, Frances suggested it would be best if she and Al weren't present. Besides she said this was their day for the movies. The fibber. I've never seen or heard of them going to the movies in the middle of the day.

TWENTY-FIVE

I hurried home to set the table, but everything was all ready for us. Frances or Al had even thought to put paper and pens by each plate. In the fridge I found sliced roast chicken, sliced tomatoes, a jello salad, a pitcher of ice tea, and lemon squares for dessert. All, of which, I'm sure she had been going to have for dinner. A note on the counter informed me there was hot French bread in the oven. This was wonderful. Perfect for a hot summer day. I barely had time to wash up before the two men arrived. For the time it took to fill our plates the talk was about the weather, the lake, and if there was a chance it would rain soon. In a few moments we settled down to eat, and the talk became more serious.

"I was flabbergasted to get Harriet's call," I said. "I'm sure she is going to want to talk about the man who killed her husband. What do I do if she asks about his wife? All that stuff about Peter Grant was in the papers. I wish we had put a gag order on that information."

"They got all of that from the South Point police, honey. As far as we knew there was no reason why Steve St. John and I should hold anything back about Peter Grant. What should Sandy do if she does start asking about Grant's wife, Doctor Morton?" Art asked.

"I'd like both of you to call me Andrew," he smiled. "In answer to your question, I wish I knew. I know what happened the last time she regressed, it was frightening. I was afraid I wasn't going to be able to get her back. She is so close to borderline that she could go either way. The problem is that even though we are now fairly certain the Emily Grant is her sister, we don't know what that information would do to her.

"Here is what I suggest." Andrew took up his pen and paper. "One: Don't mention Emily unless Harriet does. Two: Try to answer only those questions she asks. Do not elaborate. Three: Be prepared for anything. If she passes out, do not move her or allow anyone else to do so. It is imperative that I speak to her before she regains consciousness. I will be parked down the block. Here is my cell phone number. Four: Stay calm no matter what kind of questions she asks. Recently, since her husband died, she has had yet another personality show up. She becomes this . . . ah . . . wanton woman. Her voice becomes quite loud, and she cusses like a stevedore. The last time this person emerged, she made some inappropriate suggestions to me."

Both Art and I were sitting there with our mouths hanging open, our forks held in suspended animation. Poor Andrew was extremely uncomfortable. He had probably hoped he would never have to tell anyone about this new personality, but Harriet had forced his hand.

"I don't feel that either Art or I should go with you, since she didn't ask that you bring anyone else. Evidently this is to be a woman to woman talk. I wish I could help you more, but I've given you all the ammunition I have. All I can do is wish you luck. If you don't need me, I will follow you back to the police station where you can tell Art and me what happened. Will that be satisfactory with you both.?"

We nodded our heads, as Art squeezed my hand. After the men left I cleared off the table, trying to calm my nerves. While in the CIA, I was well briefed on what to expect from the enemy, but this was something else.

On my way to Harriet's I consoled myself with the fact that William would be there if I had any trouble. If all else failed and she became violent, I could knock her out with my crutch. Thinking about the crutch got me to thinking about the operation. If it is successful I think I'll brush up on my karate techniques. With steel bones I should be able to knock anybody cold. Not a bad idea in my line of work.

Day dreaming and driving do not go hand in hand. Before I

knew it I was parking in the Logger driveway. Getting out of my car, I straightened my shoulders and marched up to the front door. I was more nervous than I had been on some of my missions for the CIA. Today, I'm dealing with several different personalities that can change from one to the other in a split second. Lord have mercy, I prayed, as I rang the doorbell.

Harriet Logger answered the door herself. "Good afternoon, Miss Shores. I'm so glad you were able to take time to come and see me," she said, leading the way into the front room. She had tea and cookies setting on the coffee table. The silver service she was using was elegant. The cookies were undoubtedly homemade. There were flowers everywhere; their perfume was overwhelming. The double doors at the far end of the room were open to the view of the garden through lacy white curtains. The green and white decor had a calming effect on me, and I hoped on Harriet also.

I took the chair she indicated and asked her to please call me Sandy. She agreed, but only if I called her Harriet. She was looking lovely and refined in a pale pink A-line dress. She made my lemon yellow pant suit look frumpy and out of place.

"Is William ill?" I asked.

"No." She hesitated for a moment. "No, I gave him and the housekeeper the afternoon off. I wanted to speak to you about personal things that I didn't want anyone else to hear." Those beautiful brown eyes looked at me beseechingly.

Oh, boy! I thought. No William, no housekeeper. Only myself and my crutch between Harriet and who knew what. Okay, we have the playing field lined out, I thought, so let's start the game.

"Sandy, I asked you here today to try to explain to you why I have acted so strangely the few times I have been in your presence. It is a rather long story that goes back to my childhood, so I hope you will bear with me. May I offer you some tea before I start?"

I said I would enjoy that. From the way the tea pot shook in her hand, I could tell that her stress level was high. She suggested I help myself to the cookies, and more tea, if I wanted it, while she talked. Fleetingly, I wondered how close it would be to Doctor Morton's version.

"I was the result of a kidnapping and rape my mother experienced many years ago," she started. I tried to seem shocked, and evidently I succeeded, for she patted my arm. "Don't worry. My mother loved me deeply, perhaps even more than my . . . sister, because of the rape."

When she said the word "sister" I thought for a moment she was going to lose it. Instead she got up and walked to the window that overlooked the driveway. I tensed waiting for whatever might come. After a short time, she came back to her chair. She appeared calm. I felt myself start to breathe again.

"I'm sure you didn't know I had a sister. Few people are left in Myrtle Woods who did know. I'm sure Luther Pritchard, my mother's husband, made it worth their while to forget that fact."

Luther Pritchard! I wanted to raise my fist in the air and holler "Yes." Now, if only Emily would mention him also.

"Luther was unable to accept the fact that my mother would not abort her pregnancy, and insisted on having me. I'm sure it must have been the first time she ever stood up to him, in view of what happened later. When I was four, my sister came shockingly close to being abducted from her bedroom. The only thing that saved her was the fact that my father was having guests that night for some kind of a political meeting, and one of the men had to leave early. My father walked him out to his car, and returned to his meeting by way of the kitchen. He was in time to catch a man taking Em . . . my sister out the window."

She paused to take a sip of her tea, looking right through me. For the moment, she seemed to have forgotten I was in the room.

"I must explain about the type of man Luther was. My father . . . how inappropriate for me to call him that. Every day of my life, from the time I started talking until the time he left this house for good, he reminded me that he was not my father nor did he want me to call him father, daddy or any other name that would indicate to anyone that he and I were related. It was a hard lesson to learn. My sister called him father, but any time I did, I got slapped hard across the mouth and sent to my room. It didn't take me too long to learn not to speak in his presence.

When I wouldn't speak, even when he spoke to me, he started telling my mother that I was a deaf mute and should be put away. I believe the only thing that kept me sane was the love my mother and my sister lavished on me when he wasn't around. Then . . . then when I was four, that horrible man took my sister from me. He told me it was all my fault that she was nearly kidnapped. He said to punish me, I would never see her again."

Harriet's voice had risen hysterically on the last few sentences. She covered her face with her hands. "I'm sorry, I'm sorry," she sobbed. "I didn't mean to do anything. Please come back. Please," she wailed. Her voice sounded a little like a child, but not the way it had before. Should I call Doctor Morton? She hadn't fainted, so I decided to wait. Pulling my chair next to hers, I put my arm around her shoulders. Her head fell on my breast, and I held her close as she cried. It was torment to watch her fight the demons within her.

What a bastard her mother had married. How could any human treat another so cruelly? No wonder this woman has a half dozen different ways of dealing with stress. I realized that if she didn't have these personalities, she most likely would be in a sanitarium, completely withdrawn from the world around her.

Harriet sat up and wiped her eyes. "I'm so sorry. Did I make another spectacle of myself?"

"No, you certainly did not. Looking back on that time in your life is extremely stressful. If you hadn't cried, I would have been surprised. Why don't I empty your tea cup in the kitchen, so you can have a nice hot cup."

"Thank you, no. Let me do it. It will give me a few minutes to collect myself." She turned at the door, "Thank you, Sandy, for being so understanding. Somehow, I knew you would believe me."

TWENTY-SIX

She was only gone a few moments, but in that time she had managed to erase any sign of tears from her face. How does she do that, I wondered. I need to get her beauty secrets. If I cry for only a minute or two, my makeup is destroyed and my eyes are puffy for a half-hour.

I noticed her hand was much steadier as she poured us both more tea. Perhaps getting past the part about her sister had been the worst of her memories. She settled back in her chair and continued her story.

"Growing up, I realized that my mother was telling everyone I didn't have a sister, whereas I was determined to keep her memory alive. Finally, when I was seven my mother sat me down, and explained why I wasn't to mention my sister to anyone again. Luther had made her sign a paper stating she would forget she had another daughter, that as far as Mother and I were concerned, Em . . . Em . . . . my sister never existed. We were never to attempt to find her; we must never allow our picture to get in the paper, in case she might see it and come to us. Mother was to wipe out any proof that would even suggest that my sister had lived in this house. If she didn't do these things, she was told, the two of us would be badly hurt. We wouldn't be killed, he said, that would be too easy, but mutilated to the point where no one could stand to look at us. I still have trouble believing anyone would threaten another in that way, but even as a child, I knew he meant it. From that day on I never spoke about my sister to anyone until I was nine. For some reason I started having nightmares about her. In each one, she was being held against her will, and was calling to me to help her. It was so real, I didn't know what to do. Over and over my mother kept reminding me that I mustn't mention her to anyone. Finally, Mother took me to Doctor Morton, a psychiatrist. I don't know if he believed me about my sister or not, since Mother kept denying it, but he appeared to believe me. He was able to help me understand that the reason I was having those dreams was because I truly blamed myself for her near kidnapping. Doctor Morton helped me to understand that I had nothing to do with anything bad that happened to my sister, despite what my mother's husband had said. The doctor told me that my mind thought she was dead, since no mention could be made of her to anyone else, but my subconscious was refusing to believe that to be true. He felt the dreams were a way my mind and my subconscious were at war with one another. It took many sessions, but he taught me to keep the hope alive that I would someday see Em . . . Em . . . oh, I'm sorry. I can't say her name. I guess I've been trained too well."

"That's perfectly understandable, Harriet," I said gently, patting her hand. "Would you like to take a few minutes, and talk about something else? Maybe your flower garden? From what I can see from here, it's beautiful."

Harriet grabbed that line like a swimmer going down for the third time. For the next twenty minutes or so, we strolled among the flowers. She knew all their names, where it was best to plant them (sun or shade), and the best time to plant. (spring, summer or fall.) It was a short botany lesson given under ideal conditions. In her garden, Harriet totally relaxed. All tension melted away; her face became alive with the joy of the moment. She was gracious and entertaining. When she smiled, I caught glimpses of the beautiful young girl she must have been.

When we returned to the living room, I asked Harriet to tell me about her childhood after her sister was taken away.

"I had what I believe was a happy childhood, in spite of what had happened. Most of that I attribute to my mother. She was determined that I would be an adult she would be proud to call her daughter—kind, good-natured, honest, and faithful. She taught me how to dress well, the most flattering way to fix my hair, how to walk and carry myself. The finished product is much like what you see today. Although, with a few less pounds," she laughed lightly.

It was the first time I had ever heard her laugh; the sound was delightful. She went on to describe meeting Paul Logger at college, how they fell in love, and how after graduation he refused to discuss marriage until he had established himself.

"He was too proud to accept any financial help from my mother or from the trust fund she had set up for me. It was five years before he was ready to take the responsibility of a wife and children. Both of us wanted children, but it was not to be," she said wistfully, a far-away look in her eyes.

"Because we couldn't allow any pictures to get into the papers, we had a quiet wedding with Paul's parents and my mother present. I had told Paul about the paper my mother had been forced to sign, and he in turn told his parents, after swearing them to secrecy. Sounds like something out of a mystery novel, doesn't it."

She reached for her cup. I could see the animation slowly fade as she sipped her tea. "I wanted to be perfectly honest with Paul about the rape that fathered me, and Luther's threat. None of that changed Paul's mind. He loved me very much, you see. Everything went along smoothly for many years. The only blight on our lives was the fact that I couldn't conceive. We tried everything—pills, examinations, charts—anything and everything anyone suggested, but to no avail. By the time we tried to adopt, the agency told us we were too old at thirty-seven to be considered. That seems strange these days, doesn't it, when women are giving birth at forty and fifty.

"Nevertheless, Paul and I made a wonderful, fulfilling life for the two of us. We became deeply interested in several charities around town, especially those involving children. We both loved golf and traveling. Every chance Paul got, we would take off to visit some new spot. It was getting harder and harder to keep our pictures out of the paper. This made me desperately afraid. Mother was getting quite elderly. I didn't want anything to upset her this late in her life. The more frightened I became, the more lapses of time would occur when I couldn't recall where I had been. In the beginning I was unaware of what was happening to me. Slowly, over time, these other personalities within my body began taking over whenever they wished. It got so I never knew who I was going to be or what I might say next. It was making me a prisoner in my own home.

"Twelve years ago I started going back to Doctor Morton. Even his wisdom failed to have any effect on those other women within me. Eleven years ago, I was returning from a session with the doctor when I had a nasty accident. I ran a stop sign without even realizing it, and hit another car broadside in the intersection. I'm thankful I was the only one hurt. I suffered a broken leg, a broken jaw, and several broken ribs. I was in the hospital for several weeks, and confined to my bed for several more."

Once more I could see she was desperately trying to keep control of the conversation. I could tell one of the personalities was fighting to get out. I found myself clasping my hands together as tightly as she was hers, trying through sheer will power to help her to remain the one in control. Doctor Morton hadn't said so, but somehow I felt that if she could get through the rest of the afternoon as herself, she would be well on the way to controlling her life.

She had stopped speaking for a few minutes. She sat rigid in her chair, her feet close together and flat on the floor, her back as straight as a ramrod, her eyes closed, her head bowed, her hands clasped ever tighter in her lap.

Without looking up or opening her eyes, she started to speak in a slow, controlled voice. "It was then that my husband evidently had an affair—no, that's not correct—when he evidently had sex with his secretary." The last two words went straight up the scale. She's losing it, I thought. Instinctively, I reached over and clasped her hands in mine. She quickly wound her fingers around my hands. I remembered the strength she had displayed the first time she came to my office, but that was nothing compared to now. She held my hands so tightly I could feel my engagement ring starting to cut into my little finger, but it didn't matter. I was willing to donate a little blood if it would free this woman from her demons.

Harriet took a deep breath, and, still hanging on tight to my hands, she continued, her voice again under control. "I don't know why Paul refused to accept the responsibility for her baby. My best friend tells me it was because he was afraid I would ask for a divorce, and he didn't want to lose me. He told my friend it only happened the one time, would never happen again, and, for the life of him, he couldn't figure out why he had sex with the secretary in the first place. She was young, and inexperienced; he didn't even enjoy it. I do know it was late at night, he was frustrated because we hadn't had sex for several weeks, and it would be many more before we could. We were used to having sex almost every night. For whatever reason, I do blame him for not telling me. Perhaps we could have done something for the child that would enable him to hear, who knows?"

"It may not be too late, Harriet," I said. "If you would like to do something, perhaps I could talk to the Fullers when they get back from Arizona."

"Arizona?"

"Yes, yesterday we found out where Doreen Fuller is, and Mr. Fuller and Tracy have gone to get her. I must tell you that Mr. Fuller is a proud man himself, much like your Paul, so it may take some time to convince him to accept your offer."

"Oh, Sandy, please try. I feel if I could help the boy to hear it would make up for some of the agony he has gone through. Tell the Fullers I will never make any claim on the boy . . ."

"His name is Tracy."

"On Tracy," she acknowledged. "All I would like to do is help him to hear if it is possible, perhaps to pay for any special school he might have to go to, and to pay for a college education. If they don't want me to pay for it all, maybe they will let me pay for half. Please, Sandy, ask them," she begged.

"As I said, they are going to be gone for several days, but I'll do what I can. How generous of you, Harriet."

"It's something that should have been done ten years ago."

"May I ask how the business is doing? Were you able to stop a crash of the company stock?"

"Yes, as a matter of fact. I called a meeting of the board of directors, and with their help the business is doing fine. The directors appointed Ronald Miller as president. I'm sure he will do a good job. Paul had every confidence in him. I'll be president of the board of directors, since I have the majority of the shares. I'm going in two or three mornings a week to work with different departments, so I can learn more about the business. Ron and the board members thought that would be a wise thing to do."

"That's wonderful, Harriet. It sounds like you have the majority of your problems all straightened out. And may I say, you did a wonderful job talking to me today. I was impressed."

"I did do well, didn't I? I must talk to Doctor Morton soon, and get his opinion. Is it possible I can rid myself of these other personalities? How blessed that would be," she said with tears in her eyes.

I was aching to suggest all kinds of things concerning Emily, but I managed to keep my mouth shut.

"Now, Sandy, it's your turn. Please tell me what happened to Paul. I want to know everything." Harriet settled back in her chair. She seemed at ease, her hands clasped loosely in her lap, her feet crossed at the ankles; the perfect picture of the well-bred woman of a time nearly forgotten.

"Are you sure you want to know everything? Some of it will be painful for you to hear. Don't you think you have gone through enough for one day?" I asked.

"No, I feel I must know exactly how he died. Only then can I pray for his soul," she answered softly.

She left me with no alternative. Keeping my voice impersonal, I told her about Peter Grant luring Paul to the boathouse; about making him take off his clothes, and forcing him out into the lake to drown in payment for getting his daughter pregnant. It was here her tears started, as she whispered, "Paul . . . . oh, my poor darling, didn't know how to swim." I told her about Peter jerking Paul's necklace off, and taking it home to his wife ("I knew it!" she interjected in a tearful voice); about him putting Paul's tie back on after he was dead. I finished by telling her about Peter towing Paul's car back to the lake front park; and finally, about folding and leaving Paul's clothes by the edge of the water. I was not about to tell her about the amputation. She was in enough misery as it was. I made the quick decision that if she ever hears about it and asks, I would pretend I didn't know about it.

We sat there in silence for several minutes. Tears were chasing each other down her cheeks. I'm sure she would have been sobbing loudly if she hadn't had her handkerchief pressed tightly against her lips as she rocked back and forth in misery. Is it possible well bred, wealthy people are taught not to cry out loud? If so, that's too bad. Sometimes people need to let the whole world know how badly they feel. I sat down beside her and put my arms around her. She clung to me and sobbed; it was like listening to a child. I thought, oh, no, not now. As her tears began to subsided, she sat up, wiping her eyes.

"Thank you, Emily," her voice normal. "Poor Paul. What agonies he must have suffered for the past eleven years. He must have been terrified that my friend would tell me the truth. And then to die in that manner! I loved him a great deal. I probably always will. I can't begin to tell you how much I miss him. Basically, he was a sweet, loving man, and that's the man I'm going to remember." She took my hand and held it as she said, "You have been sweet to put up with me today. I truly feel that you have helped me more than I will ever be able to tell you."

Now what do I do? Call her attention to the fact that she called me Emily, or let it go and accept her gratitude. Sorry, Doctor Morton, I thought, I can't let a chance like this pass me by.

"Harriet, do you realize you called me Emily a moment ago," I said. Her beautiful eyes opened wide in surprise.

"I did? I did! I haven't been able to say her name for years. Even when Doctor Morton said I should be thinking about seeing her again someday—even then I couldn't say Em . . . Emily. Emily, Emily, Emily," she said tremulously. "Oh, Sandy, you are a miracle worker. Thank you, dear girl, thank you," she said, giving me a hug.

"I wish that was so, Harriet, but it was you who took control of your life today. If there's a miracle worker here, it's you," I said, returning her hug.

"I'm going to call Doctor Morton, and tell him what has happened. I'm sure he will be surprised. Finally, some of the sessions he and I have had are beginning to show results." The doctor's answering service connected her to his car phone. He told her he was nearby and would be there shortly.

"Thank you again, Sandy," she said, as arm in arm we walked to the front door. "I feel you played a large part in my successful attempt to take charge of my life. Please come and see me again. Next time we will talk about your exciting life," she promised.

"Not much to tell there," I told her. "However, I would enjoy coming again."

"Bring your young man with you, will you?" she called out to me as I was going down the front steps to my car.

"Sure, I'd love to," I answered.

Doctor Morton drove into the drive as I was leaving. I gave him the a-okay sign and caught a thumbs up from him as we passed.

TWENTY-SEVEN

It was after five before I left Harriet's place. I stopped by the police station to let Art know I was on my way home. Immediately he wanted to know what happened, but I asked him to wait until after dinner because it would take quite awhile to tell him everything in detail. He agreed under protest, telling me I wasn't playing fair. I gave him a wave as I hurried home.

One would never know from his appetite that Art was anxious to hear my news. He went through baked sole, twice baked potatoes, green beans in stewed tomatoes, and bread pudding as if he had all the time in the world.

During dinner I told them what Doctor O'Conner said about replacing my leg. "I'm wondering if we shouldn't wait until after the operation to get married," I said to Art.

He stopped chewing, a shocked look on his face. "Why would we want to do that?"

"I was thinking if we wait, I might be able to walk down to the lake normally. You know how much I want to do that."

"Yes, I know, but let's consider all the possibilities. Number one and foremost, I don't think I can wait another two to three months. Either we get married as planned or we live together in sin." Art held up his hand when I started to speak. "Second, what will the weather be like by that time? The rains are sure to start by mid-September. I don't believe you want to be married by the lake in the rain, do you?" Again he held up his hand. "Number three, if you delay this wedding by so much as an hour

I will not be responsible for what Marie will do. She might go stark raving mad and kill us all. I rest my case."

By the time Art finished we were all laughing. "Okay, okay, we will go ahead as planned. But, Art, you know that little item I was talking to you about earlier in your office?" He looked puzzled. "You know, that little thing I wanted to be able to walk with...."

"Oh, you mean the baby," he exclaimed.

Frances and Al were looking at us like parents who have just been told their beloved daughter is pregnant. I was so embarrassed. "No, no, calm down," I said to them. "I told Art that is the reason I want to have my leg done. I want to be able to walk the floor with our baby, and ... um ... if I'm pregnant they won't operate." I wasn't about to take this conversation any further.

"Oh, I see what you mean," Art said, as the light dawned in his eyes. "Well, I don't mind waiting a few months to try to get you pregnant, but I sure as hell don't want to wait for the wedding"

"I think we've carried this subject as far as I wish it to go. I'll agree the wedding will be as planned, so let's change the subject, shall we," I said, pushing my chair back.

Before anyone could say anything more the phone rang. It was Doctor Morton. He had taken Harriet Logger out to dinner, and had stopped by his office to call us.

"I thought you might want to know that Harriet has asked me to try and locate Emily—to verify if she is dead or alive," he said.

"Is she ready for that kind of trauma already? Isn't it possible that something like that would make her revert back to her childhood?" were my questions.

"I'm going to put off finding Emily for a week or more. That should give her time to continue facing these other personalities in her body. Each day that she is successful will make her stronger in fighting them off completely. I think it would be a good idea for me to clue Doctor Davidson in on what is happening. He would be the best one to tell us how soon we can bring the two women together."

"Let me put Art on the phone so you can tell him your idea," was all I said. For once, I didn't jump in and monopolize the conversation.

Art and Doctor Morton agreed that it would be a good idea for the two doctors to discuss the case, as long as Art and I were there. "That was something I was going to suggest," Doctor Morton said. "There have been some things that have happened that you both know more about than I do."

The final decision was that Art would call Doctor Davidson the next morning to see if we could see Emily, then make an appointment for everyone to get together.

It was ten the next morning before I received a call from Art. "We have an appointment with Doctor Davidson and Doctor Morton at twelve for lunch in South Point. At one-thirty we can talk to Emily. Does that timetable fit yours?"

"No problem here," I answered. "Is Doctor Morton riding over with us? If so, I'll meet you at your office at eleven. Okay?"

Art said he wasn't sure about Doctor Morton, but to come at eleven anyway. I hadn't even taken my hand off of the phone when it rang again. It was Marie.

"Good news about the dress, hon. The cleaners promised it will smell brand new when they finish with it," she said.

"Wonderful. And you will keep it for me?"

"You bet. I'll call when it's ready and we can go pick it up together. I went ahead and bought that dress I told you about because I love it and can wear it elsewhere. You can see it when you and Art come over on Sunday. If you don't like it, I'll get something else." She continued for a few minutes with other plans she had in mind.

"I'm completely in your hands," I told her. "Tell me where you want me on the wedding day and I'll be there. I'm sure any plans you make will be what I would have wanted. All kidding aside, Marie, I wish I could tell you what it means to me for you to be in charge. I have so many things going right now there is no way I could do justice to a wedding. You are a sweetheart to do this, and I love you dearly."

"Aw, shucks, t'aint nothin'. What are friends for anyhow?" she drawled and hung up before I started crying. She could always tell when I was getting weepy.

When I arrived at the station both men were outside by Art's police cruiser waiting for me. I didn't know about the guys, but my palms were sweating. How were these women going to react to the realization that they had existed this close together all these years?

The two doctors compared notes during lunch and agreed that both childhood stories were technically identical. There was no doubt in anyone's minds that the women were sisters. Doctor Davidson suggested that Art and I go in and speak with Emily to get the rest of her story. When she has finished both Doctor Davidson and Doctor Morton would step into the room and Doctor Davidson would tell her about Harriet. I was glad to hear that he would be in the room when she learned the news.

Emily was a different woman today from the one we had visited a few days ago. I had to admit that yes, makeup and a becoming hairdo do make a big difference. After welcoming us, she told us how much better she felt after getting all of the horrible things Peter had done to her out in the open.

"There isn't much more to tell. The last ten years of our married life was something you would only expect to find in a soap opera. I'm positive that Peter would have killed me if he had thought he could get away with it. I'm ashamed to admit it, but I enjoyed making his life miserable.

"Two years ago an army buddy of Peter's stopped by. Peter's reaction when he saw who it was made me wonder what was going on. It was during that visit that I found out Peter had been a cook, not the war-torn, brave serviceman in the trenches he wanted everyone to believe." Her laugh was like water rippling over stones. A beautiful duplicate of Harriet's.

So that's where he learned to carve. I thought about the amputation of Paul Logger. I'll give him credit where credit is due. It was a professional job.

"Believe me," Emily continued, "I milked that for all it was worth. I realize now that I was as horrible to him as he had been to me, perhaps even more so. It makes me ashamed of myself. But now it is over. I've asked for and received forgiveness from God, so now I can put the whole thing behind me." She lay back on the pillow, serenely happy.

Art stepped into the hallway and signaled the two doctors.

Doctor Davidson greeted Emily and introduced Doctor Morton. I noticed that Doctor Davidson stayed right by Emily's bedside. Unobtrusively, he started checking her pulse.

"Emily, you referred several times to something that happened in your childhood. I wonder if you would mind telling us about that," Art asked.

She lay quiet for a few minutes. We could see several emotions flitting across her face. Then slowly, with many starts and stops, she told us almost word for word the same story that Harriet had told me. When she told us what happened between her parents—Luther Pritchard and Anna Brocall—we had absolute proof that the two women were sisters.

"I think about my sweet Harriet often. I even drove by the family home once hoping to see her, but I guess it had been sold because all I saw was a giant of a man standing in the doorway." Tears welled up in her eyes. "I doubt now that I'll ever see her again. Oh, Howard."

Doctor Davidson sat on the bed, calming her down. Watching them, I realized this man was the love of her life. "Emily, dear, the sheriff and Sandy think they know where she's living."

She sat up quickly, her eyes shining. "Where is she? When can I see her? Are you sure it's my sister, Sandy?"

"We are positive since you told us of your childhood. It was nearly word for word what Harriet told me. We do have one problem, though. Doctor Morton can explain it to you better than I can."

Emily watched him fearfully, expecting to hear that something terrible had happened to Harriet. We could see her visibly relax as Doctor Morton patiently explained how fragile Harriet's mind was at this time; about the numerous personalities that occupied her body; and how she was fighting to regain control of her life. Emily was full of questions and he answered them all.

"I see," Emily said. "You say you have told her you will try to find me. How long is that expected to take?"

"As soon as you are released," Doctor Morton said. "Doctor Davidson and I both feel it would be better if she didn't come to the hospital. He tells me you should be out of the hospital within a week."

"If that is all it takes to see Harriet, I'm ready to go home today," Emily stated firmly.

"Now, now, dear," Doctor Davidson hushed her. "You aren't as ready as you may think you are. You must stay in the hospital for a few more days. I want to make sure you are completely healed and ready to be up and about. If you had someone to care for you at home it would be different, but I can't even be sure I would be there at night if . . . "

"Surely we can get a visiting nurse or someone for a few days, Howard," Emily interrupted him.

"Yes that's a possibility," the doctor conceded. "I'll call the visiting nurse's office and see if someone is available." Turning to us he said, "Emily is coming to my house when she leaves the hospital. I don't want her returning to that house she shared with Grant—too many bad memories. Besides," he said with a smile, "I'm hoping to convince Emily to marry me as soon as she is strong enough."

Emily blushed. I gave her a hug, while the men shook hands with each other.

"I'm so happy for you, Emily," I said. "Art and I are getting married on the thirty-first of this month. I hope all of you will be able to come."

"We would be delighted," they all said.

While the men continued to discuss how best to break the news to Harriet, Emily and I spoke about life and its strange twists and quirks. How many other lives had Luther and Peter ruined? Thank God, there was no way we would ever know.

TWENTY-EIGHT

Sitting in my office the next day I decided to put my notes of both cases in order. In the midst of arranging the Doreen Fuller case it suddenly dawned on me that we hadn't ever located Jasper's car.

I called Art to see if they had located it and had forgotten to tell me. "Hi, it's me," I said, when he answered the phone.

"Good morning, light of my life. What can I do for you today?"

"Was Jasper Grant's car ever found?"

"Son of a gun, I'd forgotten all about it in the midst of all the other excitement," Art exclaimed. "I meant to send some of the boys over to the other side of the lake to look further down that old logging road where he hid yours. Since it appears he killed Jasper there, it stands to reason that's where the car is."

"I was thinking the same thing. What happens to it once it is found?"

He thought for a moment. "Since it is all paid for I imagine it would go to his next of kin. Either his mother or sister, I suppose."

"I might be a tad sentimental, but I think it would be wonderful if Emily got it, if she wants it," I said. "Granted, it's not something she can have around forever to remember her son by, but for a few years every time she gets into it she could remember Jasper." Not sentimental, did I say? All it took was my last few sentences to put a lump in my throat.

"I don't see why not. If it has been in the woods all this time I won't vouch for its condition, but I'm sure Emily has the wherewithal to get it fixed as good as new. I'll send Ed and Billy Ray out right now to see if they can find it."

The car they found was far from being the beauty it had been a few months previously. Hundreds of birds had been using it for a nesting place, as well as several small animals. The cloth top had been torn to shreds, the upholstery was in tatters.

Art called me when they got the car back to the station and I hurried over to take a look. I had to agree with Art that it would take a lot to get it back to its original state. Art decided to have the car stored at the station until we could talk to Emily. Neither of us was looking forward to telling her about Jasper.

"You know I've been thinking about calling Doctor Davidson and seeing if he thinks it would be better for him to tell Emily about Jasper's death," Art said. "Then if she wants more details we can furnish them to her. What do you think?"

I thought for a few moments. "Yes," I said slowly. "That probably would be the best way to go. Maybe he can take some of the pain away by telling her that Doreen is on her way home. Why don't we call his office right now?"

The doctor agreed it would be best for him to tell Emily about her children, promising to call us if she wanted more information.

The rest of the day seemed to drag, until about four o'clock when the ringing of the phone jerked me awake.

"Sandy Shores, Investigations," I said crisply.

"Hi, partner," a well-remembered voice from my CIA days answered.

"Jake! How are you? It's good to hear your voice. How are Sue and the kids? Are you going to be able to come to the wedding?" As usual I was full of questions, giving him no time to answer.

"We are all fine, yes and yes," he laughed. "We couldn't let you get married without us. We are going to drive out. Give the kids a chance to see the country. We will take our time so it will probably take us eight days if we stop to see all the landmarks and stuff. I figure we will pull into Myrtle Woods at the latest on Saturday the thirtieth. How does that sound?"

"No, no. Can't you start out sooner so you will get here on the twenty-seventh or twenty-eighth? We've got to have a few days to catch up on everything, and for Art and me to show you and Sue the countryside."

"Yeah, sure, we can do that. We didn't want to arrive too early and be in the way while you were getting ready for the wedding."

"No problem. Everything is under control. My best friend is taking care of everything. She's a perfectionist, so I'm standing back and letting her take charge. I can't wait to see you all. I'll bet the kids have grown like weeds."

"That's for sure. Have you heard anything in answer to our letter concerning the mole in the CIA organization?"

"Not one word. I was going to ask you the same thing when you got here. It's been eighteen months, but I suppose these things take time. Let's talk about it while you're here."

"Agreed. For now, I better sign off," Jake said. "We have a lot to do to get ready if we are going to leave on Sunday. See you soon."

I sat holding the receiver, as if I could keep him in the room with me as long as I didn't hang up. How silly can one person get, I wondered. Hanging up the phone, I locked the office and rushed home to tell Frances the first of the wedding guests were on their way from DC.

After dinner Art and I walked down to the lake and talked about the spy I was sure must be in the organization—perhaps even the director himself. "It seems to be taking far too long. Most likely they are going to ignore us," I said bitterly.

"Now, honey, it's only been what—seventeen, eighteen months? This type of investigation must be done carefully to make sure they get the right person. I wouldn't jump to conclusions yet. I would be surprised if you heard much before another six months."

"I suppose you are right. I told Jake we'd talk about it when they get here."

"Feel like visiting Mrs. Logger tomorrow," Art asked me.

"Sure. What's happening?"

"She called me this afternoon when she couldn't reach you

to invite us to tea. Can't you see me with one of those cups with the handle I can't get my finger through and one of those silly little sandwiches."

"Yes, I can visualize that. You'll be like an elephant in a china shop," I laughed. "I wonder what she wants?"

"We'll know soon enough," he answered solemnly.

The next day did not bode well for enjoying tea in the garden. The eerie sound of a wild wind whistling around the corners of the house woke me up early. Opening the curtains I saw that the wind was lashing the lake into a fury.

"Where in the world did this storm come from?" I asked Frances as I stepped into the warm, sweet-smelling kitchen.

"Al heard about it on the late news. It has something to do with that El Nino phenomenon that is causing all the floods and stuff in California. He can tell you more about it than I can. I hope you don't have to go anywhere today. I don't like that wind," she said worriedly.

"Only out to Mrs. Logger's this afternoon. Maybe it will let up by that time," I said, trying to reassure her.

I picked up the phone when it pealed its summons. It was Art telling me he wouldn't be over for breakfast. "Trees are falling all over town. We are going to call in extra help to keep people away from the wires the trees are dragging down with them. You better call Mrs. Logger. Tell her we won't be out this afternoon. Even if the storm lets up, I'm going to be busy working with the power company to get things cleared up. Got to run. I'll call later, Babe."

"Be careful, honey," I said into the dead phone. I relayed Art's message to Frances and Al, who had walked in as I was hanging up the phone.

"If this wind don't let up, it's gonna be bad," he said. "I'm worried about that old pine out front. If she goes, she'll hit the house for sure. I better call Mac."

Mac, who lived next door, was Al's best friend. Before he retired a few years ago he was a forest ranger. There wasn't much Mac didn't know about trees.

Breakfast was a hurried affair. Frances wanted to get some food cooked ahead in case the electricity went off. I convinced her it would be a good idea for me to do the breakfast dishes, so she could get to her baking. It was her opinion that since she was the housekeeper, she should do all the cleaning up. It gave me a clue how worried she was when she let me tidy up for her.

I called Mrs. Logger to tell her I doubted that Art and I would be out for tea, only to find out she was getting ready to call me to cancel the appointment. She told me she had already lost two large trees in the back yard. Luckily neither hit the house nor any wires. We agreed to put off our date for tea until the following Friday.

"I have something I want to ask you and Chief Landow to do for me, but I don't wish to discuss it over the phone. I will look forward to seeing you Friday," she said cryptically as she hung up.

Now what could she mean, I wondered. I was glad I had called her because it gave me something to think about other than Art out in this awful weather.

I wandered to the front window and saw Al and Mac out by the big old pine tree. The tree was whipping from side to side in a bizarre dance; its limbs reaching to grab the men. Even to my untrained eyes it seemed to be moving more loosely than the other trees in the yard. I watched as the men began pounding metal stakes into the ground about ten feet in front of the pine. I held my breath as Mac climbed the swaying tree to wrap two stout ropes around its trunk and tossed them down to Al. It became clear what they intended to do when they tied the ropes tightly to the metal stakes. Now if the pine fell it would fall away from the house, not into it.

"That's quite a plan," I congratulated them, as both men shed their rain clothes on the back porch, brushing pine needles from their hair.

"I've done the same thing several other times with those old trees that are a danger to homes around the lake. After the storm I think it would be a good idea for Al and me to cut it down. It is dying, and it will only get worse," Mac stated.

"Yes, I guess so," I said sadly. "I hate to see it go though. I spent many a day playing up in those wonderful old limbs when I was a kid."

The three of us sat there drinking mugs of good hot coffee, each thinking their own thoughts, as we watched Frances bustle around the kitchen. Suddenly Frances spoke, "My gosh, look at that. What is it?"

We all rushed to the windows. Marching across the lake was a curtain of rain that looked like a horde of locusts descending on Myrtle Woods. As the rain curtain overtook the house we all drew back swiftly from the windows in fear. I realized I couldn't even see the lake, the rain was so heavy.

It was exactly four hours later when that old majestic pine tree sighed and tumbled to the ground. To me, it was like losing a friend. The sound of the tree falling sent me running to the front window. I could not believe what I saw. All over the neighborhood lay tree limbs looking grotesquely like severed human body parts. Several cars were smashed flat. It was a war zone.

I don't know how many times I went to the phone to call Art. I needed reassurance that he was okay, but each time I stopped myself. I knew he wouldn't want me to tie up the phone when someone with a real emergency might be trying to get through. It was the middle of the second day of the storm before he stopped by for a few minutes. He looked terrible—red-eyed, unshaven, wrinkled clothes.

As I took him in my arms, I felt him sag wearily against me. "Thank goodness, you are okay, sweetheart. Are you getting any rest?" I asked.

"Yes, some. I'm grabbing what sleep I can on the cot in the precinct. There are so many things happening all the time that I've got most of my men on duty twenty-four hours a day. This is a bad one. I stopped for a minute because I knew you would be worried. Now I've got to get back on the road. May I have a cup of coffee to take with me, Frances?"

Bless Frances' heart. While we were talking she had quickly

wrapped up several sandwiches, some of her homemade cookies, and a thermos of coffee.

"I love you, Frances," he said. "What say we run off and get married?"

"Oh, you," she laughed. "I don't think Al or Sandy would approve."

With a hug for Frances and a quick kiss for me he was gone.

Fifteen minutes later the electricity went out. For the next twenty-four hours we sat in the light from the old-fashioned kerosene lamps Al had stored in the basement for emergencies.

It was three days later, Thursday, before the sun shone brightly again and the clean-up began in earnest. The power company was working around the clock restoring power. Those in town actually got off lucky; many damaged cars, a few trees, masses of large limbs, several lines down, but generally Art felt we were lucky. The river had risen exceedingly fast, but the dam had held. The spillway built years ago to handle the winter overflow was able to handle the run-off. If the dam had broken there would have been far more damage done to the low-lying farms around Mountain View. As it was several farms lying close to the river did flood; over a hundred people had to find alternate shelter. Sometime during the violence of the storm Emily's house in South Point had been struck by the single bolt of lightening that flashed during the storm. The house and all its bad memories burnt to the ground. In a way it was a blessing. Now she would never have to set foot in that house of horrors again. Yes, there was good and bad caused by that wild storm. I'm sure no one wanted to see El Nino return anytime soon.

Friday dawned clear and bright. Birds sang and flowers raised well-scrubbed faces to the sun; it was a beautiful day to be alive. Art had slept around the clock, showered, and shaved. He was his old handsome self when he arrived for breakfast. While we ate he told us some of the true stories of human and animal heroics that took place during the storm.

"One in particular I will never forget," he said. "We were called out to a small house by the lake that was about to be swamped. A woman called because she was annoyed by the barking of the neighbor's dog. When we arrived it was to find that the neighbor, Mr. Stokes, was being pulled up the path that ran down to the house by a big yellow dog. It's hard telling how long the dog had been pulling and barking trying to get help. Each time the water got close she would pull him up a little way further. It was truly amazing. Mr. Stokes had had a heart attack and was dead by the time we got there. His dog put up a fuss when we took him from her. She didn't want to be separated from him, but it was necessary. She was a sorry looking mess and so sad when I dropped her off at the Humane Society. There is no other family, so I don't know what will happen to her. She is truly a wonder dog." I saw tears form in Art's eyes. The dog had made a great impression on him.

"You know, I've been wondering if it might not be a good idea for me to have a dog at the office. I never know what type of person will walk through that front door next," I said.

"That might be a good idea," Art said, hope dawning in his eyes. "Why don't we go take a look at her after breakfast. Right now she is in pretty bad shape. Her hair is terribly matted and, of course, she is mud from her nose to her tail. Sadie is the name that was on her collar, but I guess you can change it if you two hit it off."

I turned to Frances to get her permission to have a dog in the house. All she did was nod her head. The story of Sadie had gotten to her also.

Later, when we walked into the Humane Society, Sadie was lying on a rug in the office. I knelt down beside her and ran my hand over her noble head. She was a beautiful Labrador. The bath they had given her brought out the golden color of her coat that was now unbelievably soft. All the matted hair on her stomach and legs that Art had told us about had been cut off.

"Hello, Sadie, how are you, old girl?" I asked softly. She looked up with those sad, sad eyes when I spoke her name, but her tail never moved. She was definitely in mourning. I had seen this happen to the dogs we used in certain situations for the CIA when their owners died in the line of duty. "You are beautiful, Sadie. Would you like to come home with me?" Again I got the look, but no other response. However, when I stood up, she came to her feet to stand quietly beside me. It was as if she had understood what I said.

"Shall we go, girl?" With great dignity she walked beside me to the car. I left Art to pay the fees needed to adopt her. Right then, I wouldn't have trusted my voice to speak without breaking into tears.

When we arrived home, Sadie stood for a few minutes looking at the lake before she entered the back porch. Slowly she entered the kitchen and I introduced her to Frances and Al. Gravely she shook hands with them both before coming to sit beside my chair. Automatically my hand reached to pet her.

"Welcome to your new home, Sadie. I hope you like it here with us." She placed her chin on my lap as she gave one thump of her tail.

That afternoon when we went to see Mrs. Logger, Sadie rode along with us. When we stepped out of the car she never offered to jump out. Instead she hopped into the drivers seat and sat there with watchful eyes.

"I think that is a good watch dog you have there, Miss. Shores," Art said smiling.

"I know. Isn't she wonderful?" I rang the doorbell, and as we waited I noticed the grounds were immaculate. No one would have ever known this house had recently come through the worst storm of the decade.

William opened the door and asked us to follow him. Funny, I thought, William kind of grows on a person. Each time I saw him he was less frightening and more endearing. He showed us into the library where Harriet's beautiful tea service waited with a variety of sandwiches and cookies. "Madam will be with you in a moment," he said as he went out, closing the door behind him.

The odor of a multitude of different flowers lured me to the

French doors. As I expected, the garden was in beautiful shape. It must have taken many workers to make it this picture perfect so soon after the storm, I thought. I had turned to call Art over to see the view as Harriet walked into the room. She was gorgeous in a form fitting jumpsuit of creamy velvet with a wide crimson belt. Her crimson shoes matched the color of the belt exactly. Wouldn't you know that the first thing that popped into my head was of Dorothy in the Wizard of Oz and her crimson shoes, followed by the silly thought: I wonder what would happen if Harriet clicked her heels together. I stepped forward to meet Harriet as she came to give me a hug.

"Hello, Sandy, I'm so glad the storm is over and you two could come and see me." Smiling she shook hands with Art. "Welcome, Chief Landow."

"Please call me Art," he informed her.

With a smile, she nodded acceptance. "And you will call me Harriet, as Sandy does. That is so much nicer than all that formal miss-mash, don't you think?"

"Indeed I do," Art replied.

While we were getting seated Harriet asked about some of the things that had happened to the town during the storm. While she poured tea, Art told her some of the same stories he had told us at breakfast ending with the story of Sadie. "Sandy adopted Sadie this morning or maybe it was Sadie who adopted Sandy. One can never be sure with dogs. She is beautiful . . . well trained and polite. In fact, she is waiting for us in the car."

"I would like to meet her when you leave," Harriet said. "I personally think it is a good idea for Sandy to have a dog on guard at the office. You never know what type of person she might meet next. I have taken the liberty to furnish you with a somewhat larger cup for your tea, Art. I know my husband hated those little cups."

"Thank you, I appreciate it," Art said gravely, as he picked up a cookie, ignoring the tiny sandwiches.

"I suppose you are wondering why I asked you here today, so let's get that out in the open and then we can sit and visit.

When Andrew . . . Doctor Morton, visited me last week I asked him to try to locate my sister Emily. Later, I realized I was asking a great deal of a person unfamiliar in tracing a missing person. That's when I decided to ask you two if you would take the case for me. Did Sandy tell you, Art, that she refused any compensation for finding out who murdered my husband?"

Art shook his head, looking at me like I was crazy.

"I didn't feel I could rightfully do so," I defended myself. "Harriet's case was solved because of the Fuller case."

"Well, that's true," Art said grudgingly. "I see your point."

"So," Harriet said brightly. "If I hire her to find Emily she can't refuse payment this time."

Oh, what a tangled web we weave, I thought. I wouldn't be able to accept payment this time either since I already knew where Emily was. I glanced at Art and knew he was thinking the same thing.

"I'll be glad to see if we can find her, Harriet. Why don't I talk to Doctor Morton to see if he has discovered anything that might help me," I said.

"Will the rate be the same? Two hundred a day and expenses?" Harriet asked.

"Yes, but let's wait a bit until I talk to Doctor Morton. He may have a line on where she is already," I finished lamely.

I could see Art smiling as he took a sip of his tea. He knew the pickle I was in.

With our business out of the way, we spent the afternoon being shown around the garden and the house. The house had four bedrooms, three baths, a library, formal dining room, a dream kitchen that I was sure Frances would die for, and a large sun room where, Harriet told us, she took most of her meals now that she was alone.

"I realize the house is too large for me, but I hate to give it up. Paul and I were so happy here. The house is full of wonderful memories."

The exact opposite of your sister, I thought. It seemed poetic justice to me that the daughter with the worst possible beginning turned out to be the happiest of the two.

We hated to have the afternoon end, but at six o'clock it seemed time for us to leave. Harriet walked out to the car with us to meet Sadie, who accepted her with the same grave handshake she had accepted all of her new family earlier that day.

"She is a beautiful dog. Perhaps I'll go to the Humane Society and see if I can find a friend there. Maybe an animal would keep the evenings from being so lonely," Harriet said, with a hint of tears in her eyes.

Art and I discussed Harriet's request on our way home. "There is no way I can charge her this time either since we already know where Emily is. I'm going to call Doctor Morton in the morning and see if we can't hurry the meeting of the two women," I said.

TWENTY-NINE

The next day, as it was Saturday, I called Doctor Morton at his home. In detail I went over Harriet's request to us the previous day. "I was wondering what you would think about having the two women meet today or tomorrow."

"Let me talk to Doctor Davidson, and make sure Mrs. Grant has been released from the hospital. I'll see what he thinks and I'll call you right back."

Within thirty minutes he called. "Doctor Davidson said Emily is "chomping at the bit," as he put it, to see Harriet. He even had to threaten to take her back to the hospital if she didn't calm down. He told me it is entirely up to me when they meet. If I think Harriet is ready for that much emotional stress, it is okay by him."

"And is she ready?" I held my breath.

"I think so," he said slowly. "She thinks a great deal of you, so I wonder if you could come with me to break the news to her."

Try to keep me away, I thought. "I'd be delighted," I said in a normal tone of voice. "What time?"

"How about right now? I'll call Harriet and tell her we would like to come over; that we have some news of Emily."

I hesitated for a moment. "Doctor, don't you think one of us should be with her when she gets that call?"

"Hum-m-m-m, you could be right. I'll call her and ask if I can come over. I won't mention you. When she sees both of us, I'm sure she'll know something is up."

"Okay, if you think that's best. I'll be there in twenty minutes."

Quickly, I told Frances what was going to take place. I called the station, but Art was in a meeting. I left a message for him to call Frances the minute the meeting was over, so she could fill him in. Grabbing my purse, I told Sadie to stay home with Frances and raced out to my car.

When I arrived, I found there had been a change in plans. "I was thinking that it might be best for you to go see Harriet by yourself. She likes and trust you. I believe the news will be easier to accept coming from you." Doctor Morton stood ill-at-ease, a hopeful look on his face.

"I—I . . . sure, why not. What would you think if I suggest we take a ride," I said slowly. "I could take her to South Point before even bringing up the subject of Emily. That way she won't have that much time to get nervous."

"I think that will be all right," he said thoughtfully. "I will go to Doctor Davidson's immediately, so I will be there when she meets Emily, but I'll stay out of sight until they actually do meet."

"Let me call her and see if she is in the mood to take a ride." When I got Harriet on the phone I talked about little everyday things, like I didn't have a care in the world. I told her I was thinking about taking a ride, and asked if she wanted to come with me. She thought that would be pleasant. "I'll pick you up in about fifteen minutes." It wasn't until I hung up that I realized how nervous I was. My forehead was wet with perspiration, and I could feel rivulets running down my back.

Doctor Morton escorted me to my car. Taking my hand in his, he said he felt this was the best way to tell Harriet about Emily. "Don't worry. You will do fine," he told me. He gave me Doctor Davidson's home address before driving off in his car.

Don't worry. Yeah, right, easy for you to say, I thought. I had time to go by and see Art before starting out on my adventure. I needed his impute on this crazy scheme, but when I arrived he was still in his meeting. Well, I thought, evidently I'm on my own. Squaring my shoulders, I got back in the car and headed for Harriet's.

She must have been watching for me because before I had time to get out of the car she was coming out the front door.

"What a nice idea, Sandy. I'm so glad you thought of me."

"I thought we might drive toward South Point, and see what the storm did to that area. Okay?"

"Of course. Anywhere you say is fine with me. Getting out of the house for awhile is wonderful."

I hope you still think so when the ride is over, I thought.

On the way to South Point we talked about Sadie, the Logger Company business, the price of grass seed, and how Ronald Miller was working out as the new president. Was I imagining it or was her voice warmer when she spoke of Miller? I asked her some pointed questions about him: age, martial status, ambitions. She told me he was her age, a widower, and seemed quite happy to continue as president of the company. Listening to her words and her tone of voice, I was sure Harriet thought more of him than she allowed herself to realize. It would be wonderful is she could find happiness again, I thought.

We were drawing near South Point and I knew the time had come to prepare her somewhat for the coming meeting. "I have done a little research to see if I could find Emily," I said in an offhand manner.

She became still. "And?"

"I believe there is a possibility she may having been living right here in South Point since Mr. Pritchard took her away from Myrtle Woods."

"Are you sure?"

"Fairly certain, but not positive. If you are up to it, I would appreciate it if we could stop and meet Mrs. Grant, although she doesn't wish to be called that any more. Her husband nearly killed her and she is still recuperating." I went on to tell her what Emily had gone through personally, plus the fact that her daughter and son were still missing. "Her name is Emily, so I'm hopeful that we have the right person, but I don't want to get your hopes up too high. Do you think you feel like meeting her?"

"Yes, of course. That poor lady. Even if she isn't my sister, she sounds like she could use a friend."

Yippee! I have her in the right frame of mind, I thought, as we pulled into the driveway.

The doctor answered the doorbell. I introduced them and explained that Harriet was looking for her sister whose name is Emily; that I thought there might be a possibility that his patient might be the correct person. I'll give him credit, he didn't even bat an eyelash.

"Won't you come in? Emily is in the sunroom. I'm sure she would enjoy having company," he said as he led us into a room flooded with sunlight from the high windows. Emily was lying on a white wicker settee dressed in a filmy, pale blue negligee. The light seemed to flow around her in a heavenly glow.

I stayed in front of Harriet as we stepped into the room. "Emily, I have a friend with me that was so sorry to hear about the problems your husband put you through. She thought maybe you could use a friend." With that I stepped to one side, so the sisters were face to face at long last.

For a few breathless seconds they stared at each other. "Emily?" Harriet said hesitantly.

"Harriet? Oh, Harriet, my darling sister. It is you, I know it," Emily exclaimed.

I think all of us felt our hearts stop as Harriet fell to the floor. Doctor Morton rushed forward and knelt beside her. "It's all right. She has only fainted. Everyone please be quiet while I bring her out of this. We will have to hope one of the other personalities hasn't taken over. She has been doing so well."

"Oh, Howard, what have we done?" Emily whispered.

"Sh-h-h-h, please," Doctor Morton begged.

We all stood like statutes while the doctor spoke softly and gently to Harriet.

"Harriet. Harriet, this is Doctor Morton. Can you hear me? When you regain consciousness you will be yourself. Don't listen to anyone else. Fight to be yourself, Harriet. I know you can do it. Emily is here, Harriet. Your beautiful sister is waiting to talk to you. You and she are together just as you had always hoped you would be. Harriet, can you hear me?"

We held our breath as Harriet's lashes fluttered and her eyes slowly opened. "Oh, doctor, did I make a spectacle of myself again?"

"No, Harriet, you did what I expected you to do when you saw your sister for the first time after all these years, you fainted. How are you feeling now?"

"I—I'm fine." Her eyes flew to Emily who had knelt beside her and had taken her hand. "Emily, is it really you?"

"Yes, dear," Emily said, her eyes bright with tears. "I'm so happy to have found you after all these years. You are so beautiful."

The two doctors helped their patients to their feet and left them hugging and kissing as if they would never get enough of each other.

I felt tears form in my own eyes. I noticed that Doctor Davidson's and Doctor Morton's eyes were wet as well. Taking both gentlemen by the arm, I stepped out into the hallway.

"Mission accomplished, I believe, so I don't think I'm needed here anymore. Doctor Morton, would you please see that Harriet gets home?"

"Of course. I congratulate you, Sandy. You handled that exactly right today. I hope we can work together again some time."

"I'd like that," I said.

The happiness I felt slowly dissolved on my way back to Myrtle Woods. I remembered Harriet speaking of Pritchard's threats if the two women ever tried to see each other. Was it possible in this day and age that there was still someone alive who would carry out Pritchard's commands? I drove directly to the precinct to see Art.

"You should have been there," I told Art. "Their happiness brought tears to everyone's eyes. They look so much alike there is no doubt they are sisters. But, Art, I'm concerned about Luther Pritchard's threats. Remember what Harriet told us would happen if she or her mother ever tried to find Emily?"

"Yes, I remember, honey, but I believe you can rest easy. I started procedures to check out that possibility immediately after Harriet shared her story with us. Through some contacts I have in Washington I believe the last person Pritchard could force to do something like that, Lew Fingers, died last April in Portland in an automobile accident. This guy had no relatives. In fact, he had been a recluse for years, with little contact with anyone except Alec Manning, Luther's attorney, who died shortly after Fingers. So I'm positive the ladies are completely free of any danger."

For a few minutes I could only stare. "What?" he asked.

"What makes you like you are?"

"What do you mean."

"It's as though all these people are your personal charge. As if it is your duty to protect and care for them all," I said in wonder.

"Yes, that's true. Sam Jones, the last chief of police said those exact words to me when I got elected. He said that's what being the chief is all about. I've tried to follow his philosophy," Art said gravely.

I could tell he meant every word. I moved to him to give him a kiss and I whispered in his ear, "Sweetheart, you are going to make a great father."

Darned if he didn't bush.

"Checking up on Fingers paid off for me in a big way," he said smugly.

"How?"

"Remember when we where discussing the hit and run accident that killed Ken Holdburg, Mrs. Brocall's attorney? When I was talking to the Portland police, they told me that Fingers had admitted killing a guy several years ago in a hit and run somewhere here in the valley, but he died before he could give them a city. One of their detectives had been spending countless hours going back over old flyers trying to find a connection. They were getting ready to call me when I called them. I pulled the case out of the archives and found that the coroner had listed finding red paint on Holdburg's clothes. I sent them the type of paint and they called me back a few minutes ago to tell me it matched the car. So I not only found there was no one left to bother the sisters, I also solved a case in the process."

"That's wonderful news, honey, both about the case and for

Harriet and Emily. Let's call and tell them, although I doubt they have even thought of those threats yet," I said.

"Let me call Doctor Davidson. He can tell the ladies when the time is right. Besides I want to feel like I had some part in this happy day," Art said, trying to look like his feelings had been hurt.

"Of course, you goose. You do that and I'll see you later for dinner." I practically danced to my car. What a great day it had turned out to be, I thought. I didn't know that the news waiting for me at home, would make it an even better day in the life of Sandy Shores, Private Investigator.

I was so engrossed in recalling everything that happened that afternoon that I didn't even notice the new car sitting in the driveway until I pulled in. Now who is that, I wondered as I started up the walk. Suddenly the front door flew open and this bundle of suntanned arms and legs threw itself at me. I couldn't help it, I couldn't keep my balance. Over we went on the grass, scaring my attacker into stillness.

Hi, Sandy, I'm home. I didn't hurt you, did I?

Tracy was home. I was so happy to see him that it wouldn't have mattered if I broken my good leg. Luckily, all I got out of the fall were skinned knuckles on the hand that held my crutch.

Hello, sweetheart, it's so good to see you. I didn't think you were ever coming home, I signed to him as he helped me up.

That was all he needed. Almost faster than I could follow he told me about going to Arizona to get his mama. The way he said "mama" with such pride made me realize immediately he was no longer my little boy. I felt my heart break a little, yet I was happy for him. He kept up a steady barrage of swiftly flying fingers telling me about visiting the Grand Canyon, Hoover Dam, and Lake Mead on their way home. He was telling me about renting a houseboat on Lake Mead as we walked through the house into the kitchen. Dale stood up to welcome me as Tracy went over to sit by Sadie. With his arm around my shoulders Dale turned to introduce me to a young woman sitting at the table.

"Sandy, I'd like you to meet my wife, Doreen."

I'm sure my mouth dropped open. Standing to greet me was a lovely young version of Emily.

"How do you do, Sandy? I've heard so much about you from Dale and Tracy. How can I ever thank you for taking care of Tracy while I was . . . away."

Her voice was Emily. If I had turned my back and either Doreen, Emily or Harriet had spoken, I wouldn't have been able to say which one it was.

"Hello, Doreen. I'm so glad to meet you. I can't get over how much you look like your mother." I nearly spilled the beans about her Aunt Harriet, but I caught myself in time.

"I know. Everyone tells me that. It's quite a compliment, I think."

"Yes, she is a lovely woman."

"Is she all right?" Doreen asked hesitantly.

"Yes, she is going to be fine. As Art told Dale when he called for updates, all she needs is plenty of rest and relaxation. Did Art tell Dale about her voice? You sound like her now or should I say she sounds like you?"

"Honestly? That's wonderful news," she said, her eyes shinning. "I know how much she hated the voice she had after the . . . uh . . . accident."

The way she hesitated made me aware that she knew exactly what had happened when they had to operate on Emily throat.

"Honey," she said, turning to Dale. "I want to go see her as soon as we can."

I was certain Emily couldn't stand much more excitement today, so I tried to deter her until tomorrow. "Right now she is staying at Doctor Davidson's house under a nurse's care. That was the only way the doctor would let her leave the hospital since her house burnt down during the storm."

"Oh, no," Doreen cried.

"It's just as well. She told me she hated that house and never wanted to return to it. I'll let her tell you all about it. I do suggest that you call Doctor Davidson before you go over to South Point.

That would give him a chance to prepare her for the visit. She doesn't know that we found you yet," I said, taking Doreen's hand in mine.

"I see. I'm sure you're right, but I'm so anxious to see her," Doreen said.

Dale spoke up quickly. "Why don't we call Doctor Davidson right away? Maybe you can even speak to your mother."

"Could we do that?" Doreen asked me.

Of course, I told her, and giving her Doctor Davidson's number, I took her in the front room so she would have some privacy. Only a few minutes had passed when Doreen came back into the kitchen.

"We can visit mother at ten o'clock in the morning. I'm glad she is staying with Doctor Davidson. He has always taken good care of her. She is sleeping right now, but he told me he will break the news to her this evening during dinner. He told me he wouldn't be surprised if she insists on calling us then. Oh, I can hardly wait to see her," Doreen smiled. Turning to Tracy, she told him what she had said to us. She had a way to go before she would be up to speed in signing, but that didn't seem to matter to Tracy and Dale. I could tell they were both proud of her.

"Now, tell me all about your trip," I said to Dale. "Tracy was giving me some clues such as Grand Canyon, Hoover Dam, and Lake Mead?"

For the next two hours we discussed Rotten Apple Ranch, Doreen learning sign language, all the sights they stopped to see on their way home. Doreen was signing to Tracy all during our conversation.

She caught me watching her. "I like to do this. It keeps Tracy informed on what is going on, and it gives me lots of practice."

"I think it's great. I can't believe you've been signing such a short time."

She blushed. "I had a good incentive," she said, with a loving look at Tracy.

We told them about the terrible storm, about losing the big tree out front, how Art had checked on their house and it seemed to have weathered the storm. I was longing to tell Doreen about Harriet being her aunt, but I knew it wasn't my place to do so. However, I did feel free to tell them that Harriet wanted to talk to them about Tracy being examined by the best doctors available.

"She has read quite a bit about how they're now able to insert a small hearing aid in the ear enabling many deaf children to hear. She is a nice woman, Dale," I said, as I saw his face begin to cloud up. "She told me she will never make a claim on Tracy, that she only wants to help him as much as possible. She wants to discuss college tuition when the time comes. May I suggest you not let your pride get in the way of accepting the help that could make a big difference in Tracy's life," I said gently.

"Yes, I think it would be a good idea to talk to her. Don't you, honey?" Doreen asked.

"Well, okay," Dale said grudgingly. I think if Doreen had asked him to go jump in the lake he would have done it. "But let's give ourselves a few days to get settled."

We had been so engrossed in talking that we hadn't even heard Art come in the house. His "Hello, everyone" made us all jump. Now that he was here, the Fullers had to tell the story of their trip all over again. We could tell Tracy was glad to see him because he jumped up from petting Sadie and went over to give Art a big hug. I could see that Sadie had made another conquest. Tracy was never far from her side. If I wasn't careful she would soon become the most spoiled dog in town.

When we were at the office she immediately took over as guard. She automatically seemed to know what was expected of her. She would lie close to the wall near the front door, so that when the door was opened it hid her. I wanted to put her sleeping pad near my desk, but she wouldn't have it. If I didn't put the pad near the door she would insist on sleeping there on the floor. Finally I acknowledged defeat and acquiesced to her preference. I didn't want her to get used to going with me everywhere, so I started leaving her home if I was going out on an errand. When she was left at home, she followed Frances from room to room or napped on the rug by my bed.

THIRTY

Sunday was a do-nothing day. I knew I needed it, and I was sure everyone else did also. After church Art and I went over to spend the day with Marie and Roger.

In all the excitement of the past few days I had forgotten all about Tracy's friend, Matthew, so it surprised me when he opened the door in answer to our knock.

"Good afternoon. It's nice to see both of you again. Won't you come in? Marie is in the kitchen and Roger is out on the deck."

I had forgotten was his adult way of speaking. It tickled me and I could see the laughter hiding in Art's eyes.

"Hello, Matthew. It's nice to see you again," I said, as I gave him a hug. Art, knowing how grownup he liked to be treated, shook hands. Those two headed for the deck, while I made my way to the kitchen. Marie and Roger's place is a wonderful mix of antique and modern. The house from the outside had an old-fashion look, but several skylights brought light into every room. To walk into the kitchen was like walking into the kitchen of tomorrow. Every modern gadget available could be found hiding in totally unexpected places. The whole back wall was glass with French doors opening out to the deck in both the kitchen and the dining room. There were few flowers or shrubs in the front lawn, but every kind of flower and bush could be found in the backyard. A riot of color greeted my eyes when I entered the kitchen. I loved this room. I don't know how many times I had wished I could do a glass wall in my place, but when Dan Corbett, the builder, had checked it out he decided he couldn't do it because the back wall of my house wasn't strong enough.

"Hi, sweetie," I called out, coming through the swinging door. "What's happening?"

"Not much," Marie answered. "I'm putting some steaks in to marinate for dinner later. Roger wants to showoff at the grill tonight."

"Sounds good to me," I told her.

I sat on a stool watching her work. There is no wasted motion when Marie cooks. I had often wished I was even half as good a cook as she is, but now that I had Frances I no longer thought about it.

"When I finish here, let's go upstairs. I got the wedding dress back yesterday and I want to show you the dress I bought. There are a few other things I'd like to use in the wedding that I want your okay on."

"How did the dress come out? It didn't fall apart from age when they cleaned it?"

"No," Marie laughed. "If anything, it is more beautiful than before."

I was glad to hear that. I had been having a recurring dream that the dress went to shreds when it was cleaned, we couldn't find another, and I had to be married in my bathing suit because Art wouldn't delay the wedding even one day. Me and my imagination!

Marie put a couple of dishes in the refrigerator, called out to Roger that she was taking me upstairs, and that no men were allowed. Roger's and Art's comments followed us up the stairs.

She was right. My dress was lovely. Over the years the satin had turned a creamy color that couldn't be duplicated. Of course, I had to try it on again. We spent some time deciding how I should wear my hair. I would have been happy wearing it like I always do, but Marie wouldn't hear of it. A special day needed a special hairdo, she told me. She brought out the dress she wanted to wear. It was perfect. It would bring all the garden flowers down to the dock. The off-the-shoulder design would show off her beautiful tan. The other things she had to discuss were napkins with our names and the date on them and tiny champagne glasses to hold mints and nuts at each place serving.

"Since it is a brunch, we—Frances and I—thought we would have fruit platters, scrambled and eggs Benedict, baked ham, roast beef, waffles, muffins, punch and champagne. And the wedding cake, of course. What do you think?"

"Good gosh, Marie. How can the two of you do all that? Who will be in charge of making the waffles? How are you going to keep everything warm?" As usual I was full of questions.

"That's all taken care of," she told me blithely. "We are renting the warming tables from a place in Mountain View; Roger will take care of the waffles; Keith Drumm will cut the ham and beef, and his wife, Louise, will be in charge of the serving up the eggs Benedict. All Frances and I have to do is see that the warming trays are kept full."

"Oh, that's all," I said sarcastically. "Marie, honey, all that is too much. You and Frances will be exhausted. I wanted a simple little buffet. I wanted everyone to be free to mingle and enjoy the party."

"No, it sounds like a lot more work than it will be. If it makes you feel any better, the evening before the wedding you can help get the fruit on the trays and put the ham on the biscuits for the eggs Benedict. We will have to keep you busy because you can't see Art that night. Roger and Keith are giving him a bachelor party, while Louise comes over and helps us."

"They are?" I exclaimed. "What fun. Well, okay, if I can help put things together I guess it will be all right to have this elaborate shin-dig."

"Where are you two going on your honeymoon,"

"I don't have the slightest idea. Art is making all the arrangements. I told him to surprise me. For myself, I would like to rent a cabin up in the woods, but I realized that wouldn't be fair to Art."

"In what way?" Marie asked

"I have done so much traveling during my days with the CIA that I'd be happy if I never saw the inside of another plane. The only traveling Art has done was when he was in the army, so he may want to go some place exotic, like Bora Bora."

We were both laughing as we came downstairs to join the guys on the deck. Roger offered us a cold beer, but both of us joined Matthew in drinking pop.

"Tracy and his family are going to pick up Matthew on their way back from seeing Doreen's mother," Roger said. "You have missed him a great deal, haven't you, Matthew?"

"Yes, sir. He has informed me that he purchased a gift for me at the Grand Canyon, and also that his father bought a new car, so I am most anxious to see them."

Art and I were in the process of telling them about Doreen's mother, and some of the hardships she had experienced lately, when the doorbell rang.

"I'll get it," Matthew yelled, already halfway to the door. Now that sounded like a real little boy, I thought. It was the first time I had ever seen him act or speak naturally.

It didn't last, however. Within seconds he was back with Tracy, telling everyone goodbye in his grown up voice. He shook hands with Art and me, told Roger and Marie he would be back in time for dinner at seven as they had previously agreed. The thought crossed my mind: if he talks like that now what will he be like at forty or fifty? I could only wonder.

We all waved to Tracy and I told him *"Have a good time."* They were a strange pair as they ran out to the car. One all boy and the other already a pompous middle-aged man. What would it take to change Matthew—to help him realize it is possible to be serious and still have fun? A miracle, I decided.

Marie turned to me, eyes shinning. "Isn't Matthew something? Roger and I wanted you two to be the first to know that we are thinking of adopting him."

For the next few minutes it was complete bedlam—all of us talking at once.

"When did you decide?" I asked.

"It's only been in the last few days," Roger answered. "I knew I had grown to love him, but I wasn't sure how Marie felt about it. When we finally got up nerve enough to broach the subject to each other, we found out that each of us was afraid to ask the other about it. I think we talked through the night. The next day at work I was exhausted."

"To me, too," Marie said, sitting in the circle of Roger's arm. "I didn't think the day would ever end."

"What does Matthew say about it?" Art asked.

"That's the problem," Roger said, seriously. "We haven't said anything to him because we want Sandy to do a little checking for us." Turning to me, he asked, "Would you be willing to go up to the convent and talk to the nuns for us? We need to know if there is any way to find his birth mother. We both think the nuns would speak more freely to a private investigator than they would to us. We wouldn't want to go ahead with the adoption, and then have someone suddenly appear and claim him as their own. I don't think either of us could stand that after what happened to Adam." For a moment his face had a haggard look, as he drew Marie close and kissed the top of her head.

Tears were choking me as I told them I would be happy to do what they asked. "I'm wondering if it might be a good idea for you to come with me, Marie. No," I said quickly, "not on that first visit. Better I find out what I can. If it looks promising I'm sure the nuns will want to meet you both."

"You don't have to do this until after the wedding, sweetie," Marie spoke up.

"Not to worry. I'll run up there tomorrow. After the wedding is the honeymoon, and then the possible operation on my foot. The trip to the convent is too important to put off until all that is done."

"No use in arguing," Art held up his hand as Roger started to speak. "You should know by now how she is once she is given a problem."

"Hey, watch the way you talk," I kidded him. "And speaking of problems, have you decided who is going to be your best man?"

"I have finally decided to have Ed and Billy Ray draw straws. I can't decide between the two after what we all went through at the Grant house. Too bad I can't have two best men."

"No, Art," Marie spoke up. "That would throw off the whole

symmetry of the wedding party." She gave him a smile to offset the curt words.

"I know," Art said. "I'll decide soon."

"There has to be time for them to get their tuxedos adjusted," Marie prodded him.

"Okay, now." I could tell that no matter what she said, the stress of pulling the wedding together was getting to Marie. "Enough about weddings. Let's talk about something else."

The rest of the afternoon was spent in lazy appreciation of good friends, good weather, and the anticipation of good food yet to come.

When Matthew arrived back for dinner, I could see a difference in the way Marie acted around him that I hadn't noticed earlier. The mother in her kept coming up and Matthew seemed to react to her with pleasure.

That evening I called Dale to find out how long it took to get to the convent. Of course, he was curious, so I filled him in about Marie and Roger. I asked him not to say anything to Tracy until after my investigation. We didn't want anyone other than Marie and Roger disappointed. Dale agreed and gave me the phone number and the name of the Mother Superior.

Monday morning I called to make an appointment at the convent. The woman who answered had the softest voice I think I had ever heard. She told me if I could be there at one o'clock the Mother Superior would be pleased to see me. Since it would take me over an hour to reach my destination, I decided to eat an early lunch at eleven before taking off for the mountains.

It wasn't fifteen minutes later that the phone rang. Somehow or another I had a premonition as I picked up the receiver. "Hello."

"Hi, Sandy. It's Doctor O'Conner."

"Well, hi, friend. How did your paper go over?"

"Not as well as I had hoped. There are still a lot of skeptics out there. Most of the old guard doesn't believe it possible for a body part to grow its own cells. Maybe someday they will realize it can be done. But enough about me. I called to tell you I've gone over your x-rays and information I received from the hospital in DC, and I believe there is plenty of bone left in both the leg and the foot to make my approach possible. When it comes to your toes, we may have to put in metal toe joints, but I will know more about that when I see the new x-rays I've asked Bert to take. If you could find time to go to his office and get those taken before your wedding I would appreciate it. After studying those I'll know definitely what I'm going to do, and will be able to share that with you when you return from your honeymoon."

"That sounds great to me. I'll get that done right away. Then what? Do I call you when Art and I get back?"

"Yes, please. I would like to do this as soon as possible."

"And I would like it done as soon as possible, too. Thanks so much, doctor. I appreciate the call."

As I hung up I realized I was looking forward to this operation with a feeling of excitement and dread. Absentmindedly, I stroked Sadie as she leaned against me. She seemed to sense whenever I was troubled. I had told the doctor I wanted it done, so I knew there was no turning back now. I squared my shoulders and went in to tell Frances the news. But first I called Doctor Johnson's office, and made an appointment to have the x-rays taken. I didn't call Art. I wanted to wait until tonight when I could see him face to face to get his immediate reaction.

Sadie and I started to the convent at eleven-thirty. I was glad I had given myself extra time. It was a beautiful drive, breathtaking scenery appeared around every bend. Several times I pulled off of the road, and gave myself time to breathe deeply of the delicious mountain air. Sadie, too, was enjoying the trip. She stood with her feet on the arm rest, her head out the window. The few times I stopped she sat quietly in the passenger seat as if she too was enjoying the scenery.

However, I kept reminding myself that I was a working girl, so at one o'clock sharp I raised the heavy knocker on the front door of the convent. The building was massive. That's the only way to explain it. Huge stones had been used to construct the walls of the three story structure. Most of the windows on the first floor were thick leaded glass, while many of the second and third floors windows were stained glass. There must have been a multitude of fireplaces for I had noticed chimneys poking up all over the roof. The front door must have been a foot thick for I couldn't hear a sound coming from within. I turned to look at the grounds that surrounded the convent. They were immaculate. Beautiful green lawn seemed to stretch forever. Flower beds were overflowing with flowers. With the sun shining on it, it was a beautiful place. However, I could well imagine how it would repulse a visitor in the winter under dark clouds spitting snow.

I was so lost in my daydream that I jumped a foot when a voice behind me asked if they could be of help. Gathering my wits about me, I told a tiny round woman in a nun's habit who I was, and that I had an appointment at one.

"Yes. We have been expecting you. Would you please follow me?" she asked. She pushed the big door shut with hardly a sound. No wonder I didn't hear her open it, I thought. I glanced around as she led me down a long corridor. There were a few pictures of Jesus, but other than a full size statute of Him at the end of the corridor the prevailing mood was austere. I had expected that, but I hadn't expected the silence. I understood from Dale that there were close to twenty-five nuns who lived there full time, so where were they?

My guide must have sensed my discomfort for she said softly, "This is the prayer and meditation time. Each of our sisters is in her own room. That's why it is so quiet."

Could she read minds I wondered, as we reached our destination. A quiet rap on the door was answered by "Come in." My guide opened the door and preceded me into the room.

"Miss. Shores, Mother," she announced. As the Mother Superior and I were shaking hands, the tiny woman went out, shutting the door behind her with, once again, a whisper of sound.

"Please make yourself comfortable, Miss Shores. Would you care for a cup of tea?"

"That would be lovely," I told her.

She pulled twice on a cord that hung from the ceiling, then returned to her seat. "Why is it that you have come to see us, my dear."

I was beginning to understand why Matthew spoke as he did. If he had been in this mausoleum all his life, he knew of no other way to act. The children who came to school here were all deaf and unable to speak, so he couldn't learn any other way from them. Poor little monkey, I thought, he's never had a childhood.

"I am a private investigator. I have been asked to find out about Matthew Smith and to see if there is a possibility that someone could adopt him."

She became completely still. For a few moments she was a statue before she blinked. With a slight shake of her head, she said, "My prayers have been answered."

I knew that she realized I wanted the whole story, so I kept quiet to give her time to tell me in her own way.

"It was ten . . . no, closer to eleven years ago when Matthew was found on the doorstep by one of our novices. She was locking up for the night when she heard a noise out on the front steps. When she opened the door there was this tiny, bloody baby. He couldn't have been more than a few hours old."

The tea came then so she paused to pour each of us a cup. While she was pouring, the thought came to me: wait one minute! This novice heard a noise out on the step? There is no way a newborn's cry would come through that thick door. Something is haywire with this story already, but I kept my thought to myself as the Mother Superior continued.

"One of our sisters is a nurse so she came and cleaned him up, putting the necessary solution in his eyes; all the things they do. It is not my field of expertise, so I can't be more explicit," she apologized. She took a sip of her tea. "There was a type-written note tucked in his diaper. Would you like to see it?"

Does the Pope pray? You bet, I wanted to see the note. "Yes, certainly," I said primly.

She pulled out a drawer of her desk, withdrew a folder. She

started to hand it to me, but changed her mind. She searched through a few sheets of paper, took out the note and handed that to me. It was typed, which was no help. I certainly couldn't test every typewriter in all the western states, let alone those in Myrtle Woods, South Point and Mountain View.

The note read: "I am unable to care for my baby. If my parents ever found out about him I don't know what they would do to him or to me. I know he will be safe here with you. Please keep him, love him, and help him to grow into a fine man. Please, in the name of Mary, Mother of God, don't turn him over to the authorities. His name is Matthew." There was no signature; no clues as to where I should begin looking after all this time.

"So, as we know, you did take him in. Did you try in anyway to find the mother?" I asked. My voice must have been harsher than I intended because for a moment her demeanor changed.

"Of course, we did. I called all the Catholic Churches in the surrounding area asking if they had a clue whose baby he could be. No one could help me. So I asked each Catholic Church to contact the other churches in their area. Again, nothing. I asked our Monsignor for advice. He felt from the way the note was worded that the mother might want him back some day and suggested we keep him. After a great deal of soul-searching and praying about it, the sisters voted to keep him in hopes that the mother would come back. The novice who found him asked to be put in charge of his care. So it was that Norma Sheridan, who later became Sister Norma Alice, actually brought him up."

"Would it be possible for me to talk to her?" I asked.

"Wait, please. Let me finish. Two years ago Sister Norma Alice came to me and asked that I hear her confession. She had gone to the doctor's that afternoon. He had informed her that she had only a few months to live, a year at the most. The cancer that had been raging in her body for years was too far advanced. There was nothing to be done." She stopped to wipe her eyes. "Sister Norma Alice was an outstanding nun, Miss. Shores. She was loved by everyone she met. A lot of her time was spent in the Catholic Church in Myrtle Woods. She spent hours polishing the altar, and, she told me, talking to God. It was with all this in mind that I was shocked, yes, extremely shocked, to hear her confession.

"When she was seventeen she got a part in a play being produced in South Point. One night after rehearsal, the older man in the play offered to take her home since it was raining. On the way, he pulled off the road into some trees and forced himself upon her. He told her if she ever told anyone he would deny it. It was two months later that she realized she was pregnant. I asked her why she didn't go to the man and tell him of her condition. She told me that he had left town shortly after he raped her; that as far as she knew he had never returned." Again she paused to take a sip of tea.

I sat there remembering Emily's story; how her husband left town shortly after the play he was in closed, supposedly to chase after an actress. Every bone in my body told me the rapist was Peter Grant. So, this is why he left. It wasn't to chase after an actress. He was afraid of being charged with raping a minor.

The Mother Superior continued. "What was Norma to do? Her religious parents would have disowned her, if they had found out. She was sure they would be convinced it was all her fault; that she enticed the man to have sex. So she convinced her parents that she wanted to become a nun. They were overjoyed, of course, and made arrangements for her to come to us. She began putting on more and more clothes every week so by the time she came to us we thought she was a plump young lady. As the baby grew she discarded clothing to keep her figure at the size we were accustom to seeing. The night the baby was born it truly was her night to lock up. As soon as possible she retired to her room, gave birth to Matthew, cleaned herself up, and bundled the baby in clothes she had brought with her. She brought the baby to me saying she found it on the front steps. I had no reason to doubt her." The Mother Superior stopped to wipe her eyes.

"She must have been petrified that you would send him to an orphanage," I said.

"Yes," the nun smiled. "She told me she spent every spare minute in the chapel asking God to lead us in our decision. After hearing her confession, I absolved her completely. To watch her son grow into a fine young boy, considerate, loving, faithful, and not to be able to tell him she was his mother was punishment enough. I don't believe I've ever felt such compassion for another person as I did for her that day. After she gave me her confession she gave me several items to hold with the note that I had kept all those years. These additional items were to be given to any couple that might want to adopt Matthew, she informed me."

She reached into the folder and handed me a birth certificate with Norma's maiden name listed as mother. The father's name was blank. The second item was a picture of Norma when she graduated from high school. What a pretty young woman; Matthew had many of her features. The third was a letter written to Matthew that was to be given to him if he should ever ask about his birth mother. The last was a document drawn up in an attorney's office stating that after Matthew reached ten years of age, the Mother Superior of the Holy Mountain Top Convent would be allowed to sign the adoption papers in place of the birth mother should a loving couple ever wish to adopt him. The form stated that the birth mother wished the couple to be religious, believing in God and followers of his word, but the denomination did not have to be Catholic.

"Do the people who wish to have Matthew meet these requirements?" she asked.

"Yes, they do," I said. "They own the drugstore in Myrtle Woods . . ."

"Do you mean Marie and Roger Owens?"

"Why, yes."

"How odd. They are well known to many of our Sisters. The last year of her life Sister Norma Alice got all of her medicine from them. God works in strange ways, doesn't He?"

"Amen to that, Mother, amen." It nearly took my breath away the way everything was coming together. It looked like another life Peter Grant had ruined was going to have a happy ending.

I told the Mother Superior that I would have Marie and Roger call for an appointment after they had talked to Matthew. "They don't want to do this unless it is something that he wants as well.

I can't imagine him not wanting to, but I've given up trying to figure out human nature."

She walked me to my car. "Isn't this the most glorious day," she said. It was a statement not a question, and I had to agree. It was indeed the most glorious day I had seen in weeks. I introduced Sadie and she gravely shook hands with the Mother Superior. As usual when Sadie met someone new she received another compliment on her beauty. She accepted the kind words with her usual aplomb.

I'm afraid I didn't take much notice of the scenery as I drove back down the mountain. Getting back to Marie and Roger was of prime importance, and I didn't want to waste a second. However, on the way down I got to thinking. If Matthew was indeed Peter Grant's son that made him Emily's stepson, Harriet's nephew, Doreen's half-brother, and Tracy's uncle. What was I to do? I didn't dare bring this out into the open, in case I was wrong and Peter wasn't the father. But what if he was? I realized I needed Art's opinion.

As luck would have it he was pulling back into the parking lot as we drove in. As soon as I saw his face I knew something was wrong. There had been a bad accident, he told me. He had been out to tell the parents of a sixteen year old boy that their son was dead. A loaded log truck had lost its brakes and couldn't stop at the stop sign. It had taken the paramedics two hours to pry the boy's car loose from under the truck. If that wasn't bad enough, it had been the boy's first solo drive after getting his license.

"I was with the emergency crew the night we took Kitty Graham to the hospital to have Howie. I watched him grow up. Coached his baseball team. He was a wonderful kid. So much potential, and now this."

I took him into my arms, holding him tight while he cried like a baby. Once again I realized the people in this town were not only people who needed his expertise to keep them safe, they were his family. When something bad happened to one of them it happened to Art also.

I knew this was not the time to bring up my news. That could wait. Right now Art needed me. Nothing else mattered.

THIRTY-ONE

It wasn't until Art came over for dinner that my trip to the convent came into the conversation. I started at the beginning and told them the whole story.

"On my way back to town I began to think what relationship that would make Matthew to Emily, Harriet, Doreen and Tracy."

"I think I've got it," Art said. "Stepson to Emily Grant, nephew to Harriet Logger, half-brother to Doreen, and uncle to Tracy. What a mess."

"I have no proof that Peter was the father, except that timewise everything fits perfectly," I said, as I rubbed my forehead. "I'm in a dilemma. Do I tell Emily my suspicions? Do I tell Marie and Roger of Matthew's possible lineage? I feel like a little mouse running around in a maze. My personal opinion is that I get Emily, Harriet, Marie and Roger together and tell them the details. After that they can decide what to do."

"May I make a suggestion, my love?" Art asked.

"Of course. You know I value your opinion."

He smiled. "Why don't you go see Emily first, alone. Explain the situation and see what she thinks. See if she is as convinced as you that Peter was the father. Better yet, talk to both Emily and Harriet. Tell them about Marie and Roger's loss of their son; stress what great people they are. If neither of those ladies thinks it necessary to object to the adoption I don't think you need to take it any further. Sister Norma Alice may have explained everything in the letter she left for Matthew. If she does name Peter, then the truth can come out. It will most likely be several years, if ever, before Matthew has any questions."

"As usual, my darling, you are right. I'll call Emily right now and make an appointment for tomorrow, if possible. I will be so glad to get this settled. I'm praying that Marie and Roger will be happy with the outcome."

We were all enjoying Frances' wonderful apple crunch pie when the conversation turned to the accident that took the life of Howie Graham. It was the first that Frances and Al had heard about it. Both of them were as devastated as Art. They had cared for Howie off and on from the time he was born until he had started nursery school.

"Do you know when the funeral will be?" Frances sniffed.

"No, I'll know that tomorrow. I would imagine it will be Friday or Saturday. I'm sorry, love," Art said, turning to me, "that it will be so close to the wedding."

"I'm sorry it had to happen at all, but no matter what day it is, we will attend," I assured him.

"Oh, honey, you are going to be so busy. You don't need to come."

"Of course, I do," I said firmly. "I wouldn't think of letting you go alone."

"Thank you," he said, squeezing my hand. "It will be easier for me with you there."

How I love this man, I thought for the thousandth time.

"I have something else to tell you, honey," I said, still holding his hand.

"Oh? Now what?"

I went on to tell them of Doctor O'Conner's call. I watched as several emotions flitted across Art's face; surprise, sadness, disbelief.

"That's great, honey, just great," he said quietly, when I finished.

"But?" I inquired.

"But what."

"There is something you aren't saying. What is it?"

"It's nothing, sweetheart, nothing,"

"Don't do this to me, Art," I implored him. "If there is something, I need to know it now."

"Well, okay. I was talking to a friend of mine at Walter Reed Hospital in Washington, DC, and he was saying that the operation you are going to have is still experimental. That the chances of full recovery, in his estimation, are zero to none. I asked him if he had ever heard of Doctor O'Conner and he had. He agreed that the three operations that Doctor O'Conner has done have been successful, but none of them have been of the magnitude that he will attempt on your leg. I didn't know whether to tell you or not, since you seem determined to go ahead with it anyway."

I sat quietly for a moment. "Yes, I am determined to go ahead. The worst that can happen is that I will lose my leg. Now that I am positive I want to get rid of this crutch, the chance that I might be able to save my leg seems like a miracle to me. I think God told me not to take that desk job in DC, but to come home, so I would be here in this place, at this time. I think He is using me to prove Doctor O'Conner's theory to the world. When I come out healed as good as new, think how many others his futuristic approach will help."

"Then I'm with you all the way, darling," Art said. "You'll hear no more doubts from me. Actually, I think you are exceedingly brave. I don't know that I could do it."

I told him to hush up. There was no doubt in my mind that he would have the operation in a second if he were in my shoes.

Sadie, as if she knew Art was sad, came and sat beside him all evening, her head on his knee most of the time. I noticed that whenever Art talked about the funeral or my operation, his hand automatically caressed her soft head. I was beginning to think I should change her name to Doctor Sadie.

When I called Emily later that evening, she said she would be happy to see me the next day. They had let the nurse go because Harriet was staying with them to care for Emily. Good, I thought, I won't have to repeat myself.

I hung up with Emily's heartfelt thanks for finding Doreen ringing in my ears. Next, I made the hardest call of all. I told Marie and Roger that it would be a day or two before I would have any news for them because the Mother Superior had a couple of things she had to check. They both said, yes, they understood. Personally, I felt like a dirty rat.

The next day when I was ushered into the room and sat down opposite Emily and Harriet, my knees were shaking and my hands were sweaty. For a moment I wished I had Sadie beside me. So much depended on decisions that would be made in the next few hours.

I couldn't believe the difference in Harriet. She was radiant. It was like . . . like she was a flower bulb that had been lying forgotten in the back reaches of a flower shed, then one day she was planted. Before long, with tender care, she arose out of the dirt, and stood there in all her glory. That's probably way over done, but when you think of Harriet you think of her beautiful garden, and . . . oh, never mind.

After all of us were seated, I told them that I had an incredible story to tell them. When I came in Harriet had searched my face. Whatever she saw there must have told her this may not be news that Emily would want to hear. She moved her chair closer to Emily and reached for her hand.

"There is a fine young boy visiting in Myrtle Woods who has lived at the Holy Mountain Top Convent for the past eleven years," I began. Both women exchanged questioning looks. "This young fellow was born as the result of a rape involving a young woman here in South Point. I think, Emily, the rapist was your husband, Peter."

"Oh, no!" Emily was greatly shocked. "How—when did it happen?"

"Remember when you told Art and me about Peter leaving town right after one of his plays closed?"

"Yes. Oh, so I was right. I knew it had to be something more than Irene leaving."

"Yes. We think he was afraid of being charged with raping a

minor, even though he had threatened the young woman to keep her mouth shut. She was only seventeen."

"That bastard," Emily exclaimed.

"So the little boy from the convent is that baby?" Harriet asked.

"Yes, we think so, but let me tell you the whole story."

I told them Sister Norma Alice's story from beginning to end. Then I told them about Marie and Roger and the loss of Adam.

"You may have figured it out already, but Matthew may be your stepson, Emily, and your nephew, Harriet, making him Doreen's half-brother and Tracy's uncle. However, as Art pointed out, it's only a hunch on my part that Peter is the father. If Matthew does get curious and reads the letter from his mother, it may not even mention the father's name. In that case I may have made things more complicated than they need to be. To further complicate things, Tracy and Matthew are best friends."

"Is Matthew deaf also," Harriet asked.

"Oh, no. I'm sorry. I should have told you. He is normal in every way except in the way he speaks."

Their eyebrows went up in question.

"He has heard nothing but adult language all his life, so he speaks as if he is thirty years old. And he is so serious. He needs to learn how to be a little boy."

"I'm sure that Harriet and I would like to discuss this latest development. Why don't I call you in a day or two?" Emily said.

"That would be fine," I lied. No, no, no my heart said. Tell me that Marie can have Matthew right now. Of course, I didn't say that, but oh, how I wanted to blurt it out.

"I think what we all need is a cup of tea," Emily said.

"Let me get it, sister. It will only take a few minutes," Harriet smiled at me as she left the room.

"Don't you think Harriet looks good?" Emily asked. "We will never be able to thank you for your part in bringing us together."

"It was my pleasure, Emily. I'm so happy the way things turned out for you two.

"Yes, it was a miracle. Please give Chief Landow our thanks

for checking out our father's threats. It is wonderful to be free to enjoy each other after being apart for so many, many years." She was silent for a moment. "Howard told me a few days ago that my son, Jasper, was accidentally killed. Do you know anything about that, and if so, could you tell me?"

"Yes, of course, if you think you are up to it. Perhaps we should wait until Harriet gets back, so I'll only have to tell the story once."

She agreed, and went on to ask me how things were going for the wedding, so I informed her about Marie's plans for the buffet.

"She must love you very much," Emily stated.

"Yes. She has been my best friend since grade school. She is a wonderful woman. You would like her, I'm sure."

Harriet came in carrying the beautiful tea service that I had seen at her house. When I praised it, they informed me that it had been in their family for over four hundred years. It was one of the treasures their family had brought over on the Mayflower. Needless to say, I was impressed.

"Harriet, dear, I've asked Sandy to tell me what happened to Jasper."

"Emily, do you think that is wise?" Harriet gasped.

"Yes. It's driving me crazy not knowing. Please, Sandy, tell us."

I was at a loss where to start, so I went clear back to the day that the boys and I took our picnic lunch to the lake. I told them about finding the bones in the forest, but I left out the part about thinking they were Doreen's. I continued with a watered-down version of what Peter Grant did to me in the forest, and the conversation we had during that time.

"Emily, I truly believe that Jasper's death was an accident. I could tell from the way he talked that Peter did love him. When they got in a struggle over the gun Jasper had taken from Harriet's house, the gun went off and killed him instantly. Art sent for dental records from Phoenix to verify that it was Jasper who was killed. Those have arrived and they do match."

Emily was weeping softly into her handkerchief. "Another

life ruined by that monster. I . . . I know I shouldn't say this, but I'm glad, yes, glad that Peter is dead. He can't hurt anyone again." She put her head on Harriet's shoulder and sobbed.

"Jasper's remains are at the funeral home in Myrtle Point, and will be held there until such time as you feel strong enough to decide what you want to have done," I told her after she regained control of her emotions.

"We . . . we will have a funeral, of course. I guess there is no rush, is there?"

"No, ma'am. No rush. I can't tell you how sorry I am."

"Thank you, Sandy. I appreciate your telling me what happened. It means so much to me to know he didn't suffer." She sat up and wiped her eyes once again.

"Here, let me fill your cup, Sandy," Harriet said.

Heck, I'd forgotten all about the tea. As she leaned over to fill my cup I noticed she was wearing the necklace that Peter had taken off Paul J. "I see you are wearing the family necklace."

"Yes, Emily insisted on returning it to me. We have decided we will have a duplicate made for her. Don't tell anyone, but she is going to present hers to Howard when they marry. If I should marry again, which I highly doubt, I will give this one to my new husband."

"Don't be too quick to deny you will ever marry again," Emily told her, with a twinkle in her eye. I definitely had the feeling Harriet had been talking about Ron Miller more than she realized.

While we drank our tea we talked women stuff: weddings, clothes, and living arrangements. Emily told me that she and Doctor Davidson had decided to get married on September 30 in Harriet's garden. They were giving some thought to moving to Myrtle Woods, so the two women could be nearer each other.

"You and Chief Landow will be able to attend our wedding, won't you" Emily said.

"I'm not sure. I may have my leg operated on," I said. That brought all kinds of questions, so I had to tell them all about Doctor O'Conner's new technique. Before I knew it, it was five o'clock.

When I rose to leave, Harriet stopped me. "How much do I owe you, dear girl, for finding Emily so quickly."

"Nothing," I said and then laughed at the expressions on their faces. "You see, we were fairly certain we had the right person before you ever asked me to look for her. So it is the same situation as it was with Paul. The case the police had asked me to help them on was the one that solved both cases you asked me to take, Harriet. I would be remiss in my duties if I accepted fees from two different sources for the same solution. Besides, it gave me so much pleasure bringing you two together that I would have done it for nothing."

"I told Emily that is what you would say, so we want to give you and your young man a little wedding present. And may I say it gives us great pleasure to give this gift to you both," Harriet said.

She handed me a small beautifully wrapped box. "Thank you both so much. I'll put it with the rest of the gifts that are beginning to arrive. We plan on opening everything at the reception. You both will be there, won't you?"

"Wouldn't miss it," they said in unison.

That night at dinner I told Art about informing Emily of how Jasper died.

"Poor little sweetheart," he said, pulling me close. "You've had a lot of emotional ups and downs the last few days, haven't you?"

"How true. I wish they could all be ups, but without the downs I wouldn't appreciate the ups, I guess."

"Now that is a profound statement," he said, teasing me. The little tussle that followed ended in a long, sweet kiss. Definitely one of my ups for the day.

I was glad I had Sue and Jake's arrival to look forward to or I'm afraid the next day would have been interminable. Sue had called from Denver to say they had some car trouble, but they still expected to arrive sometime late Wednesday night. They had offered to hole up somewhere and come in early Thursday morning, but I wouldn't hear of it.

All day Wednesday I kept busy cleaning the guest bedrooms,

polishing everything in sight to a shiny luster, putting on clean bedding on the twin beds in the bedroom the kids would use. Even though Frances kept the bathrooms shining, I cleaned them again for good measure. When I finished, Frances kept Sadie and me running back and forth to the store. I had never known her to forget half of what she needed. We arrived back from our second trip as she was hanging up the phone.

"Wait, Miss. Hello . . . hello. Oh, darn," she said. "It was a lady from Washington trying to reach you. I was hoping I could catch her, but she hung up."

"Did she leave a message or a number?"

"Nothing. She said she would call back."

"Was she calling from the state of Washington or Washington, DC?"

"I don't know, dear. She didn't say, and I never thought to ask. I'm sorry."

"No problem. It must not be important or she would have left a message."

When we arrived back from our fourth trip to the store, Frances informed me the same lady had called back. She still wouldn't leave a message or a phone number where I could reach her. How strange, I thought to myself.

It must have been about four-thirty when the phone rang. My stomach lurched as I ran to answer. "Hello?"

"Hi, lovely lady. Is your husband around?" Art asked in a deep voice.

"You must have me confused with someone else. I'm not married," I answered, my voice all fluttery.

"I say, that's good news. I've still got a chance then, right?"

"Only if you work fast. I'm getting married on Sunday."

"Well, then I better get crackin'. If I come right over could we sit in the swing on the porch and pitch a little woo?"

"Humm, sounds delicious to me."

"I'm on my way." He didn't even say goodbye.

I hardly had time to run a comb through my hair and change my shirt before he pulled into the driveway.

"What's your big hurry, handsome?" I asked him, leaning seductively against the porch railing.

For an answer he drew me into his arms and gave me a long kiss. When we came up for air he said, "I haven't had enough of those lately."

"Me, neither," I whispered, as he drew me close again. The porch swing welcomed us like an old friend, and the vines climbing the porch hid us from those passing by on the street. Sadie, who was never far from my side, flopped down at our feet.

Then wouldn't you know it, the phone rang. I knew Frances would answer it, but still my heart skipped a beat. Would it be Emily or Harriet? When the screen door opened Art reluctantly released me from his embrace.

"Phone, Sandy. It's that lady from Washington calling," Frances said.

I took Art by the hand and walked in to take the call in the front room as Frances headed back to the kitchen. "Hello?"

"Miss. Shores?" I acknowledged that I was she. "Hold one moment, please. President Wilton wishes to speak to you."

I turned wide-eyes on Art. The President, I mouthed to him. My hand gripping the phone immediately became clammy. I could feel sweat forming on my forehead. I could feel myself getting tongue-tied and I hadn't even said anything.

"Is this Sandy Shores, formerly a member of the CIA?" asked the familiar voice of the President.

"This is Sandy Shores, yes sir." I motioned for Art to get on the phone in the den. "What can I do for you, Mr. President?"

"Has Jake Cummings arrived for the wedding?"

"No, sir." How did he know Jake was on his way, I wondered. For that matter, who told him about the wedding? Was I being spied on? I thought I'd left all that behind me when I retired.

"Do you expect him soon."

"They've had some car trouble, sir. He will be in sometime late tonight. How did you know about my wedding?" I blurted out.

He chuckled. "From your fiancé, Chief Landow. You see, Sandy . . . may I call you Sandy?

"Yeah, sure." Oh, great. What a way to talk to the President, I thought.

"When my secretary, Mrs. Lincoln, couldn't locate you earlier today, I had her call the police station. I was quite certain with your background that you would be working with them in some capacity. Chief Landow was kind enough to fill me in on your plans. It is imperative that I see you and Jake together to discuss a matter of national security that you two brought to my attention some months ago. Are you following me?"

"Yes, sir," I answered. Now I knew it was the President. They must have found the mole in the CIA organization, I thought excitedly.

"Due to the seriousness of the matter there are others close to me who must not know we are meeting, therefore I can't have you come to Washington. I had hoped to see the two of you at the Portland airport on my way to China, but that won't be possible now since I'm leaving within the hour. My plans are to return early Sunday morning. I will be landing in Portland at five a.m to refuel. With your permission I would like to come to Myrtle Woods, have a quick meeting with you and Jake, attend the wedding, if I may, and return to Portland by one o'clock. "

Attend our wedding? The President? My mind went blank.

Art could see I was dumbfounded, so he took over. "Mr. President, this is Art Landow. We would be honored to have you come to our wedding. It takes about two hours to reach Myrtle Woods from Portland, so you should arrive here between seven and seven-thirty. The wedding is at ten-thirty, so there should be plenty of time to meet with Sandy and Jake before Sandy has to start getting dressed. For your safety, we won't tell anyone but Jake and his wife, Sue, of your impending arrival. It will also make protecting you much easier. Is that satisfactory, sir?"

"That would be wonderful, Art, except I'd rather no one knows about this but you, Sandy, and Jake. Jake can fill his wife in later. Agreed?"

"Yes, Sir."

"One of my men will see that I get out of the airport without being followed. It will be heaven to have a few hours to myself.

It's been several months since I've pulled one of my famous disappearing acts. I'm thinking I may even wear some kind of disguise to make your job easier. Here, let me put my secretary, Mrs. Lincoln, on the line because I've got to run. Please give her directions on how to get to Myrtle Woods from Portland."

"Yes, sir. One more thing, sir. Will you be bringing any secret service personnel or should I have a few plainclothes men among the guests?"

"I will be alone. If no one knows I'm coming, I'm sure your men will work quite well. Thank you, Art for your cooperation. I'll see you both on Sunday. Are you still with us, Sandy?"

"No, I think I fainted when you said you would like to come to the wedding," I gulped.

"I'll see you Sunday morning about seven or so." He was laughing as he gave the phone to his secretary. I decided to let Art give her the directions and hung up.

When Art walked out of the den I was all over him like a swarm of locust. "Why didn't you tell me about this? When did you talk to him? Did he say anything else to you about why he wanted to see Jake and me?" Every time he opened his mouth to speak, I shot him another question.

"Silence," he bellowed. "Come out on the porch." He didn't say another word until we were seated in the swing. "In answer to some of your questions: I talked to him shortly before coming over here. I didn't tell you because I wanted to see your reaction when he called." He ducked the punch I threw at him. "He didn't tell me what he wanted to speak to you both about, but I got the impression it was important."

"It sounds to me like he has an answer to our inquiry into the mole problem. It must be someone pretty high up from the way he talked. Do you think he will drive down here from the airport by himself?"

"It wouldn't surprise me. He's crazy enough to do it. I'll have four of the boys in plainclothes here by seven Sunday morning. I'll tell them it's to keep the gifts from being stolen, then if the President does stay for the wedding he will have some protection.

I'm sure if I told Sadie to guard him she would do it, don't you? Of course, the fact that no one knows he is coming will make everything easier. Too bad we can't tell Frances. I'm sure she would want to fix something special for his breakfast."

"I'll think up some reason for her to make something special."

"I guess I won't meet him until I come at ten, huh?" Art said wistfully. "Of course, if I insisted on showing up here at seven, everyone would know something was up. What we don't want to do is make people wonder. Whew! Can you believe it? The President at our wedding. That will be one to tell the grandkids, won't it?"

"I hope I don't faint," I said worriedly.

"You, faint," Art hooted. Jumping up, he hurried out of range of me and my crutch. "That will be the day!"

"You—you . . . if I could run you wouldn't be making remarks like that," I yelled, banishing my crutch like a saber. Even Sadie ran for cover.

THIRTY-TWO

It was close to eleven that night when Sue and family pulled into the driveway. They were all exhausted. Sue is normally a vivacious, stunning blonde with every hair in place, always looking as if she had just stepped from a page of Vogue magazine. Getting out of the car, she looked like she could lie down and sleep on the grass. Her hair was unruly, her smile barely there as she gave me a hug. They must have slept in their clothes for the last couple of days. Greetings, unloading the car, everyone meeting Frances, Al and Sadie, and getting the kids settled took almost an hour, so it was past midnight before I got to speak to Jake alone.

"I can't tell you how much it means to me to have you guys here," I said, giving him another hug.

"Hey, there was no way we could let my wife's best friend get married without us. After all, doesn't Art have to ask me for your hand?"

"What a hoot," I laughed. "I'd love it. I think you should come on serious in the morning when you meet him and broach the subject to him then. I'd give anything to see his face."

"I'll do it," Jake said, going right along with the joke.

"Come out on the porch. I have something to tell you."

I led him out to the porch swing to tell him about the call from the President.

"It must be a can of worms for the President to take a chance to come here by himself. Art must be a nervous wreck."

"Not really. He is a cool guy under fire. Later, I'll tell you about what he and I went through on a case we were working on together a few months ago. The important thing is that you don't say a word to anyone. I'm sorry, friend, not even Sue." I said, as I saw the question coming. "That was the only stipulation that the President made. Art and I are hoping he will wear some kind of disguise; horn-rim glasses, and maybe a wig. We'll have to wait and see."

Jake and I talked for another half-hour trying to guess who the mole might be. When the President said "others close to him must not know he is meeting with us," did that mean there was more than one mole? Good grief. I couldn't speak for Jake, but that thought blew my mind. Finally, we gave up and tottered off to our beds, too befuddled to make any sense of anything that late at night.

I set my alarm for seven, so I would be dressed when the kids woke up. I decided I could take them down to the lake after they had breakfast, and give Sue and Jake some much needed rest. As so often happens with the best laid plans of mice and men, my plan didn't work. I think the kids must have been up with the birds because when I walked into the kitchen they were up, dressed, talking to Frances, petting Sadie, and in the midst of eating their breakfast.

Twelve year old Robbie was an exact copy of his dad. He had the same dark hair, green eyes with those long, long eyelashes, even the dimples. It wasn't fair that ten year old Carolyn didn't get the dimples because she was such a little mouse. She could have been my daughter. Her hair wasn't the beautiful blonde of her mother nor the deep brown of her father; rather it was a cross between Jake and Sue. Like I said: mouse. The only thing she had going for her was her beautiful skin, and a quicksilver smile. When she bestowed that smile on you, you felt as though you'd been blessed.

They were dressed in swimming suits and robes, ready to hit the lake. I grabbed a banana and two hot muffins and followed them out. They were a joy to talk with, each finishing the other's sentences. Everything they had seen on the way across the country was a big deal. It was a good hour before they began to wind down.

"It is beautiful here, Aunt Sandy," Carolyn said, immediately falling back into the old nickname. "I wouldn't mind living here."

"Me, too," Robbie told me. "Especially if we had a house right by the lake. I can't believe how clear this water is." He had been throwing a stick in the water for Sadie to retrieve. Of course, each time she came out she shook water all over us. The kids thought it was great fun. They had never lived where they could have a pet.

I had told the kids the story of Adam, so they understood why I didn't want them in the water without an adult other than myself present.

"Where were they having the birthday party for Adam?" Robbie asked.

"Down the lake about a fourth of a mile," I said. "I'll take you down there sometime while you are here. Lots of kids love to swim out to the raft."

"That is such a sad story about Adam." Carolyn said as she looked out across the lake.

"Yes, it is. Especially since he was Roger and Marie's only child."

I was going to say more, but Frances called down to say that I had a phone call. I told the kids they could stay and play in the sand as long as they didn't go in the water. They promised, helping me to my feet. Telling Sadie to stay, I hurried as fast as I could to the house. Please, please, let it be Emily, I prayed.

"Hello, this is Sandy."

"Sandy, Emily here. Harriet and I have talked about it and we have decided that since we have no way of verifying that Peter was the father, we won't contest the adoption. What I would like you to do is to ask Mr. and Mrs. Owens to come here tonight without Matthew, if it is possible. Harriet knows them, and she said they were a lovely couple, so I'm sure I will like them. After you all get here we would like you to tell the whole story of Matthew again. Then we wish to approach them with an idea. Harriet would like to be Matthew's substitute grandmother. As Tracy's grandmother I'll be doing all the things for Tracy that Harriet wanted to talk to Doreen and Dale about doing. What do you think?"

"What a wonderful idea, especially since the boys are best friends. Both Marie's and Roger's folks died young, so I'm sure they will be open to the idea."

"I know I'm asking a lot of you, Sandy, when you must be so busy with the wedding taking place on Sunday, but . . . " Emily said.

"No, no, it's perfectly all right. I would like to see this settled to everyone's satisfaction. I'll call Marie and make sure they are free tonight. What time did you have in mind?"

"Would seven-thirty be all right? Tell everyone not to worry about dinner. Harriet and I will have a small buffet laid out."

"Perfect. I'll call you back in a few minutes," I said.

A call to Marie and Roger assured me they could go to a meeting with me tonight, but what was it all about? I told them I would explain later, and told them not to eat. A call back to Emily and everything was arranged.

Now I had to find someone to take care of Matthew. I was sure the letter from his mother was the way for Matthew to find out about this triangle when he was older.

I wanted to shout with joy when I hung up the phone, but apparently Sue and Jake weren't up yet, so I squashed that desire. Instead, I hurried into the kitchen to share the news with Frances.

"Frances, Frances, guess what? Marie and Roger can adopt Matthew. Yes!" I said quietly, my fist in the air. "Isn't that wonderful?"

"Yes, dear girl, I'm happy for them all. Is that what the call was about?"

"Uh-huh. Now I have to find someone to take care of the boys for tonight. Any suggestions?"

"I have one." Sue had been standing behind me all during my discussion with Frances. When she spoke, I think I jumped a foot.

"Oh, Sue, you startled me."

"I'm sorry," she said, giving me a hug. "If it will help you, why don't Jake and I take all four children out to dinner, and then to a movie?"

"What a great idea,?" I said, giving her a hug. "There's no theater in this town, but there is one in Mountain View, and believe me, Tracy and Matthew know how to get there."

Jake walked in about that time, so we had to explain our plan to him. "Sounds like a good idea to me," he said.

So it was decided. I called Marie and Doreen to make arrangements for the boys to be here at five p.m. for their night on the town. I called Art and let out such a whoop he swore he could hear me without use of the phone. He was as delighted as I was with the way things seemed to be working out.

"Do I get to go with you tonight?" he asked, like a little kid wanting to be invited to a party.

"Of course," I assured him.

The rest of the day was spent visiting with old friends. I took them down to my office. They were impressed with what we had done to the old house. I impressed on them that there was plenty of room for another desk when Jake decided to retire. We drove slowly around town, stopping at the police station to give the kids a tour while Jake and Art visited. Then we went to the park, and while the kids waded in the lake, the three of us caught up on old times.

"By the way, Sandy, I told Art he had to ask me for your hand," Jake smiled

"And?" I asked, not for a minute believing Art would do it.

"Darned if he didn't do it. Surprised the heck out of me. That man truly loves you, you know."

"Yes, I know. I'm fortunate he waited for me."

That turned the talk to the mole we hoped would be caught. A couple of times I had to stop myself practically in mid-sentence to keep from mentioning the President's upcoming visit. It was so good to see them again. Jake was interested in what I had been doing in my work, so I told him about Peter Grant, what happened in the forest, and of Harriet and Emily.

"Whew! I thought Myrtle Woods was a quiet little town. We may have to rethink moving here, Sue," he said.

"Hey, I thought that was decided before I left DC."

"I know, little friend. I was only teasing you. I'm going to take early retirement. Sue and I both feel we've got to get the kids out of DC. It's not the right atmosphere for growing children."

"I've never worried about Jake before when he was off on a case," Sue said quietly, "but after what happened to you, Sandy, I'm on pins and needles now until he returns. I will be so glad when he is no longer with the Agency."

Jake put his arms around her shoulders and hugged her close. "I'm afraid if I don't retire soon, she'll develop an ulcer."

"It's not that bad, you goose," she said, hitting him lightly on the chest.

"For whatever reason, I'm quitting at the end of this year. I've already handed in my resignation."

"What great news," I said. "I'll start looking around for another desk for the office and . . ."

"Whoa, whoa. Let us decide for sure that we want to live here. Sue wants to check out the schools and we will want to look at a few homes. Also Art was asking me if I would like to go to work for him. We were discussing it while you two were giving the kids the tour."

"No fair," I said, "I had first claim, remember?"

All in all, we had a peaceful and relaxing day. I hadn't realized how much I needed it. We hurried home at four, so the kids could get ready for their night out. They were both anxious to meet the boys. Jake and I were sitting at the kitchen table talking to Frances when Carolyn walked in. I stared. What a transformation. Her hair was swept up in a French roll with a few loose curls hanging around her face. Her tan she picked up today showed off her frilly pink dress to perfection.

"Carolyn, you look beautiful," I told her.

She blushed, thanking me for the compliment.

"She does dress up nicely, doesn't she," Jake said, his voice full of pride.

"Why the notebook and pencil, sweetie," I asked her.

"I figure Robbie and Matthew will be talking, so I'm going to talk to Tracy with my pencil."

"Why, what a sweet thing to do. Tracy will appreciate it. I'm sure he sometimes feels left out when he is with people who can talk."

"I'm going to ask him if he can teach me to sign. I've always wanted to learn," she said, from the circle of Jake's arm.

"You continue to surprise your old dad, sweetheart," Jake said, kissing the top of her head.

"Oh, daddy, you aren't old," Carolyn giggled.

What a beautiful child, I thought.

Sue and Robbie came in about that time. Both of them were clean and shiny, but dressed in everyday clothes. I could easily see who the clotheshorse was in their family.

It was only a short time later that the boys came. It only took minutes to see that the kids were all going to get along great. Matthew was careful to include Tracy in the conversation, however, when he realized that Carolyn was prepared to communicate with Tracy, he relaxed.

THIRTY-THREE

After we saw everyone off, I nonchalantly wandered into the kitchen with Sadie to talk to Frances. "What are you going to do with your night off," I asked her.

"This is a godsend, believe me," she said. "It will give me time to get the rest of the cake layers made and in the freezer. Did you know that Rob and Carolyn have asked if they could watch me decorate?"

"Oh, gosh. Won't that make you nervous?"

"It will be like old times," she exclaimed. "Our son and his friends used to crowd around to watch. I'm looking forward to it."

"When are you going to do that? On Saturday?"

"Yes, bright and early Saturday morning. That way I'll have the rest of the day to goof off."

"Oh, yeah. I can see you goofing off."

"No, it's true," she insisted. "If there is anything special you want for Sunday morning breakfast, now is the time to order it."

Talk about playing right into my hands. "Well, let's see. What would you make if . . . oh, if the pope or the president were coming."

Frances laughed. "The pope or the president, huh?" She thought a minute. "I'd most likely make my fluffy orange rolls. They won first prize at the State Fair some years back," she said proudly.

"First prize! They must be delicious. Why haven't you made them for us before now?"

"Oh, I don't know. Too many other good recipes out there, I

guess. Besides," she smiled, a twinkle in her eye, "I only make them for special occasions. Now I suppose you are going to want them for Sunday morning?"

"If it's not too much trouble," I said humbly. Was I putting on a good act or what?

"Of course, dear girl. I should have thought of making them before this. After all, what is more important than a wedding? I better make a double batch," she mused more to herself than to me. "Art will want something before you two start down to the lake. And there will be those four young men he told me he was sending over to watch the gifts, although why he thinks he needs that many, I'll never know. Yes, certainly, a double batch. Orange rolls, scrambled eggs, juice and coffee. How does that sound?"

"Wonderful. I guess I better quite talking and get dressed if Art and I are going to be at Marie's on time." I walked out of the kitchen feeling extremely proud of myself.

On the way to South Point I told Marie and Roger a little bit of Matthew's heritage saying that he might be related to Emily Grant.

"Oh, dear," Marie said, "do you suppose that she will want to bring him up? Is that what this meeting is about?"

"Don't worry, dear heart. I've talked to her, and she says she is too old to even think about bringing up a child. I think probably what she wants is to meet you two and satisfy herself that Matthew is going to have a good home, should he wish to be adopted."

They both sighed in relief at my explanation.

When we arrived, Harriet took over the hostess duties to make Marie and Roger comfortable. Both she and Doctor Morton knew Marie and Roger, but Doctor Davidson and Emily had to be introduced.

After everyone was seated, Emily said, "I think it would be best if we get our discussion about Matthew out of the way first. Then we can relax and enjoy the small buffet my sister and I have arranged, if that's satisfactory?"

Everyone agreed, so Emily asked me if I would tell how

Matthew happened to be living at the convent. Everyone sat spellbound as the story unfolded. I ended by telling everyone about the items, including the letter, that Sister Norma Alice left with the Mother Superior.

"There is a possibility that Emily's husband, Peter Grant, is Matthew's father. The timing is correct. He was in a play, one of the other members of the cast was named Norma, he did leave town immediately after the play ended, and he was gone for a year. However, it could all be a coincidence. There is no way of knowing for sure without exhuming Peter's body and doing an DNA test against blood drawn from Matthew." Marie's face went white. She knew all about Peter Grant and what he had done to me and Art.

"May I take over now, Sandy?" Emily asked. Turning to the others she said, "My sister and I do not see any sense in subjecting Matthew to a procedure of that nature at this time. If and when he asks about his mother, I'm assuming he will be given the letter?" She looked inquiring at Marie and Roger, who nodded their heads in agreement. "Then I suggest we wait until that time to see if Peter was named as the father. Personally, I have a feeling she won't name anyone. I'm sure she would have been afraid of hurting her parents too much. Harriet and I did a little sleuthing on our own and found out that Norma's father died of a heart attack a year ago. A few weeks after the convent notified her mother that Norma had died, her mother died also, probably of a broken heart. It is a sad story. Peter had a knack for ruining lives. I have no doubt he had a hand in this also," she said bitterly.

Harriet took her sister's hand. "What we are trying to say is that all of us in this room give you our blessing. We think you two will make wonderful parents for Matthew."

Marie broke into happy tears, "Oh, thank you, thank you. You have no idea how much this means to us. Now, if we can convince Matthew that it's what he wants also."

"There is one other little thing," Harriet said hesitantly. "If we can figure out some way to do it, I would consider it a great honor if you would let me be Matthew's substitute grandmother."

"Why . . . I don't know," Marie said, looking at Roger.

"Mrs. Logger . . . "

"Harriet, please."

"Harriet, how would we do that? I mean I think it's a wonderful idea, but . . . " Roger was saying.

"May I suggest a way," I asked them all. All their faces turned to me. "Why don't you, Emily, have Tracy and Matthew over as often as possible. When Matthew sees how much love there is between you and Tracy, perhaps you could tell him about your sister, Harriet, who is longing to be a grandmother to someone. Then you could ask Matthew if he would consider being her pretend grandson."

For a few minutes no one said anything. Then everyone started talking at once:

"Good idea."

"It might work"

"Leave it to Sandy to come up with something."

"Roger, what do you think?"

Roger waited for the hubbub to die down, then he suggested his own idea. "I suggest that we get Matthew and Mrs. Log . . . , Harriet, together as often as possible; either at the drugstore, our house, or here at Emily's. Then let Harriet ask Matthew in a few months if he would like to have her as a grandmother; that she truly wants a grandson. Then let nature take its course."

Everyone agreed with that idea, so Emily stood up and said, "Let's eat!"

On the way home later Roger said quietly, "Now it's up to Matthew. I can only pray that he will want to become our son."

"When he says yes, as I'm sure he will, call the Holy Mountain Top Convent, and make an appointment with the Mother Superior. She wants to visit with the three of you before she signs any papers." Digging in my purse I found the phone number for the convent. "Here is the phone number. If you lose it, call Dale Fuller. He has it."

When we arrived at the house for them to pick up Matthew, the kids were having a wonderful time. Al had gone to the basement and dug out some old games I played with when I was a kid, some the kids had never heard of before. They were having as much fun giggling about the game itself as they were about how it was played. A few minutes after we arrived Doreen showed up to get Tracy, and soon we had the house to ourselves again.

"How did it go?" Frances asked.

"It was wonderful. Everyone loves everyone; one big happy family. Since we have no idea what his mother told Matthew in her letter it is the consensus of the group that Marie and Roger should go ahead and adopt him. If and when he reads the letter—well, the family will cross that bridge when they come to it. One interesting thing happened though. Harriet Logger would like to be Matthew's surrogate grandmother."

"Really?" exclaimed Frances. "You would think she would like to be Tracy's since her husband . . . oh, I think I understand. Since Doreen and her mother are rid of that monster, Peter Grant, Emily is free to be Tracy's natural grandmother. That kind of leaves Harriet out in the cold. Poor lady. She has wanted a child all her life."

"Yes, and now she may have the pleasure of being a grandmother. It was decided, however, that it will take some time for Matthew to get to know her before the subject is even broached. Right now the primary question is Matthew. Will he want to be adopted by Marie and Roger? It all depends on him now."

There was nothing to do but wait.

When I awoke the next morning, my first thought was: hey, girl, tomorrow is the day. For the first time I felt a little nervous. Why, I asked myself. Then it dawned on me. I wasn't nervous about the wedding. I was nervous about the President walking into my house in the morning. I could only hope I didn't make a fool of myself by saying something stupid or tripping over my own feet. Oh, come off it, I told myself. Consider it an assignment. You've never goofed up one of those, my inner voice said. That was true enough, I thought, squaring my shoulders and heading for the shower. But, golly, the President in my house. Wow! Every time I thought of it my tummy did a flip-flop.

"What are you doing up at this hour," Frances asked, as I walked into the kitchen. "We were all going to let you sleep in. Everyone is up and they've all gone down to the lake, except for Al. He will be glad you are up. He is itching to mow the lawn."

"If I might have a cup of coffee and a muffin I'll head for the lake also."

"Is that all you are going to eat? What's the matter? A little nervous?"

Yes," I answered her truthfully. Boy, if she only knew why, I thought. "Are you making icing for the cake?"

"Yes. Tell the kids if they want to watch me they better get up here pretty soon."

I said I would, yelled at Al he could mow the lawn, and hurried as fast as I could to the lake. When Frances said they were all going to let me sleep in, she neglected to say that "all" included Art, Tracy, and Matthew, as well as the Cummings family. Art had brought a lawn chair down for me to sit on, making it easier for me to get down to the sand. I watched Matthew to see if I could tell if he had been asked yet, but I couldn't get a clue. The message Art gave me with his eyes and a shrug of his shoulders told me he didn't know either. Of course, I thought, with his adult thinking Matthew might look at adoption differently than the ordinary child.

I relayed Frances' message, and it was a good thing I was sitting down or I'm afraid I would have gotten trampled in the rush. I would have liked to join them, but I had promised Frances a few days ago that I wouldn't watch.

"Having you watching would make me nervous," she had told me. "I like the kids hanging over the table, but the bride? No way." I had laughed, and promised her I would stay away.

It was so pleasurable to relax. Sadie lay by my side, her head in my lap. The day was beautiful; not a cloud in the sky. By mid-morning it would be hot enough for everyone to be thinking about bathing suits and cool lake water. I had not gone swimming in front of anyone but Art since I had come home. I had always begged off and acted as the lifeguard. I was embarrassed by my bum leg that made me look like an injured frog moving through the water. I knew it would have to get hot enough to boil eggs in the lake before I'd get in the water.

Sue had regained all her vim, vigor, and vitality. She look radiant. Every hair was in place once again. The pretty sundress she was wearing, and the golden tan she had acquired since arriving, made her look like a model. Yet I had never known her to flaunt her beauty. She described herself as a mid-western farm girl and proud of it. I knew that Jake was her whole life. Every time he left on a mission, she started preparing for his homecoming. 'One in a hundred million' is the way Jake described her to me once.

We discussed everything under the sun except that subject that was most on the minds of all of us, except Sue, the CIA mole and the President's visit. To get my mind off it, I asked Sue if the town measured up to my description of it.

"Yes, it's everything you said it was. We truly like it here. The kids love the lake. I still need to talk to someone about the schools before we make up our minds.

"That's wonderful." I was pleased. "Have you talked to any real estate people? Looked at any houses?"

"I don't know when you thought we had time to do any of that since we got here," Jake chided me. "What we have decided to do is stick around for a few days after the wedding and see what's out there. Frances knows a real estate lady who has kids in school and we are going to talk to her on Monday. We offered to move into the motel after the wedding, but Frances wouldn't hear of it. I hope you don't mind."

"Of course not. You know my house is your house for as long as you want to stay. I hope you can find what you want. It will be wonderful to have you living here. And by the way, Mr. Ludlow, this man," I said indicating Jake, "is going to be my working partner, so don't get any ideas about stealing him away."

"But . . . . "Art started to say.

"No buts," I said. "Of course, I may loan him to you once in awhile as long as you remember he is working out of the Shores & Cummings Investigations office."

Art held up his hands in surrender, but Jake decided to get into the act. "Shores & Cummings, huh? Why not Cummings and Shores? I like the ring of that."

"Better yet," Art said, "how about C & S Investigations?"

"No, no," I said giggling, "I've got it. I've got it. How does S & J sound."

"Not as good as J & S," Jake said laughing.

"That's enough out of all of you," Sue interjected, laughing as hard as the rest of us. "Hadn't we better wait until we see if we're staying before we change the name of the office?" We all had to admit she was right.

We were having such a good time that we didn't realize it was time for lunch until the kids came trooping down the path. The boys were each carrying a pizza box, while Carolyn and Marie brought a cloth to spread out on the sand, paper plates and cold pop. While everyone was getting settled with their plates, I asked the kids how the cake was coming.

"It's going to be beautiful," Carolyn said. "Mom, we have to move here because I want Frances to make my wedding cake, too."

"But that's years away, Honey."

"I know, but Frances told me she would make it, God willing."

"I'll drink to that," I said holding up my pop. "To Frances."

"To Frances," everyone chorused, their pops held high.

Marie was busy taking pictures. She told us the candid shots would be the best pictures of all to look back on in the years to come. The years to come, I mused. Like maybe fifty or sixty? I could only hope.

It wasn't long before we were all eating slower and slower, even the kids were pushing their plates away, when Marie dropped her bombshell.

"Matthew, have you told anyone yet?"

"No, I thought it best to wait until you arrived," he answered. "May I do it now?"

Marie nodded her head. I could tell she was close to tears and didn't trust herself to speak

"Marie and Roger have done me the great honor of offering to adopt me."

The kids went crazy, jumping up and hugging everyone and each other.

"Wait, wait," I called out. "We haven't heard what Matthew told them."

"Why, surely, you would have no doubt, Sandy, what my answer would be. After all, it is something I've been praying for all my life. I would have to be crazy not to say yes." He suddenly yelled, "And believe me, I'm not crazy. I said yes, yes, yes!"

The kids formed a circle chanting "yes, yes, yes" over and over. Sadie, excited by all the hubbub, raced around barking and jumping up on the kids. All those who could stand were giving Marie and Matthew hugs and kisses. I wanted to get in on it too, but I couldn't get my balance to get out of the lawn chair. Darn it, I thought, and then there she was, kneeling by my chair. We fell into each others arms.

"I'm so happy for you, sweetie," I whispered in her ear.

"It is all because of you that this happened, Sandy. How can I ever thank you."

"Oh, poo. I had nothing to do with it. Well, maybe a teeny, tiny bit," I said, laughing.

Marie dried her eyes. "Yeah, yeah, a teeny tiny bit. Everything, is more like it."

"What did Matthew do when you and Roger asked him?"

"Oh, Sandy, it was so comical. He sat there a minute, then in that grown-up language of his, he said, "Are you telling me that you two exceptionally fine people wish to have someone like me live with you from this day forth?" It was as if he was afraid to believe it, but when we told him yes, it was like . . . like he got his childhood back, is the only way to explain it. He started dancing around, hugging first one of us then the other, acting like a kid for once. Well, you saw him a minute ago. Don't you think that's a change?"

"Definitely. Too bad Roger couldn't be here to see this."

"Yes. He wanted to be, but since he is the only druggist in town—well, you know how that goes."

She settled beside my chair while we watched the kids. For the first time Matthew seemed to be trying to act more like a young boy instead of an old man.

Frances called down a few minutes later to tell the kids she was going to be putting the flowers on the cake. That's all it took. In seconds the beach was void of children.

"I wish I could go and watch, too," I said wistfully.

"I peeked in to collect the kids when we arrived with the pizzas, and it is going to be beautiful," Marie said. "I told Frances not to worry about dinner. Roger is going to pick up fried chicken, jo-jos, and two or three salads when he closes the drug store tonight. We will all eat together and then the men will run off with Art for his party. Doreen is coming over to keep an eye on the kids, so we can get the trays of food ready. Just think, girlfriend, tomorrow is the big day. Did you think it would ever happen this way?"

"To be truthful, I dreamed of this day over and over. I've loved Art since we were kids, but I had to get the wanderlust out of my system. I would have never been truly happy if I hadn't." Then silently, I said to myself, oh, Marie, if you only knew how big a day tomorrow is going to be.

Suddenly I felt freezing cold. I shivered, thinking of the old saying my mother used to say. 'It means someone is walking over your grave,' she told me more than once. Now why would I remember that, I wondered, as I hugged Sadie's warm body against me.

THIRTY-FOUR

Art wasn't the only one surprised with a party after dinner. The men left at seven o'clock. Doreen came at seven-thirty bringing Emily and Harriet. Ruth, Doctor Johnson's nurse, was the next to arrive. Then all my other women friends began filing in until we had about twenty people in the house.

"What in the world are you all doing here?"

"It's a surprise party for you, ninny," Marie said. "Okay, everybody, bring in your gifts," she called out.

There were gifts everywhere—on the front porch, in the porch swing, in their cars, even one that Frances had hidden in the basement. What a grand time we had. Art and I got so many lovely bed and bath things. New towels, sheets, pillowcases, piled up around me. I reached for the one that Frances had brought in last, and was surprised to discover that it was quite heavy. When I took the last of the wrapping off we all broke into gales of laughter. It was a cookbook!

"Frances, what does this mean? You aren't leaving us, are you?"

"No, not to worry. This is the first cookbook my mother ever gave me. I thought while you were laid up after your operation I could teach you a few of the better ones."

"What a great idea," I said. "Maybe I'll get good enough to surprise Art one of these days."

Everyone there wanted to know what kind of operation I was going to have, so I filled them in. Many of them felt it was too futuristic for them to even comprehend. Then the talk turned to whether or not we planned to have a family . . . pure women talk.

It was then going on nine o'clock so everyone moved to the kitchen to help get the trays of food ready. By ten we were done and everyone but Marie had gone home.

"See, I told you it wouldn't take long," she said impishly.

"Yes, but you didn't tell me we would have twenty people helping out," I scolded her. "It was a fun party though, wasn't it? I appreciate all the work you've done."

"Hey, I couldn't let my best friend get married without a shower, could I? Now, I better get Matthew to bed so he will be in good shape tomorrow."

"Aw, Mom," he said.

He said it so naturally that for a minute it didn't register. When it did my eyes flew to Marie's. She had an arm around Matthew, her lips on the top of his head, her eyes shut as if in prayer.

She raised her head, her eyes moist. "I will be here at nine in the morning to fix your hair, Sandy. And yes, I'll bring the dress," she said, as I opened my mouth to speak. With a wave to Frances and a hug for me, she and Matthew were out the door.

I told Frances I was going right to bed, but first I wanted to tell her something. Art and I had decided I should tell her the President was coming. We certainly didn't want her to have a heart attack when he walked into her kitchen.

"Yes, dear, what is it," she asked, preoccupied with trying to find room in the refrigerator for some of the trays of food. "That's the best I can do. I'll have Al take the rest to the refrigerator in the basement."

I sat there and waited until she was giving me her undivided attention.

"Remember when I told you about the spy that Jake and I thought was in the CIA?" She nodded. "And that I wrote a letter to the President? And that Jake and I were getting upset because we hadn't heard anything about the outcome?" Again she nodded. "Well, we are going to find out what is going on tomorrow morning when the President comes here to talk to Jake and me and to attend the wedding."

For a full minute she stared at me, not saying a word.

"The President of the United States is coming here?" I nodded. "Will he be here for breakfast?" I nodded. "I will cook for the President?" Once again I nodded. "Oh, mercy. Oh, my," she said twisting her apron. "What should I make?"

"First thing I want you to do is sit down," I told her. "Remember when I asked you what you would make if the Pope or the President was coming for breakfast? Okay, we are having your famous Fluffy Orange Rolls, juice, eggs and coffee, and that's all we want," I said firmly. "If we have anything else we won't be able to enjoy the buffet after the wedding. Promise me you won't make anything else for breakfast."

"I promise," she said in a meek little voice. "But, oh my, the President! Wait until I tell Al."

"I'm sorry, dear, but you can't tell Al. Neither can Jake tell Sue. No one but Art, Jake, myself, and you can know his real identity until after he leaves. To everyone else he must be just another wedding guest. We decided to tell you rather than risk you having a heart attack if you should recognize him."

"I understand, Sandy. Thank you, dear, for the warning."

"He may come in disguise. We aren't sure of that yet. But whatever we can do to make his visit a pleasant experience is what we want to do. Above all else, we must remember not to call him Mr. President. Think of him as my uncle. Yeah, Uncle Charley is what we'll call him. That way it will make it easier for Art's men to protect him."

Again a chill ran over my body. What the heck? Was I coming down with something. Heaven forbid, I thought.

"Yes, I understand, Sandy," she said, sounding more like herself. "The poor man actually has no time to himself, does he? Well, we will make sure he enjoys himself tomorrow. What time will he be here?"

"We expect close to seven. If you could have some coffee ready, then after he talks to Jake and me, we will have breakfast. Okay?"

"Okay, dear. And, Sandy? Thanks for telling me. I think I would have had a heart attack if he had suddenly walked in."

I gave her a kiss on the cheek. "That's what we were afraid might happen."

"Oh, you. Go along now," she said, all flustered. "Go get your rest. You will need it tomorrow, that's for sure."

I was up at six, showered, dressed in new jeans, a clean blouse and new tennis shoes. I combed my hair every way I've ever worn it, and finally decided on the style I've been using for months. You can't make a silk purse out of a sow's ear, I remembered Mama saying. With one last look in the mirror I decided it was the best I could do.

I walked into the kitchen where Jake and Sue were having coffee. I had poured myself a cup when I heard the sound of a car in the driveway. Setting my cup down, I hurried to the door to find someone climbing out of a car in the drive way. A car driving slowly past caught my attention. I froze. It couldn't be!

Jake, who was close behind me, felt my tension. "What, Sandy? What's the matter?"

"My God, Jake, that General who caused all my injuries is driving by. Get back, quick. It looks like he has a gun. Oh, no, the President."

'The Executioner', as I had nicknamed him, was a little hard to recognize because of an ugly cut on his face that ran from the outer edge of his left eye down past his neck and disappeared into his shirt. But there was no mistaking those burning eyes and that cruel mouth. I thought I saw a rifle pointed at the house. The President, at least I was fairly certain the person getting out of the car was the President, would soon approach the porch.

Not giving a thought to my own safety I dashed out the door. "Uncle Charley, how great to see you," I yelled. I dropped my crutch as I jumped off the porch into his arms.

"Quick," I hissed in his ear, "help me into the house." I tried to keep an eye on the car as it drove on by, as the President half carried me into the house, but I lost it. Once in side, Jake handed me my crutch.

"Are you sure it was him, Sandy?" he asked.

"What is going on?" the President asked, confused.

"I'm sorry, sir," I said, still peering out of the window. "I'm sure the man who drove past a moment ago is the same man that inflicted my injuries on me during my last tour of duty. Remember the Korean general I nicknamed "The Executioner?"

"Yes, but that was in North Korea. And you think he is here? For what reason?"

"I would think to kill Sandy. He probably lost face in a big way in his country when she escaped. I wonder why it has taken this long for him to trace you down? I think I better get my gun," Jake muttered, hurrying from the room.

"Uncle Charley, I want you in my bedroom. You will be safe there until we make sure everything is okay. I want to load my gun, too. I better call Art and ask him to get over here immediately with his men. We certainly don't want any more people hurt than necessary."

I thanked God for speed dial as I picked up the phone.

"That won't be necessary," hissed the soft voice that I remembered all to well. The President and I wheeled at the sound of his insidious voice. "Hang up the phone, Shores. My work here will be over in a short time. I do not wish to harm innocent people. Only Miss. Shores interests me."

In the kitchen doorway with Al, Frances, and Sue standing in front of him was the Korean general. He had a 350 Magnum handgun pointed at Sue's head.

I started forward. "Take your filthy hands off . . . "

"Stop, unless you want to see her head blown off and these others shot," he thundered. "I'm sure you know that I mean what I say. Past experience should have taught you that much."

He gave an impatient wave of the gun at the President. "You there, head for the basement with the rest of these people."

Thank God, the Korean doesn't realize he was looking at the President of the United States, I thought. I have to admit that if I wouldn't have known who he was either, except for his eyes and that well-known voice. He had on a full beard and mustache combination, dark glasses, and a baseball cap. His jeans were filthy, his T-shirt grimy with a hole in one sleeve. Even his tennis shoes had holes in them.

"Go with him, *Uncle Charley*," I said with emphasis, looking President Wilton right in the eyes.

I could tell he wanted to say: Now, wait a doggone minute, I am the President of the United States.

"Go," I said, again. "And none of your back talk either."

The four adults made their way down the basement stairs; Sue and Frances softly crying; Al and Bill Wilton stoic, not saying a word. I thanked my lucky starts that Robbie and Carolyn had spent the night with Matthew, but, oh, how I wished they hadn't taken Sadie.

THIRTY-FIVE

After he locked them in the basement, he pushed me into the front room. "Now perhaps you are wondering why I have hunted so long, and come so far to find you. Sit there," he demanded, pushing me into a chair, "and don't try any of your tricks on me. I'm here to finish the job I started in Korea," he informed me.

Well now, I thought, that sounds pretty definite and on my wedding day, too. The more I thought about it, the madder I got. This low down, sneaky, contemptible little man was about to take my life on the day I was going to have all my dreams come true.

"Why have you . . . ?" I started to ask.

"Quiet!" the general thundered. In the midst of his yell, I thought I heard a door open. Jake! I knew I had to keep the General talking, so he wouldn't hear the board that creaked in the hallway.

"But all I was going to say . . . ," I tried again.

This time he lurched at me with the gun raised overhead threateningly. "I am warning you, Shores, for the last time," he voice was nasty. "If you so much as open up your mouth again, it will be for the last time."

Believe me, I knew he meant what he said, but right now it didn't matter what happened to me. Those in the basement were far more important. I had to give Jake a chance to get to this crazy varmint. I knew if he killed Jake and me, he would never let those in the basement go free. If nothing else, he would set fire to the house and let them die in the flames.

"When your Navy Seals broke into that warehouse and rescued you, I was cut up so badly I was expected to die. Because of you my face is like this." He pointed to the ugly scar I had seen earlier. "When I was in the hospital I made a vow to hunt you down and have the pleasure of killing you myself. I wanted you to know who was pulling the trigger. I wanted to see terror in your eyes instead of that blank stare you gave me before."

Blank stare? He must mean the trance, I guessed.

"So say your prayers, Shores. You've breathed your . . . "

"No, you've breathed your last, you son-of-a-bitch," Jake yelled.

The Korean spun around, screaming and firing several shots at Jake, who got off one shot before jumping behind the door jam. I jumped up, grabbed a large vase that must have weighed twenty pounds and brought it down on the General's head. He had turned to me at the last second and fired again. Even as his bullet grazed my arm, he fell to the floor, out cold.

I ran to Jake. He was sitting on the floor, holding a bloody handkerchief to his forehead. "Jake, that looks bad."

"I know, but you know how head wounds bleed. I'm sure it's just a scratch," he said, his voice weak.

"Sit right there," I answered, grabbing up a dishtowel and wrapping it around my arm. "I'll let the others out of the basement and tell Al to bring up some clothesline to tie up that varmint."

I thought Frances and Sue were going to faint when they saw the blood running down my arm, but that was nothing compared to how they reacted when they saw Jake. Sue sank to the floor beside him, holding him close. Frances stood there wringing her hands, saying, "Oh, dear" over and over, her face white. I was afraid she was going to faint, so I grabbed her arm. "Frances, call 911. NOW!" I thundered when she didn't move. Quickly, she did as she was told.

Minutes later, Art ran into the house. "We got a report of several gun shots . . . Sandy, darling, what happened?" He practically knocked the President down in his haste to get to me. "Are you all right? Has anyone called 911? Who is this guy?

And who is that guy," he asked, pointing first at the Korean, then the President.

You can imagine the look on his face when I explained that one of those *guys* was my Uncle Charley. The way I emphasized *Uncle* helped Art realize he was looking at the President of the United States. He held me close as he shook hands.

"Sorry I wasn't here when you arrived to welcome you, *sir*. I hope the rest of the day is much quieter." With Sue and Al in the room the best Art could do was to stress the "sir" in his remark. "Sandy, let me look at your arm." He took a quick look and said, "I think he only grazed you, but it's deep, so we better have a doctor look at it. We'll follow the ambulance to the hospital."

We could hear the ambulance coming long before they pulled into the driveway. Quickly, they loaded Jake on the stretcher, helped Sue in the back with him. When they found out Art was bringing me, they pulled out and headed up the street, sirens screaming. Art, the President and I were right behind them in the police car. Art wasn't about to let the President out of his sight again.

We all thanked our lucky stars when the doctors told us that both wounds were superficial. All of us were back at the house within the hour. Jake was warned to take it easy and lay down as much as he could. He had been shot before while on assignment, so he assured them he knew what to do. Orange juice and rest.

"It's just like giving blood," he told us on the way home. He was determined to attend the wedding, so no one had to force him to get in bed when we arrived. Everyone wanted me to lie down also, but I shrugged them off. Yes, it hurt like the devil, but I wasn't going to let the General win and ruin my wedding day.

When Art pronounced to those who had remained at the house that we both would live, I believe every eye in the house filled with unshed tears.

Art had instructed two of his men to take the Korean to jail before we left for the hospital. They were to hold him under double guard until someone from Washington could come to get him. He told his men to come right back. He wasn't taking any more chances about guarding the President.

After we got back, the President took a shower and came out looking much more respectable. Sue served us coffee, then took a seat at the kitchen table next to the man she thought was Uncle Charley. He had kept on the fake beard, but even with that Sue made the remark about how much he resembled the President. Uncle Charley told her that people said that all the time. She seemed content with that explanation. We could only hope that others would too.

While Frances started breakfast, Art, Al and I went to check out any damage made during the shooting. Most of the bullets the Korean had fired were embedded in the walls and ceiling. We decided to leave them where they were until such time as we decided to redo the room. Frances volunteered to get the blood out of the carpet while we were on our honeymoon. During the wedding we decided to shut off the front room to keep people out. It was the best we could do for now.

"Are you sure it won't bother you to see the bullet holes every time you come into the room?" Art asked me.

"It will be a reminder that we got the best of that devil. Right now I smell something wonderful being cooked, and I'm starving. Let's go eat."

I glanced at the clock. "Can you believe all this happened in a total of an hour and fifty-five minutes," I said to one and all.

"Seemed more like four or five hours," Al commented dryly.

All the others agreed that it did seem like hours. "I guess having to sit in the basement, knowing we couldn't help you two, made the time crawl," President Wilton said.

"Al," Frances said firmly, "I want you to get another key made for the basement door. Hide it down there where it isn't too obvious. If there is a next time, God forbid, we will be able to get out of there."

I think the laughter that followed was more relief than anything else. I laughed with more than a hint of tears when I realized how close I had come to missing my wedding day.

THIRTY-SIX

During breakfast we agreed not to say anything to anyone about what had happened. The sleeves of my wedding dress were long and would hide my bandage. We would say that Jake stumbled on the beach and hit his head on a rock.

Jake called out from the bedroom that he wanted to go down by the lake and rest down there. He cautioned Sue not to treat him like a mother hen, so she let him have his way. After we ate, Art went home to get into his tuxedo, while President Wilton, Jake and I went down to the lake. The President was quiet. We had settled down on the blanket I had brought with me and a good two minutes went by before he began to speak.

"What I have to say to you is classified information. You both were right to suspect a mole in the CIA. We have proof that it is the head of the organization, Wendell Smyth. The problem is that he is married to my Secretary of State, Millie Smyth. My advisors have recommended that I get in touch with your group and ask them to hang in there a while longer. The announcement will be made, and Wendell will be taken into custody, as soon as my lawyers can tell me if Millie has to be relieved of her appointment. The big questions we are still trying to answer are did she know about his activities. If so, was she a partner in delivering some of the information on one of her many jaunts overseas? I hope not. I like Millie; she does a whale of a job for me and the country as a whole."

He was quiet again for several minutes. "So, if you would please write your people?" It was a question.

"Sir, may I suggest that I enlist the aid of my wife, Sue? After all, we can't expect Sandy to write letters on her honeymoon, can we? With Sue's help, I'm sure I can get the letters out right away. We won't say anything other than that we may have good news soon, that we can expect to know in a few weeks if there is a mole in our department . . . you know, I was thinking as I was talking . . . what if we have a mole in our group who would inform Smyth. Perhaps it would be better to ask the rest of our group if they have heard anything. By the time we hear back from all of them, your questions about Mrs. Smyth may be answered."

The President rubbed his lip in thought. "You may have something there, Jake. Yes, have Sue help you, and do as you suggested. Sandy, you may also share what I have told you with Art. I'm quite impressed with that young man. I wondered if he would like to come to Washington and work for me."

"No, sir. I don't even have to think about it. I'm positive he wouldn't even consider it, but you can certainly ask him if you wish," I told him firmly.

"I may do that," he chuckled. "I made a decision this morning while I was sitting in that basement. I was fairly certain none of us would get out of there alive if you two didn't pull off something. I can't begin to tell you how impressed I am with your actions. When I get back to Washington, I'm recommending you both for the Medal of Honor."

We stared at him. "Sir, we were attempting to save my life. I hate to say this, but you weren't the main focus of our attention," I said.

"That's right, sir. There is no need for a medal," Jake insisted.

"Can you stand there, both of you, and tell me truthfully you never gave a thought to your President down in the basement?" Neither of us said a word. "That's what I thought. So I will make the recommendation."

"Thank you, sir," we said together.

I saw Marie waving from the porch and knew it was time to get my hair done. "Gentleman, I hate to leave you, but it's time to make the bride beautiful." I put out my hand. "Mr. President, it is a pleasure to have you here. I hope you don't think too badly of us for that little bit of excitement we had earlier."

"Thank you, Sandy. Actually, since everything turned out okay, that excitement made my day. I haven't felt an adrenaline rush like that since I was in the war. I'm sorry I wasn't more help to you two, but perhaps it is best that it happened the way it did. Before you go, Sandy," he took my hand, "may I wish you and Art years of happiness. And if you wish to introduce me to your guests as the President, it will be all right."

I saw the wistful look on his face and made my decision. "Why, thank you, Uncle Charley. It will be a pleasure to introduce my favorite uncle, and remark how much he resembles the President."

He studied me a minute, smiled, and gave me a kiss on the cheek. "Thank you, Sandy. This day will live in my memory forever."

As it will in mine, I thought, as I worked my way back up the path.

While Sue was working with my hair I thought I heard the phone ring. Frances didn't come to get me, so if it did, it wasn't for me. When Marie came to help me get dressed, I told her that I had snagged my arm on a nail in the basement. I don't think she believed me for a minute because she examined the bandage and said, dryly, "Must have been an awfully big nail."

I stepped out of my bedroom in all my finery at ten o'clock sharp, followed by Sadie. She acted like she knew what had happened here earlier because she had refused to leave my side since they had brought her home. Art was waiting in the hall. When I came down the hall he stepped into my view. I believe both of us caught sight of each other at the same moment. Art was so handsome in his tuxedo it took my breath away.

"Sweetheart," Art said, "you are gorgeous." He raised my hand to his lips.

"I was thinking the same thing about you, my love," I whispered.

We exchanged a long kiss until Sadie made a sound in her throat that sounded like: That's enough of that, you two.

"Are you ready?" he asked.

"Yes," I said tremulously.

"I'd like you to meet my best man," Art said, turning me around. Coming down the hallway was the President all dressed in a tuxedo.

"How . . . what . . . ?" I choked out.

"Art called me to see what size tuxedo I wore. When it was the same size as the officer that was going to be his best man, Art asked me if I would like to have that honor. I jumped at the chance. I hope you aren't disappointed."

"Disappointed! I'm thrilled. I can't believe it."

"Do you still want your guests to know me as your Uncle Charley? I could understand if you don't."

"No. Oh, no, you are still my uncle," I started to giggle. "Who in their right mind wants to be upstaged on their wedding by . . . the President." I whispered the last two words because Marie was coming out of my room.

Art introduced Marie to the President as my Uncle Charley. She sent a puzzled look my way, but before she could speak, President Wilton handed her the small bouquet she was to carry, complimented her on her beautiful dress, and hustled her out the door.

"Whew," I said. "That was close. Marie knows I don't have an Uncle Charley."

"You can tell her later, love. It's time for us to go," Art said, as he stood my crutch in the corner.

I was shaky enough without my crutch, but thinking of the wedding service yet to come actually made my knees knock as we walked the path to the dock. How good it felt to grab the bar that Art had built for me. Whether we wanted her or not, Sadie had decided to become a part of the wedding. She followed us out onto the dock, and sat at my side all during the service. Everyone kidded me later about having such a beautiful blonde bridesmaid.

In no time at all the service was over, and everyone was following us up the path to the garden with Sadie leading the way, her beautiful tail waving back and forth. It seemed that God had every flower in the garden blooming for this day. Al had hurried ahead of us up the path to get my crutch and have it waiting by the garden fence. We stood by the gate into the garden to give everyone a chance to speak to us. All the men were giving me kisses: all the women kissed Art. Many told the President how much he resembled the president. He gravely thanked each one, telling them how much he appreciated the compliment. Several times he looked at Art and me, barely able to control his laughter. He stepped up to us as the last guest went past. He shook Art's hand, gave me a kiss and a hug, and whispered "Thank you" in my ear.

We cut the wedding cake as soon as the reception line was over, knowing some people, including the President, had to leave early. Someone had brought all the gifts from the house so we set about opening them. There were many lovely vases, tablecloth and napkins sets, gifts certificates—the gifts were varied and many. The one that made the biggest impression on us was the little box from Emily and Harriet. It held a check for ten thousand dollars! Neither of us could believe it. We both went over to give them a kiss and a hug.

I thoroughly expected the President to leave by noon, but at one-thirty he was still mingling among the guests. Watching him, I was glad everyone thought he was my Uncle Charley. He seemed to be having a good time.

It was two o'clock when Art whispered in my ear, "We have to be leaving soon, dear. Shall we go in and change?"

"Wait. Let me throw my bouquet first."

Art announced that all single women were to gather at the bottom of the porch steps to try to catch the bouquet. Emily even managed to get Harriet in the group. After the flowers bounced from hand to hand a few times, the bouquet ended up in Harriet's hands. I happened to catch the look on Ron Miller's face and decided we wouldn't have to wait long for another wedding.

Art had told me to dress as if I were going to meet the queen, so my going-away outfit was a mauve suit and a white blouse with a fluffy lace insert. Mauve shoes completed the picture. While Marie was helping me out of my dress, I told her about the President, after swearing her to secrecy.

"You mustn't even tell Roger until after the President has been gone two hours. That will give him time to get back to the airport. Are you surprised?"

"Surprised? It's a good thing I didn't know it before the wedding. I would have probably fainted when he took my arm." We both laughed at that picture.

When I was ready to go, I found Art waiting in the front room. He took an orchid out of its box and after several tries managed to get it pinned on my jacket. Marie had disappeared, so we decided we better get going rather than wait for her to return.

When we stepped out the door onto the front porch we found her, the President and all the other guests lining the walk. In the driveway stood Art's car decorated with balloons and streamers. Across the trunk was a "Just Married" sign.

We walked to the car as quickly as I was able, pelted along the way with birdseed and good wishes. What a perfect day and a perfect wedding!

THIRTY-SEVEN

"So, husband," I said, snuggling close, "where are we headed?"

"Ask no questions and I'll tell you no lies, wife," Art answered, giving my hand a squeeze.

It was approximately forty-five minutes later that we exited the freeway to a highway that ran between a wide river and some high rocky cliffs. There was one place where the water came cascading down the mountain, rainbows flitting through the water. Art pulled into the lookout along with many other travelers to let us stretch a bit and watch. It was fascinating to try to catch sight of a rainbow. They came and went so quickly.

"It won't be long now, honey," Art said, helping me into the car.

True to his word, it was no more than thirty minutes before we pulled into the magnificent grounds of the Rushing Water Hotel.

"May I help you, sir?" the desk clerk asked.

"Yes. I have a reservation for Mr. and Mrs. Landow." Art couldn't help smiling as he glanced at me.

It hadn't hit me until I heard it out loud. Mrs. Art Landow. Sandy Landow. It sounded wonderful. No more jokes about the ocean, the sand or sailors. Then I realized I had a whole bunch of decisions to make. Should I keep my business name as Sandy Shores? If Jake came to work with me, what would we call the business? Cummings & Landow? Landow & Cummings? Did we want every nasty that came into town to know I'm related to the Chief of Police? This was bigger than I had thought it would be.

We would have to talk it over. I came out of my daydream as Art took my hand to take me up to the Honeymoon Suite.

Art tipped the bellhop, pushed him through the doorway, closed and locked the door. Gently he took me in his arms, being careful of my injury. One long kiss led to another and another and . . .

Every night we found a fresh rose and chocolates on our pillows. It was an unforgettable experience. We hated to go when it was time to leave. On the way home we decided we would spend each anniversary there, reliving our wedding night.

I felt so different when we pulled into the driveway that somehow I expected everything there to be different, too. But it was all the same—same house, same Frances and Al coming around the corner to greet us. It all seemed so surreal. I shook myself mentally as Art helped me out of the car.

When we reached the front door, Art handed my crutch to Al, picked me up in his arms and carried me over the threshold. We were both laughing so hard when he finally made it through the door that he nearly dropped me.

Frances was full of womanly questions. "How's your arm?" "Where did we go?" "Was it fun?" and the most crucial one, "What did we eat?"

As usual Al let Frances do all the talking. It was a good hour before the two of us ran out of questions and answers. Sometime during our conversation Art and Al had slipped out to the back yard, and were engrossed in man talk.

When they came back in from the yard, Art's face was a thundercloud. He came to me immediately and put his arms around me.

"What? What's happened?" I asked.

"I'm sorry to have to tell you this, dear, The General escaped when they were transporting him to DC. They think he is headed back here."

"Oh, no." I looked at Art with stricken eyes. "Of course, he's coming back. He is nothing, if not tenacious, and he hates me with every fiber of his body." My tears came uninvited, as I buried my head in Art shoulder. "I'm sorry," I hiccuped. "I thought I was through with him."

"There, there, sweetheart." Art patted my back. "We'll get him. I want you to promise me that you won't go anywhere unless I or one of my men are with you. I think we can rely on Sadie to protect you at the office, but don't leave unless one of us is there to follow you. Agreed?"

I could only nod, because my arm that hadn't bother me for several days had suddenly become extremely painful.

I dried my tears and while Frances started dinner I went to call Marie and tell her we were home. Of course, she and Roger wanted us to come right over. Frances anticipated her invitation and stuck a piece of paper under my nose: Ask them over for dinner. I'll make Matthew his favorite hamburger, she had written. I did, and they came.

Needless to say, we talked long into the night. We rehashed the wedding, and the fact that "Uncle Charley" was the last to leave. Matthew was the only one there that night who didn't know that Uncle Charley was actually the President. When we told him, he didn't seem fazed by the news as he announced nonchalantly, "Way cool."

No one remarked on how many times Art checked the doors and pulled the curtain back slightly to search the grounds. The General had been free for two days. He could arrive any time. When a week lengthened into two weeks, then into a month with no sign of him, we began to think maybe he had given up and gone back to Korea. I fervently hoped so since the time was drawing near for me to go to Seattle and have the operation on my leg. If the General did return and found I wasn't around and Frances was alone I could imagine what he would do to her. The mental pictures weren't pretty.

THIRTY-EIGHT

I'm a lousy patient, so I'll skip what I went through right after the operation on my leg. Everything went as Doctor O'Conner had hoped it would. He attached the steel rod encapsulated in the cells to the knee that the doctors gave me at Walter Reed hospital. Secondly, he attached his revolutionary designed ankle to the steel rod, and then he placed steel toes in place of my own that he found smashed to "a pulp," he told me later. The ankle and the toes are going to make it somewhat more difficult for me to learn to walk again mainly because of the extra weight.

Art, bless his soul, came to Seattle every weekend. Poor guy, he never knew what to expect. Half of the time I ranted and raved about everything: the sheets were too rough, I was too cold or too warm, a fly in the room was too noisy, and on and on. Thinking back on it, I'll bet there were times he wished he had never bothered to drive all that way to see his bitchy wife.

After more weeks than I care to think about, Doctor O'Conner signed me out of the hospital with the instructions that I could do anything (he winked at Art) and go anywhere, as long as I didn't put any weight on my leg for six more weeks.

"I will want to x-ray that leg every two weeks, but I imagine you would prefer to be home instead of up here. Am I right?"

"Such a silly question," I answered. "It is truly okay to do anything as long as I don't put any weight on it, right?" I wanted to make sure.

"Well, yes," the doctor said thoughtfully. "Things like eating or sleeping or making love or . . . "

"I get the general idea, doctor." I couldn't believe I was actually blushing.

It wasn't a pleasant ride home. I had to sit in the back seat with my leg stuck out in front of me. We stopped often, but still I was as jumpy as a cat by the time we reached Myrtle Woods. I hadn't thought going right to bed would feel so good. It was wonderful to be back, even if we were going to have to make the trip to Seattle every two weeks.

I think everybody I knew visited the first few days I was home. Both Tracy and Matthew were growing like weeds. It surprised me to learn that Matt, as he preferred to be called, had asked about his birth mother. Sue gave him the letter, she told me, and by the time he had finished, he was crying. He handed it to her to read. When she finished, they cried together. Nowhere did his mother name his father. The one time she did refer to him, it was "an older man" who forced her to have sex. She never used the word rape, making her a saint in my eyes. What young boy wants to think he is a product of that horrendous deed? Deep in my heart, I still felt it was Peter. The time frame was too close for it to be a coincidence. Emily and Harriet were glad also that Norma didn't mention Peter by name. It saved a lot of possible heartache for everyone concerned.

The days crawled by. I was at that stage of recovery were I was beginning to think I would never walk again; that I was going through all of this for nothing. Depression was settling in and it was difficult to remain upbeat in front of everyone. The trips to Seattle did get easier, thank God. Doctor O, as I was calling him by that time, had a nice surprise for us as we were preparing to leave his office after my latest exam.

"Sandy, I've talked to Doctor Davidson about continuing your therapy in Myrtle Woods. I have complete confidence in his ability, so if you don't mind, he will be in charge. If he thinks something needs my attention he will either send you back up here or I will make the trip down there." Art and I were delighted.

I'm sure I must have looked a little like Frankenstein. I had pins that connected to rods on the outside of my leg from the knee to the toes. Doctor O told me that inside my ankle was a small, intricate version of a true ankle. This ankle replacement was something that researchers had been attempting to invent for years without success. What I wanted to know was why I was learning to use all this steel stuff if they were going to take it off in another month.

"You haven't been on that leg for close to three months and the muscles are quite weak from non-use. By learning to walk with all that stuff attached, it should be a breeze to walk when it's all removed," Doctor O told me.

Well, let me tell you it wasn't easy. I don't know how many times I ended up in tears of frustration. It was as if my ankle had a mind of it's own. It would bend at the most inopportune times causing me to stumble over my own feet. Doctor Davidson called Doctor O'Conner to ask if it was natural for the ankle to do that.

Doctor O'Conner was waiting for me when I came in for my therapy the next day. I knew whatever he had to tell me was not good news when I saw Art in the room. He put his arm around me and led me to a chair.

The doctor's voice was not quite steady when he said, "Sandy, I'm sorry to have to tell you this, but the ankle replacement has failed. I will have to go back in and fuse the metal implant I put in. I'm devastated over this. It is the first one that has ever failed, and it is the one I most wanted to work."

"Is the rest of the leg okay?" I asked, afraid of the answer.

"The rest of the . . . oh, yes, everything else is fine."

"Will I be able to walk without a cane or a crutch."

"Of course. I'm sorry. I should have realized you would be concerned about the rest of the procedure. Yes, fusing the ankle will have little effect as far as walking is concerned, running will be slightly more difficult. I was so sure I had the problem of ankle implants solved. Well," he said, wiping his hand over his face, "I guess it's back to the drawing board for me. In the meantime, let's take care of that ankle."

"Is this going to slow up my progress?"

"Yes, we must give the fusion time to mesh. It will mean

another week in the hospital and two of partial bed rest. But," he held up his hand as I started to speak, "the work you have done so far to strengthen your leg muscles won't be lost. I expect you to be out and walking on your own within two more months."

"Okay," I said resignedly, "let's get it over with."

We made arrangements to report to the hospital in Seattle the following Monday. Art walked beside me to the pickup where Al and Sadie were waiting for me.

"Chin up, sweetheart. Hang on to the thought that you will be able to walk normally in a few more months," he said, putting my crutches in the back seat. "I'll see you later."

I told Al the bad news. "Well, hey now, that's not so bad," he said when I had finished. "I know several of my service buddies who had to have their ankles fused. If I hadn't known they'd been operated on, I wouldn't have believed it."

That perked me up considerably. I'd never known Al to lie. Sadie leaned against me offering love and encouragement as Al put the pickup in gear.

We were three blocks from home when we heard the ambulance coming. Al pulled over as it went screaming by. I felt a chill course through my body. I knew something terrible had happened, but before I could say anything a police car came toward us, sirens blowing and lights flashing. We were surprised when the cruiser pulled up in front of us, blocking our way. It was Art! He came running to my door and jerked it open.

"Quick, Sandy, you and Sadie get in my car. Al, Frances has been hurt. Now wait," he said as Al jerked to put the pickup in reverse. "It's not life-threatening, so take it easy. I'm going to take Sandy to South Point to stay with Emily. I'll see you at the hospital and fill you in on what happened."

"Tell me. How bad is it," I demanded when Art and I started toward South Point.

"Not as minor as I would have Al believe, but I didn't want him to get in a wreck on the way to the hospital. All I can figure is that the Korean came back and he must be insane. For some reason, Frances had all the doors locked, which I've never known her to do. When he couldn't get in he started running around the house shooting out the windows. As close as we can figure, Frances was up on a stool either getting or putting something away in a closet. One of the bullets entered near the top of her head at the back and exited two inches later at the top of her skull. That caused her to tumble backwards, breaking her wrist as she fell. The paramedics tell me they are more worried about the loss of blood than anything else."

"It's all my fault," I murmured, more to myself than to Art.

"I knew you'd feel that way, honey, but don't blame yourself. It was just a freak accident. I think you should stay out of town until we catch that SOB. I'm sure he won't want to talk this time when he sees you, he'll just start shooting."

The unemotional detached feeling that I always got prior to starting another assignment stole over me and suddenly I was Sandy Shores, CIA. I knew what had to be done.

"Turn around, Art." My voice was hard, demanding. "We're going back."

"What? There is no way . . . "

"Please, don't argue with me. I know what has to be done. That snake is after me. It won't matter where you take me, he'll find me. Anyone who gets in his way will be killed, I'm positive of that. I have to be the bait. There is no other way to catch him."

"No, Sandy, I won't allow you to do this."

"Yes, you will, Art." I looked him straight in the eye. "I know how to take care of myself. This is the sort of thing I was trained for. Believe me, I will do this with or without you."

Art stared at me. "I've never seen you like this, Sandy. All right, I'd rather be involved than let you do this alone. Tell me what to do."

On the way back to Myrtle Woods I outlined my plan. "First, call someone who can get all the windows replaced today. We will go to the hospital while that is being done to be with Frances. When we get to the house this evening I want you to pull all your men off." I could see he was getting ready to speak. "Don't interrupt. Sometime this afternoon I want one of your men to sneak Sadie in to the house from the beach. I don't want the General to know I have any protection."

"I don't like it. So many things could go wrong," he worried. "If I should lose you . . . "

"Nothing will go wrong. I'll have my gun. I know the layout of the house—he doesn't. This time I'll have Sadie, something he won't expect."

"This time? You mean to tell me you have done this before . . . made yourself the bait?"

"Yes, a couple of times, so see you don't need to worry."

"That's easy for you to say, Babe, but I'm going to be worried sick. Yes, Yes," he held up his hand. "I know. You have done this before, but, damn it, I haven't."

At the hospital I left Art making arrangements to get the windows fixed. Inside I found Al sitting by Frances' bed, holding her hand.

"How is she?"

"Doc says she might not regain consciousness for a few days. Says that's the way it is with head wounds. He thinks she's gonna be okay. What ya' doing here?"

I told him I had insisted in coming back when he told me how badly Frances had been hurt. I wasn't about to tell him what was planned for that night. Frances was the same when we left four hours later.

"I had to call in every glass company from here, Mountain View and South Point, but I've been assured the windows will be repaired by late afternoon," Art told me as we drove away.

When we pulled into the driveway, I could feel "The Executioner's" eyes on me as Art helped me up the steps. I smiled wryly to myself. I had immediately fallen into the old habit of thinking of the General by his nickname. He was determined, tenacious, and hated me with a passion. I should have known he wouldn't go back to Korea without executing me first. I stood on the top step surveying the houses across the street. Immediately, I knew where he was hiding. Directly across from us was the Adams house. Don and Jean Adams had taken their kids to

Disneyland, so the house was empty. They had no pets, had stopped their paper and had a timer that turned on a light in the front room at seven in the evening. The whole neighborhood had assured them we would keep an eye on the house, but there was no reason for anyone to go inside. I knew the General wouldn't shoot me from a distance. He would want to see the fear in my eyes before he pulled the trigger. I was going to have to stay on my toes tonight if I wanted to stay alive.

Art was right. Workers swarmed over the house putting final touches on the windows that were reflecting the rosy evening glow of the sunset. Art played his part well. He ordered all his men back to the station and from the sidewalk, in a loud voice, told me to stay inside and keep the doors locked. As he turned to walk toward his cruiser I saw that he was crying. If the truth be known, I felt weepy myself. Straightening my shoulders I turned toward my bedroom. I had a lot to do in the next hour. I hurried to lock the front and back doors. I wanted to leave the back door open, but I knew that would look suspicious and we might miss another chance to apprehend the SOB, as Art insisted on calling him.

I had been training Sadie to silently lie in wait until I gave her a signal, then she was to charge anything that was between us. I wasn't one hundred percent sure it was going to work. She had the tendency to growl low in her throat at the crucial time, so I could only pray that she would perform correctly this time. I certainly didn't want her to get shot.

I brought in extra pillows and made a human form in the bed, arranged a wig I had used last Halloween, messed up the bedspread and general left the bed in disarray. I dug through the closet for extra bullets for my 38 Special, then positioned Sadie, leaving the closet door open just enough for her to rush out. Hopefully, anyone coming in would not see her until it was too late. I grabbed my cell phone, laboriously got down on my stomach and slowly began to pull my body under the bed, keeping my gun and my cell phone in front of me. I had known this would take time because of the pins in my leg, but I hadn't counted on the pins getting hung up in the rug. Each time they did pain would shoot through my leg. I was sweating by the time I was in place. I bent my elbows slightly and brought my hands together around the trigger of my gun. By raising my chin slightly I could sight right down the barrel. Art was to wait for my call before entering the house. No call meant I didn't win. The luminous dial on my watch said seven-thirty. The last of the sunset was fading. I left my gun in position, folded my arms and rested my forehead on them. I knew it wouldn't be long now.

THIRTY-NINE

I must have dozed off, although that seems impossible, as keyed up as I was and as uncomfortable. Trying to place the noise that had awaken me, I heard Sadie give a soft whine. Oh, no, I thought, not now, sweet dog. As quietly as I could I shushed her, praying she would hear me. My leg was trying to cramp up from being in one position too long, but I found I couldn't move. In my sleep I had turned slightly and the pins had gotten embedded in the carpet. I heard the noise again and realized it was someone picking the lock on the back door. It was nine o'clock. The moonlight flooding the room was too bright for comfort. I could see Sadie plainly as she rose to her feet, her hackles rising, a silent snarl forming on her lips. Everything depended on her now. I prayed God would protect us both.

He was cautious, I'll give him that much credit. It seemed to take him forever to soundlessly check the other rooms. Suddenly his feet appeared in my bedroom doorway. Come in and check the bed, I urged, don't shoot from back there. As if he heard me, he took three steps quick steps into the room. He was so intent on the form on the bed that he didn't notice Sadie getting ready to spring.

"Now!" I yelled. Sadie hit "The Executioner" hard, knocking him to the floor before he had time to turn and shoot. His head hit the floor directly in front of me. Moonlight illuminated his dazed face. He shook his head and in so doing, caught sight of me. Surprise, disbelief and hatred flitted across his face, in that order. Somehow, he had managed to hang onto his gun when he fell and I could see him bringing it up to shoot me. I fired. The bullet bore a neat hole in the middle of his forehead. I had no choice but to lie there and watch life drain from his body. His blank stare was unnerving. I tried to touch his face to close his eyes, but he was inches beyond my reach. Trembling, I picked up my phone to dial Art's cell phone, trying not to look in his face. Before I could finish dialing, Art burst through the kitchen door.

"Sandy? Sandy, where are you?"

I had to clear my throat twice before I could speak. "Here, under the bed," I called. Stupid man. If "The Executioner" had won, Art would have died the minute he stepped into the bedroom.

"Under the bed?" he was saying as he flipped on the light. "My God," he whispered. Before him was "The Executioner", dead, the back of his head blown away. Sadie was straddling the Korean's leg, glaring at him, daring him to move. She was not making a sound, but her lips pulled back in a savage snarl. I had to call her off before she would let Art come in the room. She had performed perfectly.

It took three men to get me out from under the bed. Two to hold it up and Art to get my pins loose from the carpet. First though, he lay down beside me and kissed me. He didn't notice that I was not responding. "Please don't ever put me through this again," he begged.

Never mind him, I wasn't about to put *myself* through anything like this again. It was the first time I'd ever taken a life. But, all that was beside the point. What made me coldly angry was that Art had entered the house without making sure which of us was alive. He had taken the chance of being killed and I didn't understand why he would do such a foolish thing.

Art put his arm around me and took me out to his cruiser. "We are going to be staying with Marie and Roger for a few days. That's where I spent most of my time waiting for your call, which by the way, never came."

"If the General had won, and you had burst in like that, instead of waiting for my call, you would be dead," I said in an unemotional, cold tone.

"If you were dead, I would have had no reason to live, Sandy," he said, softly. "I knew what I was doing. I had a stakeout on the beach. I was informed when that SOB entered the house. The boys and I were outside waiting to hear a gunshot. I made the others wait to hear your voice before coming in. They were safe. You have no reason to be angry."

I saw the misery in his eyes. Even that didn't deter me. "I'm used to having orders followed. The order was wait for my call."

He pulled over to the curb. Turning to me, he took my chin in his hand and made me look at him. "I've learned that one shot always means that someone has died. I knew that you would want to be sure he died if you had to shoot, so you would be close to him. It would have been impossible for whoever shot first to miss. Am I right?"

"Yes, that's true. However, following orders has been drilled into me for so long, I expected you to obey them." I took a deep breath, trying to calm down. "I . . . I . . . give me a few minutes to get out of my CIA persona and back among the living."

We sat there for several minutes wrapped in each others arms.

"I hope none of the boys come by or we could get a ticket for making out on the street."

That struck me funny and I starting laughing. The ice that had gripped my emotions since I pulled the trigger, started to melt. My laughter turned to tears. "I've never killed anyone before," I sobbed.

"I could tell. It wasn't the phone call as much as having to kill, right?" I nodded. "It will take a while to get over it, sweetheart. You may even have to go to Doctor Morton."

"Me, go to a shrink? Oh, come on. I'm sure I'll be able to handle this. However, it may take hours of tender loving care from you. Of course, if you don't feel up to it . . . " I said, trying to make light of a dreadful experience.

"Oh, I think I can handle that assignment. I just hope it's some place more comfortable than this car."

We were both laughing as he pulled away from the curb, but I was still freezing somewhere in the region of my heart. It would take time, he was right about that. I could still see the General's dead eyes staring at me. I couldn't help but wonder if that was the way I looked when I was in the trance.

Marie and I went to the hospital the next day to see Frances. She had regained consciousness, thank God, but she was confused as to why she was in the hospital. She'd ask Al why she was there, doze off, wake up and ask him all over again. Typical concussion symptoms, the doctor had told Al.

"Probably be better tomorrow," he told us in his blunt way. The hospital had put Frances in a double room so Al could get some rest on the other bed, since he refused to leave her side.

"I can't imagine a big city hospital doing that," I said to Marie. She had to agree.

The next day she was coherent, although still weak from loss of blood. Al had told what had happened to her, but she wanted to hear the whole story again from me. I started with my ankle operation failing (what a shame, she said), continued on to the repair of the windows (every one of them?), to my capture of the General. I wasn't going to upset her with the truth about what happened until she was much stronger.

"When you are released you'll be staying with us while Sandy is in Seattle getting her fusion done," Marie told her.

"Oh, dear. I don't want to be any trouble. Couldn't Al take care of me?"

"Nope. Can't cook. Don't want to learn," Al stated.

"You aren't going to be any trouble, dear," Marie said, laughing. "I'll be feeding Al and Art and it will be much easier if you are right there."

Frances finally agreed, which was a relief. I had been wondering if I was going to have to put off the fusion until she was well. With Frances taken care of and me in Seattle, Art would have time to get the house redone inside and out. The bloody carpets in the front room and our bedroom would be replaced, the bullet holes from the General first visit would be patched, and the rooms would all be painted an off-white.

"You won't know the place when you come home," he told me. I didn't doubt it for a minute.

There was no fuss about the General's death. Our State Department was instructed to send his body back to Korea. President Wilton called to tell us that there would be no repercussions. We both thanked God for that.

The next seven weeks were a combination of wins and losses. It was as if I went two steps forward and three steps back, but slowly we made progress. The day finally came when I was able to fulfill one of my dreams—I walked down to the lake by myself. True, Art was right behind me in case I had a problem, but I made it.

Having the ankle fused didn't bother me a bit. There were a few minor difficulties, but nothing that I couldn't do another way. What I couldn't get used to was my beautiful, beautiful new leg. After they took all the pins and rods off and the small holes where they had been, healed, I would catch myself running my hand down my leg. I couldn't believe this wonderful limb actually belonged to me.

A few months later we were attending a high tea at Harriet's. Inside, this time, because the weather was turning colder and most of the flowers had died. Emily took my arm and pretended she wanted to show me something on the other side of the room.

"I think we should get prepared for another wedding soon," she whispered to me. "Every time we have Harriet over for dinner we ask her to bring a friend and guess who the friend is? Ron, of course."

Before we could say anything more Harriet came up to talk for a few minutes.

Emily and Howard had gotten married while I was in the hospital the first time. They had bought a house close to Harriet, so the sisters can visit each other often. Now, thinking about Harriet's possible marriage, I go around humming the Wedding March. Art has the audacity to call me a matchmaker.

We did make the decision for me to keep my maiden name for the business. Art agreed that it wouldn't be wise for newcomers or drifters to know of our relationship. Both of us were happy that

I would have Sadie with me, especially after how well she followed my cue to attack the General.

In late November Jake and family moved to Myrtle Woods. They chose a new house being built over on the other side of the lake. It was near where Peter Grant did his best to rid the world of my presence, but I will never remind them of that. I'm just glad to have them here. The first thing they did was get a male golden retriever.

Sadie wasn't sure she liked this other four-legged creature coming into her house and her office. Eventually, they got it straightened out between themselves and decided to be friends.

The family was just getting settled when Jake and I got a call to come to Washington for an awards ceremony. True to his word, the President had recommended both of us for the Medal of Honor. Sue, Jake, Art and I were planing on making the trip together when, at the last minute, Art couldn't go. Two of his men called in sick with a vicious strain of flu that was going around. There were two others on vacation, which left the police station with a skeleton crew. There was no way Art could leave.

"Tell the President to take lots of pictures for me," he told me when he informed me he couldn't go. I promised, not knowing how I would arrange it.

Jake grumbled all the way to the airport about having to pack again before he'd even gotten unpacked.

"Do you see this?" I asked, rubbing two of my fingers together. He said, mystified, that yes, he could. "That, my friend, is the smallest violin in the world playing your sad, sad song."

"Okay, okay, I get the message. No more griping on my part."

Art held me tight and gave me a long kiss when he dropped us off at the airport. "Safe flight, darling. Hurry home."

"I will. I'm missing you already," I said.

Art clasped Jake on the back, wishing him a safe flight. With a hug for Sue and a last wave, he drove away. Watching him out of sight, I allowed the tears to spill over.

Sue, full of understanding, handed me a Kleenex. "I know how much you wanted him to be there."

The weather from Portland to Chicago was perfect, but when we took off for Washington, we hit a bad storm. The pilot asked us to keep our seat belts fastened. The storm was massive. We couldn't go around it nor get above it. It rained hard, tossing the plane around like a cork in a creek. Sue handled it well, but many others on board were air sick. Even I, who had flown in weather like this numerous times, was feeling a little queasy. Jake, bless his heart, slept all the way, not waking until we were preparing to land. When we reached the hotel there was a message to call the President. He expressed disappointment that Art had not been able to attend the ceremony.

"I was looking forward to showing him around," President Wilton said. "Perhaps talking him into coming to work for me."

I made no reply to that silly statement.

It rained hard all through the night, but the next day dawned bright and clear. The Washington Monument, framed by the blue sky and the rain-washed trees, was a beautiful sight from my hotel window. I was in my room getting dressed, when I heard a knock at the door. Oh, great, I thought, and me in my slip.

"Who is it," I asked, struggling into my robe.

"Telegram," a deep voice called out.

"Slip it under the door, please.".

"Sorry. You have to sign for it, Ma'am."

Breathing a sign of exasperation, I pulled open the door. Standing there in all their splendor were what looked like half of Myrtle Woods. Art, Frances, Al, the three Owens', and the three Fuller's. I stared, not believing my eyes.

"Well, don't just stand there. Aren't you going to ask us in," Art asked, a big grin on his face.

"How . . . when . . . who's . . . ," I stammered.

"You can thank the President," Art said, giving me a kiss. "He thought you should have us here to applaud when you get your medal, so he flew us here this morning in Air Force One." All of them were clearly in awe of what a President could do by picking up a phone.

"And that's not all," Frances said, her eyes shining. "When

we get ready to go home we will all go back the same way. All of us, including you and Jake and Sue. Isn't that something? I can hardly believe it. Right, Al."

"Right."

"But who did you get to work in your place, Art?"

"That's the other thing. He sent a fellow from the FBI as an extra body in the station until I get back." Art shook his head, still unbelieving.

Everyone settled in the front room of the suite, while Art came to help me finish dressing. Words like, "I can't believe . . . ," and "I'm so happy . . . ," filled the air as I put on my dab of makeup, and slipped into my suit. On the way to the White House Tracy and Matt rode with us in the limousine, their eyes like saucers. Neither of them could stop signing and talking about the President's plane.

If you have never seen an award ceremony, imagine the American flag fluttering in the breeze, while hundreds of proud young men snap a salute to their Commander in Chief as they march pass the review stand. It brought tears to my eyes.

When the President pinned the ribbon on my chest, I thought I'd burst with pride. "Were you surprised to see Art and your friends?" he whispered. "Totally. Thank you so much," I whispered in return. "It's the least I could do," he answered. I blinked away sudden tears again. I couldn't figure out what was wrong. I'd been queasy since I'd gotten off the plane, I cried at the slightest provocation, I felt tired, then hot, then cold. I realized I must be coming down with that nasty Asian flu when I didn't want anything to eat at the reception.

When my head started pounding I knew it was time to get back to the hotel. I was looking around for Art, when the President came by, grabbed my hand, and took Jake and me into an alcove off of the main part of the room.

"I can't thank you two enough for realizing there was a spy in our depths. When I think how many of our CIA operatives gave their lives because of that bastard . . . sorry, excuse the language, Sandy."

"That's okay, sir. I believe we used some of the same when

we realized what was going on. Smyth's wife didn't know what was happening?"

"No, that's the sad part. She has had to take a short leave of absence to try and deal with it. I hope everything works out for her. She is a wonderful person and, I can truthfully say, the best darned Secretary of State this country has ever had. I'm sorry you two aren't coming back to work for me. As I said before, with that leg of yours, you would make one heck of an agent, Sandy."

"I've been wondering how you knew."

"About your leg? Elementary, my dear, elementary. I found out who your doctor was when I came for the wedding. Since the moment you first arrived at the hospital in Seattle I have been kept informed of your progress. I was sorry when the new ankle didn't work, but in watching you walk, I can't see that it made much difference."

"No, sir, it didn't. I was extremely fortunate that the rest of the operation was a success. I wish more people were aware of Doctor O'Connor's work. I think many could be helped right now, even if he doesn't have the bugs out of the ankle replacement yet."

"I think I can take care of that today. Congress passed a bill this morning that I will sign as soon as I get back to my office. It gives Doctor O'Conner a two million dollar grant to continue his work in that area. Also, I'm adding him to the list of specialists that the doctors at Walter Reed hospital can call in to assist on some of their cases."

"That's great. Oh, thank you, sir, thank you." I was the one giving the hug this time.

We started home the next day. I, for one, would be glad to get there. I felt like I'd been gone a year, instead of two days. I knew I was really sick when I didn't want to spend time with Tracy and Matt.

They tell me it was a beautiful day when we landed in Portland, but it could have been raining for all I knew. Even flying in all the luxury of Air Force One, I got so nauseated I thought I was going to lose everything I'd eaten for the past three days, which wasn't much. Thank goodness that never happened, but I felt like death warmed over when the plane landed.

"Do you want to stay over in Portland for the night, honey?" Art asked, concerned.

"No, I don't think so. Get me to the car, so I can lie down. Boy, whatever this virus is, it sure hit me hard," I said weakly. Even when recovering from the ordeal with The Executioner, I couldn't remember being this sick.

I thanked the heavens above that Art had his car at the airport. Sue and Jake took Al and Frances home with them, so I could lie down in the backseat of our car. I'm sure Art must have exceeded the speed limit because it didn't seem to take any time to reach Myrtle Woods

When we reached home before Frances did, but when she came in she took over. She found me in bed and before I knew it, she was making me some hot chicken soup. That didn't sound good to me, but rather than hurt her feelings, I said I'd try it. Art had planted himself in the chair by my bed and wasn't about to move. It was good to be home in loving hands.

The next morning I did feel better; although still a little queasy. So I was up and about before anyone knew I was awake. I told one and all that I felt one hundred per cent better. In the middle of rehashing the last two days, I got nauseated again. I excused myself, went in the bedroom, and got into bed fully clothed. That's where they found me fifteen minutes later. This time, over my protests, they called the doctor. Art must have made it seem like a matter of life or death, because within the hour Doctor Johnson was there. He asked everyone to leave while he did his examination. Art wasn't happy about being ordered out, but with a kiss on my cheek, he went.

"All right now, Sandy, tell me when you got sick, how long has it lasted and how you feel right now."

I told him about feeling nauseated on the plane and how that feeling got worse and worse.

"Did you actually vomit?"

"No."

"Kept feeling like you were going to, huh?" I nodded my head. He pushed in and there on my stomach, asking if that hurt or if this hurt.

"No," I said each time. Then he squeezed gently on my breast.

"Is your breast sore?"

"Yes, a little."

"Well, I'll tell you, Sandy. I think you are pregnant. Now, don't get all excited until I examine you in the office. I think for the rest of the day you better stick to soda crackers, maybe a little soup tonight. I'll see you tomorrow in the office. Have Art call and make an appointment."

"Wait, doctor. Don't tell Art yet. Let's make sure first. I don't want him disappointed again," I begged. "Please, tell them it's a virus or something."

He agreed, and left after telling Frances nothing but bed rest and crackers for me today. I could hear her asking Art how much he trusted that doctor, anyway.

"Not feed a person. What is he trying to do, starve her to death," she grumbled.

To make a long story short, the tests Doctor Johnson performed the next day did verify that Art and I were going to have our baby. I don't know who was the happiest: Art, Frances, Al, Sue, Jake, Marie, Roger or me. Doctor Johnson only had one thing to say. "Didn't I tell you this would happen as soon as you quit trying so hard." How right he was.

When I called Marie to tell her the news I had enough sense to hold the phone at arms' length. Otherwise, I'm sure her congratulatory scream would have broken my eardrum.

EPILOGUE

It's been seven months now since that fateful day. I've been getting bigger and bigger. Friends keep telling me I'm going to have twins, but Doctor Johnson can only find one heartbeat. Darn, I'd love to have twins. A boy and a girl—get it all over with at once. We told Doctor Johnson we didn't want to know the sex of the baby before hand. We may be crazy, but we both think not knowing is half the fun.

Jake and I finally came to a compromise and named our business Myrtle Woods Investigations. Not very original, but easy to remember.

The other day, Jake was telling me that soon there won't be enough room in our office for both of us. I cuffed his ear as I walked past his desk.

While I was puttering around the office this morning, I came across those unsolved case files that I had brought over from the police station so many, many months ago. Idly, I began to read one. When I had finished I had several questions jotted down on my notepad. Immediately, I called Art and asked if he had time to see me.

I lumbered into his office a few minutes later, and handed him the file. I wanted to know if he recalled what had happened. He was brand new on the force then, and had actually been assigned to the case, he told me. He was able to answer all my questions in detail, as if it had happened yesterday. I asked him how he could remember it so well when the case was now over twenty years old.

"I'm not likely to forget a case that involves a child," he said quietly. "I wish you would delve into it. Perhaps you will find the key we need to solve it."

Who knows? Maybe I will.